THRILL KILL

THRILL KILL

William Vanderberg

A Division of Shapolsky Publishers

Thrill Kill

S.P.I. BOOKS
A division of Shapolsky Publishers, Inc.

ISBN 1-56171-353-X

For any additional information, contact:

S.P.I. BOOKS/Shapolsky Publishers, Inc.
136 West 22nd Street
New York, NY 10011
212/633-2022 / FAX 212/633-2123

Manufactured in Canada

10 9 8 7 6 5 4 3 2 1

DEDICATION

This book is dedicated to the men and women of the Fifth District, Metropolitan Police, District of Columbia.

> Carry the banner proudly
> For those of us who have gone before
> Some who made the supreme sacrifice
> *Held it very high indeed.*

ACKNOWLEDGMENTS

Special thanks to my agent, Sasha Goodman-Waters. For me to believe wasn't enough. I needed someone to believe in me.

Heartfelt gratitude to Ben Pedrick for I know you truly care. You, my friend, are the salt of the earth.

PROLOGUE

HE FLICKED HIS greasy calloused thumb against the keen edge of the serrated blade. Lifting the cold steel into the crisp air, its shimmering silhouette gleaming against the backdrop of the strangely glowing moon, he felt the bestial urge to raise his head and howl into the shrieking wind.

"Double yer pleasure, double yer fun, it's two chinks, it's two chinks, it's two chinks in one," perversely laughed the lurking figure, chanting the twisted lyric over and over again. Gazing fondly at the glistening stainless steel blade, he couldn't help but think that it was his kind of night, brutally cold, damp, blustery, the kind of night where nothing stirred, not even a mouse. Bent over in spasms, hacking up huge globs of phlegm, his insides raked with burning fire, he still smiled.

"Son of a bitchin miserable black lung," mumbled the coughing man, as he sent a long arc of mucous and blood laced spittle splattering against a nearby rock.

"Yeah. I don't know how much longer I've got. But, fer sure. Fer real sure. I know how much time you've got, little Miss Chop suey. Not too Goddamned much," he muttered under his breath, parting some tangled branches and eyeballing his little china doll. The slant eyed bitch was about to feel his own personal brand of hari kari rip open her greasy gook guts. Nothing could ruin his fun. Taking out two of the rice eaters with one shot would be an added delight.

Suzie Choi's whole body tingled with joy. Nothing, nothing in this wonderful world, could ruin her day. Suzie Choi was wrong, dead wrong. Walking down the dark deserted path, her numb hands rubbing her protruding stomach, she could only dream of the life that she was about to give birth to. Her baby would be beautiful, a joy to her family, a pride to her hard working husband. It would be their first. Unfortunately, for Suzie Choi, it would also be their last. She walked on, glad for the chance to get out of the house, the chance to smell the budding cherry blossoms, to feel the sting of the whipping wind. It all made her feel so very much alive.

Looking to her left, down the steep slope, she paused to watch the tranquil flow of the murky canal, its peaceful waters reflecting the shadowy moon beams. A strong gust swooped across the rippling currents, rustling the thick shrubs lining the canal's entangled banks. Suddenly, Suzie Choi felt uneasy, the hair on the back of her neck tingling with fear. She froze, the snapping crunch of some nearby twigs sounding strangely like a graveyard full of brittle bones rattling in the gusty wind. It was almost as if she was being watched. No, that wasn't it. She couldn't quite put her finger on the queer sensation.

Quickly, she turned around, stumbling on the exposed worn roots of a nearby oak. Before, she had always liked it this way, alone out here all by herself, no one to interrupt her daydreams. Now, briskly hurrying down the empty pathway, she prayed to see someone, anyone. Yes, that was it. She didn't feel like she was being watched. It felt almost as if she was being stalked.

"Oh no. Not him. Not the Carver," gasped Suzie Choi, desperately fleeing down the desolate walkway.

Slinging the high-power rifle over his shoulder, he shinned up the thick limbs of a nearby tree, the radiant moon bathing the landscape in a bleak portrait of foreboding gloom. Still, he climbed higher, wanting to get a better line of sight. He had tracked her, just like all the others. Now, all that was left for him to do was to answer the primitive call of the wild and bury his drooling fangs into her nice round belly. She was coming. He could sense it. The air around him crackled with static electricity, sparks flying like flickering fireflies. The hair on his back bristled. He felt super charged. It was the magic hour, the witching time, the moment to seal her carcass in the eternal tomb of death.

Carefully, he surveyed the now familiar urban landscape, constantly licking his brown stained lips in eager anticipation of the ultimate high, the thrill of the kill.

"There she is, waddlin' down the path like a two legged pot bellied stove," he whispered in the wind as he watched the terrified woman stumbling down the deserted trail, her long black coat fluttering out behind her in the cold stiff breeze. Well, the slant eyed good witch of the west was about to meet the wicked warlock of the north. Her northbound train life was about to get permanently derailed, Carver style. He'd make sure that she drowned in the salty brine of the cruel sea of death. He'd take her out right through that cute little chink throat of hers. Then, he'd hollow out her ching chong guts, just like all the others.

He watched as the split tail gook passed his lurking form, scurrying down the eerie pathway of death, her petite rotund silhouette highlighted in the moon beam's luminous rays. Locking the scope's cross hairs on the back of her smooth neck, he waited patiently. Like any game animal, she'd freeze when she felt the vise of death clamp her body in its fateful grip. He laughed silently as the terrified woman stopped suddenly. She was about to panic and bolt like a frightened rabbit. He sniffed the rank air, smelling the stale odor of sweat and fear. It was all over for her and her fairy tale dreams.

"Don't worry. Be happy," snickered the concealed murderer, holding his breath and squeezing the trigger of the powerful weapon.

Fortunately for Suzie Choi, she died instantly, her throat disintegrating in a boiling explosion of bloody tissue and cartilage, most of which splattered against the bark of a nearby oak. She had gone down easier than a white tail doe, figured the heinous butcher, scrambling down the branches of the sturdy tree. Most likely she'd probably gut out easier than one, too, being such a scrawny little bitch.

Descending on the mangled woman, the scurrying man unsheathed his stainless steel hunting knife, its serrated blade shimmering in the moon's ominous glow. Without hesitation he plunged the razor sharp blade into her soft round abdomen and began his gruesome hacking ritual. He just couldn't believe his good fortune. How many men ever had the ultimate pleasure of performing an abortion at the same time that they were dressing out a prized trophy kill?

"This is one little ornamental brat that will never live to lick a lollipop," bitterly muttered the callous murderer, slicing out the dead watery fetus, and then holding it up in the dismal night air.

Rhonda Renee Bell stared through the high power scope mounted on the 30.06 rifle, its cross-hairs aligning themselves on the walking form, following it as it slowly moved along the obscure walkway. The dimly lit path was cloaked in a hazy shroud of moonlit darkness, a flicker of light from a passing car's high beams briefly illuminating the solitary figure. It was definitely a woman, her long jet black hair shimmering in the eerie nocturnal gleam. She couldn't make out the face. The petite woman was starting to run, stumbling away from the tattooing cross-hairs. Rhonda Bell had to see the face. That would tell her everything. God, the fleeing woman was pregnant.

A cold sweat coated Rhonda Bell's entire body, her pulse

racing. Banging against her heavily breathing chest, her heart pounded wildly. Terror gripped her tall lean frame, droplets of perspiration trickling down between her full breasts. She sighed in relief as the figure disappeared behind a huge tree. Then, the cross-hairs immediately picked up the female form as it instantly reemerged from behind the protection of the concealing tree trunk. Gasping, she tried to scream to the fragile looking woman. Why couldn't the woman hear her warning shouts?

Rhonda Renee Bell watched in horror, unable to help, as the small silhouetted figure clutched at her throat and staggered against a nearby tree. The powerful murderous weapon kicked high into the air, slamming its wooden butt into the shoulder of the callous human hunter. The sharp cracking of the rifle followed instantaneously in a deafening roar, the scope framing the moonlit sky. He moved quickly, covering the short city block at a brisk walking pace so as not to arouse any undue suspicions. Creeping through the shadows, he kept the rifle concealed underneath his long black London Fog trench coat.

The dream was slowly fading in a periphery of shadows and darkness. He was pulling out a long bladed hunting knife from a camouflage colored sheath attached to his belt. Bending down, he slowly slid its finely honed edge into the woman's belly, gutting her like a slaughtered pig.

Rhonda Bell lost her vision in the netherworld of nightmares which bombarded her sleeping mind. Startled, she reached under the mattress and grabbed the two inch .38 special Smith and Wesson revolver. Leaping out of bed, clothed in a Redskins football jersey, she charged down the hallway and burst into her sleeping son's room. She flipped on the light, leveling the revolver across the small stiflingly close bedroom enclosure. Her heart pounded with terror.

Dropping the revolver to the carpeted floor, she ran to her ten year old son's bed and wrapped her long graceful arms around his soundly sleeping body. She hugged the murmuring boy to her bosom, smothering him in an unbridled expression of total and absolute love. For, above all else, he was the only reason for her existence in the insanity of this cold, cruel world. He stirred, and began to wake. Quickly she released her trembling arms from around his vulnerable frail form and allowed him to reassume the pose of peaceful tranquillity which she had almost interrupted in her haste to protect him from a menacing beast that was as real as life itself.

She gently lowered her five foot nine inch frame to the soft mauve colored carpet of the tiny bedroom, sitting cross-legged in the middle of the floor. Her breathing became much steadier as the tingling spasms of the prickly feeling adrenaline rush began to slowly subside. The tiny droplets of perspiration coating her back began to evaporate, causing a chill to penetrate her otherwise heated body. A bead of sweat formed on her slowly heaving chest and trickled down between her full breasts, disappearing in a line of moisture before arriving at the indentation of her navel.

Rhonda Renee Bell, known simply as Bell or Ronnie to her co-workers and friends, depending on their degree of intimacy with the young thirty year old single mother, looked down at her dark forearms. Rows of goose bumps protruded from her otherwise smooth skin. There were so many things reeling through her head. She had to put them in some kind of logical order. Everything was there, right in front of her. The answer was so close at hand, so obvious. She just couldn't quite put her finger on it.

She shook her head violently, trying to clear the cobwebs of confusion and the shadows of uncertainty which lurked in her mind. This, unlike any other investigation she had been involved with in her first year on the homicide squad, was becoming a personal matter. Lately, a shred of apprehension had begun to weave its way into the very core of her being. She was starting to become afraid. The fine line between fantasy and reality was being obscured in the shadow dance of death being played out in the streets and alleys of her hometown, Washington, D.C. Her once clear perspective was becoming tainted with doubt. She didn't know whether she was the hunter, or whether through some cruel twist of fate, she had suddenly become the hunted.

Picking up her service revolver, she raised her graceful frame off the bedroom floor and turned to walk back out into the hallway. She paused at the doorway, hesitant to turn off the light. Why was it that darkness always scared her? So much of her life had been, and still was, spent not only in the darkness of night, but also in the darkness of life. Being born in the very same drug infested ghettos, which for the last nine years of her adult life she had been sworn to protect, was both a constant source of accomplishment and shame.

Tonight, she felt no shame in the black race, only a sense of pride that she, a black woman, was in the front lines leading a desperate hunt to find a crazed serial killer. Rhonda Bell didn't have to read about it in Sunday's edition of the Washington Post.

She instinctively knew that out there somewhere, in the nocturnal void of the D.C. night, lay the disemboweled body of a young Oriental girl, the butchering bastard's twelfth victim in five months. There was one other thing she knew for sure. It wasn't one of the brothers who was murdering her fellow human beings and then gutting them like animals in a slaughterhouse. This satanic beast was cloaked in a white skin, the pale color of death.

After church, tomorrow morning, she'd drop her son off at her mother's house in Southeast D.C. and go downtown. She was scheduled to work the four to twelve shift. Sunday noon-time dinner had suddenly lost its appeal. She'd go into work early. Maybe something would break in the case. She fell to her knees in front of her double bed, and prayed like her mother had made her do since she was a little pig-tailed girl.

The prayer was always the same. When she was a child it was on the wall of her room, above the bed. And still, it was above her bed now. She bowed her head, closed her eyes, and prayed that God would carry her along the troubled path of life. She needed his help more than ever. If only she could see the vision of the single set of feet in the sand. The footprints would then be his, and only his. But, she still saw the two sets as she walked along, next to her creator. Rhonda Renee Bell desperately needed her God to lift and carry her through this troubled time in her life.

She also prayed that when she reported for duty, her partner, Michael Anthony McCarthy, wouldn't be drunk again, not that she could blame him. Not many human beings had to live with such a terrible burden of suffering. There was simply no way to change the past. What was done was done. Ronnie Bell could only absorb so much of her partner's pain. He'd have to lift himself out of the darkness of despair. Ronnie knew that Mac was close to swallowing the cold steel barrel of his own gun. She could only imagine what it must be like, having to live with such tormenting agonies.

Nobody, not even Ronnie Bell, could ever dream of just how horribly Michael Anthony McCarthy really felt. Every night his drunken mind conjured up hordes of flesh eating demons, coming to devour him in a frenzy of ghastly death. No other police officer had ever done what he had done. No other D.C. police officer had ever killed another D.C. police officer in the line of duty. His was the friendly in the familiar phrase friendly fire, the friendly fire that had snuffed out the innocent life of an young cop.

The frigid northern winds of winter's deadly hawk whipped through the trembling city, snatching away the breath of spring. It was unusually cold, the bleak winter trapping the terrified inhabitants in a dank bloody slaughterhouse of human flesh. Beware, the season of the haunting hunt is upon the asphalt jungle, its fearful unrest strangling the reeling city. He loved this place, this place where the shadows run from themselves, this place of demons and ghouls, this place of misery and death. Welcome to this place. Welcome to Washington, D.C., the grim stalking grounds of the Capital Carver.

CHAPTER 1

THE CROSS-HAIRS of the 30.06 bolt action Winchester rifle locked onto their target. There was a crisp chill in the early morning air. The slowly melting frost glistened as the rising sun's rays filtered through the valley, surrounded by an endless panorama of mountains stretching as far as the eye could see. Their slopes and rounded tops were ablaze with the resplendent colors of Autumn. Forests laced with vividly colored trees mingled with intermittent patches of cleared land which sprouted withered yellowing cornstalks and formed a patchwork quilt of glorious beauty.

Ray Carson Carver watched the warm breath from his lungs crystallize as he exhaled into the frigid morning air. He could almost hear the crackling noise of the semi-frozen leaves laying on the frost covered ground as his quarry stepped from the edge of the hedge row and entered the clearing. This would be an easy kill. The sun was behind his back, barely over the horizon, blinding any attempt by his hopelessly doomed prey to see its callous stalker. There was no breeze, eliminating the only other chance at possible salvation the unsuspecting victim had.

Ray Carver decided to savor the moment. He lived for the hunt. Maybe even more, he lived for the kill. The hunt was the foreplay. The kill was the orgasm of his life. He felt the deep rooted aching of lustful anticipation which preceded each of his times of need, times that were becoming increasingly more regular. Their intensity demanded that every fiber of his being answer their persistent call. They forced him to satiate the familiar tingling sensation much as a sexually aroused man would seek a prostitute to satisfy his throbbing member. To cum, he had to kill.

Re-focusing his vision through the cross-hairs, he tightened the wrap of the rifle's brown leather sling around his left arm, steadying the weapon against the trunk of the slender birch tree it rested against. He felt the numbing cold in his right hand as he thumbed off the metal safety of the lethal weapon. Just for kicks, he'd take this one out right through the left ear. He'd pulverize its inferior mind into a boiling mass of churning brain matter.

The cross-hairs framed their mark. Without hesitation, Ray Carver squeezed the trigger of the powerful weapon. The startled whitetail deer never even heard the booming discharge as the copper jacketed projectile, traveling faster than the speed of sound, mangled its brain into a fiery explosion of grizzly jelly. He watched through the scope, fascinated, as the buck's head snapped upward and then disintegrated into a blood-red mush. The once regal animal staggered with the force of the impact and collapsed against a row of dried yellow cornstalks, their crisp rustling sounds snapping loudly in the now perfectly still frosty air.

Ray Carver slung the bolt action rifle over his right shoulder and began the slow meandering walk towards the fallen eight point buck. Somehow, the tormenting demons kept calling to him. There needed to be more blood letting. Their voracious appetites were consuming his mind and body in an insatiable quest for ultimate fulfillment. The thrill of these mundane executions was waning. He needed more. The idea began to take shape in his twisted mind.

He crunched across the thawing leaves and disheveled cornstalks which carpeted the crumbling plowed furrows of the field. Huge masses of dark grey clouds were already beginning to fill the sky. He sniffed the air. It felt like snow might be in the offing. The temperature was steadily dropping. The wind raked the shuffling rows of cornstalks with gusts of swirling air as dawn broke over the far horizon, only to be immediately smothered in a stormy looking black mass of swiftly moving clouds.

Standing over the fallen buck, he glanced into the shadowy woods at the field's edge. Many of the trees were already barren, their leaves littering the crimson carpeted ground. He propped his rifle against a nearby rotting fence post. Its rusted barbed wire lay tangled in the undergrowth, long ago having relented to the harsh battering winters.

He reached into his right pant's pocket and withdrew the small circular can of Copenhagen snuff which had imprinted its ring, much like a tattoo, on the outside pocket flap of his worn jeans. It served to act as a brand, telling the rest of the world that here stood one Ray Carson Carver, who was an ex-underground coal miner retired on black lung. It told them that he was a tough son of a bitch, a mean bastard who could kick ass, drink whiskey, and chase pussy with the best of them. Placing a pinch of the finely ground tobacco between his teeth and gum he spit out some of the rancid juice in a long arc, wiping the dribble with the sleeve of his black and red wool plaid jacket.

He paused as he withdrew the long blade of the hunting knife out of its sheath. It signified the beginning of the sacrificial ritual.

He gutted all his kills, even when he simply left them there to rot, as he would this one. He slid the cold steel into the warm furry belly of the dead deer. Steam formed in the cold clear air as the animal's hot innards were exposed to the plunging outside temperature. The smell of death reeked from the slaughtered whitetail, a scent unlike any other odor he had ever experienced. The sweet perfume of putrefied flesh permeated the crisp autumn air.

It was this, his twenty-seventh kill of the year, that changed the course of his life and the lives of many others. Suddenly, the realization came to him. His futile attempts at vindicating his bloodlust were falling far short of satiating his all consuming need. It was like balling that slut wife of his. The thrill was gone. Baby, the thrill was really gone.

He had always known the answer. Deep inside the demented recesses of his conscious-less brain stirred the solution. Being the hunted might be more thrilling than being the hunter. He realized that he could be both if he played his cards right.

Finishing the evisceration of the lifeless animal, he wiped off the blood covered stainless steel knife blade on a corn stalk and slung the rifle over his shoulder. Slowly, he began the walk back to his four wheel drive Dodge Ram pick-up truck. Today was special. It was his birthday. But, even more than that, it was the day of the undead. A flock of cawing crows circled overhead, in the dark grey stormy sky. Soon, they'd be picking the carcass and its steamy innards to pieces in a feeding frenzy of carnivorous lust, thought the solitary figure, as his demented mind turned the circling crows into blood sucking vampire bats.

The ghost of the headless horseman galloped across the rustling cornfield. The whistling wind carried the agonizing moans of countless multitudes of tortured souls on its chilling journey across the bleak lifeless field. Visions of a carnival of carnage flickered through his head as he conjured up scenes of murderous ghoulish slaughter. From the darkest caverns of his insane twisted mind arose the haunting premonition. His sordid seance with the images of the devil's disciples of doom had finally answered his prayers to end his miserable life. On this day, the thirty-first of October, Halloween, Ray Carson Carver decided that it was his time to die. This, he figured, could be the greatest birthday present of them all.

But first, he'd go coon hunting, and the best place that he knew of to find coons, the human variety, was in Washington, D.C.

CHAPTER 2

WHILE RAY CARVER prayed for his life's fulfillment in death, Danny Money, sometimes known as Easy Money to his fellow police officers of the Washington, D.C. Police Department, was praying to a different god. Bent over, on his knees, he pleaded for the agony to end. He swore he'd never do it again, no way. The moment of his salvation had to be close at hand. His guts must be bone dry by now.

Danny took one last long look at the smelly puke stained porcelain bowl and heaved a wretched gagging mess of lumpy bile like slime into the stinking toilet of Clancy's Bar and Grill. He knew one thing for sure. It was the first, and the last time, that he was ever going to let that fucking low life partner of his talk him into eating a bowl of, yes they're delicious, chitlins. Boiled pig's guts, no matter how much hot sauce you put on them, were still guts.

Officer Essex Johnson, a.k.a. the Bud Man, wondered how long his partner could possibly puke. He looked over at Clancy, affectionately called Tiny by the police regulars, in reverence to his six foot six, three hundred pound frame. The huge black bar owner winked back at the Bud Man as he drew the off duty officer another mug of Bud from the dwindling keg. The Bud Man drank nothing but Bud. Period. End of story. He took a swig of the golden nectar of the gods and belched.

"You know, Tiny," he said. "The only two things you can get anywhere in the world are Budweiser Beer and Coca Cola. And since you need a third ingredient, whiskey, to make Coke drinkable, you might as well stick with Bud. It has everything you need. In can, bottle, or keg variety. Ain't it a fucking fact of life?"

"You ain't sayin' shit, Bud Man. It's the gospel. It sure 'nuff is."

"You getting your white ass out here for another beer or you gonna puke in the shitter all morning?" yelled the Bud Man as he pounded on the flimsy bathroom door. He had to piss like a race horse. Just for good measure he added, "Tiny's got some more chitlins boiling on the stove." He chuckled as he made sure to fan some of the nauseating odor wafting up from his bowl in the direction of the now silent bathroom.

"He's fallen and he can't get up," joked Tiny, trying his best to mimic the helpless old lady's line in the pathetic Medic Alert commercial that made him wonder if an early death was really all that bad.

"Fuck you and your chitlins," hollered Money, his voice echoing in the flushing toilet bowl. The Bud Man, who thought chitlins beat Cheerios for breakfast any morning, returned to his seat at the bar to wash down his latest mouthful of the delectable chewy morsels with a long swallow of his favorite elixir. He had been trying for the entire first year that they'd been assigned together, to get his partner to taste some good steamy guts. He figured, this morning, with Tiny's help, he had finally ended his gastronomic mission. And, what a fitting ending it had turned out to be.

That son of a bitch, Money, had scared the shit right out of his black ass last night, on midnights, when he had pulled their patrol car, Scout 150, into that sunken alley while he was sleeping. That bastard, Money, had had the balls to line up his open passenger side window directly next to a fenced in used car lot full of ass chewing Dobermans. And then he had the audacity to bang the fence with his nightstick to set them off in a frenzy of teeth baring savagery.

Startled at the ferocious barking, the Bud Man awoke to find himself eyeball to eyeball with six flaming eyed murderous looking killers. The fact that the fence separated him from the savage beasts never registered as, in the darkness and being still groggy, he never even saw it. He was sure he was dead meat. His heart was in his throat as he threw up his arms to protect his face from the impending maiming he was about to receive. It was then that he caught a glance of that white prick partner of his, laughing his ass off, silhouetted in the scout car's illuminating headlights.

The Bud Man had taken it in the ass at the check off window this morning. But now, he had evened the score. Tonight at roll call he was going to bend Money over and ram the high hard one home. He might even bring in a baggy full of warm chitlins and leave it in Money's locker. Or, better yet, he could deliver it personally in the roll call room. Money wiped off his smelly face with a wet paper towel. The nauseating stench of vomit permeated the bathroom stall. He had to get his shit together. No way he could let the Bud Man see him like this. Tonight's roll call would be bad enough. Pushing open the creaky door, he headed directly for the nearest bar stool and resolutely ordered another draft beer. Despite having no wish to put anything other than

Bromo-seltzer in his already queasy stomach, he couldn't show any sign of weakness. The ravenous howling roll call room wolves would tear him to shreds.

Tiny decided it was time to open up for business and unlocked the front door. Two of the regulars, leaning against the steel door in anticipation of their first steadying drink of the day, tumbled into the musty smelling bar as Tiny swung it open. Within minutes all the stools were taken and the vagrant looking overflow began to settle into the red vinyl booths, their torn cushions like the back seat of a junked 57 Chevy.

The Bud Man and Money had been stopping into Clancy's ever since their first patrol together. It was only a few blocks outside of their beat, an area envied by no one except maybe the rats and roaches, animal, insect, and human variety alike. Tiny lived above the place and welcomed their presence almost any hour of the night or day.

He kind of missed Ronnie though. She had been Money's partner for five years. Money had been different around her. More than once he had sworn he had seen a sparkle in their eyes when they looked at each other. If ever there was a white boy that he'd condone taking up with one of the sisters it was Money. He loved him like a son. Ronnie had ended up in Homicide Squad and Money had more than once said he never wanted to be anything more than what he was, a uniform scout car officer, patrolling the beat.

"Hey, man, you ever hear from Ronnie anymore?" questioned Tiny, hoping he wasn't opening up any old wounds. "Yeah. I still talk to her once in awhile. Don't see her much though," lied Money who had spent all yesterday morning and half of the afternoon at her apartment, making love to her. Ronnie was that one special lady who turned him on like no other.

"Sheet man, I'd fuck that bitch's brains out if I had the chance. She's one fine lookin' fox," added the Bud Man, pushing his glass forward for another refill.

"A fine lookin' sister like that would never give your pitiful black ass a chance. She's got too much class for you. Your nigger ass is lower than snake shit," laughed Tiny as he filled up the Bud Man's glass with Miller Genuine Draft, positive that the Bud Man wouldn't be able to tell the difference by this time, anyway.

"You ever sample some of that fine black pussy? She's probably screwing some lieutenant downtown, in homicide squad," pressed the Bud Man, looking over at Money.

"Hey man. She's a friend. Lighten up. O.K.?"

The Bud Man, discerning that he had just broached a rather touchy subject with his partner, decided to back off. He couldn't help but think to himself that he'd sure as shit wished he could get in her drawers. He'd take her through the changes if he ever had the chance.

Unable to swallow the 'gag a maggot' brew that he suddenly found himself sipping on, the Bud Man spit out the nasty tastin' shit and shouted, "Tiny. Pour this motha fucking panther piss down the drain and give me a Bud, man. Miller is for faggots."

Tiny, in total amazement, shit canned the glass of Miller and handed the Bud Man a can of Bud, on the house. Now he knew, beyond any reasonable doubt, why they called the Bud Man the Bud Man. Money, deciding to top the morning off with the proverbial shooter and a splash, bought himself and the Bud Man a shot of Seagram's 7 and a brewski on the side. Sweating bullets, Tiny made sure that the golden, foamy elixir was pure unadulterated Budweiser.

Soon thereafter, both officers staggered out of the dingy hole in the wall bar and were blinded by the bright D.C. sunshine which lit up their ghetto world in a cleansing bath of false purity. Daylight made everything look so safe. Nothing was as it seemed. In their world there was no black and white, only flickering shadowy twilight.

"Later, man," shouted the Bud Man as he opened the door of his brand new red IROC Z-28 Camaro, the pride of his thirty-seven years of existence on the face of this miserable scumbag-infested planet. He watched Money drive away in his yuppie ass white BMW convertible, and made a mental note not to forget the chitlins.

Danny Money was heading for home. He wasn't going to his townhouse in Greenbelt, Maryland. He was going where his heart was, to visit a tall dark skinned woman who had stolen his soul. To him, she was the black magic woman of whom songs have been sung. He called her his brown sugar. There were times when he wanted to ask her to marry him. Then, there were those terrible times when he felt not only the whites, but, also the blacks, stare with a penetrating hatred as the two of them walked down the street holding hands, or laughing the carefree lover's laugh of happiness.

Alone, with her and her son, he wanted to take care of them for the rest of his life. But, in public, he was afraid. The deep roots of racial prejudice lay in the cold hearts of too many of both races. He wasn't afraid for him. He was afraid for them, Ronnie and Darnell. Physically, they might get hurt. Spiritually and emotionally, they might die. He owed them a commitment. Ronnie would never ask him for one, but Darnell's eyes said it all. He'd have to fight his own conflicting feelings. He'd have to sort things out for himself. Deep down inside Danny Money really knew the answer. It was only a matter of time.

CHAPTER 3

DETECTIVE RHONDA BELL sat in the Homicide Squad roll call room and half listened as Detective Sergeant John Gregson routinely plowed through the official bullshit lookouts, descriptions, and explanations of the four homicides which had occurred during the previous two eight hour shifts. It didn't take a doctorate from Harvard to figure out that three of them were drug related. The locations revealed more than any eye witness ever would, if you could even find one. The drug trafficking corners where they were wasted were well known by everybody.

Her mind was on the two men in her life, Danny and Darnell. If only everything could work out. She knew it was hard on Danny. He had fallen in love with a black woman. It was worse on her. She was head over heels in love with a white man and was afraid of losing him, not to another woman, but to a sick society which judged your emotions by the color of your skin. How could she bear him children and expose them to this inherent hate? How would people treat Darnell if she and Danny were man and wife? Ronnie felt like she was sinking in a cesspool of human waste.

Ronnie Bell also knew something else. She knew her body glowed with the warmth of spent passion. Thinking about their brief afternoon liaison of less than two hours ago, her thoughts drifted to the tumultuous, shattering orgasms and the sweat soaked abandon of lovemaking which had driven her to the brink of total ecstasy. When she took him he was hers for as long as she wanted. No other man, not even her first lover, had made her feel the way Danny did. In her heart, she knew the answer. It could be no other way.

Her late afternoon wet dream was interrupted by the guttural voice of Detective Lieutenant Bow Wow Bowser who had aptly acquired the deserved nickname when, in uniform, he had bitten off the ear of a violent suspect and consequently secured himself a revered place in police folk-lore. Right now his legendary status, with all that his appropriate nickname implied, was unleashing its unrestrained fury onto the cringing forms of the ten homicide squad detectives sitting in the tiny roll call room.

His meeting with the Assistant Chief had not gone well. Homicides were up almost thirty percent, topping the six hundred mark for the first time; which, related into simple terms, meant that an upstanding D.C. resident had about a one in one thousand chance of ending up in an early grave, abruptly deposited there by a never ending variety of insane circumstances. All of these premature applicants to the D.C. Morgue honor roll needed a rational explanation for their impromptu demise which, in turn, had to be supplied by the frustrated detectives of the overworked homicide squad.

At this moment, the rational explanations, in Bow Wow Bowser's opinion, were not coming fast enough. In an uncontrolled fit of vehement rage he flung his clip-board against the far wall, prompting Ronnie Bell's partner, thirty three year veteran Mike McCarthy, to calmly ask, "Lieutenant, does this mean that my sabbatical to the Sorbonne has been disapproved?"

Bow Wow Bowser flew into an even greater rage at McCarthy's smartass remark and stormed out of the roll call room muttering obscenities to himself, his face the color of crimson death. Mike McCarthy couldn't help himself. He felt pretty spry today.

As Bow Wow Bowser smashed into the swinging roll call room door McCarthy yelled, "Lighten up Lieutenant. Chill out. You look like a heart attack lookin' for a place to happen."

Mike McCarthy pulled Cruiser 311 out of the basement motor pool of downtown police headquarters, heading for Fourteenth and T Street, NW, to make a preliminary assessment of the early evening's incessant parade of hookers. He couldn't help but feel a little disturbed. In all his thirty three years on the force he had never felt so helpless. Murder, in this drug crazed city, had become like honey to a bear, only in this case it was more like shit to flies. Respect for law and order had vanished in the race riots of the sixties and the protests of the seventies. Now, they fought a deadly war of survival in which they were both outnumbered and outgunned. The enemy, like the shadowy Viet Cong, was virtually invisible to all but the most savvy of street cops.

Detective Mike McCarthy missed the old days, the days when footpatrols were the pulse that ran through the police department's veins. Now, hot shot jockeys raced their shiny blue and white patrol cars through the congested streets and avenues, answering the incessant radio runs, never bothering to get out of their four wheeled world. Things were always happening too fast. Sometimes you had to slow down. Every once in a while had to stop and smell the roses.

If Mike McCarthy had learned one thing in his countless years policing the streets of the Nation's Capital, it was a simple thing. Don't make people earn your respect. Give it to them regardless of who they appear to be. Answering radio runs wasn't solving crimes. Solving crimes walked hand in hand with understanding the people whose lives you were sworn to protect. Compassion was the key to unlocking the gates of justice.

Rhonda Bell smiled as she looked over at Mac, an informality he had finally allowed her. His wavy grey hair, streaked with an occasional burst of reddish brilliance, was combed straight back, hardly wavering in the gentle breeze that wafted through the slowly moving unmarked tan cruiser. His threadbare navy blazer did little to make a fashion statement, nor did it conceal his protruding stomach which, like the disease bearing the same name, had, years ago, 'dun lapped' over his belt.

The puffy red faced man in his middle fifties was, for all practical purposes, a throwback to another age, an age of laughter and joviality. Somehow, through life's twists and turns, he had stumbled into an age of violence and an era of death. That, more than anything, was why Ronnie Bell had come to love working with this rumpled old man.

Despite his sagging chin and the rolls of flesh that hung over his yellowed shirt collar, to her, Mac was a hero. He treated her people, the black people of her city, with respect. A large piece of her generous heart now belonged to this out of vogue warrior who had become like the father she had never known. Inside, where it really mattered, they were so much alike. They both dreamed of gingerbread men, in a land filled with murderous evil, a land that was about to explode into a bloody killing ground where a living dead man stalked his human prey.

Even at this very moment, Ray Carson Carver was truckin' down his own personal highway to hell, heading for the Capital, his newly designated happy hunting ground. Tonight he would bring down his first real kill. He'd take out a coon, a buck coon. In his mind, it was only natural that a bitch coon would be next. All in due time. He didn't even need a license for this hunt. He inserted the cassette tape into its slot on his truck's dashboard. It was the first rock tape he had ever bought. Good ol' foot stompin' country was his style, not rock. But, this song had really tickled his fancy.

He just knew that Jonny boy couldn't be one of them freaked out long haired dopers. This boy knew too much of what he sang. You could hear it in his voice. His music came from his guts. Singin' bout six gun lovers and goin out in a real bloody blaze of glory. That's the way real men die. This Bon Jovi guy really talked turkey, thought Ray Carver, as he spit out the window and laughed to himself. The kill was such a thrill. He only hoped that the news media would give him a good handle. Damn, the Night Stalker was already taken. He liked that one.

The Bud Man eased Scout 150, their blue and white marked patrol car, to the curb in front of Ricky's sometimes used Auto Sales, and all the time numbers joint. He glanced over at the tall lanky frame of his dark haired partner. Money was almost too much of a pretty boy. His finely chiseled delicate features contrasted sharply with the Bud Man's thick lips and wide nose. Money's fair skin was on the opposite spectrum of the color scheme. The Bud Man looked down at his own shiny jet black skin and concluded, once and for all, that black is beautiful even if white was might.

Despite his looking like a white version of Arsenio Hall, the Bud Man couldn't help but like Danny Money. The guy had style, but unlike most white boys, he was cool, a real blue eyed soul brother. Damn, the Bud Man was sure Money was screwing that fox from homicide, Bell. She was one fine filly. Maybe, with any luck, figured the Bud Man, she'd get tired of that puny white meat and go back to her own kind. He'd be more than willing to reacquaint her with some big black oak. If not, it was her loss. He made it a rule to keep his hands, and everything else, off another man's territory. Danny Money looked out of the passenger side window of Scout 150 and watched the fat human ball of fluorescent orange saunter down the driveway. Slick Rick, himself, was already walking down to meet them.

"Hey, man, the motha fuckas got me. They snatched one of my cleanest rides, man," shouted the excited owner.

"Cleaner than a chitlin', I bet," stated the Bud Man, snickering as he swore he saw his partner wince at the sound of that most dreadful of culinary delights.

Money opened their scout car's report box, removed a stolen auto report form, and prepared to listen to Ricky's shuckin' and jivin' bullshit. As their field investigation progressed it was becoming obvious that Slick Rick had got nailed for one piece of shit 1985 brown Thunderbird with three hubcaps missing and slight left rear fender damage that still contained a yellow paint mark from the striking vehicle. What a slimy office, reflected Money, as he excused himself to finish the report and lookout in 150.

Slick Rick followed them all the way to the scout car, bitching, and complaining incessantly about the worthless good for nothing local punks. Money couldn't help but compliment Ricky baby on his orange polyester leisure suit.

"Rick, you must have really looked hard to find that suit, man," he said.

"You're cleaner than a chitlin', brother. And, that's a fact, Jack," remarked the Bud Man, looking for another painful reaction from his beleaguered partner.

Slick Rick replied, "Shit, man, this motha' fucka' be bad. Got it down on H Street. At Gorgeous George's Clothes Emporium."

Money figured about as much, and couldn't help but add, "Shit, looks like it came from Saks. Thought I saw one just like it down there last weekend." Jesus, Money wished somebody other than the Bud Man could hear this. He really had Slick Rick going.

The Bud Man glanced in the rear view mirror as Money was about to air the stolen auto lookout. An elderly couple in a beat up looking Oldsmobile was pulling in behind them. Probably got lost on their way home from some street corner preacher's "pass the plate and pay for my pussy" social, figured the Bud Man, as he prepared to give directions to the dapper couple.

As the old black man approached the patrol car the Bud Man could see that the old boy was extremely upset about something. By the look in the man's eyes this wasn't just going to be any simple direction-giving bullshit session.

"Officer, they just about ran me and my old lady off the road. Smartasses. Called my wife an old bitch. They're driving like maniacs all over the place," wheezed the old man excitedly.

The Bud Man replied, "Relax, sir. What the fuck? Oh, excuse me, sir. What the hell are you talkin' about?" The Bud Man, like most every police officer, sometimes forgot that the f-word wasn't everybody's everyday language. He made a mental note to try and get his fucking act in order.

"Where'd this shit go down, sir?" asked the Bud Man politely, figuring his four letter words were getting a little better.

"It happened in Trinidad Terrace. About five blocks away. Just a bunch of young black punks."

Money inquired, "Can you describe the vehicle that they were driving?"

"A brown T-Bird, officer," replied the old man as his wife hollered out the window, "And it was sure 'nuff a beat up looking wreck, officer."

"Couldn't be my ride, man," shouted Slick Rick from the car lot. "My shit was clean, real clean."

Money pretended to ignore Slick Rick's obvious bullshit comment. "Any paint or damage on the vehicle?" he asked.

"It weren't no cream puff officer," answered the lady. "It even had a two-tone paint job. Yellow on the side."

Money keyed the radio mike, "Scout 150."

The dispatcher answered, "Go ahead 150."

Money stated, "I believe a stolen vehicle described as a brown Thunderbird. Hub caps missing. With a yellow paint streak on same is in the Trinidad area. Occupied by several black males."

The dispatcher replied, "O.K. 150. 151 you respond to the vicinity and assist 150."

"151 responding to Trinidad and Neal," stated the despondent Emancipation Proclamation Jones who wondered why in the hell he had ever volunteered to work with Spic N' Span Spiegel. He should have been at Jasper's listening to some tunes and sipping on some cognac while he perused the fine lookin' bitches. He wouldn't ever volunteer for jack shit again.

Spiegel stunk like unwashed drawers. Damn, the son of a bitch must never even splash any water on his stinkin' white ass. His hair looked like his head leaked 10W-40 oil, thought Emancipation Proclamation Jones, as he disgustedly looked at his partner, whose wrinkled light blue uniform shirt hung half out of his grease stained dark blue pants. At least the nylon jacket covered the embarrassing looking shirt, figured Emancipation, glad that he didn't have any traces of Spic N' Span's acne covered oily face.

Man, he'd been lucky this afternoon. True to his nickname, he had spent the better part of the day living up to his favorite "Baby, I'll set you free rap," and stroking some guy's old lady into a sexual frenzy. Jesus, he loved it when they talked.

"Give it to me, baby. Harder. Harder. Get it, baby." His dick was starting to get stiff just thinking about it. Then, the bitch had started screaming, music to his ears. He loved that even more.

So much so, that he forgot that they were in her condo, with the window open.

The fucking concerned nosy neighbors had called the police. How the hell was he supposed to know that her old man was a D.C. police officer from the Sixth District. Even worse, the brother was on duty, patrolling the very beat where he lived. Emancipation Proclamation Jones had managed to crawl out of the second floor bedroom window just as one excited policeman entered his own house, gun drawn, looking to bust a cap in somebody's ass.

His luck, in all his twenty-nine years, had never failed him. Gasping in panic, he had fallen out of the window into a garbage filled dumpster which broke his fall, and fortunately not his leg. Emancipation Proclamation Jones had run down Division Avenue and jumped into his black Corvette convertible and was last seen leaving the neighborhood at a high rate of speed.

The Bud Man drove 150 onto Trinidad Avenue and turned left on Childress Street. It was still early enough in their shift that the usual incessant din of neighborhood activity was at a minimum. As he slowly cruised east on Childress Street, he couldn't help but feel the pulsating excitement throbbing through his composed outer being in anticipation of the chase. Who needed drugs? This had to be the ultimate high. "C'mon you mother fuckers. C'mon I know you're up here," mumbled the Bud Man.

It happened so quickly that all thoughts simply vanished with the huge adrenaline rush. The brown T-bird was turning left on Childress from Holbrook Street. Shit, the Bud Man knew he couldn't avoid it. They were driving right past him. The jig was up and the chase would be on before the trap was set. The Bud Man and Money tried not to look at the occupants as they slowly drove past Scout 150, heading west on Childress. The two vehicles passed within three feet of each other. The Bud Man knew as soon as he swung around to make a u-turn the T-Bird would be booking. He slammed 150's steering wheel right and left in quick succession, forcing the patrol car into a tight U-turn that would put them right on the T-Birds' ass.

Black smoke was already pouring out of Slick Rick's creampuff as the driver of the stolen car floored the gas pedal.

"Son of a bitch!" yelled the Bud Man. He couldn't make the turn. "Goddamned shit turning radius is screwin' us again," muttered the frustrated officer. He slammed the brake and threw the gear shift into reverse, 150's squealing rear tires burning rubber as he tried to get behind the escaping car. Now he had enough room. The Bud Man slapped the shifter into low and floored the gas pedal. The T-Bird was already through the intersection of Childress and Trinidad, heading south on Trinidad. Money was fumbling with 150's mike. Jesus, he wished Ronnie was still with him. The Bud Man was O.K. But, Ronnie was something special, both in and out of the patrol car.

Money finally keyed the mike. "150 priority, 150 priority," shouted the excited officer as the dispatcher answered, "All units stand by. Go ahead with your priority 150."

Money yelled, "We're in pursuit of a 1985 brown T-Bird occupied by four black males heading south on Trinidad. Towards Neal. The vehicle is out and reported stolen."

"151 is at Trinidad and Neal," replied Emancipation Proclamation Jones who prayed that his moment of salvation from this afternoon's close encounter of the fuck up kind might possibly be at hand.

The Bud Man flipped the switch that activated the red pulsating visibar lights and turned the siren knob to 'yelp' as the chase was now on in earnest. They were closing in on the T-Bird as it approached Neal.

Money knew the rats were heading for their hole, wherever it may be, and advised 151 to remain at Trinidad and Neal. The brown T-Bird began to slow as Money saw Emancipation Proclamation Jones and Spic N' Span Spiegel, in 151, approaching head on to the fleeing vehicle. The passenger side door opened and two of the occupants made their dash for safety. The T-Bird continued to slow. Out of control, it bounced over the curb and imbedded itself in a wooden telephone pole, its flimsy hood and trunk simultaneously flying open.

The driver threw open his door and extended his leg to the curb in an attempt to make his escape. Emancipation Proclamation Jones eased the left front bumper of 151 into the door, pinning the driver's left leg with a sickening crunch and securing at least one arrest for unauthorized use of a vehicle. The fourth passenger, in sheer panic, climbed over the screaming driver and dove out the window.

Money popped the portable radio out of 150 and began the foot chase down Neal St. Shit, no way Jose, figured Money as he started to suck air, his holster wildly flopping against his right leg. This dude was rolling. It was worth a try. "Halt or I'll shoot," he yelled in the direction of the fleeing juvenile.

"Fuck you. And your slow white ass. I knew you'all couldn't

jump. But, you can't beat feet, either," shouted the juvenile over his shoulder as he disappeared around the corner of a nearby building, Money throwing his nightstick down the middle of the street in frustration.

Danny Money walked back down Neal St., towards the scene of the crash. Emancipation Proclamation Jones was mocking his tired white ass unmercifully while Emancipation's prisoner was still hysterically screaming about his broken motha' fuckin' leg that needed immediate medical attention. Spic N' Span Spiegel was reading the suddenly wilting suspect the required warning of rights, his rancid breath gagging both Emancipation Proclamation Jones and the recoiling prisoner.

The Bud Man had hit paydirt. At least these asshole punks had good taste. He gleefully looked down at a case of shiny silver Budweiser cans that lay in the cluttered trunk of the abandoned T-Bird. The best news was that it was still cold. He walked over to 150 with his precious cargo in hand and opened the Scout car trunk, quickly depositing his prized haul. This was confiscated property that wasn't going on anybody's Found Property Book.

The Bud Man headed 150 towards the Fifth District Headquarters to handle their share of the impending paperwork. Jones and Spiegel had taken the collar, now they could have their spoils, a seven AM trip to D.C. Superior Court, the next morning. Money and the Bud Man would be toasting their victory with a cold one while Jones and Spiegel got writer's cramp.

Ray Carson Carver reached the Capital Beltway and began to circle his happy hunting grounds just as the Bud Man and Danny Money sat in 150, behind a vacant warehouse, sipping their first cold beer of their first night on another four to twelve shift. This tour of duty was off to a monumental start. Only three hours had passed and already they had felt the thrill of a heated chase and had managed to avoid the bulk of the much dreaded paperwork.

While Danny Money and the Bud Man were enjoying the fruits of their recent victory, Ray Carver's loins were throbbing with the lustful anticipation of imminent human bloodletting. He couldn't even remember the first four hours of his trip. Everything, except the impending snapshot of death, framed in his mind, was a blur of unreality.

He exited on to the Baltimore-Washington Parkway and headed southwest, towards Washington, D.C.. Brown lines of tobacco juice drooled down through the heavy growth of his stubbly beard, staining the corners of his sinister mouth. His deep brown lifeless eyes revealed no emotion. They were simply two murky bottomless pools of death's remorseless eternity. His balding head, encased in a dirt and grease covered camouflage cap displaying the yellow insignia of the Caterpillar company, CAT, pounded relentlessly.

Reaching into the pocket of his tan hunting vest, he removed the pack of Camels and placed one of the unfiltered cigarettes between his moist discolored lips. Not many could chew snuff and smoke a Camel at the same time, figured Ray Carver, proud of his virile manhood. Then again, not many could do what he was about to do. Not even the new generation of coal miners had his balls. They were punks, just like most of their old men.

CHAPTER 4

"HEY, RONNIE, let's grab a cup of coffee," suggested Mike McCarthy, pulling the detective cruiser into the parking lot of the McDonald's at New York and Florida Avenue Northeast. So far it had been pretty quiet. He hoped it stayed that way.

They looked inside the packed two story McDonald's and then cautiously entered, neither detective wanting to walk into a robbery in progress with them being the guests of honor. Making sure to secure a table which faced the entrance they sat down and unconsciously began to watch every suspicious person coming in or going out of the bustling fast food restaurant.

"How's Darnell doing?" asked Mike McCarthy, sipping on his three sugar, three cream, large cup of coffee.

"He's doing real good. Mama's watching him tonight," answered Ronnie, dunking the tea bag in and out of her cup of hot water. Lately, her mind had been wandering a lot. Except for Darnell, this job used to be her life. Danny Money had changed all that. She got a case of old fashioned goose bumps every time she thought about him. Her whole body glowed with a warm prickly heat when he touched her. Right now, even her face felt flushed.

"The old boyfriend been bothering you anymore?" asked Mike McCarthy, sensing that Ronnie was daydreaming about something other than solving homicides.

Mac knew her ex-old man, from the old days, when Mac had been assigned to the Narcotics Squad. That piece of shit was trash, the kind of human garbage that infected everything it touched with the cancerous sores of rotten sickness and death. He had busted the bastard once and the low life had spit in his face. Mac was glad Ronnie had finally set herself free from the vile scum of the decaying ghetto. Now, if she could only find a man that loved her for what she was, a sensitive fragile woman who had blossomed out of the manure covered fields of asphalt where she had been raised. Her ex old man, that no-good hard-ass prick named Fred Frost, would end up with a bullet in his head, one way or another, figured Mac. He had more than a faint suspicion that her old uniform partner, Danny Money, was messing up her head. He only hoped Money didn't intend to mess up her life. This poor girl had had it rough enough. She needed tenderness and love, not fast talk and mind games.

"No, everything's cool. He's left us pretty much alone," lied Ronnie, thinking about the biggest mistake in her life that had resulted in creating her biggest pride and joy. Why had she ever slept with that bastard in the first place? She had thought she loved him. She had even let him move in with her. Then, one month, she was late. The next month she knew she was pregnant with their child. She was elated. Naively, she dreamed of how he would take her in his arms and ask her to marry him.

Well, Prince Charming had hit her instead, calling her a stupid nigger bitch for not being on the pill. Then, the beatings had started, beatings that vividly reminded her of her childhood when a countless assortment of men had used and abused her mother, and then finally they had starting abusing her. She knew all about users and hurt. Sometimes, when she dropped Darnell off at her mother's house, the son of a bitch would follow her. She wasn't afraid for herself. She was afraid for her mother, Darnell, and even Danny.

Her ex-lover, Freddy Frost, had threatened to kill Danny if he ever caught them together. She knew he was more than capable of doing just that. It bothered him that she was giving her body to any man, let alone a white man. Ronnie knew that he was living with some woman that had borne him a son. The woman's two daughters stayed with them too, in a row house, on Orleans Place. While she and Danny dealt justice, that bastard and his bitch dealt drugs and violence. In the inner city ghetto where he now lived, where he and Ronnie had been raised, he was a big shot. The street dudes called him Frosty, Frosty the Snowman. His kind of snow melted in your nose, not in your hand.

Orleans Place was a bad place, a place where demons danced in your head. Nobody wanted to go to Orleans Place. Many of those that went never returned, becoming human fodder for the ruthless cold blooded drug lords that ruled there. Orleans Place was a sanctuary for those that only wished to sample the worst vileness that life had to offer. It was whispered that even the ex-mayor had been seen on Orleans Place, quenching his appetite for Frosty's snow.

When a blue and white D.C. police car turned on to Orleans Place, on routine patrol, it was said that dead men rode in the car. The thing that bothered Ronnie most was that the scout car always bore the same number. Orleans Place sat right in the middle of Scout 150's beat. Danny and the Bud Man were the human ghosts of the living dead that the homeboys talked about. She had been lucky. She had got out of there alive and, God help her, she'd never go back to that life. Every night she prayed that Danny wouldn't die in that cesspool of drugs, violence, and death.

The Bud Man popped open his second can of his favorite nectar. Deciding to relieve himself, he opened the scout car door and strolled over to the unlit corner of the dark warehouse. Danny Money glanced at the massive muscular back of his broad shouldered partner and then dotted the last 'i' on the recovered stolen auto report. Now, he could finish his beer in peace.

"Scout 150," called the dispatcher.

Money picked up the mike and disgustedly answered, "150 is 10-4." Sometimes, this job could be a pain in the ass. The Bud Man was walking back towards the car, smiling, eager to suck down his next brewski.

"Scout 150. Check for the unconscious man. Under the Anacostia Bridge, 1925 hours," assigned the dispatcher.

"Shit," muttered Money, under his breath. That's all they needed, to find some puke covered shit stained wino laying under the bridge. The Bud Man wasn't too pleased with this radio run either. He pictured a more dire scene, a bloated human carcass, laying there ripe, just waiting to burst its greasy grimy gopher guts all over his clean uniform. Worse yet, to add insult to injury, it was starting to rain.

After ten minutes of driving up and down the river bank of the stinking polluted Anacostia River, shining the spotlight, and walking through all the trash that lined the river shore, Money just couldn't help himself. He keyed the mike. "The only thing dead down here is the fish, 10-8," stated the chuckling officer as he put 150 back in service. I crack myself up. That was great, thought Money, laughing to himself. What an original radio transmission. It could go down as a classic to be talked about for years. I might become a legend, he figured as he listened to the dispatcher's curt acknowledgment.

No sense of humor in the Communications Division. It didn't matter. It was worth it, thought Money, grinning at the Bud Man, who couldn't have agreed more.

The Bud Man headed 150 down Benning Road. He couldn't decide whether tonight's main entree would be a rib sandwich or some hot spicy chicken wings. The only thing that Benning Road had more of than chicken wing carry outs and seamy bars was churches, the ones where the collection plate was some fast talking self appointed slickster's payroll check. The more services he could hold, the more Cadillacs he could buy.

The Bud Man hated these so-called preachers. The scumbag maggots sucked the poor ignorant people dry. Sitting in front of the Islamic church of the Benning Road Brothers and Sisters, smoldering in anger, the Bud Man decided to do a little preaching of his own. Inspired, he abruptly pulled 150 to the curb and, without saying a word to Money, immediately proceeded to begin issuing a barrage of parking tickets to the car that he knew belonged to the Reverend Oral Arsenio Ames. He was absolutely sure that the good reverend's first name denoted his sexual preference with his parishioners, not his ability to honestly convey the word of God. The Bud Man knew for a fact that asshole Oral spoke with a forked tongue. The slimy weasel had his pink Cadillac parked in front of Tommy's T house, on Maryland Avenue, almost every afternoon. Tommy's T house being the rent by the hour version of the ghetto Hilton.

Just as the Bud Man finished his self ordained gospel mission and neatly tucked the fourth violation notice under Oral Ames' windshield wiper, this one for the heinous crime of having dirty tags, the Reverend Oral Ames burst out of the swinging double doors of his dilapidated house of worship and immediately jumped into the bulky officer's smiling face. Oral Ames, his pudgy body decked out in the shiniest peach colored suit Money had ever seen, stood eyeball to eyeball with the Bud Man. The narrow sidewalk was beginning to overflow as the milling congregation spilled out of the crowded church, joining the lookyloos that had already gathered around Oral Ames' pink Cadillac.

Reaching over to the Cadillac's windshield, Oral Ames slowly pulled the tickets out from under the wiper blade and proceeded to tear them up, one by one. Money watched in anxious anticipation. The Bud Man continued to smile, never laying a hand on the outraged preacher. Oral Ames dropped the tiny shreds of torn paper on to the wet road, making his one mistake of the damp drizzly evening. The Bud Man saw the opening that he had been silently praying for. He grabbed the preacher's flabby arm and spun him around against the rain covered Cadillac, advising Oral Ames that he was under arrest for depositing trash, which was what he was, anyway.

Money grabbed his nightstick and popped the portable radio out of its console. He rushed over to help the Bud Man handcuff the struggling preacher who, in an unconscious digression, began to mother-fuck the two officers with a smoldering verbal tirade, shocking his stunned congregation into hushed silence. Then, all hell broke loose.

Oral Ames, his senses returned, called for a jihad against the unholy infidels of brutality and oppression. Without a second's hesitation, they answered his desperate call for a holy war and charged towards the bewildered officers.

Money ducked just in time to avoid the brick that came hurtling through the air, disintegrating the rear driver's side window of Scout 150 into an explosion of shattered glass. The Bud Man began to retreat towards their scout car, making sure to keep Oral Ames between him and the pressing crowd. At least Oral baby would eat the first mouthful of flying fist, he concluded. Money pulled the mace canister out of his Sam Brown belt and sprayed a steady stream of the blinding liquid into the first wave of charging assailants. They staggered back, but, incensed to an even greater rage, resumed their attack. Money, knowing that this was about to become the twentieth century version of the Battle of the Little Bighorn, depressed the portable radio transmitter and screamed, "150, 10-33, 2300 block of Benning Road!"

Emancipation Proclamation Jones, cruising 151 down Maryland Avenue, less than three blocks away, floored the scout car gas pedal, sending a plume of black exhaust smoke rising into the misty night air. This shit beat doing the boring paperwork on ol' Hop-a-long. The poor bastard's leg was really broken. Damn, the son of a bitch was still screaming when the ambulance had come to the Fifth District to take him to D.C. General Hospital. Besides, having Spiegel for a partner wasn't all bad, figured Emancipation. The mother fucker could write some powerful shit. He could talk trash and Spiegel could write reports. Not a bad basis for a partnership, thought Emancipation Proclamation Jones. If only Spiegel didn't stink like rotten toe jam.

Spic N' Span Spiegel turned on the red lights and siren and advised the dispatcher that they were now only two blocks away. Answering a 10-33, a police officer in trouble call, was like mainlining adrenaline. If it didn't get you high then you had lost the edge. Spic N' Span Spiegel hadn't lost the edge. He loved this job. All he had ever wanted to be was a Washington, D.C. police officer, like his father before him.

He was as proud of his father as any young man that had ever walked the face of the earth. To him, his father had become a saintly legend, his ghost walking the footbeat that had taken his life, a footbeat on Orleans Place. Sometimes, Spic N' Span Spiegel drifted into states of abysmal depression. He was ashamed of himself, embarrassed that he'd never live up to the towering image of the beat cop that his father had been, an image he revered like no other.

His wandering mind was snapped back into the harsh focus of reality as Emancipation Proclamation Jones abruptly skidded 151 sideways, across the wet slippery pavement, wildly sliding the careening scout car in the direction of the violent looking crowd surrounding 150.

Danny Money was in a bad way, about to be buried in some even deeper shit. Two black men held him in a choke hold while a lithe young black woman began punching the side of his face, her wildly flailing fists pummeling his reeling head. Out of the corner of his eye he caught a glimpse of the Bud Man wildly swinging his nightstick like a cavalry sabre, never letting go of Oral Ames, who was absorbing as much punishment from his own holy warriors as he was from the desperate Bud Man.

Money knew his ass would be history if one of his assailants managed to get his gun out of his holster. His nine millimeter dangled precariously from the flopping swivel holster. His right hand, tightly clasped on the handle of the semi automatic Glock, was the only thing preventing either one of his attackers from grabbing the pistol. The girl was really hurting him now, her sharp nails raking his cheeks, drawing blood. She spit in his face, all the while yelling a steady stream of obscenities into the damp night air.

The violent crowd momentarily disintegrated into a churning mass of panicked humanity as Emancipation Proclamation Jones, caught up in the frenzy of the moment, slid Scout 151 into their reeling midst, knocking several of the combatants to the oily pavement. Scout 151, sitting in the middle of the suddenly retreating army of Islam, its red lights flashing and its siren still screaming, gave Danny Money the opportunity he needed.

He kicked his right foot into the young girl's shin, her leg buckling under the painful force of the staggering blow. Spic N' Span Spiegel, seeing no other alternative, crawled out of Scout 151's passenger side window and dove head first into the wild melee, knocking over the man that was still reaching for Danny

Money's gun. Emancipation Proclamation Jones, screaming, "Praise the lord, baby. I'm gonna set a whole lot of you mother fuckers free," charged in the direction of the small group of assailants that still surrounded the Bud Man, his huge blackjack swinging wildly in the dim glow of the misty night.

Money, finally freed from the two men, thanks to Spic N' Span Spiegel, pulled his own leather encased lead blackjack from his right rear pocket and raised the lethal weapon high over his head. The crazy bitch was coming again. Only, this time, her right hand held a razor knife. The crazed woman lunged at Money, the pointed edge of the blade barely missing his gasping throat. Danny Money jumped up in the air, and with all the force he could muster, he slammed the descending blackjack into the attacking girl's forehead, right between her eyes. The wicked weapon cracked into the girl's head with a sickening thud. The girl staggered back, clutching at her bloodied head as she fell to her knees.

Fearing that he had killed his crumpling assailant, Danny Money leaned over, hoping she was still alive. He had no desire to kill anybody, let alone a young girl.

Danny Money almost made the biggest mistake of his life. The recovering girl reached out and wildly swept the razor blade across his chest, slicing open his nylon uniform jacket, barely missing his skin. Bewildered, Money grabbed the girl's flailing arm and wrestled her to the slick pavement in a punching and scratching free for all that ended abruptly when Emancipation Proclamation Jones, having just finished his liberation of the Bud Man, jammed all four inches of the barrel of his gun down the gagging throat of the wild eyed hellion. Just for good measure he added, "It ain't as big as my cock, baby. But, it'll set you free even quicker."

Sirens wailed from every direction as unit after unit of blue clad reinforcements screamed on to the ghetto battlefield, their flashing red lights casting an eerie glow on the suddenly calm scene.

Danny Money looked down at the convulsing woman who was flopping around like a fish out of water, the cold steel barrel of Emancipation's pistol still stuck in her quivering mouth. Spic N' Span Spiegel handcuffed the struggling woman, wondering how the hell this mess had ever got started in the first place. The Bud Man told Oral Ames to watch his head and then purposely slammed his skull into the transport car's door frame, simultaneously punching him in the side of the face for good measure. The Bud Man felt great. He'd given ol' Oral baby a little taste of his own kind of fire and brimstone.

While the Bud Man preached, Ray Carson Carver smiled. He wasn't so sure that the sign was meant for him. In his mind, instead of Welcome to Washington, D.C., the sign should have read Welcome to the Valley of Death, a sink hole full of human shit to act as his own personal game reserve. There were all kinds of trophy kills just waiting to feel the lethal sting of his poaching prowess.

The D.C. Police were the game wardens of this target rich killing zone. He was going to help them. His skills were far superior to theirs. To keep the hunt and the kill exciting he'd leave signs, just like a predator leaves his droppings. He wanted them to find him at a time and a place of his own choosing. They'd play the game by his rules. But, first, he had a mission. It was all so clear. There was so much easy prey wandering around on these asphalt trails.

Ray Carson Carver drove his grey Dodge Ram pick up truck down New York Avenue, towards the heart of the city, its empty gun rack creating a false illusion of compliance to the city's strict gun control laws. Underneath a blanket, hidden behind the front seat, lay one of the many tools of his trade. The 30.06 Winchester rifle smelled of gun oil and cleaning solvent. A finely tooled tan leather sling hung from its frame. Its burled walnut stock gleamed with the rich glow of dark polished wood. The barrel, covered with a fine sheen of oil, shimmered a dull charcoal color. A powerful Bushnell scope crowned the pristine weapon, having never before aligned its deadly accurate cross-hairs on this kind of game, human prey.

The misty drizzle continued to seep out of the low hanging black clouds. A light fog was beginning to settle under the flickering city street lamps. Ray Carver slowed as he approached the red light at New York and Florida Avenue, Northeast.

He signaled a left turn and pulled into the McDonald's parking lot. No use in hurrying. He had plenty of time. He slipped on his rumpled black London Fog trench coat. Its purpose, to conceal the rifle when both he and it had work to do.

He walked inside the packed fast food restaurant into a strange world, a world he hated more than any other, a world full of dopers, whores, faggots, lesbians, niggers, chinks, and every other kind of human shit under the sun. He had to fight the burning sensation. His head pounded unmercifully. Right this very second he felt an overpowering desire to run out to the truck and grab his rifle. He could take out a whole lot of these puke faced assholes right here. Yeah, he could splatter their perverted brains all over this shithole place. Not so long ago, hadn't some guy up in Northern California already christened a McDonald's with his own brand of special sauce? Ray Carver calmed his throbbing heart. The hunter, the hunter must always be in control.

Detective Michael McCarthy glanced up at the strange looking out of place man. Mike McCarthy knew this man, not by name, but by character. Ronnie wouldn't know this type, not the way he did. She was a city girl. This man was a foreigner to her. Mike McCarthy had seen plenty like him. They worked in the steel mills. They mined coal. They drilled oil and gas wells. They came from the hills of West Virginia, the steel towns of Pennsylvania, the back woods of Kentucky and Tennessee.

They chewed snuff and drank whiskey. They lived in shacks, shacks lined with thousands of dollars worth of guns. They drove expensive four wheel drives. They were hard men, men who beat their women and expected dinner on the table at five. These men would kill for the blood sucking unions. Yeah, Mike McCarthy, knew these men well. His father had been one. He hated that cold cruel bastard as much as he hated both them and what they stood for.

Ronnie reached over and tapped Mac on the arm. They had killed about as much time as they could. Nothing was worse than driving in the city while it rained. It didn't look like it was going to let up any. In fact, it might even be getting worse.

Ronnie Bell nodded at the hard looking man in the funny looking Cat hat and the wrinkled trench coat as she walked out of the McDonald's. Funny, Mac was usually polite. But, tonight, he had pushed the man right out of his way, almost as if he was trying to provoke him. Ronnie didn't understand why men sometimes had to be such arrogant pricks. The poor guy was probably just some farmer, vacationing in the big city. He looked kind of lost. She almost felt sorry for him. The city could be so frightening to these down to earth country folk.

Ray Carson Carver sat down at a table in the far corner of the restaurant. He spat a chew of snuff into an empty paper cup. It made him sick to see a white man with a nigger bitch.

The only thing he hated more was to see some blonde white slut with a buck nigger. Before his killing spree was over he'd see to it that he took out one of each. Tonight, he'd solve half of that problem. He chuckled, to himself and wiped the drooling tobacco juice off his stubbly chin with the sleeve of his black trench coat.

Ray Carson Carver was about to be baptized, reborn in a series of cold calculated kills. He slowly cruised the grey pick up truck deeper into the dark foreign jungle. In his mind, the crumbling buildings, the rickety shacks with their barred or boarded windows, the abandoned rusting cars, and the garbage laden streets and alleys, all became the familiar gloomy mountains, the barren fields, the bleak forests that he called home. Strange human animals scurried through this asphalt and cement jungle, their passing forms shadowy reminders of the prey he had so often stalked. They traveled the same habitual pathways, never suspecting the lurking danger of the one who would send them to their final slam dance of death.

Something called him to this mystical place. He couldn't quite put his finger on the reason. But, he turned off Florida Avenue into an even murkier land of gloom. Suddenly, he was just there, materialized into a dark void of wretched humanity, a void blacker than the deepest depths of any dank soggy forest he had ever seen. Wispy clouds of rainy mist blew across the spooky street in fine sheets, obscuring the dim glow from the flickering street lamps.

He looked down this mysterious corridor of impending doom, seeing only a watering hole where all kinds of human game congregated for their final drink, a drink that came in the form of amber liquid, white powder, black, red, and yellow pills, spots on images of Bart Simpson, and hazy clouds of pungent smoke. Here lies the doorway to hell. Ray Carver had yet to meet its gatekeeper, Frosty the Snowman. But, he knew that he himself bore the honor of turning the key, opening the vile lock, and unleashing a torrential gale of bone chilling fear across the false facade of the Nation's Capital.

Squinting as he peered through the moist clammy fog, he gazed up at the black and white street sign. In the swirling mist he could just barely make out the name, Orleans Place. It seemed like such a shit hole of filth. Ray Carson Carver concluded that he was probably doing the city a favor, eliminating another useless fuck from the welfare roles. He had found the worn trail. Tracks and signs were everywhere. His lips curled slightly upwards. On their tobacco stained corners, there suddenly appeared an evil mocking grin. He was, as the military would say, in a target rich environment. Now, he would do what every good hunter would instinctively do. He'd pick his spot and wait for a prize trophy buck. This prize would die in the street of the damned.

Danny Money sat in the holding area of the Fifth District cell block. He had had just about enough action for one night. It seemed to him that a week of four to twelves had been compressed into the first seven hours of this, their first night, on the hectic shift. He was more than just plain tired. A bone weary exhaustion had crept into his lanky frame. He was sore, his muscles aching from his twelve-rounder with the Islamic forces of the so called reverend, Oral Ames.

Shit, maybe after all this he shouldn't even plan on sucking down a few cold ones with the Bud Man and Tiny tonight at Clancy's. Instead, he ought to get some sleep. First thing tomorrow morning he'd be looking at Emancipation's face and sniffing Spic N' Span's musty smelling drawers at court while he tried to talk the flunky Assistant United States District Attorney into charging the slimy bitch that had scratched the shit out of him with Assault on a Police Officer.

Damn, he knew it was hard getting an APO to stick. The U.S. Attorney's office didn't give a shit. Their criteria for APO was, and would most likely always be, the same old bullshit. If you weren't cut, shot, or similarly maimed they wouldn't charge or prosecute the case. Instead, they'd most likely tell him to walk the papers over to the Corporation Council, having reduced the charge to a Disorderly Conduct misdemeanor. In fact, Danny Money knew that they wouldn't even go forth with prosecution for Possession of a Prohibited Weapon either, the razor knife not constituting their bullshit definition of PPW.

It wasn't hard to figure out. Why should they care? It wasn't their ass that was on the firing line. At four o'clock they'd straighten their yellow paisley ties or pull up their pantyhose, get in their BMW's, and head for the Maryland or Virginia suburbs. Then, they'd probably tell their spouses what a tough day they had had while they downed their first vodka martini. Danny Money was beginning to feel the first surges of burning contempt for these arrogant pricks. The faggots and dykes at the U.S. Attorney's office talked too much about things that they knew too little of.

Danny Money knew that his power, the right to take away an individual's freedom, or even his life, was the heaviest burden to bear. Sometimes you sweat bullets just worrying about making one little mistake and ending up in the same place you were trying to put the other guy. The line between cop and criminal was a thin tightrope of hypocrisy that had no net on the bottom. To stumble meant to die. His power was more immediate while the attorney's power was ultimately more absolute, hidden in a incongruous web of protective layers. Danny Money concluded that he hated attorneys as much as the Bud Man hated self ordained preachers.

He shook himself out of his mind wandering daydream as he looked up and watched the Bud Man wave good-bye to Oral Ames. Strutting out the front door of the Fifth District Station house, the arrogant preacher turned and flipped the Bud Man the finger. "You ain't nothin' but a white man in a nigger's skin! You Goddamned Oreo. Next time your black ass is mine, pig."

The Bud Man digested this little tid bit and then ran to the door and hollered back, "Yeah, mother fucker. And you ain't nothin' but a fuckin' slitherin' reptile. Your sleazy tired ass is gonna be doin' time, instead of doin' bitches, if you mess with me again. You punk bastard."

With only thirty minutes to go until check off, Danny Money considered hiding out in the 5D station and avoiding any further street headaches. Best of all, it would allow himself and the Bud Man the precious time to make a few personal phone calls. He still had a chance to line up some fresh pussy for tonight. There were plenty of phone numbers in his wallet. But, as good as some of them were, they still couldn't keep his attention like Ronnie. She was in a class all by herself. Sometimes he cringed when he wondered how she had managed to get so good. Other times he just laid back and enjoyed the ride of his life. Lately, his dick was starting to feel the vibrations from his heart. And, this was getting real scary. He didn't know if he could ever give that last little bit of himself to Ronnie. Or, anybody for that matter. Where he came from, he seriously doubted if they'd welcome the two of them with open arms.

The Bud Man was already in the telephone room, picking up the receiver of the nearest phone. He could use some pussy and at this point he wasn't above beggin' for it. Danny Money, motivated by what he thought at the time to be an attack of guilty conscious hollered, "Let's roll. We've still got thirty minutes."

The Bud Man slammed down the receiver just as he heard the first ring of possible relief on the other end of the line and, muttering to himself, followed Money out the back door and into Scout 150. Unknowingly, both officers were about to become two different people. What they were was much less than what they would become. The hunt was about to begin. Already, the wheels of death were beginning to turn, about to roll over their first victim in a fateful savage grip of crushing finality. Like a steamy cloud of clammy mist, rising out of the murky bogs of a fog en-shrouded river of doom, a rancid dragon's breath of gruesome death began to seep out of Orleans Place and spill across the Nation's Capital. Ray Carson Carver was about to leave his calling card. The mystique of Orleans Place was about to be personi-fied in gore.

Ray Carver sat wedged in the thick branches of a gnarled oak tree, swallowing the last swig of Old Grand Dad. Small droplets of rain rolled off the bill of his camouflage colored Cat hat. The night was charged with an eerie aura of desolation and gloom. He could feel the power of this unholy place. It stunk like death. An unmistakable wave of apprehension had almost scared him off. Then the burning need for ultimate fulfillment had engulfed his loins, causing him to realize that now there was no turning back. He shook with nervous anticipation, much like a young boy who was about to touch his first naked woman.

Jerome Anthony Marshall kissed his girlfriend goodnight. It was late and they both had to get up early for work. He couldn't help but think it was nice of her parents to buy the pizza, leaving them alone downstairs to watch television, while they went up-stairs to bed. Sometimes Jerome Marshall was ashamed of what he had to offer his woman. He was still trying to get his G.E.D., but mostly he was just trying to save enough money to get them out of this miserable drug infested ghetto. The problem was that they couldn't get very far, very fast, on what he made changing tires. She said it didn't matter. She loved him for what he was, not what he could become. Anywhere they were together it was home.

Jerome Marshall smiled to himself as he joyously leaped over her parent's backyard fence. It wouldn't be long now. He was going to surprise her tomorrow. He was going to sign the lease on a one bedroom apartment just off of Maryland Avenue. It would be their new home. It would be his last thought.

There, in the shadows, a tall man jumped the fence and bounded down the garbage filled alley. Ray Carver wrapped the sling of the 30.06 rifle tighter around his left forearm. He sighted through the powerful scope. He would only get one shot. He had to make it count. The figure jogged past graffiti covered garages, quickly moving along the unlit alley way. For a split second, in Ray Carver's mind, the black man's silhouette turned into a leaping white tail buck. He would take him out through the lungs, making sure not to spoil the meat.

The crosshairs found the mark, zeroing in on the young buck's powerful chest. A little venison would be nice. The image of the buck faded, replaced by the smiling face of a young black man. Ray Carver winced in momentary self realization of what he was about to do. Unconsciously, he thumbed off the safety of the lethal weapon and made sure the bolt was locked in place. The heart pounding thrill of the initial anticipation was waning. It was time for the much greater satisfaction, the ultimate experience, the tantalizing thrill of the kill. Strangely, he felt so detached from the whole experience. His mind wandered. That slut wife of his better have his breakfast on the table when he got home.

He squeezed the trigger. The man clutched at his chest, reeling backwards. Simultaneously, the rifle discharged in an ear splitting explosion, a puff of acrid gunpowder slowly wafting out of its smoking barrel. Ray Carver slung the Winchester rifle over his right shoulder and quickly descended down the tree. If he'd had a little more time he could have made a good tree stand, thought the excited murderer to himself, as he stumbled to the wet ground and began to run towards the fallen figure.

The young black man was terrified. He kept trying to get up. But, he simply couldn't move. His chest burned, almost as if someone had run him through with a red hot poker. Strange sucking sounds gurgled out of the bubbling hole in his chest. He could feel the gaping wound in his back, the cold damp air stinging the moist bloody opening. His legs twitched in uncontrollable spasms. Even now, close to death, he still hadn't realized his own imminent fate.

Ray Carver quickly moved in on his fallen prey. Damn, the son of a bitch still wasn't dead. No use wasting another bullet. He felt underneath his black trench coat, under the tan and fluorescent orange hunting vest. He located the handle of his stainless steel hunting knife and withdrew it from its sheath. Kneeling down next to the quivering torso, he grabbed a handful of the victim's coarse kinky hair. He propped up his downed quarry's head, blood now seeping from the corners of the young man's greying lips. And, without hesitation, Ray Carver slit his throat.

Pulsating spurts of blood gushed out of the dying man's wheezing windpipe, the poor victim literally gagging to death on his own blood, his mutilated body begging to escape the agonizing torture that was about to be perpetrated upon it. Even before doctor's would have considered Jerome Anthony Marshall's dreams in life officially over, Ray Carver braced himself and then rammed the blood covered blade of his hunting knife deep into his prey's lower abdomen, hacking a gruesome path from his bowels to his sternum. He was used to the rank odor of steamy death. Nothing could ever take its place. Rolling the limp victim on his side, Ray Carver eased his hand into the man's moist innards and scooped them out, onto the wet ground, with cold practiced precision.

Not much difference in gutting a man than in gutting a deer, chuckled the human butcher to himself. Calmly, he reached his gloved hand inside his coat pocket and began to fondle the hard round object. Inserting his gloved fingers into the dead man's mouth, he opened his jaw and slammed the rock deep inside, splintering several teeth. The hunt would now begin in earnest. He had left sign, much like a predatory beast. It would be up to them to figure it out. Right now it was time for him to move quickly, before the vultures come. Besides, he needed to begin thinking about his next kill. It was time for a split tail. Doe season was right around the corner. And, there was no shortage of permits. No posted signs either. Ray Carson Carver had found his heaven on earth.

Goddamnit, thought Danny Money. Why hadn't he listened to his own best advice, and stayed at 5D to wait for the relief section to come out. Now, instead of sitting in the locker room, he was sitting in Scout 150 heading for Orleans Place to answer a sound of gunshots radio run. He knew one sound for certain, the sound of the ear banging that the Bud Man was laying on his stupid honky ass for dragging him out into the street when they could have coasted on government time. The Bud Man was reminding him in no uncertain terms that they got paid by the hour, not by the number of radio runs they handled.

Danny Money slowly cruised Scout 150 down the seamy one block stretch of Orleans Place. Crumbling row houses crowded both sides of the littered street, their front doors virtually opening on to the trash covered sidewalks. The entire block glimmered in unreality, the dim light from the sparse street lamps striking thousands of tiny pieces of broken beer and wine bottles. Discarded beer cans covered every space of exposed ground. Abandoned rusted automobiles took up as many street parking places as drivable vehicles. But, everywhere, the broken glass shimmered in the mystical fog.

Both Danny Money and the Bud Man knew this grim area well, too well. They knew what the others knew. Orleans place had, many years ago, been the judge, jury, and finally the executioner of Spic N' Span Spiegel's father. Orleans Place had driven other officers over the edge, sending one home, to Bowie, Maryland, where he had dispatched both himself and his wife with a bullet in the mouth. It had claimed the soul of ex-officer Don Lambert, who despite having lived through an ordeal known only to a very few, never really survived. A coked up drug dealer had got the drop on the startled officer, sticking his .357 Magnum between the terrified officer's eyes, and pulling the trigger three times. Miraculously the hammer fell on three duds before Lambert emptied his .38 special into the dealer's chest. The drug dealer lost his life. Lambert, lost his mind.

All in all Danny Money and the Bud Man agreed consistently on one thing. Orleans Place wasn't a nice place to visit. And they certainly wouldn't want, under any circumstances, to have to live there either. Money knew Ronnie's ex-live-in, Frosty the Snowman, hung on this street, dealing drugs for a living. Sometimes he couldn't understand how she could have ever got involved with such an asshole. That was one of his toughest times with her, the time she had told him about Freddy baby. She had said she was only twelve when he had first taken her, a child who thought it was a game. Jesus, Danny hadn't got laid until he was seventeen and even then he had been nervous, poking around in the backseat of his dad's Coupe de Ville with Mary Lou King. Their world's were always so different.

"Shit, there ain't no bodies laying in the fuckin' street," stated the Bud Man, noticing Money was daydreaming again.

"Might as well check out the alley while we're here. If we fuck around long enough maybe we can pick up some comp time," answered Money.

"Actually. When you think about it. What's so unusual about the sound of gunshots around here, anyway? I can't believe some asshole would call the police for some bullshit like this. They should be glad to hear shooting. With any luck some unhappy junkie wasted his fuckin' dealer. Save us all a lot of time and trouble," added the Bud Man as Money turned into the narrow alley, and shined his spotlight down the garbage strewn lane.

"Damn, I can't drive no farther down this shithole street. There's too much broken glass. And I ain't about to change no tire in this Goddamned rain," remarked Money, already opening the scout car door.

"What the hell are you doing? Let's just get the hell out of here," stated the Bud Man, wondering what had possessed his partner to, all of a sudden, become such an over zealous cop.

Money, leaving the scout car's spotlight beam aiming straight ahead, through the misty rain, shouted back, "Look's like some fuckin' wino is laying down here by this garbage."

"Forget the pukehead. Let's boogie on out of here," hollered the Bud Man, deciding against his better judgment to walk on down and back up his partner. It was easy for Money to walk around in the rain. At least he had his raincoat on. The Bud Man had left his behind, figuring there was no way he was getting out of the patrol car with only thirty minutes left in their shift. Now, he was going to get his big beautiful black ass wet just because his partner had a thing for taking wino's to the Detoxification Center. Well, what the hell, thought the Bud Man. At least, at Detox, the brother would get a hot meal and a warm dry bed.

There was nothing warm inside Danny Money's shaking body. The shadow of death was upon his soul, chilling his veins and turning his churning stomach into a bowl of quivering intestinal jelly. He turned his head back towards the Bud Man, trying to mentally escape from this grotesque scene. It was too late. Flaming red fantasies danced across the blood curdling night. Orleans Place began to weave its haunting evil spell across the twilight zone of death.

Danny Money gave in to the overpowering sensation and began to gag. Beads of sweat formed on his forehead as droplets of rain continued to roll off the shiny black bill of his police cap. He couldn't hold back any longer. His face felt flushed. His insides waxed cold. His back was suddenly soaked with nauseous perspiration. Bending over, he felt the unstoppable liquid pause at the back of his throat and then roll out of his mouth, covering the slippery asphalt in a coating of rancid puke.

The Bud Man grabbed the collar of Money's black vinyl rain

coat, trying to steady his swaying partner. Then, he too, caught a glimpse of the ghastly scene and instantly choked on his own bile filled spittle.

"Jesus fucking Christ," gasped the Bud Man staring down at the disfigured torso laying on what was left of its back, mist still rising from what remained of the man's steamy   innards.

"Shit. He ain't got any guts, man," stated the shocked Bud Man. "They're laying next to him. Look at that shit. His heart's still pumping."

"The muscle's just contracting," replied Danny Money, trying to get a hold of himself despite seeing, for the first time in his life, the entire exposed innards of a gutted man's   stomach.

"What's in his fuckin' mouth, man? He looks like a stuck roasted pig," observed the Bud Man, gazing down at the round object sticking half out of the dead man's bleeding mouth.

"It's a fucking rock," answered Danny Money gingerly touching the smooth oval object and then quickly pulling his hand away from the man's smashed face and blankly staring greyish eyes.

"Jesus. We better call for an official. And homicide squad," nervously stated the Bud Man, wishing that he was at Tiny's sucking on a beechwood aged cold one. After this he might even lay off the chitlins for awhile. Right now they weren't sounding too good. He wondered if they stunk as much as human guts. This was worse than being stuck in the patrol car with Spic N' Span Spiegel, in the middle of August, with no air conditioning.

Danny Money slowly walked back to Scout 150 and radioed for an official cruiser, a Fifth District Detective, the Mobile Crime Lab, homicide squad, and the 'you kill 'em we chill 'em, you stab 'em we slab 'em' Morgue wagon. If there was ever a time he didn't want to see Ronnie it was right now. She didn't need to get dragged into this bizarre shit, thought Money. She had enough problems without taking on what sure as hell didn't look like any routine drug related shooting he had ever seen. Danny Money almost got his wish, almost.

Detective Mike McCarthy had enjoyed this tour of duty. He was starting to sense in himself a renewed vigor for life. Recently, he had discovered a new found eagerness to report for duty. It was no coincidence that his newly acquired attitude adjustment had directly coincided with the assignment of Ronnie Bell as his partner. Damn, thought the puffy faced detective. If he was only twenty years younger and fifty pounds lighter he'd trip the light fantastic with his striking partner. They'd do up the town in style. Dinner at the Palms. Moonlight cruise on the Potomac. Maybe even take in a performance at the Kennedy Center.

Well, right now, he'd settle for one last cup of coffee and a Snickers Bar at the local Seven Eleven. In another five minutes they'd be back in the office filling out follow up reports on the statements from the four witnesses that they'd interviewed tonight. This case would be a piece of cake. Tomorrow they'd get the warrant and go lock up Rolondo Robinson. The sorry son of a bitch had lost his cool in a family argument and tried to shoot his belligerent brother-in-law. Instead, the poor drunk bastard had missed the sprawling brother-in-law and had put three .32 caliber slugs into his own wife. Fortunately, she might still live. Mac knew her old man wouldn't be so lucky if she got her hands on him.

Mac pulled Cruiser 311 on to the ramp leading down into the Police Motor Pool, located downtown under the main police headquarters building. Ronnie reached over to turn off the unmarked Cruiser's radio, knowing that once they began the descent radio communications were all but useless.

"Simulcast broadcast. Any homicide cruiser to respond to the alley rear six hundred block of Orleans Place, Northeast? Scout 150 is on the scene of an unconscious person. Sound of gunshots call. Shooting apparently just occurred," radioed the dispatcher.

Raising his eyebrows, Mac looked over at Ronnie. He prayed that some other homicide cruiser would answer up. But, somehow, he instinctively knew that this was to be their assignment. Some things in life just always went together. Like flies to shit, so went murder to Orleans Place. And, when murder went down on Orleans Place, especially tonight with Money working, Ronnie would never allow him to do anything other than turn Cruiser 311 around and haul ass.

Before he had even turned the steering wheel around Ronnie grabbed the mike and answered, "Cruiser 311 responding from headquarters."

That simple transmission was about to plunge Cruiser 311 and its two divergent partners into the most desperate hunt of their lives, a hunt so desperate that, at times, there was only one set of footprints in the shifting sands of both their lives.

Detective Mike McCarthy nonchalantly offered his hand to officer Danny Money, feeling an unfamiliar and terribly uncomfortable twinge of jealously. He hoped the stinging sensation was a result of his fatherly concern for Ronnie's fragile heartstrings and not a result of some hope he had of having her for himself. He knew it had been a long time since he had had a woman. Maybe as long as three years. But, he sure as hell better get real. No prime filly like her would want an old, out of date plow horse like him. He was just an old fart with a dirty mind.

Looking over at Ronnie's tall lean figure, Danny Money felt a little uncomfortable. It wasn't like the old days when they were uniform partners, sharing a drink and talking about kicking ass. That one little act had changed everything. About the same time that Harry Met Sally, Danny met Ronnie in the same sexual trap. And, just like the movie, everything, like magic, had changed. Nothing was simple anymore. Unlike many situations, much of their trouble was, ironically, black and white. For better or for worse when they had fallen into bed together, clutching passionately, entangled in a frenzy of lust, they had become simultaneously entangled in a struggle that had its roots as far back as the days of Cain and Abel.

Detective Mike McCarthy did not throw up at the ghastly scene. But, he got sick, sick of seeing the innocent victims of the vileness of life. Too many years. Too many bodies. Too many remorseless killers. But, never this, never anything like this. He reached inside his wrinkled sport coat and pulled out his notebook, ready to write the two words he had prayed he'd never have to put down on paper. He glanced back over at Ronnie who was still talking to Danny Money and his partner. He couldn't shield her from it. The mutilated body cried out to him, asking him to stop the madness. Mac would need everything Ronnie could give him on this one. They were in for a steady diet of sleepless nights and hectic days.

In the old days, back in the seventies he had heard some of the guys talk about it. He had listened intently while they spoke of patterns, MO's, high visibility, saturation, stake outs, quirks, threads, character sketches, profiles, and the need for the most important item of all, one lucky break. They never got one. The Freeway Phantom escaped the hunt. Mike McCarthy's hand shook in fear as he scratched the words serial killer on the torn page of his notebook and yelled for Ronnie to come over. He wondered what bizarre handle the faggot press would lay on this tormented ghoul.

Rhonda Bell looked down soberly at the grizzly scene. Silently, she closed her eyes and prayed for the dead man's salvation. Her next reaction startled her. A consuming rage engulfed her suddenly shaking body. Mike McCarthy, mistakenly assuming the gruesome murder was too much for his sensitive partner, put his flabby arm around her hunched shoulders and tried to back her away from the disemboweled body.

Ronnie would have none of this. She was incensed beyond any level of anger that she had ever before experienced. She shrugged off Mac's well intentioned display of compassion. Deliberately bending over the still steaming body, she reached out to lightly press her long slender fingers over the young man's ashen colored lips in a symbolic testimony of her resolve to track down this butchering mad man. It was the first time in her life that she had ever felt capable of killing anything. Pretty soon she'd be facing the toughest part of her job, looking into the mournful tear filled eyes of the loved ones that this young man had left behind.

She shuddered as she, like Mac, realized the ominous trappings of this ritualistic murder scene. This was the first. But, most likely, it wouldn't be the last. Rhonda Bell watched intently as Danny Money and the Bud Man roped off the crime scene with yellow plastic tape. The crowd was beginning to gather, gasping at the violent image of the eviscerated victim. Word was already on the street, filtering back to the house where Jerome Anthony Marshall had said his last good-byes, a house where a young woman, filled with the optimism of youth, was about to wake up in a cold sweat of harsh reality.

Now, Ronnie and Mac could only wait in the miserable rain. The Mobile Crime Lab van was only a few minutes away and, unlike the Columbo re-runs, there wasn't any need to mess up the crime scene with aimless wanderings and baseless conjectures.

"What's in his mouth?" asked Mac, glancing at Ronnie. "It's a rock," answered Danny Money, walking over to join the two detectives.

"Why would some asshole stuff a rock in the kid's mouth?" asked the Bud Man, morbidly fascinated by the whole grotesque scene.

"If we knew the answer to that we'd probably have our first clue," replied Mike McCarthy, incessantly jotting down notes on his observations of the crime scene. To him, his notes were like a surgeon's scalpel. When used with precision and skill, they both had the ability to remove a malignant cancer from spreading its terminal disease.

The Washington Post reported the murder on the second page of its Metro section. The small rote column contained a few vague references to another routine murder in the drug infested environs of Orleans Place. What it failed to report turned out to be of more consequence than what it actually printed. It had been late. Nobody had really cared much about another ghetto killing. Details were sketchy. The eleven o'clock news was already over.

Somehow, the gory murder escaped much of the media hype that surrounded a late evening robbery and shooting in affluent white Georgetown. Nobody paid much attention to the obscure incident. Nobody that is, except Ray Carson Carver who had just purchased a copy of the *Washington Post* newspaper. Ray Carver deserved better. He tilted his head back and rinsed his mouth with whiskey. Kicking shut the fuel door of the woodburning stove, he sat down at the dinner table and watched his wife bring his supper.

"Where's Becky?" he asked as he lit up a Camel.

"She should be home any minute now. I told her to be home by five for dinner," answered Kate Carver, his terrified wife of almost thirty years.

"I've told you this before. And, Goddamn it. I'm not going to tell you again. She gets her ass home at five. And you get my dinner on the table. If my rules don't suit you, you can both get your lazy asses out of my house. I paid for this place with my sweat. Bent over in those goddamned wet coal mines most of my life. I'm gonna beat her ass if she ain't home soon," stated Ray Carver, almost hoping his ripe young daughter of fifteen would be late. He was beginning to enjoy the thought of running his hand over her firm round buttocks. But, even more than that, he needed to teach them fucking city slickers a little respect. Before long he'd be front page news, not some second rate story assigned to some dickless dork gofer from the mail room. This coming weekend he'd go doe hunting, black doe.

CHAPTER 5

"OH, I'M SO HORNY. Oh, I'm so horny," cried out Emancipation Proclamation Jones while doing his best version of a Michael Jackson moonwalk across Clancy's bar room floor, that simple statement summing up his constant state of both mind and body.

"OH, the dude's so horny. Oh, the dude's so horny," chorused the Bud Man, trying to do a lambada with one of the ancient looking bag ladies that regularly frequented Clancy's Bar and Grill.

Danny Money shouted across the room, "E.P., you're always horny."

"Yeah. That's right. I'm so horny I could eat a horse. A mare that is. If you dig where I'm comin' from," answered Emancipation Proclamation Jones.

"It ain't where you're comin' from that scares me. It's where your simple ass is goin'," replied the Bud Man.

"Jesus Christ, Tiny. What the hell kind of shit you got on this jukebox, man? Damn. Andy Williams. Perry Como. Nat King Cole. What is this shit? You're supposed to be a brother, man. Sheet," shouted Emancipation Proclamation, staring in disbelief at Tiny's music selection, his jaw dropping to the grimy floor.

"I'm hip, man," bragged Tiny. "I've got me a little slop sloppy dog. Round abouts somewhere."

"If it's fried in grease I'll take one," shouted Spic N' Span Spiegel from the far end of the bar.

"You simple sons of bitches. It's Snoop Doggy Dogg. Rapster extraordinaire," emphatically stated Emancipation.

"Hold the mustard on that snoopster dog, Tiny. Sounds like a couple scoops of mayo might help it slide down the old gib," said Spic N' Span Spiegel, his unwashed body about to go into cholesterol withdrawal.

"Excuse me. Hello. Is anybody in there?" shouted Emancipation. "You two are friggin' extinct dinosaurs. Brontosuckus to be exact."

"Keep on keepin' on," acknowledged Tiny, shaking his head in disbelief.

"I love my car. My car. It goes boom," sang out Emancipation.

"What the fuck is he talking about?" asked Tiny, staring at Danny Money, his eyes rolling back in his head.

"Forget it. He's crazy. Hey, I got one for you. How do you stop five brothers from rapin' a white girl?" quizzed Money.

"I don't know," replied Tiny.

"Throw' em a basketball," laughed Money, hoping Tiny would appreciate a little tainted humor this afternoon.

"Hey, Tiny. My main man. How about another screwdriver?" shouted Emancipation Proclamation Jones sitting down, but not too close, to Spic N' Span Spiegel who was busy devouring a chili cheese dog, grease running down his chin and dripping on to his uniform tie.

"Jesus. If anybody ever did a lobotomy on that sick son of a bitch, Jones. When they opened up his brain all they'd find is one big pussy," commented Tiny, sending Spic N' Span Spiegel his double order of chili cheese fries smothered in onions.

"Tiny. You hear about that guy over on Orleans Place? The one that got killed last weekend?" asked Danny Money

"Yeah, man. I heard. The home boys say he was gutted like a stuck pig. That right, Danny?" inquired Tiny. Deciding to have one on the house, he poured himself and Money a shot of Seagram's 7. "You guys watch your asses out there," cautioned Tiny, knowing that very shortly the boys were going in to work another four to twelve tour. Roll call was only an hour away.

Danny Money watched Sergeant Samuel Williamson habitually walk back and forth, pacing like a caged animal, in front of the crowded roll call room zoo. The jittery sergeant looked like a palsied guard at the Tomb of the Unknown Soldier, his whole body twitching uncontrollably.

"What's wrong with that crazy mother fucker?" whispered the Bud Man to Money, leaning over in his seat directly behind his fascinated partner.

"I hear he thinks one of the guys is tappin' his old lady," answered Money, casting a quick glance in the direction of Emancipation Proclamation Jones who was vehemently shakin' his head back and forth, attempting to dispel any doubts of his innocence in this deadly serious matter.

"Man. That son of a bitch is one hurtin' dude," remarked the Bud Man. "He's a policeman in trouble."

"He's a fuckin' 10-33. 10-33 Sam," chuckled Money, equating the nervous sergeant with the ominous radio code for an officer in trouble and giving him a handle that would become a legendary part of police lore.

As 10-33 Sam, his thin brown mustache twitching with his lip's continual spasms, paced nervously and wondered which one of these scumbags was nailing his constantly smiling old lady, Detective Lieutenant Bow Wow Bowser was in the process of verbally dressing down Rhonda Bell and Mike McCarthy. Confined in his cubbyhole office and lighting up his fourth cigarette in the last ten minutes Bow Wow Bowser growled, "What the fuck's the problem here? We've got a Goddamned cut and dried situation. Some dealer just wasted his mule. The kid was probably skimmin' the fuckin' profits. Probably went into a partnership. But, just forgot to tell his dealer. Damn, it's Orleans Place. Who the fuck cares? Go lock up that Goddamned Frosty the Ice Man. He's probably involved anyway."

Detective Mike McCarthy winced as he looked in Ronnie's direction and stated, "It's Frosty the Snowman, lieutenant. And this ain't no drug related killing. We're gonna hear from this boy again. Real soon."

"Lieutenant," cut in Rhonda Bell. "I've talked to the victim's family. And I've interviewed his girlfriend's family. That's where he was the night of the murder. He was a good man. A Christian man. He worked sixty hours a week trying to save enough money so he and his girlfriend could move in together. He wasn't any damned drug dealer. He was just a decent human being who got slaughtered by some crazy butcher. I agree with Mac. It won't be long before he kills again."

"Bullshit," remarked Bow Wow Bowser. "I need this case closed. If it ain't, you'all will be back in uniform. Walkin' H Street. Pickin' up puke-faced winos. And smellin' their nice shit-stained drawers. Now, hit the pavement and lock somebody up. Real soon."

Ronnie started to protest, but looked first at Mac, who was discreetly shaking his head. Against her better judgment, she decided to defer to her veteran partner's unspoken advice. Lieutenant Bowser was an asshole, simple as that.

"What a jerk off," muttered Ronnie as she looked out the window of Cruiser 311, slowly cruising down M Street, Northwest. The swank boutiques of Georgetown lined both sides of the trendy street, their windows displaying a constant montage of products affordable only to the nose up in the air shoppers who frequented the ultra expensive shops. "Look at that one, will you. La De Da," laughed Mac, "She's got a serious case of the A & P walk." "What are you talking about?" asked Ronnie, smiling over at her grinning partner.

"When she walks, one foot points towards the Atlantic while the other one points towards the Pacific," answered Mac, satisfied that he had just about summed up the whole Georgetown scene pretty succinctly.

Ronnie had to laugh. She never could feel quite comfortable in Georgetown. Danny would bring her down here for dinner, sometimes, and that was nice. But, it was all so fake, so phony. The people smiled constantly. But, strangely, they never laughed. Maybe they were caught up in a worse prison than the blacks in the ghetto, thought Ronnie. At least her people knew how to live life to its fullest. Whether they had money or not didn't matter, for they lived life with a desperation, almost as if each day or night might be their last.

"What are we doing here, anyway, Mac?" questioned Ronnie, wondering why in the hell they weren't on Orleans Place trying to find a witness to interview.

"The lieutenant says the honkies up here are a little nervous ever since that liquor store owner got wasted on his way to his car. We're supposed to canvass the neighborhood. See if anybody saw anything. You know us honkies. We're afraid the brothers are gonna rob our homes and businesses. Pillage our neighborhoods. And rape all our white women. Don't worry. After we get us a little police freebie cappuccino we'll head over to Orleans Place and do some real police work."

Ronnie felt relieved. Once again Mac had read her mind and shown his compassion for the sensitivities etched in her soul. They had a few things to go on, things that at this point meant nothing, in and of themselves. They knew it was a 30.06 slug that had taken most of the young man's lungs and slung them, like raw meat, on to the wet, oily pavement. The jacketed hollow point found in the frame of a nearby garage door indicated, by its trajectory, that the bullet had come from a position higher than the deceased.

The medical examiner's office had confirmed their suspicion that the gutting had been both instantaneous and professional, probably done with a hunting knife containing a serrated edge. The rock, slammed into the young man's mouth, could have come from almost anywhere in the northeastern United States. The Mobile Crime Lab, as of yet, had only managed to find the expended slug. No fingerprints or any other physical evidence had been located.

Ronnie felt awfully tense. It was one week ago today when the murderer had executed his appalling savagery on an innocent young man. She felt the anxiety grip the pit of her stomach in a vice of tense morbid fear. It was the closest thing she had ever had to a divine premonition. Rhonda Bell could not help but feel that, tonight, once again, the steam roller of death was bearing down on her city, its chugging engine about to spew forth a torrent of vile homicidal lunacy unlike anything that had ever been before.

Danny Money had Scout 150 winging down Florida Avenue, towards H Street, the Bud Man holding on for dear life. Spic N' Span Spiegel and Emancipation Proclamation Jones were behind a black Chevy Van that refused to stop despite their red lights, siren, and outside speaker advising the male driver to pull over to the curb.

Danny Money careened on to H Street and spotted Scout 151 slowly weaving in and out of the congested rush hour traffic, still following the ponderous black van. Money closed in on the slow motion pursuit, pulling up next to 151. The Bud Man rolled down his passenger side window and hollered, "What the fuck are you morons doing? Can't you even make a Goddamned simple ass traffic stop?"

"Your mama," shouted Emancipation Proclamation Jones. "Go fuck yourself, you beer fartin' asshole."

Danny Money wheeled Scout 150 into a lane of oncoming traffic, almost causing the Bud Man to stain his boxer shorts. He jerked the wheel and cut back in, ahead of the creeping van. Looking in his rear view mirror, he began to cautiously pump the scout car brakes, knowing that if the van plowed into their ass end at least there was no way the Accident Review Board could say that the crash was preventable. Maybe, even better, the asshole might have insurance. Then the Bud Man and he could open their doors and grab some pavement. A non preventable accident in the line of duty was better than money in the bank. Not only could they sue the simple simon asshole, but while they did it, they'd be off on full pay reaping the rewards of life in the big city. This job had some perks that weren't even listed in the recruiting brochures, laughed Money to himself. Regrettably, the weaving van began to stop.

"Damn," muttered the Bud Man, mirroring Money's devious calculations regarding his potentially fatter bank account.

The van finally came to a complete stop right in the middle of the busy thoroughfare. Before Spic N' Span Spiegel and Emancipation Proclamation Jones even had a chance to play cops and robbers and rush the suspicious vehicle, nine millimeters in hand, the driver's side door creaked open. The totally plastered driver leaned out and then fell smack on his face in the middle of H Street.

"Shit," yelled Emancipation Proclamation Jones. "The mother fucker's drunk as a skunk. Man, I don't wanna fuck with no drunk. Me and Spiegel will be in the station all night. Fillin' out all that Goddamned paper work."

"Yeah. Its a tough job, brother. But, somebody's gotta do it," chuckled the Bud Man as he elbowed Money in the ribs.

"It ain't nothin', E.P.," added Money. "As good as your skinny black ass is at paperwork you'll still be fillin' out the forms come time for court tomorrow morning. If you need me or the Bud Man to take care of your old lady tonight just ask. Cause you'll be fillin' out papers while we're fillin' in her pussy."

Emancipation Proclamation Jones looked pleadingly towards Spic N' Span Spiegel, who was still sitting in Scout 151. Money noticed Spiegel wasn't getting the hint.

"It's your arrest, E.P. It's all yours, man. Don't get Spiegel involved. He don't wanna do your dirty work for you this time," stated the Bud Man, glancing at Spic N' Span Spiegel and then looking back at the staggering drunk who was getting to his feet, swaying like a tipsy sailor in a rough heavy sea.

Emancipation Proclamation Jones was backed into a corner. He just couldn't shame himself and let Spic N' Span Spiegel do his dirty laundry for him. He decided he'd be a man about the whole thing and do the only thing a good police officer could do. He'd improvise. That was the ticket. His plan was ingenious. He was so Goddamned lucky that he knew it would work. All he had to do was talk Spiegel into going along with it. Money and the Bud Man would keep their mouth's shut. It was all part of the unwritten code.

Nobody would drop a dime on him. And, the old drunk would thank him when he sobered up. Emancipation Proclamation Jones couldn't believe his brilliant black ass had never thought of this before. He could have saved himself a lot of hassle and the city a lot of money. Emancipation Proclamation Jones had thoroughly convinced himself that what he was about to do was an act of compassion and mercy, not a violation of general orders or accepted police procedure.

Spic N' Span Spiegel couldn't believe his partner's conniving scheme. But, he'd go along with it, no matter what. More than anything in the world, Spic N' Span Spiegel just wanted to be accepted by the others. They looked so good in their pressed uniforms and shiny brass, always attracting the glancing eyes of the ladies, always milling around, loud and boisterous, bragging about their conquests and about kicking ass and taking names. They had an air, an air of swaggering arrogance, an air that innately implied confidence, poise, pride, and self esteem.

His father had walked the beat with that same air, a proud man standing tall in the urban plains of battle. Spic N' Span Spiegel knew he didn't measure up. He just couldn't seem to get it together. God, he didn't want to bring shame on his father's revered legacy, so he let the others use him, talk him into things he didn't really want to do. It was all part of his quest for acceptance. He cared for everybody. But, nobody seemed to pay much attention to him, except when it came to his one special talent, filling out reports.

After hearing Emancipation Proclamation Jones' insane simple ass plan, Danny Money and the Bud Man decided it was time to exit stage right. They didn't want any part of this ridiculous scheme.

"E.P.. You're TAFU, dude," stated the Bud Man, shaking his head and getting into Scout 150.

"Say what? What you talkin' bout, you beer belchin' asshole?" questioned Emancipation Proclamation Jones, looking inquisitively at the Bud Man and Money.

"You're TAFU. Totally all fucked up," explained the Bud Man. "Don't worry about it E.P.," added Money. "That's one step above what I think you are. I think you're FUBAR, man. Fucked up beyond all recognition."

The Bud Man slapped Money's palms and both officers headed away from the scene at a high rate of speed while Emancipation Proclamation Jones proceeded to drag the limp babbling drunk into the rear of the Chevy van. Pulling out the unconscious drunk's wallet, he found the man's driver's license and hopefully his current address. Emancipation Proclamation Jones turned over the van's ignition, motioned for Spiegel to follow him in Scout 151, and headed for 1458 Neal Street, to take the very fortunate drunk driver home.

Spic N' Span Spiegel pulled Scout 151 behind the van which was now safely out of harm's way, parked in the owner's driveway on Neal Street. Emancipation Proclamation Jones was knocking on the door of the dingy looking row house, hoping to find the man's old lady at home. Everything was going almost too good to be true. All he had to do now was turn over both the keys and the drunk to what would surely be his very grateful wife and they were on their way, case closed. A most excellent piece of enterprising police work. He'd look like a hero, figured E.P., who, to the contrary, was about to look like the simple ass that he was. Emancipation Proclamation Jones turned around to look at Spiegel and shouted, "Man, I love it when a plan comes together." Too bad E.P.'s plan was beginning to fall apart.

Emancipation Proclamation Jones heard the front door opening just as the distinct sound of a cranking ignition pierced the otherwise quiet air. He turned to look in the direction of the now idling van, desperately groping in his uniform pants pocket for the keys he had inadvertently left in the parked vehicle.

"Oh, shit!" he yelled as he watched the suddenly revived, but still disoriented drunk, settle into the driver's seat and throw the gear shift lever into reverse, the van's tires squealing as he raced it backwards down the driveway towards Scout 151.

In a state of mesmerized shock, Spic N' Span Spiegel watched helplessly as the swerving van plowed into 151's left front fender and then pushed him and the battered police car across the street. Emancipation Proclamation Jones stared in disbelief as 151, propelled by the careening van, crunched into two parked cars. The van then spun around and crashed into a metal light pole, its horn blaring an ominous tune as the inebriated driver once again slumped over the van's steering wheel.

Spic N' Span Spiegel radioed for an official to respond to their location. 10-33 Sam answered the call, licking his lips at the chance to screw over Emancipation Proclamation Jones, sure the cocky black officer was the cocksucker that was tapping his old lady. That afternoon, more than anyone would ever know, the winds of change were in the air. Emancipation Proclamation Jones felt the first subtle twinge of doubt, his luck slowly ebbing away, down the river of destiny. Spic N' Span Spiegel's moment of deliverance was drawing nearer, both events bearing one common thread, the mystic lure of Orleans Place.

Ray Carson Carver floated down another river, the blood red river of hell's fiery inferno. He was, at this very instant, less than one hundred miles from Washington, D.C., closing in on another rendezvous with his eternal partner, death. Humming his favorite Bon Jovi tune, the Dodge pick up clipping along at seventy, he reverently stroked the gleaming barrel of the 30.06. Tonight would be the first encore in his deadly game of murder. Tonight, he'd take out the human equivalent of a black white tail.

Spitting a moist stream of tobacco juice into the empty Styrofoam cup which he used as a spittoon, Ray Carver's demented mind drifted back to thoughts of his daughter's hard young body. He envisioned her pale naked flesh calling out to him, begging him to take her in a brutal frenzy of lust. The bitch was a slut, just like her mother, her tight ass hanging out of those short mini skirts that she was always wearing.

He could see it in her eyes, eyes that would passionately roll back into her pretty little head if he ever decided to spill his juice into her wet horny pussy. Jesus, he knew she'd be tight, not all sloppy like his old lady's stretched out snatch. Once he broke her in, the little vixen would probably fuck like a mink. If she didn't, maybe he'd skin her just like one. The horny slut was an evil temptress who only lived to torture and tease his suddenly rising manhood.

Before his self ordained mission of murder ended in the proverbial blaze of glory, Ray Carson Carver would see to it that his daughter felt the magic from his throbbing wand of pleasure. Rubbing his stubbly bearded chin, he smiled, sure that his lecherous vision of lust was a self fulfilling prophesy of orgasmic delight already chiseled in the stone of eternity. He could see it in his mind. She would feel it in her gasping body.

Maybe it just might be the last thing she ever felt. Yeah, that was it. He'd give her a thrilling ride and then drive her groaning sweat soaked body right down the one way street to hell. Ray Carver glanced at the passing exit sign as he sped down the slowly darkening highway. The Beltway was just ahead. All aboard the thrill kill train of grisly death. Next stop, Washington, D.C.. Next stop, Orleans Place.

"Ronnie. Get the hell down from there before you kill yourself," shouted Mike McCarthy, watching his partner clamber up the thick branches of an old barren oak tree located in the alley behind the six hundred block of Orleans Place.

"I'm O.K. I've just got a funny feeling about this. I think this is where our killer pulled the trigger. Something about this whole thing is kind of spooky. To be honest with you, Mac. I'm a little scared on this one," stated Ronnie, looking down at Mac's thinning gray hair through the tangle of gnarly branches.

"I should be up there. Not you. Jesus. You're a lady for God's sake. You ain't no friggin' tree surgeon," shouted Mike McCarthy, trying to position himself underneath Ronnie in case she fell.

"Mac. I love you too much to let your big butt up here. Besides, you'd make a great cushion if I fell," laughed Ronnie, looking in the direction of the place where they had first discovered the disemboweled body of the unfortunate young victim. The field of fire was clear. Wedged between two branches, Rhonda Bell knew beyond a shadow of a doubt that she was sitting in the exact spot where the murderer had sighted the rifle and unloosed the .30-06 round that had sent an innocent young man to meet his maker.

"This is it. I can feel it. This is where he was sitting when he wasted Jerome Anthony Marshall. You might think I'm crazy, Mac. But, I can almost see it taking place. It's like it's one week ago. And I'm looking over the bastard's shoulder while he aims the gun. Jesus, Mac, I'm scared," stated Ronnie, suddenly trembling with the fear of an obscure future clouded in the fog of an urban war that raged on, claiming casualties at an alarming rate. Now the battleground bore a new image. The shapeless form of a cunning sniper of death floated aimlessly across the shadowy void of blackness.

In her mind, Rhonda Bell conjured up the lurid vision of countless bodies laying in the D.C. morgue, side by side. Each one with a gaping hole in its shredded stomach. Hollow lifeless souls they'd be, wandering aimlessly through the ages. How do you bury somebody without their insides, thought Ronnie, as she lowered herself from the clutches of the foreboding tree. No matter, God would accept them into his kingdom. It was this insane butcher that would fry in the fire's of hell. And, if she had anything to say about it, she would be the one to personally lower him into the scalding bonfire that would consume his vile soul.

Noticing Ronnie's shaking body, Mac wrapped his navy blue top coat around her unsettled form. He sensed an aura of uneasiness engulf his partner in a bone chilling wave of apprehension. Her deep brown eyes stared out into the dark. Almost like x-ray vision, they appeared to penetrate the cloudy night's ebony void.

"You all right?" asked Mac, squeezing Ronnie's supple shoulder.

Ronnie shook her head and answered sullenly, "No. I'm not all right, Mac. I don't even know if I'm ever going to be all right again. We're fighting a war. A war that we can't win. Mac, no matter how it ends it's always the same. We lock up some of the murderers. But, it's always after they've already slaughtered some poor innocent person. Why couldn't we, just once, stop somebody before they kill? This guy's going to kill again. Maybe even tonight. And there's nothing we can do to stop him. He's in the driver's seat. Us, we're just along for the ride."

"Listen, Ronnie. Don't let it get to you. We'll nail this asshole. He'll screw up. They all do. You're right about one thing though. It is a war. A dirty filthy rotten war with small skirmishes and all out battles. With mounting casualties on both sides. People are getting killed and wounded in action. But, we're the good guys. At least we can take prisoners. That's what makes us different. We don't have to kill our enemy to win. We win only because we hate what he does more than he loves what he does," soberly stated Mac as he led Ronnie back to the Detective Cruiser. It was time to go home.

Ronnie turned to look back at the scene of the recent murder in the dark garbage strewn alley way and quietly said, "Mac, in this war, there'll never be any cheering crowds or ticker tape parades."

CHAPTER 6

DANNY MONEY was busting a gut, laughing uncontrollably as the Bud Man described to Tiny, in intimate detail, the sequence of events which had led up to the demise of Emancipation Proclamation Jones and Spic N' Span Spiegel who were still in the Fifth District Station filling out forms to document the circumstances surrounding their unfortunate accident.

"I can't believe that asshole, E.P.. I feel sorry for Spiegel though. Anybody that's got the jungle rot as bad as he does doesn't deserve a douche bag like Jones for a partner," chuckled Tiny as he nonchalantly poured the Bud Man a beer, making sure that none of the red eyed customers noticed that the Bud Man's coffee cup was actually filled with the king of beers.

Danny Money looked at his Movado. It was almost ten. In another couple of hours he'd be laying in bed with a raging hard on, ready to bury it into Ronnie's eager body. Damn, half the time he couldn't come close to satisfying her. But he sure as hell enjoyed trying. Tonight, maybe he could talk her into letting him handcuff her. That was one fantasy, as of yet, still unfulfilled. Right now, he just hoped that they could make it to check off time with no major fuck ups.

The last thing he needed was for some lunatic to do an instant replay of last week's shift. Seeing a dead man with his guts laying next to him was not high on his priority list. Seeing Ronnie, sweating and groaning in the heat of unbridled passion, was definitely on the top of that list. Sometimes he felt guilty thinking about her like she was some 14th Street hooker. But, she had so much sexual electricity that, when plugged in, it could scorch you like burnt toast.

Danny Money was not too gung ho about leaving Tiny's and driving Scout 150 over to Trinidad Avenue just so he could look down the barrel of some asshole's rod. In fact, he wasn't too gung ho about anything except jumpin' Ronnie. Such was life in the big city, figured Money, because at this very moment he had 150 smoking down Neal Street towards 1358 Trinidad Avenue, apartment number 9, where the dispatcher had informed them that a man was threatening his girlfriend with a gun. The Bud Man gulped the last of his beer, spilling half of the swig on to his once spotless uniform shirt and tie as Money hit a pothole in the narrow street.

"Before long, you'll look like Spiegel," joked Money turning 150 on to Trinidad Avenue and barely missing three young gangsta types crossing the crowded street.

"That mother fucker's got the biggest ghetto blaster I've ever seen. His boom box is almost as big as my jamoke," boasted the Bud Man, watching one of the young juveniles stagger under the weight of the huge radio which was blaring a steady stream of unnerving rap.

"What did he have? A mini walkman?" joked Money, shining the spot light on the doorways of the look a like apartment buildings hoping to find an address.

"Sheet. The motha' fucka had a Goddamned monster jammer just a teensy weensy bit smaller than my big black slammer," replied the Bud Man, grabbing his night stick from its customary position, stuck between the adjustable headrest and the scout car's seat back.

"There it is. 1358," stated Money, pulling the car to the curb, facing the wrong way, against traffic.

Danny Money took the lead walking up the broken glass strewn sidewalk, the portable radio in his left hand. The Bud Man followed. Already having nonchalantly pulled his nine millimeter Glock out of its holster, he kept the weapon at his side as inconspicuously as possible. Sometimes the natives got a little restless when they saw the police walking around with their guns drawn. Both officers knew that in this liberal city, famous for its continual barrage of unsubstantiated innuendoes of police harassment, it was sometimes better to be sorry than safe. Nevertheless, the Bud Man had no desire to go to an early grave. He'd much rather have a chat with the wimpy faggots on the civilian review board.

Danny Money opened the torn screen door and cautiously stepped inside the dimly lit hallway, the Bud Man right behind him. He turned down the volume on the police radio which, in this narrow corridor, crackled loudly with the buzz of constant radio transmissions. Danny Money peered down the length of the hazy corridor, trying to see the numbers on the apartment doors. Naturally, observed Money, the first floor contained apartments one through three. As was almost always the case, the asshole complainant had to live on the top floor. He located the burned out exit sign, pushed open the squeaky metal door, and began the climb up the creaking wooden steps.

Danny Money glanced at the tattered moldy carpet and started the slow walk down the hallway, a greasy smelling film of thick smoke obscuring the naked lightbulbs hanging from the cracked plaster ceiling. The Bud Man followed closely, turning up his nose as he caught a nauseating whiff of rotting garbage and the rancid stink of human excrement. This building had to be one giant crack house, figured Money, as he carefully inched his way towards apartment 9, its entrance a broken wooden door at the end of the narrow hallway. Danny Money had never thought about dying. The cold swirling winds from the north whipped up the open stairway and lashed out at him, their frigid grasp momentarily stabbing his suddenly trembling body with needle like pricks of stinging pain. Right now, standing in this lonely desolate hallway, dying was on his mind. The frosty breath of hideous death hung in the putrid air. Danny Money broke into a cold sweat. The hallway began to spin. The black hand of eternal darkness clutched at his pounding heart. His knees began to buckle. He felt himself sinking into unconsciousness.

The door at the end of the hallway slowly creaked open. Suddenly, Danny Money was staring down the barrel of the instrument of his imminent death. He threw his hands out in front of his face and turned his head in a feeble attempt to stop the oncoming bullets. He dropped the police radio to the floor. It was all happening in slow motion. Terrified, he watched as the hammer slowly drew back, the cylinder rotating the next round into the chamber. The pistol exploded with a deafening roar, flame and smoke spewing out of its sparking barrel. Danny Money tried to swat the bullet away, much like a pesky fly.

Almost simultaneously he felt the powerful grasp of the Bud Man's hand on his left shoulder, steadying him in the face of the withering fire. The Bud Man laid his right arm across Money's right shoulder from behind, and drew a bead on the assailant's chest which was less than ten feet away. Money felt the cold steel of the Bud Man's pistol against his neck. The explosions were ear shattering. Spent shell casings clattered off the yellow wall and rolled across the musty carpet. Acrid bursts of gunpowder singed his hair, their floating white puffs slowly diffusing into the hazy smoke filled hallway.

Danny Money slowly sank to the cold floor, his head reeling

from the close proximity of the cracking explosions. Watching the man from apartment number nine wildly clutching at his gurgling chest, brackish looking red stains oozing down his bloody wrinkled shirt, Danny Money cupped his hands over his ringing ears. The mortally wounded man staggered forward, crashing to the floor with a tremendous thud. The Bud Man reached down and swept the fallen man's weapon out of his reach.

Now on his knees, Danny frantically began to tear at the front of his body, trying to locate his almost certain wound. Everything was dry. There were no tell tale stains on his light blue uniform shirt. He had to be hit. Disoriented, he crawled around on the blood stained carpet, groping for the police radio. He had to call an ambulance. He must be dying. God, he felt sick to his stomach, sick with fear. He could smell the fear. It clung to him like stale sweaty body odor.

The Bud Man was shaking almost as bad as Danny Money. Damn, he had to call for help. Get some back up and an ambulance. Jesus, where the hell was the gun? He had to find the Goddamned gun. It was the only thing that could save him from going to jail. Apartment doors were beginning to open, people peering out from behind their reclusive shelter.

"Get back inside. Get your nosy asses back in your holes," screamed the Bud Man, wildly waving his weapon above his head as the murmuring lookyloos continued to stare at the violent scene of death.

Danny Money, still crawling around the foul smelling hallway, gazed in horror at the glassy open eyes of the fallen victim, his face less than one foot away from the dead man's eternal stare. He heard the high pitched squeak as the door to apartment number nine slowly creaked all the way open. A shocked black female stood in the doorframe, leering down at the macabre scene. Trying to lift himself off the blood stained floor, Money staggered against the hallway wall. The woman instantly began to shriek in terror, her screams of anguish reaching an ear splitting crescendo.

Realizing that the woman was most likely gazing down at her wasted lover, Danny Money reached out to her, vainly trying to comfort the bewildered woman who was fast becoming hysterical. It was a lost cause.

"You've killed my man. You murderin' bastards have killed my man. You mother fuckers. I'll fix your ass," screamed the bitter woman, diving into Money's teetering weak kneed frame.

He fell backwards, collapsing on to the back of the dead man as the woman jumped on top of the ghastly pile, pummeling Money with a cascade of blows.

The Bud Man stood mesmerized, just staring at the grotesque scene. The dead man's body was rolling back and forth, propelled by the struggle being fought on top of his limp torso. Finally, the Bud Man holstered his gun and forced his shaking legs to move. He felt like he was trying to run through wet cement. Reaching out to grab the crazed woman, he slipped in a pool of slimy blood and only managed to grasp a clump of her bushy hair. Half of it tore out at its roots, her head snapping back with a sickening crack.

Panicking, Danny Money pushed off the struggling woman and rose to his feet. The woman was laying on top of the fallen Bud Man, flailing away and staring up at him with hate filled eyes of fiery loathing. Money felt the thick glob of phlegm splatter against his face. The woman spit again, hitting him in the chin with a slimy mixture of spittle and mucus. He had had enough. Unable to control himself he pulled out his handcuffs and, swinging wildly, lashed out at the woman's skull. The hard metal cracked into her fleshy skin, leaving a dark crimson gash across the side of her forehead. Inserting his fingers through the round metal handcuffs, he punched the woman's face, fracturing her cheek. The handcuffs cut into his hand as he battered the screaming woman, the cuffs tearing into her jet black skin like brass knuckles.

"Man. She's had enough!" shouted the Bud Man, looking out from beneath the wilting woman and finally starting to regain his composure.

Horrified, Danny watched as the woman slumped to the gooey hallway floor. Damn, what had come over him? He hadn't meant for it to go this far. He felt like a wrung out washcloth. This was wrong. It was all so wrong. He hadn't ever wanted to kill anybody. Up until now it had just been fun and games, good guys and bad guys, cops and robbers. Nobody ever died in these games. It had never really crossed his mind. He had never dreamed that another human being would want to kill him just because he was cop. There was no rhyme or reason to this madness. His mind was a confused jumble of reeling sensations. He was used to looking at death, but always after the fact and certainly never his own.

Danny Money knew that this night would change his life forever. What he didn't know was whether the change would be for the better or for the worse. Kneeling next to the beaten woman, deathly pale as a ghost, Danny Money had the distinct feeling that he had lost more than his nerve. He felt a dull ache in his penis. He reached down and adjusted his limp cock. The hollow sensation returned. His penis felt dead, incapable of rising to the hard throbbing instrument of pleasure that he knew was its favorite state. "Oh, no. God. Not this," cried out the panic stricken officer. "Anything but this." He needed Ronnie. She could help him get his shit together. This was her world. Sometimes, he felt so very much like a stranger in the life and death struggle of the inner city ghetto.

While a little piece of Danny Money died on Trinidad Avenue Ray Carson Carver felt as alive as he ever had. He was beginning to feel comfortable in his new stalking grounds, so comfortable that he decided to use the same tree stand he had used last week. Animals always followed the same familiar trails, whether human or not. If he waited long enough a nice corn fed doe would pop into his sights and he'd lop off its head.

Ray Carver decided to be patient. He turned the four wheel drive Dodge pickup on to Florida Avenue Northeast and pulled into the McDonald's where he had sat not so long ago. The two story fast food restaurant at the intersection of New York and Florida Avenue northeast teemed with bustling activity. Blue and white D.C. police cars sped by, their red lights dancing off the dark deserted buildings, their sirens blasting a shrill, almost ominous, scream of urgency that echoed across the inner city corridors.

Oblivious to these common sights, the people went about their routine, not even bothering to speculate about the destination of the speeding scout cars and detective cruisers. Another day in paradise, another night in the big city. It was a portrait of life, being painted one stroke at a time. This particular snapshot was being taken on Trinidad Avenue, in the mind of two shocked police officers and one beaten woman whose world had come crashing down in an inexplicable explosion of hatred and violence.

Ray Carver wasn't too concerned about other people's worlds. His world was the only reality. And, his world was filled with the forbidden fruits of life. Murder, rape, incest, it was all his for the plucking. And, he intended to sample it all. Right now murder was on his mind. The other thrills would have to wait.

Ray Carver sat in the back of the McDonald's watching the parade of human shit that walked in and out of the busy restaurant, his black trench coat concealing the hunting vest and Buck knife that hung from his belt. He had decided to leave the hunting tag pinned to the middle of the back of his vest. It made it all the better. It was his legal license to kill.

Looking out into the damp chilly night, he caught a glimpse of a familiar face pulling up to the carry out window. It was that fat assed Porky Pig with the tall nigger bitch. They were the two that he had seen last week. He slumped down in his chair. Why should he care? They couldn't see him, anyway. Tonight wasn't the time to take out lard ass. But, the black bitch, she'd be perfect game. He'd enjoy stroking those nice titties of hers while he slit her belly open and gutted her just like the pig that she was. He liked tall sluts. They were so graceful going down. Wouldn't it be nice to watch her thick moist lips suck his throbbing white cock? He shuddered as he thought about the sweat soaked ecstasy that she could bring him to. Then, he thought of his daughter. That would be even better.

Mike McCarthy decided it was a four cream four-sugar night as he sat at the McDonald's carry out window. In fact he'd get one of those nice fried pies to satisfy his constant sweet tooth. He ordered Ronnie her usual hot tea and some McDonaldland cookies, figuring he'd end up with half of them too.

Neither Mike McCarthy nor Ronnie paid much attention to the inside of the restaurant, their minds still trying to figure out the method to the madness of the Orleans Place butcher.

"Man, this place is becoming a real red neck truck stop," joked Mac as he glanced over at the jacked up grey four wheel drive Dodge pickup, its shiny camper top glowing under the parking lot lights. "Probably belongs to that red neck shit kicker that was in here last week."

"Mac. Everybody's not an asshole, you know. If it wasn't for guys like him we wouldn't have food on the table or heat in our homes," countered Ronnie, trying to soften up Mac's stereotypical perception of much of the human race. Ronnie knew his bark was a lot worse than his bite. He had more genuine compassion for her race than any white man she had ever met.

Mac almost drove right past the baby big foot truck without looking. He had to squint. "Damn," he cursed under his breath. His vision was going. He reached inside the pocket of his blue sport coat and pulled out his glasses. He hated the damned things. They made him look and feel so old and frail. But, he was curious. His guess was West Virginia. Those hillbilly's really loved the kind of truck you needed a step ladder to get into. Slipping his glasses on and off in one quick motion he saw that he was wrong. "What's the difference," muttered Mac. "If you've seen one red neck you've seen them all."

Rhonda Bell looked over at Mac, sitting behind the wheel of Cruiser 311. "You should leave them on. You're kind of cute with glasses. They make you look like a cuddly old professor."

"Yeah. The nutty professor," laughed Mac as he pulled on to New York Avenue and headed downtown to Homicide Squad.

"Simulcast broadcast. Any Homicide Cruiser to respond to 1358 Trinidad Avenue northeast? Apartment number nine. Scout 150's involved in a shooting. We have an unconscious subject at that 10-20," broadcast the dispatcher.

Rhonda Bell's heart leaped into her throat. Her dark face turned an ashen coppery hue, beads of sweat instantly materializing, like little dots, across her forehead. In a confused panic she grabbed for the radio mike mounted on the dashboard of the detective cruiser.

Mike McCarthy could see the immediate tension engulf his beloved partner. Again, a slight pang of jealously ripped at his heart strings. He knew what he had to do for Ronnie. It would hurt her, but he'd have to hope that she'd understand. It could be no other way. She was too deeply involved with Danny Money.

Mac reached out with his fleshy hand and squeezed Ronnie's wrist, pulling her arm away from the mike. "Leave it be, Ronnie. It's better for him if you're not there. At least not as the one that might have to send him to the trial board if they screwed up. Let somebody else answer up to handle the call. It'll be all right. I'm sure he's OK. It sounds to me like they wasted some dude."

Ronnie looked incredulously at Mac and jerked her arm away from his gentle grasp. Every female hormone, every feminine instinct, was telling her to rush to her lover's side and comfort him as only a woman could. Men were weak, helpless as little babies in these kinds of situations. She knew Danny's weaknesses. He wasn't the street savvy dude he pretended to be. He was a small town kid who was scared, a young man who had never had to see the vileness of humanity that had surrounded her entire life. He thought he was one thing. She knew he was something else. And that something else was what she loved.

She prayed for the day Danny might ask her to marry him. Then, they could leave her world of ghetto demons behind. Darnell could escape the hideous nightmares that were always holding her in their elusive grasp. Maybe, God willing, she could even have Danny's baby. It was time to stand up and be counted. Love was supposed to be color blind. But, no matter how deep her love, her pride was deeper. It was he who'd have to come to these conclusions. He'd have to do the asking, not her.

Mac reached over and patted Ronnie's knees which were covered in a pair of khaki slacks. She bent over, her tailored red blazer straining at the seams as she wrapped her long arms around her knees and rocked back and forth.

"Hey, Ronnie. If it's that important to you, we'll go. I could never hurt you, you know. In my old foolish way I love you," quietly stated Mac as he struggled with his own confused feelings.

Ronnie turned her head, a tiny tear trickling down her brown skinned cheek. She grasped his pudgy hand with her long slender fingers. Her red manicured nails pressed against his sweaty palm as she squeezed as tightly as she could.

"I know you do," she answered. "You're right. He's just part of my candyland dreams. Dreams that'll probably never come true."

"They'll come true. I'll see to it, myself," promised Mac, silently vowing that they most definitely would, no matter what the price.

They both quietly listened as Homicide Cruiser 310 answered the call to respond to 1358 Trinidad Avenue. From this point forward none of their lives would remain unchanged. For tonight, the grim reaper would sweep another carcass under the carpet of death. Soon, very soon, the womb of hell would open up and unleash its nurturing embryo of death upon the land. The Capital Carver would be born in a fanfare of media hype, choking the revered city in a lurid stranglehold as Satan knocked at its very door.

"I wonder what in the hell the rock was for?" mumbled Mike McCarthy, pulling Cruiser 311 into the underground parking garage at police headquarters and still thinking about the grisly homicide on Orleans Place.

"I've got a feeling that there's going to be a lot more questions that we haven't got the answers for before this mess is over," dejectedly answered Rhonda Bell, hoping Danny was OK, but not quite able to shake the frightening sensation that she had experienced in the killer's tree top lair. It was almost as if she was looking through the scope of his rifle, looking right at the victim as he squeezed the trigger.

Latisha Davis was not a particularly nice lady. In fact, she might even refer to herself as a bitch. God had blessed her with a body that was as stunning as any female figure that walked the face of the earth. Unfortunately, for Latisha Davis, she was born black, in the ghetto of northeast Washington, D.C., and had never had the opportunity to avail herself of the advantages of being born white, or of having been raised by parents that might have given a shit one way or another. Her mother was a junkie whore. And her father was history before she was even out of her mama's belly.

By the time she was twelve years old Latisha Davis knew that her body got her places her skin color ordinarily wouldn't have. Men, old white men, with money, would pay a lot of it to look at and touch her young tight body. They had begged her to let them do it to her. Finally, one night seven years ago, she had let four of them take her. Two Congressmen, a U.S. Senator, and some no account wanna be had deflowered her. Latisha Davis laughed out loud as she thought of that night. Not one of them had lasted more than ten strokes. The night's work had made her four hundred dollars, ten dollar's a stroke. Not bad for a twelve year old.

Latisha Davis had just turned nineteen and since that night, seven years ago, she had always kept track of her pay on a per stroke basis. She delighted at seeing how fast she could get a man off. One old pale white fart had cum in his pants just looking at her. He had paid five hundred dollars for that privilege. Somewhere along the line she was sure that she had balled a Supreme Court Justice. If her memory served her well that had cost the legal eagle one hundred dollars per stroke.

Latisha Davis should have had a lot of money. But, unfortunately for her, the white men had also introduced her to coke. Her five foot eleven inch frame had begun to wither away, dropping thirty pounds to an even one-hundred. Her breasts, once standing firm and straight, now sagged against her skinny ribs. Her long graceful legs and narrow waist had shrunk to anemic proportions. Her appetite for the addictive powder had consumed her in a voracious fire of lustful dependence. Sometimes, she'd even let them screw her for the coke.

That is how Latisha Davis ended up back on Orleans Place, where she had been born nineteen years ago. Once again, unfortunately for Latisha Davis, nothing ever seemed to go right. Tonight, walking the streets in a black patent leather miniskirt and see through lace top, her studded waist length black leather motorcycle jacket draped over her sleek graceful shoulders, she had managed to find a John who had taken her in the back seat of his Sedan de Ville. He had stroked her until she had lost count, all for fifty miserable bucks. Her stock was dwindling quickly. Latisha Davis decided that she had to change her life. Latisha Davis made the right decision one day too late.

Ray Carson Carver parked the Dodge pick up truck behind a deserted warehouse, less than a block from the alley on Orleans Place. He slipped on his black leather gloves and stroked the barrel of the powerful rifle. Tonight, he had waited longer, making sure that the streets were as quiet as possible. He looked at his watch. It was almost one in the morning. It was time.

He slipped through the pitch black veil of darkness, making sure to cover his tracks. He found that by traveling quietly in the patchwork of garbage filled alleyways he could remain unseen, the shadows concealing his creeping form. He owned the night. He, like all the nocturnal carnivores, felt that it gave him an edge. Darkness was his friend. It welcomed death with open arms.

He located the tree and scrambled up its thick heavy branches. Sniffing the air, he could almost feel another presence. Someone, or something, had been up here. He could sense it. The hair on the back of his neck stood straight up, sending a tingling shiver down his spine. The predator was master of the jungle. He had all the advantages.

Glimpsing a sudden movement on the branch above him, he froze deathly still. The cat moved cautiously, stalking its prey. Ray Carver watched as the silent cat crouched, ready to strike. He quietly slipped his hand inside his black trench coat and withdrew the stainless steel hunting knife. The cat slowly turned its head to look at the strange intruder. Almost seeming to welcome the man's presence, it began to purr.

In one fleeting movement Ray Carver snatched the grey cat by the scruff of the neck, slitting its throat before it could even shriek in terror. Just for kicks, he sliced open its belly and watched as the dead cat's innards splattered on the asphalt and gravel down below. "There's more than one way to skin a cat," he chuckled under his breath. In a grotesque salute to the vanquished predator he laid the disemboweled cat on the branch where it had stalked its last prey only to become the quarry of another, more sinister, predator. Then, in one swoop, he lopped off its head and dropped the two parts of the mutilated animal to the ground.

Ray Carver saw the solitary figure slowly sauntering down the desolate alley. Turning his camouflage colored Cat hat around backwards, its bill facing the back of his neck, he sighted the scope. He couldn't believe his good fortune. Jesus, she had nice legs for a darkie, thought Ray Carver as he watched Latisha Davis walk down the alley, her breasts bobbing heavily under the sheer white lace top. Her coat was slung over her shoulders. She was a looker. And, he'd sure enough get a good look at her real soon, figured the cold blooded murderer, tapping down the bolt and thumbing off the safety of the 30.06. He didn't want to mess up those fine big titties before he had a chance to pinch her nipples. Yeah, he'd take out this tall black split tail right through the brain. "No use spoiling that fine dark meat," he murmured as he held his breath and exhaled. Then, he gently started to squeeze the trigger.

Latisha Davis wished she could afford some better shoes. The black six inch spikes were killing her feet. She stepped up on the first stair to her apartment over the abandoned garage. The heel caught in a narrow crack in the rotten wooden step, snapping it off like a piece of dry pasta. She stumbled forward, smashing her knee on the splintering step. Latisha Davis, to her dying day, was never a lucky person. Except for that heel, she would have never felt the agony she was about to endure. The head shot would have ended her life instantaneously. Now, she was about to experience an even more gruesome fate.

For a split second, Ray Carver panicked. Then, gaining control of himself, he steadied his weapon. Having no choice, he instantly decided on a body shot and squeezed the trigger. The rifle cracked sharply, kicking into his shoulder.

Latisha Davis felt a dull thud as a cold hollow pain exploded in her side. She reached down, clutching at her burning side. A moist warm sticky goo coated her long nailed fingers. She was confused, disoriented. An empty feeling clawed at the pit of her stomach. Somehow, Latisha Davis instantly knew that she was shot. Grievously wounded, she struggled up the stairs and sought the safety of her disheveled apartment. If she could only make it inside. She had a gun in the drawer next to her bed.

Ray Carver knew he couldn't chance another shot. In this shithole, one explosion might not even be worth calling the police. Two, was pressing his luck which, so far, had been pretty good. He dropped to the ground. Staying in the shadows of the trees and bushes, he covered the forty yard distance in almost no time. The crawling slut had pulled herself all the way to the top of the stairs. She was hanging over the top railing, on the landing, unable to even scream. He slung the rifle over his shoulder. Withdrawing the knife, he followed her up the stairs like a hungry lion on the trail of freshly spilled blood.

Latisha Davis couldn't find her keys. The man was coming up the stairs after her. She felt deathly ill, drained of energy. She was weak, unable to move. The warm dark fluid was everywhere. She was having trouble breathing. Gasping for breath, she pushed at the door. It was no use. His shadow was upon her. The shadow of death covered her face. She glimpsed the dull shimmering knife and futilely kicked out her legs towards the towering figure.

Staring down at the pathetic whore, Ray Carver suddenly figured it all out. He braced himself against the door jam and began brutally kicking the groveling woman. Finally, with one mighty heave, he pushed her off the landing, her body splattering to the ground with a dull sickening thud. He raced down the stairs. Jesus, she was one tough whore. She was still breathing. He forced open the creaking garage door and dragged her limp body into the dark building. Looking around the oily smelling structure, he located a piece of rope on a cluttered shelf. He quickly tied the greasy rope around the gasping woman's ankles and threw the other end over a wooden support beam which spanned the width of the abandoned garage. He tugged frantically on the rope, hauling the woman's body, feet first, up into the air, her head several feet above the ground.

Securing the rope to an exposed two by four, Ray Carver watched in silence as the black woman's body spun slowly around, dangling in mid air like a trophy buck hanging in some proud hunter's back yard. He walked over to the helpless woman and ripped open her flimsy top, his warm breath rising in the cold garage. He fondled her ponderous breasts, pinching her nipples unmercifully. He slit her tight skirt, watching it fall to the oily dirt floor. This bitch didn't have any panties on. Grinning the lecherous grin of the eternally damned, he plunged the knife into her soft abdomen and hacked his way down to her clavicle, using both his hands to leverage the blade. He wiped off the knife on her lacy white top and sheathed the weapon. Reaching his hands into her open squishy torso he yanked down, spilling her innards onto the now sloshy ground.

Ray Carver wiped his gloved hands on the blood splattered lace top. He reached into his coat pocket and withdrew the branch, ramming its stem into the back of the dead woman's throat. He stepped cautiously out of this dark oily smelling tomb of death and, never looking back, crept slowly down the alley, away from Orleans Place, the living graveyard of the walking dead.

Mike McCarthy had had enough for one night. He was tired, tired of asking the same useless questions to the same never see anything citizens. He was beginning to believe that this, like the whirlwind arena of the uniform scout car gladiators, was a young person's job. He was feeling a little complacent as he prepared to knock on the metal door of 1222 Wylie Street Northeast, apartment number three, to ask Ms. Ophelia Johnson, for the third time, how it was that one Tyrell Richardson had been shot five times on her couch with her sitting in the same room, miraculously managing not to see anything. Jesus, he hoped she wasn't home. He didn't need to hear this same old bullshit story again.

Ronnie, sensing her partner's reluctance and needing something to take her mind off the constant agonizing worry over Danny's still unresolved fate, stepped in front of Mac and knocked, making sure that neither one of them stood directly in front of the closed door. She knew that too many police officers had prematurely met their maker, carelessly deciding to greet the potentially dangerous occupant like a Fuller Brush Man trying to sell a toilet bowl scrubber.

Mac took a deep breath, trying to force some life into his lethargic body. He sniffed the subtle delicate sweet scent of Ronnie's lingering perfume. That was just the ticket. His heart, jump-started by the arousing aroma, began to pump a steady flow of blood to his head. His vitality returned instantly, his mind wandering back to the days when he had been full of piss and vinegar, the days when his life had been showered with hope and joy, the days when his Mary Rose had decorated his world with the brilliant colors of love.

Twenty-four years of sacrifice and devotion, of happiness and harmony, of marriage and commitment were all only memories, dreams shattered by a world without guarantees, a world where the dusky Autumn of life was slowly turning into the chilling cold of Winter, a world where there was still no cure for the cancer that had drained the life out of her once vibrant body.

Mac thought back to the funeral, glad that against everyone's wishes, he had asked that the casket be closed. He wanted to carry with him the memories of what she truly was, not the fleeting glimpse of her painful suffering and what she had become. Her lovely smiling face was a joyful painting, forever etched into his lonely tired mind.

"What is it?" asked Mac, sniffing the crisp air for another hint of Ronnie's perfume.

"Chloe," answered Ronnie, glad that Mac obviously approved of her favorite fragrance.

"It looks like Ms. Johnson isn't in," stated Ronnie, almost relieved not to have to interview Ophelia again. She was beginning to sound like a bad recording of the female version of Paula Abdul's Cold Hearted Snake. This lyin' black bitch was as callous as they came. The late Tyrell Richardson had been her common law husband for the last five years. It was only four weeks after he had been murdered and she had already brought in a permanent pinch hitter, bitching about having to buy a new couch because the dead nigger had bled all over her favorite piece of furniture.

Mac and Ronnie headed back to Cruiser 311 and decided to call it a night, both detectives happy not to have to listen to Ophelia talk trash.

"I can't believe it," exclaimed Mac as he plopped down behind the steering wheel of the unmarked tan cruiser.

"Can't believe what?" inquired Ronnie, sitting on the passenger side and filing a sharp edge off of one of her shapely red nails.

"I can't believe that we made it through a shift without having to watch the Medical Examiner bag one. Maybe we're starting to win the war. The body count's dropping. At least for tonight."

"Well. That might be. But, I think we should have left sooner. That's Ophelia. Over there. In the Cadillac that just pulled up in front of her apartment. And, unless my vision is getting as bad as yours, I thing I know whose car she's gettin' out of," calmly remarked Ronnie, wondering where Freddy fit into this bizarre situation. She didn't relish the thought of having to come face to face with a past mistake, especially when her stomach was already churning, every fiber of her being exploding with spine tingling apprehension, worrying about Danny.

Mac squinted, trying to make out the two forms through the blackness, a single flickering streetlamp casting nothing more than a dim glow over the parked white Cadillac El Dorado and its two occupants. He looked over at Ronnie, her sullen face telling a tale of anguish and grief, a look he had seen before, a look of hurt, the hurt of misery and frustration known only to the frustrated children of the ghettos of the world. Whether he could see him or not, Mac instinctively knew that he was staring at one of the main reasons for Ronnie's pain. Scumbags like the Snowman perpetuated the defilement of her people. Before true resurrection of the impoverished black race could ever occur, figured Mac, terminal diseases like the Snowman had to be snuffed out forever, suffocated in their own powder of death.

Mac's puffy wrinkled face began to glow a deep shade of crimson, his head throbbing with rage. He'd fix this drug dealing asshole once and for all. With one shot he could erase Ronnie's demons forever. Reaching for the door handle of the parked cruiser, he made up his mind. It didn't take Dick fuckin' Tracy to figure it out. The Snowman had pumped those five rounds into the poor bastard's head and now he was knockin' boots with the dead man's old lady, Ophelia. This whole bad scene reeked with the stench of a soured drug deal, the Snowman adding the last ingredient, death.

Momentarily caught up in her own little world of despair, Ronnie didn't notice Mac's sudden change in temperament. Stumbling out of the cruiser's driver's side door, he caught his balance and then headed straight for the shiny El Dorado. Mac's right hand reached across his body, grasping the worn wooden grips of his two inch Smith and Wesson revolver which dangled from its shoulder holster wedged underneath his left armpit.

Ronnie was stunned, unable to move. Mac's out of character movements had paralyzed her into inaction. "Damn," she gasped. Mac was pulling out his gun, his bulky frame rushing across the narrow deserted street towards the parked Cadillac. Ronnie knew she had to move quickly, or she'd be looking for a new partner to replace what was now a dear friend. She threw open the cruiser's passenger side door and bolted after Mac, the heels of her flats clicking sharply against the pavement as her long muscular legs gracefully propelled her, like a bounding gazelle, across the pitch black street towards the shimmering Cadillac.

Fred Frost never even noticed the charging officers, his hand buried in Ophelia Johnson's insatiable wet steamy pussy while her long slender fingers unmercifully squeezed his rock hard cock. His eyes glazed over in a film of lust as she lowered her head, all the while moistening her lips in preparation to devour his raging hard on in a slurpy suction of carnal rapture. Once he busted a load in her sucking mouth he'd bust a cap into her fucking brains, silently chuckled the Snowman to himself as he fondled the .357 magnum laying next to Ophelia's wildly wriggling ass. He'd miss that juicy pussy of hers. But, there were always others willing to pay the ultimate price for a trip to never- never land.

The junkie whores were like rock and roll groupies, always wanting to say they balled the man, the prince of center stage, the main man, the king of Orleans Place. Their thrill was a short, sweet ride in the fast lane of life, devouring man-made pleasures like starving dogs. His thrill was ending their fantasy ride in a fiery crash of burning death. The Snowman was about to make Ophelia Johnson his second crash of the year. Her old man had been an added delight. His payments had been a little late once too often. "When you plays you gots to pays," laughed the Snowman, thinking about his personal collection service and the late payments that he charged his delinquent customers. His cash flow had dramatically increased after the word about Ophelia's old man had been put out on the street. A moist sheen of sweat broke out all over the Snowman's pumping body. He was about to cum and Ophelia was about to go.

Gasping for breath, his chest heaving, Mike McCarthy reached the shiny white El Dorado just about the same time as the Snowman was about to reach a boiling orgasm. Mike McCarthy flung open the unlocked driver's side door of the rocking Cadillac and jammed the cold steel barrel of his revolver into the Snowman's left ear. Shocked, Ophelia Johnson pulled her wetly sucking mouth off of the Snowman's throbbing penis, her head still unconsciously bobbing up and down. Unable to hold back any longer, the Snowman's suddenly wilting cock began to spurt its load all over his Khaki colored Dior pants, staining the wrinkled trousers with thick streaks of gooey semen.

Mike McCarthy, staring down at the Snowman's limp penis and soiled pants, was not in his usual good humor. His mind was bent on ridding the face of the earth of one more drug dealing asshole, an asshole who tried to destroy everything he ever touched, including Ronnie and her son Darnell. Mac was in a grim state of mind as he cocked back the hammer of his revolver, ready to spill the Snowman's brains all over the red interior of his big time Caddy.

Ophelia Johnson reached over and slid the six inch stainless steel .357 magnum under her short purple suede dress, her head spinning from an all day orgy of drugs and alcohol. Mac, still savagely pressing his service revolver against the Snowman's left ear, yanked the struggling drug dealer out of his car and kicked his legs out from under him. He slammed Frosty's face into the side of the rocking car. Ronnie was almost there.

"You motha' fuckin pig. Leave my man alone or I'll fix your white ass," screamed Ophelia, contemplating raising the .357 and wasting the fat bastard cop.

"Go ahead, motha' fucka. I'll be your whippin' boy. And, I'll see you in court. You'all be hearin' from my lawyer," defiantly shouted the Snowman, unaware that Mike McCarthy, having just snapped, was about to pull the trigger and send him to the big needle in the sky.

Kneeling over the Snowman's spread-eagled body, his gun still pressed to the side of the flailing man's head, Mac began to slowly squeeze the trigger. Ronnie, her mind instinctively recalling her self defense training, slammed her hand, thumb and fore finger spread widely apart, between the falling hammer and the awaiting bullet of Mac's revolver. The firing pin cut into the soft web like flesh of her tender skin and prevented the descending hammer from striking the cartridge and putting an abrupt end to one of her more serious problems.

Mac, seeing Ronnie's grimace of pain, finally regained his senses and allowed her to gently remove the revolver from his suddenly trembling hand. God, he felt sick to his stomach. He turned his back and staggered away from the terrifying scene, unable to understand what had come over him. Bending over and placing his hands against the sides of his head, Mike McCarthy began to shake like a leaf. Then, falling to his knees in the middle of the dark deserted street, he began to sob uncontrollably, ashamed of himself, sorry that he had disgraced the badge that up to now he had worn so proudly for so many years. Reaching down, he unclipped the tarnished silver badge from his belt and flung it to the ground, the tinny metal clanging against the asphalt pavement.

Still holding Mac's service revolver, Ronnie slowly walked over to her partner's rocking frame. She bent over and picked up the dented badge, wiping it off against the pant leg of her suit.

"Pretty rough treatment for something that you've dedicated your whole life to for all these years. Don't you think you're allowed some mistakes? None of us are above making mistakes. We're human beings, by God. We're not Robo Cops. We're flesh and blood. Officers like you have written the litany for the rest of us to follow. Please, Mac, forgive yourself. I forgive you," consoled Ronnie, her heart crying out to her despondent partner.

"Bitch!" screamed Ophelia Johnson, stepping out of the El Dorado, the .357 magnum pointed at Ronnie.

"Do her. Waste the bitch. Smoke her black ass," hollered Frosty, getting up on one knee and seeing a golden opportunity to do away with two gnawing problems with one bullet. Ronnie would be dead. And Ophelia, that whore'd spend the rest of her life in jail, probably convicted of killing her old man, too, once he conveniently remembered seeing her pull the trigger of the murder weapon which she now clasped in her trembling hands, figured the Snowman.

Ronnie looked down at Mac who continued to weep. He was sprawled out on the pavement like a quivering bowl of Jello. Ophelia Johnson lurched forward and aimed the powerful handgun at Ronnie's heaving chest. Her smooth shapely legs were wobbling. Precariously supported by a pair of purple spike heeled pumps, she teetered back and forth. Ronnie stared blindly, unable to react. She was frozen like a deer caught in the illumination of an approaching car's highbeams.

"I'll fix your ass. You nigger bitch. He's my man now. You couldn't keep him. You and your uppity ass self. Your holier than thou shit don't cut it no more. Not down here in the Snowman's land. I'm his woman. He wants me," shouted Ophelia, still clutching the heavy revolver which was making an unsteady pattern of figure eights as it weaved dangerously in the chilly evening air.

Mike McCarthy stayed, stomach down, on the cool pavement and prayed that Ophelia would keep jabbering on. He chanced a quick glance at Ronnie. Seeing that she still held his revolver in her hands, he decided to take the chance. If he could distract Ophelia for even a split second Ronnie could draw a bead and smoke her before she could bust a cap on either one of them. Tonight was to be one of Mike McCarthy's last lucky nights on the face of the earth. His stock, much like that of Emancipation Proclamation Jones' was beginning to plummet into the fickle depths of misfortune.

Now less than ten feet away, Ophelia took one more unsteady step forward. Mac decided it was now or never. He bolted to his feet. Leaning over almost as if he didn't want to look at the bullet that was going to end his life, he began to run toward Ophelia, the worn soles of his black wing-tips slipping on the oily street's slick surface.

Ophelia turned towards the rushing detective, one of her spiked heels catching in a tiny crack in the patched roadway. She stumbled forward, accidentally squeezing the trigger of the stainless steel .357 magnum. The deafening explosion cracked loudly in the still night air. A brief flash of brilliant flame shot out of the smoking barrel. The bullet slammed into the pavement, ricocheted between Mac's wildly pumping legs, and then harmlessly imbedded itself into the engine block of a bright pink Toyota low rider, parked, unoccupied, across the street.

Mac plowed into Ophelia with all his might and knocked the staggering woman backwards to the ground, her skull crashing into the pavement with a brittle crack. Ronnie raised the two inch revolver and leveled it on the twitching woman who still clasped the .357 in her right hand. Ronnie hesitated, the use of deadly force weighing heavily on her overburdened mind. She just couldn't pull the trigger. It wasn't the right thing to do. Laying virtually unconscious in the middle of the street, Ophelia wasn't a threat to anybody, except maybe herself. Mac grabbed Ophelia's wrist and wrenched the weapon from her limp grasp.

"Good work, Ronnie. Sometimes it takes more courage not to pull the trigger," praised Mac, clamping a set of handcuffs on Ophelia's wrists which he had pulled behind the small of her shapely back. "You're goin' down, too," he added, staring in the direction of the kneeling Snowman whose face was oozing a steady trickle of congealing blood.

Ronnie walked towards the Snowman, his lips clenched in a sinister grin. Silently, he defied her to lay her hands on him.

"You're under arrest," she calmly stated, her cracking voice revealing her inner turmoil.

"What for? I ain't done a motha' fuckin' thing. 'Cept get beat up by your honky partner for messin' around with my ol' lady. Shit. You'all ain't got nothin' on me. That's the bitch's gun. She wasted her old man with it. Right in their crib. She did him. Damn. The whore was prob'ly gonna do me too," answered the Snowman, knowing he'd be walkin' before they even finished with the paperwork on this chicken shit rap.

"That white boy pig you're fuckin'. I bet he ain't shit. Probably can't get his dick hard half the time. And I knows how much you like it. Don't I baby?" he added, hatefully staring into Ronnie's sensual brown eyes.

"Whatta you gonna tell Darnell? You gonna tell the sissy punk that that faggot white boy is his ol' man? He's my son, bitch. My son. And don't you ever forget it."

"Listen up, you piece of crap. You aren't ever going to touch my boy. He isn't yours. He's mine. I never asked your worthless black ass for nothin'. I raised him. Raised him to be a Christian boy. A boy that can walk tall. Proud of what he is. I'm teaching him that he can make a difference in this crazy world. That he can reach for the stars. And that he should help other less fortunate people realize their dreams. He's going to be a decent human being. Not a drug dealing piece of trash like you. He'll help our people. You destroy them. And, someday you'll pay for your sins," coldly stated Ronnie, leering down at the Snowman, her soft eyes blazing with the fires of frustration and rage.

Mac walked over towards Ronnie. He wanted to get the Snowman and Ophelia out of here as soon as possible. The once dark quiet street was beginning to light up like opening night of a blockbuster Hollywood movie, lookyloos beginning to congregate all over the now bustling street.

"Better call an ambulance for Ophelia. She's pretty messed up. Frosty baby needs a little cruise in the patrol wagon. That'll cool him off a little. I guess he'll have to go back and hang with his old lady down on Orleans Place now that Ophelia's out of action," chuckled Mac, taking Ronnie's handcuffs and locking them tightly around the Snowman's wrists.

"Mac. I thought you were gone. Damn. I knew how upset you were. How did you ever get it back together so quick?" asked Ronnie, startled at Mac's abrupt turnaround.

"Don't ever underestimate the power of the word. For it is truly mightier than the sword. And, don't ever underestimate your preaching ability. You, my dear, are a silver tongued she-devil who probably just saved my old tired butt from the worst case of self pity I have yet inflicted upon myself," solemnly answered Mac, a gleeful twinkle in his sparkling green Irish eyes.

"You, my man, are a classic example of the true meaning of a Big Mac attack," joked Ronnie. "Excellent, dude. Very excellent."

Ronnie watched quietly as the paramedics loaded Ophelia Johnson into the ambulance, a uniform scout car officer sitting with her in the back to make sure that she didn't disappear on the way to, or even at, D.C. General Hospital. Officers clothed in the dark blue utility uniforms of the Mobile Crime Lab scoured the surrounding scene in an attempt to secure additional evidence. Two uniform officers were escorting the Snowman into the back of the patrol wagon. Ronnie wished that they could drive him far into the darkness, disappearing forever in the black void of eternal damnation.

Mac had told her that he'd do most of the paperwork so that she could get some rest. He'd handle the arraignment, tomorrow morning, at D.C. Superior Court. It was his little way of thanking her for helping him get his shit back together. Ronnie certainly appreciated Mac's cute gestures. Sometimes, like most men, he was so predictable. But, unlike most of them, he was so genuinely sincere. Deep down inside Ronnie knew that Mac loved her as a person, loved her for herself, not for the thing between her legs that so preoccupied most every waking minute of the entire male population. She just wished she was as sure of Danny's motivations as she was of Mac's.

Anyway, she knew it really didn't matter. She'd fallen for Danny. And that made her weak and vulnerable. Love, like life itself, was so much of a gamble. He could hurt her if he wanted. She had given him more than her body. She had given him her soul. He held her in the palm of his hands, a living breathing hunk of clay to be molded into a form that would merge with his in a union of love. The last thing Ronnie wanted was to get some rest. Inside, she was a pent up ball of smoldering coals, ready to explode in an outpouring of fiery passion. She had to see Danny. She needed to hold him. To have him hold her. To comfort each other. To share a few hours of love in this violent world of hate.

"Hey, bitch. Just remember Darnell. He'll never be nothin' but a sorry ass nigger. Just like you and me. He's my flesh and blood. Not pretty boy's," hollered the Snowman from the back of the patrol wagon and abruptly ended Ronnie's romantic dreams.

She wanted desperately to strike back, but controlled herself. "Those that live by the sword shall perish by the sword," she yelled, the patrol wagon disappearing down the crowded street. Little did Rhonda Bell know how true those words of prophecy were soon to become. It was getting warmer on Orleans Place. The Snowman was about to melt.

Mike McCarthy and Rhonda Bell sat in the interrogation room of Homicide Squad filling out the papers that would charge Ophelia Johnson with Assault on a Police Officer, Possession of a Prohibited Weapon, Unlawful Discharge of a Firearm, and hopefully the recent murder of her common law husband. They had had the misfortune of finding nothing more than a half empty bottle of Hennesey Cognac in the Snowman's white El Dorado, leaving them no recourse but to charge him with Disorderly Conduct and let him go after he posted bail.

Both detectives knew that even this was a little shaky. The only disorderly person had been Mac, himself. But, the Snowman deserved a little slap on the wrist. At least if he sued them they had covered their asses by bringing him in on charges, no matter how chickenshit they were. With any luck they could link him to the gun. They both knew that he had pulled the trigger, scattering Ophelia's old man's brains all over her favorite couch. Proving it, was a different matter altogether.

CHAPTER 7

DANNY MONEY and the Bud Man sat in the Fifth District Detective room replaying their line of duty shooting, over and over again, to two pricks from the Internal Affairs Division while a couple of 5D detectives and sergeant 10-33 Sam stood by, trying to protect the two officers from themselves.

The Bud Man had broke down and admitted to the I.A.D. strokes that he had planted the gun on the deceased, stating that he always carried a throw down weapon under his uniform cap, camouflaged in his afro. The bigger the weapon the higher he had to grow his afro. He had, however, expressed some difficulty in his efforts to conceal the baseball bat that he'd like to ram up their fat stupid asses. Maybe that would remove the shit eating grins that they always wore plastered on their smug looking faces, he figured as he smiled at the two I.A.D. dickheads and wondered which one of the faggots was back dooring the other one.

Danny Money didn't have a whole lot to say to anybody. He couldn't stop thinking about his shriveled penis. He kept reaching down to adjust it, still wondering if the magical mystery of its rising growth was only becoming a vague memory. Sitting there, listening to the white shirted, grey suited, stripe tied, black loafered, mustachioed cloned clowns from I.A.D. drone on, his mind wandered. It was five am. He was sitting in Scout 150 next to Ronnie, trying to cross his left leg to conceal the hard throbbing bulge in the crotch of his dark blue uniform pants. Ronnie, cruising 150 on a routine patrol of their beat, had glanced over at his squirming form, asking him if everything was all right. Then, it had been all right, natural. Now, he didn't know.

"What's wrong?" she had inquired, giggling because she already knew both the problem and the answer.

"Nothing," he had lied in reply, embarrassed to broach the delicate subject.

Ronnie had laughed. "EMHO. That's about the only problem us women don't have."

"What the hell's EMHO?" he had asked.

"Early morning hard on," she had chuckled. "If you've got

the problem. We've got the cure."

Now he didn't even have the Goddamned problem. Danny Money was desperate. He had to find out the answer tonight, no matter who supplied it.

It had been almost two hours since he had called Homicide Squad and left a message for Ronnie, professing to have some additional information regarding the recent murder of Jerome Marshall on Orleans Place. He was beginning to panic. In his haste he forgot the cardinal rule of internal police department communication, never trust that a message will ever get to anyone, let alone the police officer that it was originally intended for. The Homicide Lieutenant who took the message had, shortly thereafter, received one of his own, one of a much more urgent nature.

Detective Lieutenant Bow Wow Bowser was in his official's cruiser, expediting across the Fourteenth Street Bridge into northern Virginia, the message from Danny Money laying unobserved in his locked office. The telephone call had come as an unexpected bonus to an otherwise dreary tour. Lighting up his sixth cigarette, the inside of the cruiser bathed in swirling wisps of thick smoke, Bow Wow Bowser conjured up visions of the sultry olive skinned woman, her smooth shapely legs pinned back against her ripe undulating breasts, begging him to give it to her harder.

Yes, Sam Williamson's old lady was the hottest piece of ass he had ever had. The horny broad was just about driving old Sambo crazy with jealousy. The dumb son of a bitch should have known, even before he married her, that no hillbilly shit kicker from West Virginia could ever handle a good Italian Catholic girl from New York. They were on fire, all the time, just dying to get jumped. Jesus, what was it that the boys over in good old 5D were beginning to call the shaky sergeant? Shit, he couldn't remember. All he could think about was her huge brown nipples, begging to be sucked. How could that asshole be working late again, missing out on those beauties?

Well his loss is my gain, figured the anxious lieutenant, pulling the unmarked cruiser into the Motel 6 parking lot, less than five blocks from the Williamson household. Slamming the car door shut, he glanced over at the dark bare window of room number lucky seven, wondering where she was. Suddenly, the light came on. Her gorgeous full figure, encased in a black transparent bra, G-string, black garter belt and lace stockings, stood framed in the uncovered window, the curtains drawn all the way back. She posed provocatively, looking like an erotic snapshot from Hustler. Damn, the crazy broad was reaching in front of her, unsnapping the bulging bra, her tits bursting forth like ripe melons.

"Yeah. That was it. 10-33 Sam. That's what the boys down at 5D were calling the wimpy asshole," chuckled Bow Wow Bowser as he rushed towards the unlocked motel room door, fumbling with the zipper of his bulging trousers.

Since Ronnie never returned his call, Danny Money didn't know anybody he could ball in such short notice. Anybody that is, except maybe Briefcase Betty Barnes. Briefcase Betty Barnes was a pale mousy woman, her shoulder length brown hair hanging in strands, looking like she was the majority stockholder in the 'little dab'll do you' company. Briefcase Betty Barnes was also a short woman, little more than five feet in height who had never before met a man that made her quiver with such physical electricity as Danny Money.

She had felt supercharged, tingling sensations exploding out of every nerve ending of her body when she had first met Danny, as classmates, in the police academy. Despite her plain Jane looks and short stature, Briefcase Betty knew that she held the key to almost everyman's lock box. Her slight frame and narrow waist accentuated a pair of thirty eight double Ds that had every octopus that she had ever gone out with drooling in anticipation. But, once they started fondling in fascination, they went reeling with frustration when she curtly ended their quest for yet another four F female victim to add to their list. Briefcase Betty was not about to join the ranks of the find 'em, feel 'em, fuck 'em, and forget 'em, society of women which had been used and then cast aside by the egomaniac assholes that made up the majority of the male population.

She did, however, make one exception to her golden rule, Danny Money. Briefcase Betty Barnes had made it very clear, from the first day that she had ever met Officer Money that she would allow him to do her, anytime, anyplace. She was more than a little hurt when he had politely brushed her aside, not knowing what an honor and a privilege she had decided to bestow upon him. He continued to turn her down over the years despite her repeated attempts to allow him the pleasure of her body, a pleasure as of yet known to no man. For, at the age of twenty-nine, Briefcase Betty Barnes remained a virgin, waiting for Danny

Money to be the right man at anytime of the day or night.

Lately, Briefcase Betty had been having some strong vibes. She'd been experiencing some mighty powerful omens prophesying a future of fulfillment and sexual bliss. It was in the air, all around her. Briefcase Betty Barnes instinctively knew that it was her time. What she didn't know was that she was having visions of the wrong man, even though she was right about one thing. It most certainly was the right time.

"Hey, Betty. It's the phone. Some jerk off named Money, from 5D, is on the line. He wants to talk to you. You gonna let him play with those nice titties of yours? Who you savin' 'em for, anyway? What are you some kind of dyke, or what?" stated Rambo Dave Roddy, Briefcase Betty's scout car partner of the last two miserable years of her very lonely life.

Briefcase Betty was incapable of hating anybody. Anybody that is, except Rambo Roddy. He, in her mind, was the pig of pigs, a low life vile scumbag who looked at women simply as receptacles for his dubious manhood. If they dissected his head, it wouldn't be water that they'd find on his brain. It'd be cum, figured Briefcase Betty as she strolled over to the telephone in the Second District station clerk's office, knowing, without even looking back, that Rambo Roddy's eyes were fixed on her undulating buttocks. She had purposely ordered her dark blue uniform slacks and light blue blouses one size too big, in an attempt to conceal her ripe body from the stares of assholes just like Rambo Roddy. It was to no avail. She had to conclude that all men were simply dogs in perennial heat.

Briefcase Betty also had to conclude that her miserable pathetic life had to change. She had not been out on a date for two years. Nobody, except the love of her life, Jasmine, her pet Persian cat, had set foot in her Northwest Washington, D.C., apartment in over a year. Despite her recent cynical reflections on the male species, she knew that she wasn't a lesbian at heart. She desired a man, a one woman man. She wanted a man that would rap his strong arms around her and tell her that he loved her, her and only her. She wanted a man that she could trust and respect. But, above all else, she needed a man to share his mind and body with her for the rest of her life.

"Why you always carry around that briefcase, baby? You keep a dildo in there or what? You need a little Rambone to set your frigid ass straight," rudely remarked Rambo Roddy, chuckling to himself despite the cold stares of several officers milling around the cellblock area.

Briefcase Betty placed her ever present burgundy Samsonite briefcase on the nearest desk, picked up the receiver, and pushed in the hold button of the archaic looking black telephone. She decided to ignore Rambo Roddy's lewd remarks. Startled at the unexpected voice of Danny Money, Briefcase Betty gasped, glad for the first time in her adult life that she was out of Tampax as the start of her unexpected period had been the reason for their impromptu stop at the Second District Headquarters Station. The women's room had been her immediate goal. That could wait. Right now, the only thing that mattered was that, after all her advances, Danny Money had finally called her.

"If you're not doing anything after check off why don't you come down to Tiny's place and meet me later," asked Danny Money, knowing that Briefcase Betty was his last chance at salvation.

"Well, I don't know. It'll be awfully late for me to drive all the way over to Northeast. Besides, I've heard about Tiny's. But, I don't even know where it is," answered Briefcase Betty, her heart pounding wildly, excited to hear the man of her dreams doing the asking for a change.

"I'll give you directions. Don't worry about the time. I'll make sure Tiny leaves the backdoor unlocked. Even if it's after hours," countered Danny Money, desperate to persuade Briefcase Betty to give it up no matter what he had to do or say.

Danny Money, in his haste to get laid at any cost, forgot another cardinal rule. This rule was not about police department messages. It was about relationships. He expected sex. Briefcase Betty expected respect, patience, friendship, and then sex. Their schedules were on conflicting courses, ready to crash and burn in a humiliating explosion of emotional extremes. Danny was too shook up to consider the feelings of another woman already in love, Rhonda Bell. And, to make matters worse, Briefcase Betty didn't even know Ronnie was a part of Danny's life.

Still on the telephone, Briefcase Betty opened her trademark briefcase and removed her Franklin Planner. She recorded the directions to Tiny's bar in the well worn date book. She hung up the phone, snapped her briefcase shut, and walked to the women's room, ecstatic over the prayed for change in her eternally desolate life. In her mind she pictured a pristine house in the suburbs, a beautiful green yard, and her baby in the always present swing. Danny Money's mind was painting an entirely different picture.

Briefcase Betty handled her most pressing immediate female problem and burst out of the ladies room, elated at the glowing prospect of starting a new life. Reality, in the form of Rambo Roddy, almost struck her down.

"You gonna let him bend you over, honey?" sarcastically cracked Rambo Roddy as they both walked out the front door of the station house, heading for Scout 80. Briefcase Betty leered at Rambo Roddy, her lip quivering in rage. She knew she couldn't take much more of his belligerent mouth. He had turned what had once been an eager excitement to get up and go to work into a living hell. For the last two years her insides had churned in anger and frustration at the thought of having to sit next to this crude animal eight hours a day.

Hers had been the misfortune of patrolling an all white neighborhood, a neighborhood so politically powerful and racially pure that Scout 80 was one of the only patrol cars in the entire city operated by two assigned white partners. This odd circumstance resulted from a telephone call from a local resident Justice of the Supreme Court who decided that racial integration had gone too far when the black officer previously assigned to Scout 80 had locked up his drunken alcoholic wife for driving her silver 500 SL Mercedes convertible into the plate glass window of Duke Ziebert's Restaurant and Lounge.

So, as a result of one of racial equality's finer moments, Betty Barnes ended up having to sit next to Rambo Roddy, her black ex-partner transferred and re-assigned to a footbeat in the ghetto projects of Southeast, D.C. Right now, despite having the most envied scout car beat in the entire city, Briefcase Betty would rather be pounding the pavement with her ex-partner, an honest decent cop, than riding with Rambo Roddy, a crude brutal man who lacked both compassion and restraint. She opened the driver's side door of Scout 80 and removed the car keys wedged between the leather folds of her black Sam Brown belt. Rambo Roddy forcibly brushed her aside, grabbed the keys from her hand, and then dropped down into the driver's seat, determined to finish the shift behind the wheel whether she liked it or not.

Briefcase Betty, against her passive nature, wanted to hurt Rambo Roddy just as she'd watched him hurt others. The arrogant officer's savage brutal streak was beginning to assert itself far beyond the accepted norms of the D.C. Police Department's strict doctrine on the use of force. His routine confrontations with the citizens were becoming increasingly violent. Briefcase Betty knew that she couldn't stop him much longer. Soon, he was bound to explode in a fit of brutality, leaving behind a slew of battered victims in his turbulent wake.

Briefcase Betty sat in the passenger side of Scout 80 and forced herself to think of teddy bears, pretty pink dresses, and Barbie Dolls, unaware that in less than two hours she'd meet her Ken. But, his name wasn't Danny Money. She turned her head. Pretending to look out the window, she closed her eyes. Briefcase Betty Barnes allowed herself a brief second of self pity. Then, her head straight, she looked around at the fashionable landscape of her uptown police world. Elegant stately row houses lined the pristine streets. Embassies and mansions sat behind locked gates, obscured by endless rows of thick tall shrubs. Huge barren trees, illuminated by dimly flickering street lamps, cast their eerie dark shadows across this shimmering land of milk and honey. Funny, thought Briefcase Betty, there were hardly ever any people walking the cleanly swept sidewalks. It was almost like the realities of life didn't apply here, in this world of untold wealth and power.

Briefcase Betty watched as Rambo Roddy turned on the red lights and pulled over a black man driving a shiny silver Jaguar sedan.

"What did he do?" she asked.

"It's not what he did. It's what he is. We don't need any spooks rippin' off these people's cars," causally remarked Rambo Roddy as he slapped his nightstick against his open palm and stepped out of the scout car, readjusting the blinding spot light beam to shine through the driver's side rear window of the idling Jaguar.

Briefcase Betty was relieved to see that Rambo Roddy was handing back the black man's driver's license and registration. She had half expected him to go upside the unsuspecting man's head. Instead, Rambo Roddy was smiling as he casually strolled back to the scout car.

"Man. That was Deputy Chief Daniels. Head nigger in charge of I.A.D. Say's he's on his way home from downtown. A couple of 5D boys wasted some mother fucker and then beat up his old lady. Sounds like some outstanding police work to me," laughed Rambo Roddy, slamming Scout 80 into a screeching U-turn in the middle of P Street.

"What did you tell him you stopped him for?" asked Briefcase Betty, hoping that Rambo Roddy had done himself in, stopping an innocent black man, who happened to be one of the most powerful police department white shirts, for no apparent reason.

"I told him I recognized his car. And just wanted to make sure it was being operated by an authorized person. The stupid black ass mother fucker believed me, too," laughed Rambo Roddy, casually brushing his hand across Briefcase Betty's knee, as he pretended to be searching for his ticket book. Briefcase Betty wondered how envied this scout car beat would still be if those that coveted it had to sit next to Rambo Roddy.

That was to be the least of her worries. For soon, very soon, the grim reaper of death would tarnish forever the high luster of Scout 80's pristine beat. The streets would run red with blood. The people of means would cringe in fear, hiding behind locked doors or fleeing the city altogether, as they sought refuge in the Boca Raton's and Monte Carlo's of their opulent jet set fantasy world. For another was soon to bring his fantasy into their urban utopia.

Ray Carson Carver, one kill away from his self imposed limit on coons, was eagerly anticipating the opening of a new hunting season. This time he'd be prowling the terrified city for albinos. It wouldn't take him long to figure out that the fattest ones grazed the rich pastures of haughty Georgetown.

CHAPTER 8

"MAN. YOU AUGHTA GO a little easy on that stuff Danny. You're gonna get plastered if you don't ease off a little," remarked Tiny, watching Money drain his third double header of Jack Daniels. The Bud Man glanced over at his disturbed partner, wondering why in the hell Money was so messed up. He had done the actual killing. And frankly, it wasn't really bothering him all that much. Money had only whacked the broad a few times. So what, figured the Bud Man as he lifted up the heavy frosted mug filled with the king of beers.

Emancipation Proclamation Jones sat next to the Bud Man on the torn red vinyl and chrome bar stool and wondered what he had done to deserve such a run of bad luck. First, the simple drunk mother fucker in the van had put his ass in the sling. And now this. Damn, he had told his old lady to stay on the pill. No, she said, it was giving her headaches. She'd use the Goddamned sponge or whatever it was. He sure as hell wasn't going to wear no friggin' raincoat. Now, he had the headache. He'd be in diaper city real soon. Mama was three months pregnant and crying because he didn't wanna talk about gettin' married. Well, piss on it. He'd marry her. He cared about her more than any of the others. And, what the hell, he could still fool around. Marriage sure as shit wasn't stoppin' too many of these other D.C. police cockhounds from cheatin' on their old ladies. The whole department was one friggin' adulterous orgy anyway. So, party on, figured E.P., who intended to do just that.

Spic N' Span Spiegel sat next to Emancipation Proclamation Jones, his grimy fingers swirling the ice in his coke. He stared down at the bubbling drink, wondering why he was always such a screw up. If only he could take charge and change his pathetic life. If only he could be like Money, the Bud Man, and E.P. Then he could stand at his father's grave, his head held high, never again disgracing the family's proud name. He needed someone to help him regain his dignity. If his self image didn't improve pretty soon he'd probably end up standing in the food line at the rescue mission, a poor homeless wretch sleeping on the grates, living another day in D.C. paradise.

The backdoor of Tiny's slowly creaked open. Spic N' Span Spiegel glanced up at the filmy cracked mirror hanging crooked behind the worn dark wood bar and got his first glimpse of that someone he needed. At first, all he noticed were the perfectly creased dark blue pants and the crisp looking pale blue shirt covered by an open three quarter length rust colored suede jacket. Then, he saw the glorious glowing face framed by the softest looking brown hair that he had ever seen. As the Goddess of all babes stepped into the dim hazy bar, Spic N' Span Spiegel sat mesmerized, still staring at the wondrous reflection of beauty in the dirty streaked mirror, unable to suppress a budding grin of exuberance. He turned on the stool, gazing at a set of tender compassionate grey eyes that melted his heart. Spic N' Span Spiegel was instantly stabbed with the pitchfork of love, totally smitten by this petite princess. Beauty, in this case, being most definitely in the eye of the beholder.

The only man in the whole bar that was staring into the eyes of Briefcase Betty Barnes was Spic N' Span Spiegel. The rest of the men, including Tiny, were lecherously eyeballing the biggest set of bodacious bouncing ta-tas that they had ever seen on an officer of the law, their jaws dropping to the floor. Briefcase Betty, her burgundy Samsonite in her right hand, walked slowly toward the off duty officers. She was definitely feeling like a fish out of water.

Danny Money moved quickly. "Hi, Betty. Nice to see you again. How's everything in the land of the 2D Squirrel chasers? Write any pedestrian violations, lately?" kidded the anxious Money.

"Hi, Danny. It's nice to see you again, too. I'm sorry I'm so late. But, you know how us women are. It took me a while to put on my beauty treatments. And even that doesn't help much," greeted Briefcase Betty, a pleasant smile breaking out across her thin lips.

"Sit down. What can I get for you?" asked Danny, motioning for her to sit down while removing the suede coat from her shoulders and introducing her to his fellow officers.

"A rum and coke would be nice. But, if you don't mind, I'd like to buy you and your friends a drink first," answered Briefcase Betty, noticing that Danny Money was looking a little drunk, despite his gracious attempts at chivalry.

Tiny had finally got past the killer set of knockers, deciding that this young lady just might be a pretty decent chick. The Bud

Man ordered another brewski. And, when Briefcase Betty commented that Bud, the king of beers, was the only beer that she drank, the Bud Man knew that he was going to like this little babe with the mega melons.

Emancipation Proclamation Jones exuberantly expressed his desire for another gin and tonic, free liquor always being high on his list of priorities. Right now, a piece of strange was not. With his recent string of troubles he'd be paying plenty, real soon. Briefcase Betty stepped off the stool and walked down to ask Spic N' Span Spiegel what he'd like to drink, her bobbing breasts slowly riding up and down in waves of undulating flesh that had the riveted attention of everyone. Everyone that is, except Spic N' Span Spiegel.

Spic N' Span Spiegel turned, his acne scarred face plastered with a friendly open grin. He stared into Briefcase Betty's dull grey eyes with a genuine longing that caused her pale face to break out into a brilliant crimson blush. There was something real about this sloppy looking frail man that touched a chord deep within her heart. Few men, if any, had ever looked at her like that, not even glancing at her protruding breasts. Briefcase Betty knew instantly that she had found her knight in shining armor, her house in the suburbs, her green grassy yard, her baby in the swing. Spic N' Span Spiegel knew only that, if eyes could speak, Briefcase Betty was writing him a sultry Harlequin Romance novel and he was turning the pages as fast as he could read them.

"Hey, Betty. How about a little game of pool?" asked Danny Money, inserting himself in between Briefcase Betty and Spic N' Span Spiegel. Wasting time was not on his mind. A couple of games of pool laced with a few drinks oughta get Betty's juices flowin'. She was probably just as hot to jump his bones as he was to jump hers, figured Money, anxious to get on with it. He had to know if he was still a man. Or had he degenerated into a limp dicked wimpy faggot? Reaching for a pool cue, he raised the shot glass to his lips and drained the burning whiskey.

Spic N' Span Spiegel turned back around on his stool and sipped his coke. He wondered how he had managed to hesitate and let the moment pass. Why couldn't he be more aggressive like Danny and E.P.? Weren't they always scoring with the chicks while he ended up alone in bed, reading another comic book and fantasizing about what it must be like to live life on the edge. Spic N' Span Spiegel failed to realize that the cartoon characters of the world were figments of writers' imaginations while he was flesh and blood, prone to all the imperfections of human nature. But, for one brief millisecond in the eons of time, Spic N' Span Spiegel was soon to become Superman, the man of steel, rising to the same giddy heights of awe inspiring heroism. The clock ticked relentlessly on, about to strike the dawning of the resurrection of his lost soul.

Briefcase Betty leaned over the pool table. Fondling himself in a desperate attempt to breathe life into his deflated member, Danny Money pressed his limp organ into the crease of Briefcase Betty's tight buttocks. Drunk, he reached underneath her bent frame and roughly pinched the nipples of her protruding breasts, all the while grinding his genitals against her resisting body. Shocked, Briefcase Betty turned around to face the offensive officer.

She didn't blame Danny. It was the liquor that was controlling his actions. Briefcase Betty understood the liquor. It was the only legal drug that these troubled ghetto gladiators could use to unloose the demons that lay festering in their disturbed minds. No matter how Danny acted she would forgive him. She wouldn't allow him to defile her or himself. Obviously, something was bothering him, something that he couldn't handle alone.

It was late. Rhonda Bell was tired. She was tired of swimming in the swirling waters of the cesspool of life. Mac was finishing up the paperwork on Ophelia and the Snowman. The butcher from Orleans Place was probably out disemboweling another poor unsuspecting victim, figured the disconsolate officer as she walked to her Ford Escort, parked across the street from police headquarters. She sat down, behind the wheel, and decided that tonight she wasn't going to sleep alone.

Darnell was staying with her mother. Right now nothing was more important to her than waking up in the morning with Danny's warm body backed against her, her long slender arms wrapped comfortably around his hard lean frame. She wanted to playfully snuggle, to touch and caress him, to breath in his comforting scent, to hold him as tightly as if she was holding on to life itself. For a few brief hours he could make her forget all about life's eternal struggle.

Being born beautiful was a blessing. Being born black, beautiful, and a woman could, in this hate filled world of prejudice, be considered a curse. The fact that she was all these, plus a cop, made Rhonda Bell's life a hard life, a life filled with inner turmoil and confusion, a life that she fully intended to use to make a difference in her little D.C. world filled with so much senseless violence and hate.

Vacations in exotic far away places were a luxury she couldn't afford. So, she settled instead for a few hours of tenderness and love, a few hours of peace with Danny. Tonight, she needed one of her little vacations in paradise. Tonight, more than any other night in a long time, she needed Danny to be there for her. She turned over the ignition and started the engine. Rhonda Bell had a strange inkling of where Danny might be. Dropping in on him, unexpectedly, was so unlike her. But, maybe a little variety and spice was good for a relationship. Anyway, that was a woman's prerogative, wasn't it?

Spic N' Span Spiegel was upset. His gritty hands trembled as they shook the glass of coke he clasped tightly against the top of the bar, its melting ice rattling against the sides. He didn't know what to do. He looked up to Danny Money, almost worshipped the ground he walked on. Now, the drunken officer was bothering Betty, touching her body against her wishes. It wasn't right. He couldn't let Danny treat her like that.

Spic N' Span Spiegel thought back to the days when his father's gravelly booming voice had delivered the message. It had been loud and clear. Always treat women with respect. They are a precious gift from God, a gift to be treasured and revered. Never, under any circumstances, lay your hands on a woman, unless it is the woman that you truly love. Spic N' Span Spiegel knew Danny Money didn't love Briefcase Betty. Therefore, he had no right to touch her. He had to follow his father's teachings. He had to try, in his own pathetic way, to carry on the family's proud name. He had to stop Danny Money, now, before things got out of hand and he hurt Betty.

"Stop it!" screamed Spic N' Span Spiegel at the top of his lungs, shocking himself with the extent of his rage. The Bud Man and Tiny, talking at the far end of the bar, turned their heads towards the shouting officer. Emancipation Proclamation Jones, finishing a marathon beer and liquor piss in the urinal, hurriedly shoved his emptied penis back into his pants, crashing into the flimsy bathroom door as he rushed out of the men's room. He had been in enough trouble to know when it was knocking at the door.

Surprised at the unexpected outburst, Danny Money dropped his groping hands from Briefcase Betty's breasts and turned around to face Spic N' Span Spiegel who was off his stool, slowly advancing towards the struggling duo.

"Leave her alone. It isn't right. You shouldn't treat a lady like that. You don't have any right. You don't love her," shouted Spic N' Span Spiegel as he closed in on the startled pair.

"Fuck off. Who asked for your advice?" yelled the drunken Money, laughing at the approaching officer.

"It's O.K. I can handle it. He doesn't mean it," pleaded Briefcase Betty, hoping to avoid a physical confrontation between the two officers.

"No. It isn't O.K. He's wrong. He's doing you wrong. Nobody has a right to violate your body. It's a gift. A gift from God that only you can allow to be opened by someone you choose. Not by someone just because he chooses you," loudly stated Spic N' Span Spiegel, ready, for the first time in his life, to defend his own principles, no matter what it cost him.

Briefcase Betty Barnes was touched. Never before, in her quiet introverted life, had anybody stood up for her like this, disregarding their own safety to come to her aid. Her heart fluttered at the thought. Briefcase Betty decided, no matter what the outcome of this unpleasant confrontation, it had been worth it to come here tonight. Otherwise, she would have never met Spic N' Span Spiegel.

Emancipation Proclamation Jones quickly inserted himself in between the two arguing officers. Damn, he didn't think Spiegel had had it in him. Anyway, it didn't matter. Money was both drunk and wrong. The Bud Man rushed over to help quell the rising emotions. Tiny, his huge lumbering frame shuffling across the wet sticky floor, had never seen Money like this. Something sure must be troubling the belligerent officer, figured Tiny, politely grabbing Briefcase Betty's arm and carefully pulling her shaking body out of harm's way.

The Bud Man, casting a quick glance at Emancipation Proclamation Jones' tense poised form, began to laugh. He couldn't help himself. Pointing at the coiled officer, the Bud Man doubled over in spasms of gut wrenching laughter. Suddenly, Tiny, seeing the source of the merriment, joined in, tears immediately welling up in his moist reddish eyes. The laughter was contagious. Emancipation Proclamation Jones began to chuckle, wondering what in the hell was so funny. Even Briefcase Betty, her fear slowly subsiding, giggled as she caught a glimpse of the hilarious spectacle.

Finally, Emancipation Proclamation Jones couldn't stand it any longer. "What's so mother fuckin' funny?" he asked as he dropped his fists and relaxed his boxer's stance.

The Bud Man replied, "You. You simple ass nigger. You're fuckin' bologna, man. It's hanging out of your pants. Damn, the son of bitchin thing is almost touchin' the ground. And your black ass ain't got no drawers on."

Emancipation Proclamation Jones, looking down at his unrestrained swinging meat, laughed, "Shit. This towering inferno don't want nothin' standin' in its way when it gets a chance at knockin' boots with some horny snatch." Now that he thought about it, he knew exactly where his drawers were. They were stuffed inside the toilet tank at randy Rhonda's apartment. The Fifth District daywork station clerk's old man had arrived home unexpectedly, causing Emancipation's premature exit out the bathroom window. "Better a premature exit than a premature ejaculation," snickered the officer to himself, as he shoved his limp penis back in his pants, making sure not to pinch the delicate skin as he cautiously zippered his fly.

"Looked more like withering heights to me," chuckled the Bud Man, slapping hands with Tiny.

Tiny, proud of his recently acquired musical knowledge, tried to perform his new and improved version of a Michael Jackson moonwalk while pointing at his groin and shouting, "Hey, E.P.. I got me some Ice Cream on the juke box, man. He's one rappin' dude."

"Bitchin, brother. But, I hope you be talkin' bout Ice Cube. If you is. We be gettin' down," yelled Emancipation Proclamation Jones, sliding across the floor to join Tiny in a impromptu duet of the butt, both men hilariously bouncing their contrasting buns off one another's behind.

"Ice Cream. Ice Cube. What's the difference," exclaimed Tiny. "I just wish it would all melt. And them gangsta wimps and the shit they sing could all run down the drain."

Realizing what an asshole he had just been, Danny apologized to Briefcase Betty and Spic N' Span Spiegel. He was one apology too short.

Rhonda Bell, standing in the unlocked rear doorway, had watched the whole revolting scene, her simple dreams of a happy tranquil life evaporating in a thick fog of uncertainty. Her stomach felt the tight grip of nauseous anxiety. She had been ready to take that last step, to come out of the closet and admit publicly that she was sleeping with a white man, a man she loved. Now she felt betrayed, embarrassed at her naive notion of trust and faithfulness. She cared so much that it ripped her heart to shreds. Her lips quivered. Her knees wobbled. Suddenly, she felt drained of all emotion. She couldn't even cry.

Danny Money caught a glimpse of the tall shapely silhouette in the doorway. Sobriety was like drunkenness. It was easy to get to either state when you wanted to. Right now, this instant, Danny Money knew he had better get sober. If he didn't deal with Ronnie now it would all be over. And, he was sure of one thing. He didn't know where this relationship was headed. But, he knew he didn't want it to end, not like this.

Ronnie turned and bolted out of the barroom door. She was suffocating, the once familiar surroundings clutching at her like a smoldering blanket of foul air. Danny ran after her, ending all doubt as to the depth of their involvement.

"It's about time Danny and Ronnie got this thing out in the open. It'll be a monkey off their backs. Nobody can deal with life. Hiding from their feelings. You've got to go for it," commented Tiny, stepping back behind the bar, glad that this had happened. He had been around a lot of hard years. He remembered times when the white boys would lynch one of the brothers for tappin' a white girl. They'd sneak off, though, to dip their sticks into one of the sisters, never admitting it to anyone, even themselves. This was all so much bullshit, thought Tiny. Everyone was just a person, not a black person or a white person, just a person.

The Bud Man, shaking his head in agreement, ordered another Bud. Now, he'd see what kind of a man Danny Money really was. If he loved the babe then he'd have to be a man and say so. Part of love was showing off your partner. Proud that he or she was what they were. Proud that they had decided to share life's pleasures and pains with you, for better or for worse. Proud to be your bud. The Bud Man was glad that he had his own faithful Bud Lady and three little brewski's, two Spuds and one Spudzette, at home to put all this bullshit in proper prospective. No matter how much he sometimes longed to bed another woman, lust could never take the place of his wife and three children. He risked his life in this shithole, everyday, just hoping they would never have to. All he wanted was for them to do better than their old man.

Emancipation Proclamation Jones glanced at Spic N' Span Spiegel and Briefcase Betty. They were talking and laughing like two schoolyard chums. Maybe, with any luck, figured Emancipation, Spic N' Span Spiegel would finally get his dick wet. He swore the rank son of a bitch was still a virgin. Emancipation Proclamation Jones picked up a deck of cards from the bar. He shuffled the well worn deck and spread the cards across the greasy bar. He picked one out, trying to guess which one. Queen of hearts, guessed Emancipation Proclamation Jones, turning over the ripped and torn card. His hand began to shake. A cold terrifying chill stabbed his heart. Mesmerized in fear, he stared at the Ace of spades, the death card.

"Hey, look. I'm sorry. O.K.? What the hell do you want me to say? Jesus. We wasted a mother fucker tonight. And then I laid a hurtin' on his old lady just because she was upset. Looking at her old man. Laying there. His chest a bloody mess of shit. Damn. You ever have a dude squeeze one off. Trying to add you to the department's honor roll of dead ass heroes? Now, I wonder if I'm even a Goddamned man. It feels dead. You understand? Dead. You want to sleep with a man that can't even get it up?" stated Danny Money, holding on to Ronnie's flailing arm as she struggled to get into her car.

"You think you're the only one whose ever had it rough? You don't know shit. You ever been raped? You ever had dirty old men fondle your privates? You ever watched your mother go to bed with two, three men a night? Trying to put food on the table because she was too proud to go on welfare. You ever been refused food in a restaurant because of the color of your skin? You ever been beaten? Helpless to do anything about it. The cops tellin' you it's your problem. Not theirs. What the hell do you know about suffering? Raised in some lily white hick town," shouted Ronnie, defiantly pulling her arm away from Danny Money's grasp.

"Ronnie. Alright. I'm sorry. I tried to call you. I left a message with Lieutenant Bowser. It was you I wanted to see. I was desperate. Crazy. Jesus. I panicked. It's never happened before. This feeling like it's dead. At least it's out in the open now. They all know about us. We have to deal with it. I'm glad. It's the way a relationship should be. What are we hiding, anyway? We're both single and I hope we still care about each other," countered Money, reaching out to take Ronnie's hand in his.

"I'm not in love with your cock. I'm in love with you. You hurt me. Real bad. All you can talk about is the state of what's between your legs. There's more to love than sex. I think you're in lust. Not love. All we ever do is screw. What are you? Ashamed of us? How about takin' Darnell and me somewhere for the weekend? How about your place? How about taking us to your hometown? How about introducing us to your family? What's wrong with that? I'm good enough for you to screw. But, we're not good enough to meet your parents. Is that it? You don't want them to know you sleep with a black woman?" angrily challenged Ronnie, pushing Danny away.

"You're right about one thing. There's more to love than sex. So, I used love to get sex. And you used sex to get love. So what? What's the fucking difference who used what to get what? The fact is that for whatever reason I've fallen in love with you. And, I'm not ashamed of you or Darnell. We're going. We're all going to my hometown. You'all can meet my family. But, right now, I want you to go home with me. I don't want us apart after all this. OK? Will you spend the night at my place? With me?," begged Danny, hoping it all wouldn't end in the back of a bar in the ghetto.

"Alright. But, if you welsh on your promise, believe me. I'm history," answered Ronnie, feeling that she had won this round, but wondering if the fight was truly over.

As Danny Money lay naked in front of the crackling fireplace waiting for Ronnie to finish her bath, he definitely decided that she was worth it. He'd fight whatever battles he had to to keep her. Love and beauty were two things that had to be color blind. They transcended the barriers of race, religion, or creed. He decided he better grow up. It was time for him to take a stand.

Rhonda Bell stepped out of the bathroom into the subtle light of the flickering fireplace. Instantly, Danny Money knew that he had made the right decision. Ronnie's golden brown skin glowed in the dancing firelight. Her tall lean model like body moved with majestic grace as she glided across the short distance, pausing briefly to lower the living room window shades. Her straight jet black hair, cut in a chin length bob, bounced saucily, rising and falling in rhythm with her firm ripe breasts, capped with stiffening chocolate brown nipples.

Straddling Danny's prone form, she reached down and grasped his limp manhood.

"Use it or lose it, baby. Tonight, I'm gonna take you ballistic," whispered Ronnie as she lowered her tight moist vagina on to Danny's slowly stiffening shaft, encompassing him in a steamy grip of mind-blowing pleasure.

"I'm all yours, Doctor Delight," replied a relieved Money as he felt the throbbing intensity of his rock hard rod slide into the slippery folds of Ronnie's clasping orifice. He pulled her upper body down, rubbing her bouncing breasts against his muscular chest. He hugged her desperately, breathing in the sweet scent of perfumed soap. Danny Money was about to go supersonic. Rhonda Bell was about to get her wish, waking up snuggled next to the man she loved.

Through all this, Latisha Davis still hung by her ankles, gutless, like a piece of butchered beef, her stiffening body dangling silently in the oily, foul smelling garage. Through all this, Ray Carson Carver sped northward, the blaring melody of Bon Jovi's Blaze of Glory rocking the speeding truck, gusts of cold wind swirling through the open driver's side window. He was almost home, home to the comforting hills of America's heart, the rural towns that had spawned this great land of opportunity. His was the cold hard land that had been forged in coal and steel, the land that was in his bones.

The old sow was still sleeping, thought Ray Carver, leering down at his plump matronly wife. He downed another biting swallow of the harsh burning whiskey and crept slowly down the hall, towards his daughter's bedroom. Quietly, he pushed open the flimsy creaking door, trying to make out her sleeping form in the pitch black room. He reached down and massaged his aching genitals, as he pictured her naked young body lying outstretched, at his mercy, begging him to give her what she'd always wanted.

He reclosed the door, steadying his wobbly knees as a bolt of ravaging lust raked his body. A couple of hours of sleep and he'd be as good as new. The Oaktree Tavern opened at ten and that was less than six hours away. Ray Carver threw his musty smelling clothes on the bedroom floor and crawled into bed, next to his peacefully snoring wife. He fell quickly asleep, his warped mind conjuring up lurid visions of hounds chasing a desperately fleeing fox. The hounds were steadily overtaking the terrified panting fox. Now they were all around him, grabbing hunks of his ripping flesh with their lunging teeth. Finally they descended upon him, chewing his insides with their frenzied snapping fangs. Ray Carver slept with a grim smile plastered across his stubbly bearded face.

"Hey, Ray. How ya' doing this morning? You didn't get any on you last night, did you?" greeted Hank Edwards, the owner of the Oaktree Tavern.

"Shit. The old hog was still sleepin' when I got in. The fat fuckin' bitch," coldly stated Ray Carver, bellying up to the oak bar.

"You want the usual? A shooter and a splash?" questioned Hank Edwards, pouring a double shot of Wild Turkey and a draught beer before Ray Carver even answered.

"Bet you was doin' some skinnin' last night. Probably bangin' ol' Tootsie Hale. Her old man still in jail?" asked Hank Edwards, pushing the drinks across the slate topped bar.

"I was doin some skinnin', alright," laughed Ray Carver, managing a cold lifeless grin, his eyes twinkling with glee.

Hank Edwards turned pale, white as a ghost. He wasn't quite sure what Ray Carver had meant. But, whatever it was, he knew he never really wanted to find out.

"You know. The old lady still packs my bucket. Every morning I get her lard ass out of bed to make my breakfast and pack my lunch. Just like the old days when I was in the mines. Bent over. Cold icy water up to my aching knees. Breathin' coal dust. And listening to the timbers shorin' up the tunnel. Creakin' like they was gonna snap like little toothpicks. Thirty years of my life, spent at hard labor, in those fuckin' mines. Now, all I got to show for it is Black Lung. And a Goddamned cheap ass check from the collieries every month," lectured Ray Carver, his mind drifting back to the old days, days when they still swung picks and shoveled coal the old way, like real men.

Ray Carver pushed his empty shot glass forward and tapped the bar with its heavy glass bottom, signaling his need for another double. Hank Edwards filled the shot glass to the top of the rim, watching as Ray Carver bent over and hacked a deep hoarse cough that sounded like his insides were about to come bubbling out of his throat. Instead, he hacked again, turning and spitting a huge glob of bloody phlegm on to the stained wooden floor. His lungs were rotting away like dead flesh in moist heat, the cancerous Black Lung devouring his innards.

Ray Carver's somber face turned a brilliant crimson as he struggled to catch his breath. Maybe one or two years at the most, figured Hank Edwards. He had stood behind the bar and watched too many slowly die like Ray Carver, wasting away to nothing, their wheezing gasps prophesying their inevitable agonizing death. Black Lung, to the miners, was little different than

AIDS, to the big city faggots and dopers, figured Hank Edwards. The only difference being, with Black Lung, at least you could stand tall and die like a man. Not hide in some back room ashamed of your cornholed ass, thought the grinning bartender as he pulled another draft to help Ray Carver wash down the chalky black dust.

Hank Edwards couldn't help but wonder about Ray Carver. There was something evil hidden in his hollow lifeless eyes. They reminded him of those cold mirrored sunglasses, only reflecting the outside world, never letting anyone look inside your soul. He had a feeling the soul of Ray Carver was black, filled with dancing demons whose courtship meant death. Hank Edwards knew Ray Carver was going to die soon. His rank cancerous breath smelled like rotting meat. He had the unmistakable feeling that Ray Carver wasn't going to die quietly. He'd never tell anyone how he felt. But, he was almost certain that the retired coal miner was going to bury a whole lot of other people in the collapsing tunnel of his own miserable life before the roof caved in on him.

CHAPTER 9

DANNY MONEY kept looking at the Fifth District roll call room clock, while the Bud Man watched the door to the sergeant's offices. Three twenty nine and Emancipation Proclamation Jones was still a no show. Spic N' Span Spiegel was squirming in his seat, wondering where the hell his partner was. Money glanced over at Spiegel. He noticed something peculiar about the frail officer, but was unable to put his finger on the exact nature of what he saw. The clock hit three thirty and Emancipation Proclamation Jones burst through the swinging door just as 10-33 Sam nervously twitched his way from the sergeant's entrance at the other side of the room.

10-33 Sam grimaced. One more minute and he could have laid a police department form 750 dereliction notice on the cockhound's ass. The corner of his lip curled up in frustration as he thought about his two timin' wife. He could only hope that Jones hadn't been out in Virginia, knockin off a quickie with his horny old lady. Somebody was sure givin' her the sausage. That was a fact, Jack.

"Hey, E.P.. That piece of shit 'Vette of yours break down?" shouted the Bud Man, trying for the last six months to get Jones riled up enough to race him and his IROC Z-28 down on V Street.

"Sheet, man. That bad ass motherfucker is a chariot of fire. It smokes both inside and out. If you know what I mean? It'll sure leave that I Flop of yours in the dust. That lean mean pussy grabbin' machine of mine can both get and kick some ass. Me and the ride can both get down and book," loudly answered Emancipation Proclamation Jones, looking around the roll call room for support.

"Lick ass. Is that what I heard? You lick ass," teased the Bud Man.

"Your old lady probably took the keys from your lyin' butt," stated Money. "She's probably out trying to find herself a real man."

"I saw E.P. gettin' off the Metrobus. Right in front of the

station house. Just a second ago," said the grinning desk sergeant as he walked in and handed the updated stolen auto sheets to 10-33 Sam and then motioned for the Bud Man to follow him back upstairs.

"Can you imagine the brother takin' a little public transportation. Ridin' the Metrobus. Listenin' to all those sisters crackin' their gum in the back seat," chuckled the Bud Man, his smug black face drawing up into an ear to ear grin as he left the roll call room.

"Lot of public. Not much motha' fuckin' transportation," answered Emancipation Proclamation Jones, hoping his pregnant old lady didn't wreck his ride or park next to some asshole who'd throw open his door and bang the side of his car. Jesus, he hated the thought of a door ding. That was worse than being bitten by a Pit Bull with Aids.

10-33 Sam began reading the roll call notification sheet, the entire room full of officers rising simultaneously to their feet and giving a standing ovation at the announcement of the passing of retired officer James Barrett who had sucked the city treasury for forty three years of blissful retirement in the hills of West Virginia. This was cause for celebration. Most of the retirees usually died within a couple of years, some even ending theirs voluntarily with a bullet to the head, unable to cope with the mundane routine of civilian life.

Danny Money pulled Scout 150 out of 5D and headed towards the McDonald's at New York and Florida Avenue. Ronnie had licked, sucked, stroked, and screwed him senseless, never asking for anything in return. He had made some toast and coffee for them in the morning. But, he was still starving. She had been anxious to pick up Darnell and get down to homicide squad. All Money could remember was that she had wanted to check the midnight shift's reports, certain that the murderer from Orleans Place had struck again. He hadn't questioned her female police intuition, figuring that he was skating on thin ice already, after last night's near total debacle. Besides, she was a special person. She did deserve better than she had been getting from him. Danny Money decided to start treating her like the woman he loved, not the black woman he screwed.

Money looked over at the empty seat that was usually occupied by the Bud Man. He had been routinely assigned to station duty pending the official justification of his shooting by I.A.D., a process that, in this case, should be a simple formality and a three day vacation from the rigors of the street. Looking back to his left, he watched as a van full of drunken looking males pulled up next to 150 and passed around a bottle of vodka, the driver taking the longest gulp of all.

"Piss on 'em. They ain't doin nothin we don't do," mumbled Money out loud, worried more about his rumbling stomach and the possibility of ending up like Emancipation Proclamation Jones and Spic N' Span Spiegel who were now driving a borrowed marked car, one preventable accident away from humping a foot beat. 10-33 Sam had viciously exacted his jealous revenge on a bewildered Emancipation Proclamation Jones and an unfortunate Spic N' Span Spiegel. Right now, vans weren't on their ten best list. Especially, vans being driven by drunk drivers. Those, they both swore to avoid like the plague.

Against his better judgment, Danny decided to stop the slowly moving van. Nobody was stupid enough to pull up next to a marked police car, sucking on a long necked bottle of Vodka. Money knew, in this unique city, there were only two rational explanations for such arrogant behavior. The first, a van full of drunken D.C. police officers, was out of the question. None of the occupants had a mustache. Cops without lip hair were like the Spotted Owl, an almost extinct species. Even before the driver's side window was fully cranked down, Money realized the second possibility was indeed a reality. Greeted by the rank odor of alcohol tainted breath followed by a verbal barrage of Russian and the inevitable diplomatic immunity card, he shook his head and threw up his hands. Why waste your time?

These embassy assholes with their fucking diplomatic immunity cards were all over the city, breaking every law that they could break, every hour of the night or day. At least, in the ghetto, you didn't run into these jack-offs very often. They were a major headache to the Second District squirrel chasers. That was where just about every nation on earth had their pompous embassy houses. Almost every race and nationality grazed the fertile grounds of Georgetown and upper Northwest, D.C., a fact that was not to escape the attention of one Ray Carson Carver.

It was a slow night, radio chatter at an unusually low level. The glowing ball of the rotund moon hung in the bleak cloudy grey sky, peeking in and out of swiftly moving dark thunderclouds. Flurries of light falling snow swirled in the gusty breeze. The city was as quiet as it ever gets, the echo of a distant siren wailing its ominous solitary warning. Danny Money turned scout 150 on to Orleans Place, hoping to get a glimpse of Frosty the Snowman's car. If he was to have a life with Ronnie he'd have to deal with the Snowman man to man, forget the badge.

He swung the scout car into the glass strewn alley, the moonlight casting a surreal glow to the dark gloomy passage. The pieces of broken glass glittered like sparkling diamonds paving the road to Camelot. Instead, this cruel hoax, this false image, paved another road, the burning road to hell. Ahead lay the hell that had already welcomed Jerome Anthony Marshall and Latisha Davis to its abysmal bowels, swallowing their empty hollow bodies in a long scalding gulp. Behind, lay the tracks of others, following the same path to this very spot, the gates to the fire that is never quenched.

Danny Money passed the thick barren oak tree, moonshadows dancing across the fluttering branches. The tree where Ray Carver had dispensed his evil magic loomed bigger than life, ominously casting an unearthly specter across the flickering landscape. The witching hour was about to chime. Strangely, Danny Money recalled what had been different about Spic N' Span Spiegel. His hair had been washed. His shirt and pants had been pressed and clean. Somehow, his pockmarked face had looked boyishly handsome.

Danny Money momentarily forgot where he was. Thoughts of love and beauty didn't last long in this breeding ground of ugliness, violence, and hate. He unconsciously stopped the car, its red brakelights reflecting into the dark shadows. He saw the partially open garage door. Not at all strange in this area, thought the cautious officer, shining the brilliant beam of the scout car's spotlight against the rotting wooden door. He pushed open the car door and walked across the alley, glass crunching under the soles of his black paratrooper boots. Withdrawing his nine millimeter, he slowly pried open the creaky garage door. Danny Money gasped. He was staring at a pair of scraped knees covered with dried blood. Glancing upward, he saw the women's ankles tied with rope. He looked downward, already bracing himself for the gruesome scene, the bone chilling spectacle.

Her stomach was slit open from her pubic area to her throat. Chunks of internal organs lay in her body cavity. Her intestines hung to the oily dirt floor like strands of stringy melted mozzarella cheese. The woman's lacy white top, streaked with blood, lay in the sloppy mess. Her skirt, looking like a tablecloth at a cannibal's feast, lay covered with human organs, almost as if spread out for display. A frigid blast of wind whipped through the foul smelling garage, the gust swaying the stiff suspended body in the shifting breeze. Danny Money panicked, raising his gun and pointing it at the disemboweled body. He turned his head away from the sickening scene and breathed deeply, trying to calm his pounding heart. He had to get a hold of himself.

He forced himself to look back at the dangling woman. Her bruised face had been beautiful. What was left of her lean voluptuous body left no doubt that this had once been an attractive woman. He couldn't shake the feeling. In his mind, the woman's face became a fuzzy indistinct outline. Then the vision cleared. He staggered backwards, tripping and falling to the cold earthen floor. In a panic, he bolted out of the musty smelling garage. He crashed into the front of Scout 150, gasping for air. His body was suddenly numb, the sickening sensation of death chilling his bones. He bent over the hood of the idling scout car, trying to get warm. It had been as plain as day. There, before his very own eyes, had hung the image of Rhonda Renee Bell, slaughtered and gutted just like the poor woman hanging in that tomb like garage.

Danny Money, his voice cracking, radioed for Homicide Squad. Specifically Cruiser 311 if they were on the air. He was beginning to feel insignificant. All his life he had valued things, material things. His townhouse was filled with things. Three televisions, a big screen and two smaller ones, a wall full of Nakamichi, Tandberg, Luxman, Yamaha, and Bose stereo equipment, designer label clothes, and his BMW convertible, these were his things. Everything in his house was in perfect order. Everything, that is, except his life.

More than ever before, Danny Money was coming to realize that things weren't what life was all about. As he sat there, in Scout 150, he began to understand what life really was. It was something Ronnie had been trying to tell him all along, in her unassuming way. It was people and all other living creatures that made life so vital. You lived for people, not for things. She had never had anything but people. He had never had anything but things. Right now, he'd give up everything he had to erase her face from the mental image of death that had popped into his mind. He was done chasing things. If it took wiping the slate clean and starting all over from scratch, then that's what he'd do to have her, decided Danny Money, watching a huge rat scurry into the garage with the nauseating realization of what, or rather who it intended to have for dinner.

Ronnie, her usually radiant chiseled face wearing a temporary mask of gloom, stepped out of Cruiser 311, the kneelength blue skirt of her double breasted Evan-Picone business suit accentuating her long shapely legs. Mac rolled out from behind the wheel and followed her across the alley, his squinting eyes scouring the surrounding area. They entered the cordoned off garage unprepared for the ghostly vision of slaughter that suddenly confronted them head on. Mac, his blue navy sportscoat bursting at the seams from the added pressure of a grey wool sweater, took out his notebook and wrote simply, Number Two Victim.

He continued to record his notes on the condition of the body and the surrounding scene. Ronnie, bursts of her frosty breath dissolving in the frigid air, relayed her observations to her note taking partner. Investigating a homicide was like brushing your teeth. To get the best results you had to follow the same routine everyday. Nothing too glamorous about walking around a stiff body realizing that this is how you'll end up someday, figured Mac, noticing a familiar looking brown stain on the dirt floor over by where the rope was tied off. As he walked closer he could see that it was fresher than the small puddles of dried oil that covered the grimy floor.

Bending over with a loud grunt, Mac reached down and touched the coarse gritty substance. He rubbed it between his thumb and forefinger, almost certain of what it was. He raised it to his nostrils and inhaled the distinctive odor. It was just as he figured.

"You wanna step outside for a minute and get some fresh air?" asked Mac, winking at Ronnie in an effort to convey the urgency of his message. His heart was palpitating. He was sure that they had their first break. And, sharing information with all the curious on lookers was not good police procedure. The last thing they needed was for the press to panic the already shaky city into a frenzy of sheer terror, creating a circus side show out of the hunt for a deadly serial killer.

"What is it, Mac? Did you find something?" asked Ronnie, glancing over at Danny, still sitting in their old scout car.

"Well. We can be sure of one thing. We ain't lookin for no brother. This mother's pure as the driven snow," stated Mac, pulling Ronnie closer.

"What makes you think our murderer's a white boy?" asked Ronnie, never even considering that possibility. In all her years on the Washington, D.C. Police Department, she couldn't remember too many times that she ever locked up a white man. Sometimes, very rarely, they had been the victims, but never the perpetrators. This could be an added twist. The only experience she ever had at getting into the head of a white man was with Danny or Mac. This could complicate things, reasoned the attractive black detective, looking longingly at Danny. As if they weren't already complicated enough, she thought, sighing as a tiny spark of passion exploded in her lower regions and ignited a pulsating surge of desire throughout her entire tingling body.

Mac brought her back to reality. "Because of this. Just smell this. It'll tell you why we've got us a white boy to find," he said. Ronnie sniffed the harsh pungent aroma as Mac held it up to her delicate nose. She had never smelled anything like it although she partially knew what it contained. That odor was distinctive.

"It's snuff, Ronnie. Snuff. Smokeless tobacco. Just like the old pinch between your lip and gum commercials. Only this isn't Skoal. It's Copenhagen. Skoal has a different smell. It's for the young kids. Hell. The hillbillies start chewin' it right after they're potty trained. The old-timers, they chew Copenhagen. And this is Copenhagen. How many brothers you know that chew snuff? Or own a 30.06? We're off and runnin' kid," excitedly stated Mac.

Ronnie kept thinking about the tree. If he had been up there she'd know. She'd be able to feel it. Almost as if in a trance, she slowly wandered over to the gnarled oak.

"I wish you could talk. I'll bet you've seen a lot in your lifetime. Haven't you, old boy?" she whispered to the thick trunk of the swaying oak. She reached out and gently touched the tree's rough bark with her soft hands. She shuddered as a vivid image of a stalking lion, its mouth dripping blood from a fresh kill, danced in her head.

"So. He was here. Again. For an encore," quietly murmured Ronnie, stepping back away from the ancient tree.

Two pink shining slits, glowing in the pitch black shadows, caught her eye. She walked over towards the unmoving florescent slits, careful not to trip over the empty broken wine and beer bottles littering the small grassy knoll under an immense protruding branch of the massive oak. The head turned away from her, a soft gentle purring noise coming from its throat. Ronnie loved cats. In fact, Ronnie loved everything that God had created. The cat slowly circled, continuing to purr in rising and falling rhythmic breaths. Ronnie bent over and lovingly stroked the cautious, but friendly feline.

"It's O.K., baby. Where's your home? You precious little kitty. I'll bet your mommy and daddy are worried sick over you. You go on home now," lovingly advised Ronnie, nudging the kitten away from the little knoll. Suddenly, she felt a horrible chill stab at her insides. Raising her hand, she noticed a thick sticky substance on the tip of her well manicured fingers. She shooed the kitten away, reaching down towards what had first appeared to be a mound of dirt. The mound was soft, like an animal's fur. She pushed the stiff form over, suddenly realizing what it really was. Shuddering, she saw the open slit in the animal's fur covered belly. Ronnie's heart raced. Her head spun. Laying next to the dead cat were the poor animal's innards, the stringy mess tangled around a long ago discarded box of Kentucky Fried Chicken.

Rhonda Bell felt the urge to kneel and pray. The harbinger of her city's death lay skulking in the ever changing shadows of eternity, shadows that blinded the seekers of truth and justice. She clutched at the tiny gold cross she wore around her long graceful neck. Her talisman was faith, faith in herself. She would find this creep. She knew it. Their paths would cross soon, very soon.

He wanted it that way. There was no other choice. That was the way it was going to have to be. Just him and her locked in the ultimate game, two predators vying for the same prey, each stalking the other. Rhonda Bell didn't cherish confrontation. But, she'd grit her teeth and bear it. She'd even spit, scratch, and claw if she had to. Her law, the law of survival in the black ghetto, had taught her to protect what was hers. And, all that she had was her dignity and her son. She'd die to protect either one, or both, if necessary.

Her people meant a lot to her, too. She'd been sworn, before God, to look out for them. Rhonda Bell began to hum as she covered the cat with the peach colored silken handkerchief from her suit's front pocket and prayed that the poor creature wasn't the little kitten's mother. Getting up to walk back to the bloody garage crypt, she began to sing. Her smooth golden voice gently carried the rhythmic lyrics across the night. For, in her asphalt jungle, the lion didn't sleep tonight. And, in her wildest dreams, Rhonda Bell never expected that the very same lion was about to awaken and devour one of her city's children in as cold blooded and savage a murder as has ever been witnessed by mankind. Even now, Ray Carson Carver was rummaging through his dank musty cellar, about to locate the instrument of his next deadly hunt. The trap, so to speak, was about to be sprung.

Emancipation Proclamation Jones was freezing his skinny black ass off. The hawk was out in full swooping force, realized the shivering officer. He reached for the handle to roll up Scout 151's open window, then decided against it. No way he was rolling up the window and turning on the heater. He'd gag himself, choked to death by Spic N' Span Spiegel's own personal form of chemical warfare.

Spic N' Span Spiegel left his window down, pretending not to know what Emancipation was thinking. It used to hurt him to know that, behind his back, they laughed at him. Now, things were a little different. Briefcase Betty had seen to that. Finally, he decided to demonstrate that fact to his partner, once and for all. Spic N' Span Spiegel rolled up his passenger side window and, reaching over to the scout car console, turned the heater up to full blast. Emancipation Proclamation Jones knew he was about to wilt in a nauseating wave of B.O. He cautiously sniffed the air for the first sign of the impending onslaught. He braced himself, ready to take it like a man. If it wasn't too bad maybe he could avoid the dry heaves. He sniffed again, shocked at the pleasant aroma. Finally, he allowed himself a full breath. Inhaling the invigorating scent, he turned his head to stare in disbelief.

"Giorgio for Men," calmly stated Spic N' Span Spiegel, smiling out the front windshield as Emancipation Proclamation Jones just about threw his arm out of joint cranking up the driver's side window in a shivering frenzy of heat seeking relief.

"How the hell can the sun be out in the middle of the day. And it be so cold?" asked Emancipation Proclamation Jones, looking up at the golden orb of the midday sun which burned bright in a cloudless pale blue sky.

"It is a little nippy. Isn't it?" commented Spic N' Span Spiegel, brushing off a piece of hair from his immaculately pressed dark blue wool pants.

"Shit. This mother fucker's colder than a nun's cunt," remarked Emancipation Proclamation Jones, wondering why he had never been more religious. Maybe if he could have seen the light he could have gotten a crack at some sister Theresa, or whatever. The priests probably had that covered anyway. They most likely wouldn't want any trespassin' on their turf, figured Emancipation Proclamation Jones, turning Scout 151 on to H

Street. It was getting time for a bank check at 8th and H Street. He'd been makin' deposits into bank teller Thelma Perkins perpetually open vault for the past two years. Non cash deposits into his own personal sperm bank that is, laughed Emancipation Proclamation Jones to himself as he began to drool just thinking about Thelma's chunky, but always horny, cottage cheese butt.

Thanks to a 911 call by a concerned citizen from the neighborhood watch program, Danny Money was just about to collar himself a pack of burglary inclined truants. The Bud Man, exonerated of any wrong doing in the hallway shooting and released back to the street, was slowly opening the passenger side door of 150, ready to lasso the whole herd when they crawled back out of the open window in the rear of 1572 Neal Street. He was beginning to get impatient. Fifteen minutes had gone by and they still hadn't come out. Patrol Wagon 29 was waiting out in front, two houses down, hoping to drive the whole thievin' herd into the back of the wagon despite police department orders barring the transportation of juveniles in its cold steel belly.

Finally, his patience worn to a frazzle, the Bud Man got out of 150 and crept around the side of the house, to the front door. He'd move things along a little. He rapped his wooden nightstick against the glass screen door. Looking up, he saw a head bob out of the upstairs window and then disappear back inside. That was all he needed. There was definitely a burglary in progress and that gave him every right in the world to break down the door and jack up some smart ass juvenile jive turkey punks. He smashed the glass in the screen door, stepped back, squared his massive muscular shoulders, and charged into the flimsy wooden door. The door stood firm. The Bud Man didn't. Bouncing off the reverberating door, he staggered backwards, tripped over the porch steps and tumbled into an open garbage bag full of shit covered Pampers.

The veins stood out on the Bud Man's face as he sat on the cold cement, his left arm buried to the elbow in the rank smelling bag. His whole body shook in rage as, unable to restrain himself any longer, he charged wildly into the wooden door screaming, "You're goin' down. You're all goin' down." The door gave, splintering off its hinges under the crashing impact of the Bud Man's fevered onslaught. Inside, the terrified juveniles scattered in every direction, running into each other as they fled the wrath of the incensed Bud Man.

"Freeze. All of you little turds freeze. Or, I'll wax your black butts," screamed the Bud Man at the top of his lungs.

"Man. We was just trying to have a little fun," stated one of the juveniles, retreating toward the kitchen as Money, finding the back door unlocked, walked into the confused scene.

"Yeah. Some kind of fun. You little snot nosed brats were just rippin' off whoever owns this house. What, you gangstas need some more drug money?" asked the Bud Man, rounding up the scattered juveniles.

"We don't use no drugs, man. This is my mother's house. We just be doin' a little partyin'. I didn't want none of the nosy fuckin' neighbors to tell my old lady we was skippin' school," stated another juvenile, the pounding bass of "Mama Said Knock You Out" booming out of two humongous speakers in the living room. Thinking about his own little brewskis, the Bud Man figured he'd like to knock out a couple of these wise ass punks, never mind waitin' for mama to do it. If he ever caught his boys skippin' school he'd put a hurtin' on their skinny black butts. His little spudzette, she'd never play hooky. She was a straight A student. Damn, them two spuds were a couple of little troublemakers, thought the Bud Man, deciding to ground them anyway, just to teach them a lesson.

The Bud Man began to feel a rising lump of crow meat insinuate itself into his quivering throat. With any luck he could talk the kid and his old lady into accepting two new doors and an apology. Damn, the complainant who had originally called hadn't even left their name or address. No matter what the outcome, the end result was undoubtedly going to be him, bent over at the check off window, takin' it in the butt from that skinny son of a bitch Jones and the rest of those 5D faggots.

At about the same time the Bud Man was impersonating a battering ram, Lieutenant Bow Wow Bowser was grilling Mike McCarthy and Rhonda Bell on the progress of the murder case, finally conceding that it looked like the beginning of another Freeway Phantom serial killer nightmare. He only hoped, for all of their sakes, that it had a happier ending. This time, if they didn't catch the sick son of a bitch all of their asses were gonna fry. They couldn't afford to be foulin' up again in front of the entire nation.

"Lieutenant. We're doin' everything we can. Why don't we hike up the uniform patrol? Or, stake out the place? We can set up a detail from eight at night to four in the morning. So far, he's only struck in that alley behind Orleans Place," pleaded Mike McCarthy, wondering why the high strung lieutenant kept glancing at his watch.

"O.K., Mac. I'll set up an old-clothes detail from eight to four. What about the clues?" questioned the anxious lieutenant, figuring if he could get these bozo's to wrap up this case he'd have a little more time to spend with 10-33 Sam's old lady. He was supposed to be out to her place in thirty minutes. That would give him a couple of hours with her hot wop ass, before old crazy Sambo got home.

"So far we've got a rock and a branch. Both stuck in the victim's mouth after death. He's using a hunting knife with a serrated edge to gut them. And a 30.06 to bring them down. Our guess is that he's white. The Mobile Crime Lab sent the snuff specimen to the F.B.I. Lab. No sign of sexual abuse on either victim. No pattern as to who's next. No witnesses as of yet. No fingerprints on anything. No material evidence at the scene, except for the slugs. Both came from the same weapon. We're researching that to find out what make and model," reported Mac, adding, "I hear the press already got their grubby little hands on some of this stuff."

"Yeah. You bet those cocksuckers. Oh. Excuse me, Bell. those dick lickers are in our shit. They're on my ass like a gigantic hemorrhoid. They've already come up with a cute little name for the son of a bitch," stated Bow Wow Bowser, motioning for the two detectives to leave his office. He'd better call her and tell her he'd be a few minutes late. That even got her hornier. Damn, sometimes she could make him cream right over the phone.

"What's that, lieutenant?" quietly questioned Ronnie, looking over her shoulder as she left his cluttered office, the usual dense cloud of cigarette smoke hovering at eye level and making her nauseous.

"The Carver. The fuckin' Capital Carver. Sweet, isn't it?" replied Bow Wow Bowser, picking up the telephone as Ronnie quietly shut his office door, both detectives wanting to get as far out of barkin' Bow Wow's sight as was humanly possible.

"Mac. That gives me the creeps. The Capital Carver. That's gruesome," remarked Ronnie as they took the elevator down to the motor pool at police headquarters.

"Yes. But, it does have such a nice poetic ring to it. I don't know why they didn't call him the Human Hunter. Or, the Gnarly

Knife, or maybe the Ghetto Gutter. That's a good one. The Ghetto Gutter. That's just great. All the little kids can read that and grow up normal. Can't they? Sometimes, the press makes me sick. You know I read this article about this guy somewhere out west. He has his podunk little tattler newspaper print the names of women rape victims. Yeah. Great idea. Respect the rights of your fellow human beings. A poor woman. Humiliated at the most demeaning act that a man can perpetrate on her. Then, she has to open up her town's local newspaper and see her picture and her name spread all over the front page. Wouldn't it be great if some fag gave that jack-off a little backdoor visit. Down the old dirt road. And, then the women could take out a full page ad with his name and picture in their own newspaper. Small town America. Sometimes, it's no better than this," lectured Mac. "Sorry Ronnie. You didn't need to hear that. Just an old frustrated man blowin' smoke."

"It's the way you feel, Mac. I know it. I know you. It's refreshing to hear a man stand up for us for a change. So many times they just don't understand. The greatest gift we can give a man we love is our body. It's our own sacred package. When we open it freely and give ourselves to someone we care about it's beautiful. When somebody rips it open and steals it from us it's as if they've stolen the sanctity of our soul. They've taken what we didn't want to give. They've used us like so much garbage. They've cheapened the gift. They've attacked one woman. But, they've raped us all," replied Ronnie as Mike McCarthy drove Cruiser 311 out into the cold afternoon sun, feeling alive for one of the last times in his fifty six years on the face of the earth.

"Let's do a little door knockin' down on Orleans Place. Maybe we can dig up something. At this point there ain't much else we can work on. A white man, prowlin' around down there. If he looks like the typical snuff chewin', cap wearin' redneck jerk from somewhere out in East Jesus, he ought to stick out like a sore thumb," remarked Mac, cruising down H Street.

"A face. A vehicle. Anything would go a long way. The rock and the branch sure don't mean anything to me. How about you, Mac?" questioned Ronnie, crossing her long shapely legs.

Mac, hearing the rustling stockings, glanced over at Ronnie's model like body and sighed, "Ronnie. You are sure as hell one beautiful lady. I hope the man you love appreciates what it is you have to give to him. And, no. They don't mean anything to me either. That's because they're just the first. Believe me. He plans on giving us plenty more." Ronnie shuddered. She hoped there wouldn't be too many more.

Suddenly, the police radio crackled. Mike McCarthy, feeling the piss and vinegar fires of years long forgotten, decided to enter the fray. He could sense it. Today was a special day. Mike McCarthy was right. It was a special day, special to the fiendish mental hobgoblins that sap men's souls.

"We're less than a block away," excitedly hollered Mac, listening to the dispatcher's simulcast broadcast of a robbery in progress at the D.C. National Bank at Eighth and H, Henry, Street Northeast, Fifth District units Scout 150 and Scout 151 responding Code One.

"Lights. No siren," remarked Ronnie under her breath, rolling down the window and placing the magnetic flashing red light on top of the steadily accelerating cruiser. They didn't need to broadcast their arrival to the robbers. She knew Danny and the Bud Man would be running silent, too. She had her doubts about Emancipation Proclamation Jones and Spic N' Span Spiegel. E.P. had a tendency to be a little excitable, a little over dramatic. Not that she could blame him. His nerves were probably always on edge, constantly trying to duck all those jealous husbands. Spiegel, he was a nice guy. He could make some woman a wonderful husband. If only he'd clean up his act a little bit.

"Jesus Christ. There they go. Across H Street. They're runnin' up Eighth Street. You see 'em? You see 'em?" shouted Mac, weaving the unmarked cruiser through H Street's perpetually heavy traffic.

Rhonda Bell had been watching the front door of the bank as two of the hold up men, dressed in black trench coats, burst out of the front door and began running across H Street. Almost immediately two other black men, dressed in green army fatigue jackets fell in behind them. Must be the lookout men, figured Ronnie, reaching for her two inch .38 special, clipped on to the waist of her skirt, the leather holster concealed by her suit jacket.

"There's four of 'em. Be careful," hollered Mac, screeching the tires of Cruiser 311 as he banked into a tight skidding turn, right, on to Eighth Street. Rhonda Bell took one last glance down H Street as the cruiser headed up Eighth, right behind the four fleeing hold up men. Her last clear vision was of two marked police cars, one behind the other, screaming down H Street, red lights flashing, closing in quickly on the bank building.

Emancipation Proclamation Jones was in the tunnel, the zone, his eyes focused on the D.C. National Bank, three blocks up the street. Everything else was passing by in a blur. Thelma Perkins wasn't going to end up sucking on the barrel of a shotgun if he had anything to say about it. In fact, right now, his adrenaline pumping like a gusher, he was ready to lay it all on the line. He'd be damned if his kid was going to come into the world with a chickenshit coward for an old man.

Spic N' Span Spiegel was thinking about Briefcase Betty Barnes. All he wanted to do was to make her proud of him. No matter what happened he was determined to stand tall and proud like the man she was making him believe he could be. He felt honored to know her. Nobody had ever been a stronger wind beneath any man's wings, thought Spic N' Span Spiegel. Gritting his yellowed teeth and pulling out his Glock nine millimeter, he prepared himself to confront the most terrifying enemy of any police officer, the unknown.

Danny Money had Scout 150 dead on 151's ass end. Looking down H Street, he caught a brief glimpse of running figures crossing the street, followed by what looked like an unmarked detective cruiser in hot pursuit. The Bud Man, his fingers sore from filling out the truancy reports from Neal Street, squeezed the oversize wooden grips of his pistol as he pulled it out of its black leather holster. Somehow, he had the feeling that this was no prank call. Despite the fear, this was the brief moment in life that no drug could ever hope to imitate. This is what got most cops hooked, unable to cope with the mundane routine of civilian life after this most powerful of all narcotics got into their blood stream. Most people, if they ever knew what it was like, would trade one year of their boring life for a few fleeting moments in the danger zone.

"We're on 'em. We've got their ass. Get ready, Ronnie. They're armed, I can see the guns. Don't take any chances. Waste 'em if you have to," excitedly screamed Mac, deathly afraid of seeing Ronnie get hurt in this certain impending shoot out.

"I'm OK, Mac. Just watch out for yourself. I'll take the one on my side. You take the one on yours. Forget the ones in front. They'll be history before we can nail these two," shouted Ronnie, forcing herself to take deep breaths. The moment of deadly confrontation was at hand. She braced her low heeled pumps against the cruiser's floor boards, her left hand on the door handle, her right squeezing the handle of her revolver.

Mac pulled up next to the fleeing suspects and slammed

on the cruiser's brakes. The car skidded sideways as Ronnie threw open the passenger side-door. Crouching behind the open door, she leveled her revolver on the gradually slowing black man on her side, less than twenty feet away. Mac threw the gear shift into park and dashed out of the unmarked car, pulling his two inch revolver out of its worn shoulder holster.

"Freeze, asshole!" hollered Mac, drawing a bead on the other black suspect who turned around abruptly, facing Mac, his pistol still grasped in his right hand and pointed in Mac's direction.

"Don't shoot, man," desperately cried the suspect confronting Ronnie as he dropped his revolver to the pavement.

Mac cringed, then pulled the trigger. The ear splitting explosion cracked sharply in the frigid afternoon air.

"He's a police officer, man," screamed the other man, finishing his sentence one second too late. He watched in horror as his Fifth District old-clothes tactical partner doubled over, clutching desperately at his wounded stomach. Mac, his ears still ringing from the thunder clap discharge, turned to look at the other man in front of Ronnie. His shocked eyes, glazed with horror, told a woeful tale of anguish. Suddenly, Mac realized what he had just done. He had shot an innocent man, a cop doing his job just like he was. God, he prayed the man wouldn't die.

Ronnie, trying to stay calm, looked over at Mac, his sweating face turning white as a sheet. The trembling man in front of her slowly pulled back his fatigue jacket to reveal the shiny silver badge of the Washington, D.C. Police Department. The badge, clipped to his black leather belt, sparkled in the glinting rays of the cold yellow sun. Mac dropped his pistol and ran towards his wounded fellow police officer, now doubled over, kneeling on the cold pavement next to the curb.

"Call a fuckin ambulance," pleaded the other old-clothes officer, running over to help his fallen comrade.

Rhonda Bell turned and ran to the homicide cruiser. Grabbing the mike, she yelled, "Cruiser 311 emergency. Police officer shot. 700 block of Eighth Street Northeast. We need an ambulance. Officer is in serious condition."

Mike McCarthy was beside himself. He wrapped his arms around the young wounded officer and rocked him back and forth. The officer, a dark stain spreading across the front of his grey sweatshirt, his hands covered in blood, looked up at Mac's pale sweating face. "I should have dropped my gun. How would you know, man. I should have dropped my gun," whispered the dying officer, staring blankly into oblivion.

"It's OK. Don't talk. There's an ambulance on the way. You'll make it," gasped Mac, desperately looking around for Ronnie. He needed her strength. He was sinking into the deepest depths of despair. He'd never shot a man before. He was sick. Suddenly the wounded officer felt as heavy as lead. Mac let the limp man's head fall back into his cradling arms. The young officer's brown face turned ashen grey. His soft brown eyes lost the spark of life, reflecting instead, the dull brackish yellow glaze of death. The rhythmic rise and fall of his heaving chest stopped.

Ronnie, sensing the life ebbing out of the fallen officer, gently pushed Mac aside and lay the wounded policeman carefully on his back, across the curb. She pinched his nostrils shut and lifted up his neck. Covering his mouth with hers, she blew deeply. After several breaths she locked her hands and pressed forcefully on his sternum, trying to revive his stilled heart.

Danny Money and the Bud Man rushed to the scene, pushing back the growing crowd of curious onlookers. Emancipation Proclamation Jones and Spic N' Span Spiegel cautiously entered the bank, hoping that the party was over. Thelma Perkins, her plump body quaking in fear, swallowed up Emancipation Proclamation Jones in a tidal wave of quivering flesh. E.P. knew, for certain, that he'd be gettin a little trim this evening. Thelma was sure looking grateful to see him.

Danny Money and the Bud Man couldn't believe their own eyes. They were looking at one of their own 5D brothers layin' in the street, bleeding all over the place, a bullet lodged in his belly. Rhonda Bell knew it was over. She had seen plenty of death in her day. Despite her arms burning with muscle fatigue, she was going to stay with this boy until the ambulance got here, the wail of its shrill siren finally sounding in the distance.

"How'd it happen?" asked the Bud Man, looking over at the other Fifth District old clothes tact man.

"He shot him. That fat mother fucker over there. He busted a cap on my partner, man. Shit. I oughtta bust a cap on his fat ass. We was chasin' the two hold up men from the bank. Workin' H Street detail, man. We was on their asses. We would've had 'em. Then this big-shot bozo the clown from downtown comes rollin' up. And, now my main man's history," answered the old-clothes officer, staring in rage at Mike McCarthy.

"He turned towards me. He didn't drop his gun. How the

hell was I supposed to know he was a cop? Jesus, we thought he was one of the look-out men from the hold up," stated Mac, looking over at the ominously still officer, Ronnie still giving him CPR.

The ambulance crew paramedics looked at one another and shook their heads. The young cop was dead. His epitaph would not be a pretty one. Fire was fire. Friendly or not, they both left you just as dead.

"You murdered my partner. You fat piece of shit. Left him lyin in the gutter of this filthy stinkin' street. Why don't you go tell his old lady and his baby what your honky ass is gonna do for them now," hysterically shouted the old-clothes officer, jumping up and down and pointing his finger at Mike McCarthy's solemn slumping frame.

"That's enough. You've said enough. All your wolfin' isn't gonna help bring him back. This isn't anybody's fault. Nobody murdered anybody. This is life. It ain't always beautiful, brother. In fact it can get real ugly," yelled Rhonda Bell, having listened to all of the nonsense that she intended to.

"Who are you, bitch? You sound like some Uncle Tom whore to me," shouted the old clothes officer, stepping in front of Ronnie's lean torso.

"Get outta my face, boy. Because, if you don't I'm gonna forget that I'm a lady and kick you right in your wrinkled little balls. You dig where I'm comin' from, brother," quietly stated Rhonda, the shocked officer stepping aside to let her pass.

"Nice work, Ronnie," complimented Danny Money, walking next to her towards Cruiser 311.

"You wouldn't have really blue balled him. Would you?" he asked, opening the door for Ronnie who smiled as she slid into the cruiser and straightened her skirt. "What do you think? You're supposed to know me so well."

Danny Money figured he better not answer that one. It, like a woman, was a two edged sword.

Lately, Mike McCarthy hadn't done much drinking, not since he had buried himself in the bottle after his wife had passed. Tonight, he fully intended to finish the bottle. Then tomorrow, he'd open another one. He opened the back door of his small three bedroom ranch house in Bladensburg, Maryland, and let in his two Lhasa Apsos, Hoss and L'il Joe. They, like Ronnie, had always brought joy to his life. He kneeled down and hugged the two animals, hoping their total acceptance of him, with all of his faults and human failings, would uplift his spirits. Right now, after killing a fellow officer, whether justified or not, he felt like the most miserable wretch on the face of the earth.

Mac kicked off his black wingtips and walked into what had been their bedroom, a room filled with memories of laughter and happiness. He looked longingly at the empty bed where images of passion and love had succumbed to the reality of pain and suffering. She had died in that bed, in his arms. He had held her until morning, talking to her all night, saying everything he had always wanted to tell her. In the morning he had kissed her good-bye, their last kiss, alone, together. Then he had called the ambulance to take her body away from him. Her memories were with him always. That, nobody could take away. That morning he had closed the bedroom door, never again sleeping in their bed. He had moved his things to another bedroom. Her's still lay undisturbed in their room. Love was different than old soldiers. If it was real, it never died or faded away, thought Mac as he shut the door and walked back to the kitchen.

He reached up into the cupboard and pulled down a glass. Walking over to the built in pantry, he grabbed the dust covered bottle of Dewars and poured himself a generous helping. His hand shook as he raised the glass to his quivering lips, not even wanting ice to cut the potent scotch whiskey. Tonight, nothing was going to dilute his medication, thought the despondent detective. Slipping the shoulder harness over his head he laid the empty holster on the dinette table and stared off into oblivion. His service revolver, his self designated murder weapon, had been confiscated pending the Internal Affairs investigation into the shooting.

He almost forgot. Before he got good and plastered he better feed his kids. The big girl, Hoss, would never forgive him. L'il Joe wouldn't mind. All he wanted to do, twenty four hours a day, was play with an old worn out fuzzy tennis ball.

"How's daddy's girl?" asked Mac, petting Hoss's head as she jumped up on his lap eager for attention. Him and his wife had loved watching the westerns together, especially Bonanza. There weren't any Bonanza's left today. Instead, there were only the Young Guns type crap with all their blaze of gory glory, with all their violence and killing, thought Mac as he walked into the kitchen to fill the kid's dishes and get them their after dinner Meaty Bones. Good God almighty, he hated that song. Funny, he hadn't thought about it in years. In fact he'd only heard it a couple of times. But, right now, it had popped into his head.

"When you're goin down, it ain't in no Blaze of Glory," muttered Mac out loud, his mind visualizing the Capital Carver dangling from the end of a hangman's noose.

Staring down at his daughter, laying on the couch watching TV, Ray Carson Carver was asking himself the same question. Daddy's girl was about to get her tight little ass spanked if she wasn't careful, thought the wheezing ex-coal miner as his body was raked with a guttural coughing spasm that was tearing apart his innards. Catching his breath, he pictured her pale white buttocks covered with juicy red welts as he blistered her ripe behind and then turned her over for the real fun.

"Dinner's ready and on the table," yelled his wife, Kate, from the aromatic smelling kitchen. Ray Carson Carver took his seat at the head of the table and motioned for his wife to bring him a bottle.

"Tell that daughter of yours to get her ass in here, now. If she don't I'm a gonna take the strap to her. You hear me, woman?" coldly stated Ray Carver, pouring himself half a glass of Old Grand Dad. He didn't have time to screw with no split tails tonight, figured the hacking ex-miner, spitting into an empty cup and wiping his mucous covered mouth with the sleeve of his plaid wool shirt. He had himself a little journey to make. He might as well take out a black fawn down on Orleans Place. "That shit hole of humanity was like a fuckin' game preserve," chuckled Ray Carver under his breath. Soon he'd have to move on. There wasn't any white meat there, only dark.

"Noah loaded them up by the two's. Me, I take them out by the three's," he laughed out loud, spitting up a mouthful of his dinner on to the linoleum kitchen floor.

"This slop ain't even fit for pigs," shouted Ray Carver at his cowering wife, deciding that it was time to relive the thrill, the thrill of the kill.

CHAPTER 10

"JESUS CHRIST," blurted out Danny Money. He was unable to move. He stood staring at the most stunning woman that he had ever seen, his chin bouncing off the floor. Rhonda Bell was literally taking his breath away. He had always known she was beautiful. But this, this was something else.

"Well. Are you gonna make me stand outside all night? Or, are you going to invite me in?" asked Ronnie, convinced by the admiring sparkle in Danny's eyes that she had indeed done good. Danny couldn't take his eyes off her.

"Let's talk," she whispered in her most sultry voice, knowing that she definitely had the upper hand in this episode of the battle of the sexes. Danny still hadn't closed his mouth. She had taken him by surprise, ambushed him. No phone call. No pre-arranged date. That is how she had wanted it. Tonight, she was going to find out if her and Danny had a future together. If he was for real she'd know it. Marriage and family is what she had in mind. Anything less and she'd bait her hook for another fish in the proverbial sea. She knew exactly how the evening was going to start. And, more importantly, how it was going to end. The main course, the one between the appetizer and the after dinner mint, was the only unknown. It would be up to Danny to pick the right entree off of her menu.

Ronnie stepped inside, pausing in the ceramic tile foyer as Danny removed her scarlet lined black cashmere cape. Fumbling with the closet hangers, his darting eyes glancing back at Ronnie's enticing silhouette, he motioned her into the white carpeted living room. Despite her impoverished ghetto childhood, Ronnie had learned how to dress, just like she had learned everything not relating to the basics of survival. She had read. She had devoured and then absorbed every magazine or article that she could get her hands on, every book from Ebony and Cosmopolitan to National Geographic and Ladies Home Journal. Tonight, she felt just a little bit arrogant. Maybe, it was she who should be on the cover of this month's Cosmo, thought Ronnie smugly. She could shame a lot of those covergirl models with tonight's display.

Danny Money stumbled as he crossed the living room into the kitchen, a little confused by Ronnie's unexpected visit. Ronnie stood in front of the brick fireplace pretending to look at two Ansel Adams black and white photographs hanging over the mantle. In reality, she just wanted to give Danny one more look at her ravishing profile. Her clinging one piece black knit mini barely concealed the bottom of her gently rounded buttocks. In the rear, it dipped down to the small of her back, revealing the lean golden brown profile of her smooth skin.

The collar of the black dress wrapped around her neck, leaving a gaping hole in the front, subtly revealing the upper most folds of her firm ripe breasts. Her long muscular legs, encased in sheer black nylons, seemed to grow naturally out of a pair of spike heeled black shoes which wrapped sensuously around her graceful ankles. Glimmering in the dim light, her gold earrings dangled below her gently sloped shoulders. For all practical purposes, Detective Rhonda Bell was loaded for bear.

"Would you like a drink?" asked Danny, his voice cracking with emotion.

"White wine, Sauvignon Blanc if you have it. That would be nice," answered Ronnie, sitting on Danny's grey leather living room couch, her knees tightly clamped together.

"How about Chablis," he inquired, looking in the refrigerator, glad that at least he had a bottle of Gallo. If they would make the shit in a fifty five gallon drum for three ninety nine that's what he'd buy, figured Danny, wondering if they still made Boone's Farm Apple Wine. He reached for a can of Coor's Light. He only kept it around to piss off the Bud Man. Then, deciding that this wasn't shaping up into a beer type night, he grabbed the Jack Daniels and poured it over ice.

He carried the drinks into the living room and sat them down on the black marble based glass coffee table. He hesitated, undecided as to where he should sit. It was usually so easy. He'd just sit next to Ronnie. But, tonight she was kind of intimidating. Somehow he felt his heart flutter, his head spin. It was almost as if he was on a first date with an inviting woman that he was trying to seduce. Only this time, the tables seemed to be turned.

Ronnie picked up the stem of the wine glass and sipped the fruity drink, her pouting lips leaving a distinctive ruby red outline smearing the rim of the leaded crystal. Danny, a little confused, sat in the sofa's matching grey leather chair. He took a long swallow of the burning whiskey, his eyes still fixed on Ronnie's alluring profile. Ronnie looked deeply into Danny's sky blue eyes. They could make a beautiful baby together, she thought, sighing. But, back to the business at hand. Step one was completed. She was in total control of the situation. A curious thought crossed her mind. If it was so easy for women to control men, how come men controlled the world?

"Danny. What are your plans for your life? Where do you want to be five years from now?" she asked bluntly, crossing her long legs in a subtle whisper of silky softness.

Danny stammered. Then, he answered, "Well. I guess I just want to be in the Fifth District. Sitting in Scout 150. Maybe, I'll try the detective gig for a while. They've been after me to transfer upstairs to the 5D detective office. I don't know. I've never really sat down and thought about it. I sure don't wanna end up like that partner of yours. Just hangin' on to the J.O.B. Whenever he retires, he's dead. He ain't got shit."

"He's got me, Danny. I'm his friend. I care about him. Not what he's got. You're talkin'. But, you're not saying anything. You didn't say one word about who you wanna have around you to share your life with. Mac's lonely. Are you any different? You don't know him. He had a lovely wife. They were happy together. Now, she's dead. And, he's alone again. But, at least they had their time in the sun. The question here is, are we going to have ours? Because, if not, I'm outta here. I'd like to be your wife. But, I don't plan on doing any asking. That's your job. If it doesn't turn out like that I can be a lot of other things. I'm not afraid of life without you. But, I'd be really excited to face it with you. I know it wouldn't be easy. If you would ever marry me you'd have to marry Darnell, too. You know who his father is. We either see past this black and white thing right now and bond together like two people in love, or we say good-bye. I'm not interested in being anybody's piece of meat on the side."

Danny Money took another swallow of the Jack Daniels and stared into Ronnie's sensual brown eyes. He had never been this close to a binding commitment before. But, he knew that she was right. The simple synopsis was shit or get off the pot. If Ronnie had been white this whole thing would have been so easy, thought Danny. He would ask her to marry him. He'd even adopt Darnell. He knew he loved her. That wasn't even a question. Life wasn't a game. It wasn't a dress rehearsal for anything. The performance was now. Maybe, if Ronnie had been white, he wouldn't even have loved her, figured Danny. Because, if she was white she wouldn't be Ronnie. Despite himself, Danny Money was growing up.

"I'll shit," quietly stated Danny, getting up and walking over towards Ronnie, a huge smile stretched across his boyishly handsome face.

"What did you say? What the hell are you talking about?" she replied, suspiciously glancing at the growing bulge in Danny's blue jeans.

"I'm talking about us. I said you're right. I'll quit bein' an asshole. And, that ain't easy for a man to do. But, one step at a time. When do you want to meet my parents? How about next weekend?" inquired Danny, taking Ronnie's warm hand and drawing her up off the couch.

"Next week would be just fine," answered Ronnie, melting into Danny's arms. Locking her right leg around his left, she gently rotated her pelvis against his stiffening manhood. Danny could hardly contain himself. Wildly, he ran his hands all over her smooth bare back. She reached between their writhing bodies, firmly grasping the hard outline of his penis. In a fit of fiery passion, Danny grabbed her shiny jet black hair and tilted up her head, burying his tongue in her mouth.

Well, figured Ronnie, everything on the menu had been just fine. Now, she'd have to cut off the dessert cart at the pass before it wheeled her into the bedroom. "I have to get home and pick up Darnell. I've really got to get going, baby," wryly smiled Ronnie, teasingly licking Danny's ear.

"I was hoping you'd spend the night," responded Danny in frustration, feeling a little bit like he'd been pleasantly had.

"Believe me. You'll have plenty more nights to be with me," said Ronnie, opening the closet door to get her wrap.
Danny put the cape around her shoulders and massaged her graceful neck. "By the way. You can bring Darnell, too. You're both part of the same package," he said, kissing Ronnie good-bye.

"I'd like that. By the way. I love you," she replied, stepping out into the cold moonless night air, feeling as full of life as she'd ever felt.

Danny watched as she disappeared into the engulfing darkness. Suddenly, much like two hands strangling the life out of a struggling victim, a heinous chill clutched at his pounding heart. He wondered what Ronnie's partner's wife had died from. Somehow he felt empty, cold. A bleak blizzard of doom covered the horizon in a swirling tempest of terror. In his mind, a dark solitary figure trudged through the heavy snow, the only hope for the unlucky victims caught in its unexpected fury. Might that figure be Ronnie, curiously thought the shivering officer, wondering if he had remembered to tell her how beautiful she was or how much he really loved her.

Ray Carson Carver didn't love anything, anything that is, except death. And with that in mind, he was making ready to strike again. One fawn, grown into mature adulthood, could spread his seed repeatedly. One fawn, dead, could spread his rotting useless flesh under a mound of filthy dirt, figured Ray Carver, preparing a little preemptive strike plan to take out a colored boy. Bloodsport was what it was all about. "My sport. Their blood," he laughed out loud as he pulled the four wheel drive pick up into the last rest stop before he reached Washington, D.C. He'd grab a couple of Z's and be up with the chickens, ready to peck out the eyes of the first little nigger boy that stepped into his deadly trap.

Ray Carver awoke at three a.m., the front windshield of his four by four covered with spider webs of frost and ice. Damn, he'd forgot to turn the tape off. Funny, he thought. Ol' Jonny Bon Jovi's boy woke up in the mornin' and didn't know where he was a goin'. And, Jonny said only the Good Lord knew where he'd been. But me, I knows where I'm a goin'. And, where I've been, the Good Lord don't know a damned thing about. Them unholy places are for the devil and me. And, neither one of us is runnin' away from shit. Put that in your pipe and smoke it, Jon boy, silently chuckled Ray Carver, wondering if maybe he shouldn't write his own Goddamned lyrics and set the record straight.

He stepped outside the cab, into the crisp frigid air, his breath distinctively visible in the black void of the moonless night. Looking up, he noticed a few pinpoints of flickering light, hardly discernible in the cloudless sky. No matter. For this next kill he wouldn't need the illumination of the full, stalking moon. For, today, he'd show them just how skilled and versatile a hunter he was. The true mountain man, the true sportsman, must be a jack of many trades, reasoned Ray Carver, reaching behind the driver's seat and clutching at the cold steel of the jaws of death.

He looked around the dimly lit rest stop. Parked big rigs idled throatily in the distance. Motor homes sat quietly, ready to resume their nomadic lifestyle at the break of dawn. Like a worn animal trail littered with scat and other signs, the highway beckoned. He had to get moving, but first, he'd leave his own sign chuckled Ray Carver, unzipping his fly.

Lieutenant Bow Wow Bowser's all night detail on Orleans Place was already figuring that this, like every other get ready to get ready police detail that they'd ever been on, was a fucking waste of their time. Most of their long boring night had been spent debating whether the bars on all the window's were to keep the mother fuckers that lived there in, or to keep the rest of the mother fuckers out. Finally, leaving their concealed positions in what they referred to as blood bath alley, they concluded that a mother fucker was a mother fucker no matter whether he was in or out.

The consensus of opinion on the Capital Carver was that he was most likely a limp dicked faggot who just might be doing the city a favor. They had never seen so few dealers, mules, pimps, and whores on Orleans Place's now deserted street corners. Overall, crime was at a standstill and, besides, there would have been at least two homicides down here anyway. They weren't totally convinced that the Carver should be caught. In fact the yea's outnumbered the nay's when they took an impromptu vote to put him on the city payroll. His first official duty, to clean out the drug infested guts of the city's worthless elected officials. This morning, when they checked off at four, it was all still a big game.

The game ended in the very alley that they were leaving on this cold grey morning. After today, the rules would change forever. Everybody would unanimously decide that it was time to play some real hardball. Some would even say that from this day forward, in the Nation's Capital, certain things would never be the same. The glowing white ambiance of the Lincoln Memorial seemed to fade to a dull yellow. The Washington Monument suddenly looked weathered, never again reflecting its peaceful image on the once serene reflection pools. The Capitol Building's shiny dome began to look tarnished. Almost as if by magic, the regal white purity of 1600 Pennsylvania Avenue dissolved, peeling and cracking chunks of paint falling to the well manicured lush green grounds. Behold, the man cometh. The time is at hand. He brings a terrible swift sword of fury. He is about to plunge it into the bowels of the city and open up the gates to hell. Few would ever remember the bleak dismal dawn which broke that cold Monday morning. Nobody, however, would ever live to forget Tuesday, the twilight's last gleaming.

Ray Carson Carver parked his pickup truck in an empty lot behind an abandoned warehouse. It was a little after five am. The dark deserted streets, void of any traffic, were eerily quiet. He walked slowly, staying away from the streetlights, crouching in the shadows. "The night doesn't belong to Michelob. It belongs to me," snickered Ray Carver, his sinister unshaven face twisted up into an evil mocking grin. Reaching underneath his London Fog trench coat, he touched the cold metal of the .357 magnum blue steel revolver he wore in a leather shoulder holster. His stainless steel hunting knife dangled from his wide brown belt, buckled at the waist with an oval grey metal Kenworth belt buckle. His faded blue jean bottoms hung over tan Timberland hunting boots. He wore a pair of leather working gloves. The real instrument of the hunt lay in a battered canvass knapsack, behind the driver's side seat of his pickup, waiting like the jaws of a Great White shark.

This was only a scouting mission. The hunter had to be patient. Stalking game meant waiting. He had to find the trails they followed, pick the prey and then separate it from the protection of the herd. That's when the bloodthirsty predator went in for the kill and finished off his helpless victim. Ray Carver was no less the predator. He'd use the same process. "Don't mess with Mother Nature," he chuckled as he slithered through a tangled mass of thick shrubs partially concealing an old dilapidated metal storage shed, its bent rusted doors hanging half open. Ray Carver crawled into the impromptu blind. Reaching into his rear pocket for a pinch of Copenhagen snuff, he settled in to wait for the witching hour, the back of the school play yard less than two hundred feet away.

Ray Carver rubbed his hands together and looked at his watch. It shouldn't be long now, reasoned the patient murderer. The sun's golden orange fluorescent ball was beginning to climb slowly, revealing itself over the eastern horizon. It's reddish tint reminded him of the old sailor's adage, red at night, sailor's delight, red in the morning, sailors take warning. His morning was red, blood red. Soon the scent of a fresh kill would permeate the foul city air.

They'd all better take warning. The Capital Carver was about to bury his deadly fangs into the jugular of another weak straggling defenseless victim.

He lurked in the shadows, watching silently, as small groups of children passed in review. A roving herd heading for its watering hole, surmised the demented killer. Groups of two and three, even four and five young kids passed. Ray Carver paced back and forth in the little shed. It was getting late. Soon the bell would sound and the moment will have passed. Yes, there he was. Ray Carver's eyes momentarily glowed with frenetic zeal. He stared at the young boy. He was alone, running late for school. The pudgy little crumb snatcher was a ripe one indeed. He would skin out at about seventy five or eighty pounds. Just like a plump veal calf, his meat would be tender, marbled with greasy road maps of fat. Now, all that was left was to wait for the right moment. "Cut him out of the herd and the rest was child's play," mumbled Ray Carver, tightening his hand around the handle of his hunting knife.

"Hey, Money. Check this out. Last night me and the Bud Lady tucked the brewskis into bed. I left a couple of aspirins and a glass of water on the nightstand next to mama's side of the bed. When she came out of the bathroom she asked me what they were for. I told her that they were for her headache. She said she didn't have a headache. That's when I told her if she ain't got a headache there ain't no reason we can't get it on. Sheet, man. I stroked the woman all night," laughed the Bud Man, pulling scout 150 into the Florida Avenue Cleaners to pick up his laundered uniform shirts.

"Shit. Your tired ass probably didn't bob more than three times. I've heard you ain't nothin' but three strokes and a joke," chuckled Danny Money, wondering when they were going to have any time to do a little police work. Between picking up laundry, dropping their cars off for a detailing, stopping for coffee, and figuring out where they could get a free dinner, there wasn't much time left to do any patrolling. It was still early, not yet six. The four to twelve shift was just beginning to heat up. The Bud Man's long night was just beginning to catch up with him. Money took over the wheel. The Bud Man drifted into never-never land. It was time for revenge, the chokin' chitlin variety of the savory dish.

Danny Money headed for the Northeast Farmer's Market. There he could find the means of his retribution. Making sure to radio for 151 to meet them at the busy wholesaler's market, he finalized his plan. He needed witnesses. E.P. and Spic N' Span would do just fine. The Bud Man was coppin' some serious z's, his mouth hanging wide open as he sucked in log sawing breaths of the scout car's warm heated air.

"What it is?" asked Emancipation Proclamation Jones, getting out of scout 151 and staring curiously at 150 pulled directly in front of an idling tractor trailer, its bright headlamps shining straight through 150's front windshield.

"I'm gonna take you to school, brother. Just watch and learn. You're about to see the Bud Man stain his drawers," answered Danny Money, wishing he had a camera to catch all the action. A camcorder would have even been better.

Walking back to 150, he quietly opened the driver's side door and sat down behind the wheel. He was careful not to disturb the Bud Man whose head had fallen off the seat back, laying at a forty five degree angle against the rolled up passenger side window.

"Look out!" screamed Danny Money, laying on the scout car's horn.

The Bud Man, opening his groggy eyes, looked out the front windshield at the glaring headlamps of the idling big rig. Seeing his life pass before him as the fatal collision with what he perceived to be a speeding truck seemed imminent, he threw open the passenger side door and dove head first into a crate full of stinking rotten tomatoes, put there by Money after careful consideration as to the Bud Man's point of impact with the pavement.

"Cowabunga, dude!" hollered Emancipation Proclamation Jones, running around the back of scout 150 to get a better look at the simmering Bud Man laying on the street, his upper torso covered with squishy rotten tomato juice. Even the usually somber Spic N' Span Spiegel couldn't contain himself. He chuckled at the embarrassed Bud Man, making sure to contain his laughter as much as possible. He knew the pain of being teased, humiliated, and made fun of. That was an intense personal suffering he didn't wish on anyone, least of all on one of his police comrades.

Danny Money had scored the big one. It was time to offer the peace pipe. The last thing he wanted was the Bud Man's powerfully muscled arms choking his white ass. Danny had a decent build. The Bud Man spent two hours a day pumpin' iron. He was beginning to look like the black version of Randy "Macho Man" Savage mixed with a little dash of the Ultimate Warrior, figured Money, bending down to offer the silent Bud Man a lift to his feet, uncertain as to the Bud Man's state of mind.

"You smart ass honky mother fucker. You finally did it, didn't you? Got even for those chitlins, huh? Well, my big black butt deserved it," chuckled the Bud Man, letting Money help him to his feet.

"Sheet, man. Your nigger ass smells like it ain't seen no water in a month," jived Emancipation Proclamation Jones, making a hasty exit stage right as the Bud Man took a menacing step in his direction.

Danny Money cleared the Fifth District and put 150 back in service. The Bud Man, having cleaned up and changed uniforms, suggested that they cruise on over to the alley rear of Orleans Place. All day he had had a creepy feeling tingling through his body. The nagging sensation wouldn't go away. He kept thinking about his kids. He knew they were safe at home with mama, but, an uneasiness had settled over him. He felt edgy, anxious, almost as if a heavy cloud of nervous energy had settled over his body. Somebody, or something, was trying to tell him something. He could sense it. The message wasn't loud, nor was it clear, but, it most certainly was ominous. He spotted a pay phone and instantly motioned for Danny Money to pull 150 to the curb. Reaching into his pocket, he pulled out a quarter and rushed to the telephone. He was scared. He had to make sure his family was safe. Something was wrong, very wrong.

Ronnie was on her own tonight. Mac wouldn't be back for a couple of days. There was no way that I.A.D. could find him at fault. Damn, every old clothes police officer knew better than to turn around with a gun in his hand. What choice had Mac had. Ronnie was afraid if it had been her, instead of Mac, she'd have probably shot, too. She banged the steering wheel with her fist, frustrated with her rollercoaster life. There were always so many lows and so few highs.

Last night she'd been high, proud of her performance at Danny's. She had felt it. She had seen it, lurking beneath the surface, ready to burst out of his sparkling blue eyes. He was hers. From now on things would be different. Only one of two things could happen now. It was inevitable. Either he would end the relationship or marry her. Rhonda Bell had no intention of being any man's skin toy shack job. She'd give him anything he wanted, anytime he wanted it, but ultimately, it would have to be with that little band of gold on her left hand. Rhonda Bell thought of the beautiful babies that they could make together. Then, she began to cry.

Pulling Cruiser 311 to the curb, she wept quietly. She hated it when her period was near. It made her feel so sensitive, so caught up in every little tragedy of life. Intimate little images of neighborhood girls skipping rope and laughing danced through her head. She had never been one of those happy little girls in their pretty pink lace dresses and black patent leather shoes. In fact none of her childhood friends had. In her mind the girls' faces were always white.

Rhonda Bell gripped the steering wheel tightly. She steadied herself. She had to keep the dream alive. One day her people's little girls would jump rope and giggle, too. Just a chance at an equal life, that's all they really wanted. Rhonda Bell, like the Bud Man, didn't know why she was daydreaming about kids. Suddenly, her mind focused on Darnell. She shuddered, the hair on the back of her neck tingling with an eerie crackle of static electricity. She had to find a phone and call her mother. She had to make sure Darnell was alright. Damn, that Capital Carver was making her nervous. At least the whole city wasn't caught up in the frenzy, not yet, sighed Ronnie, fearing that it wouldn't be long before they too would wonder where their kids were.

Ray Carver huddled in the back of his pick up, pulling the fluffy down-filled sleeping bag over his balding head. It was almost time. The cold grey dawn was only a couple of hours away. He had slept peacefully, undisturbed. He hadn't seen a soul back here, behind the abandoned warehouse. A couple of times he had noticed the circular arc of a search-light beam flicker across the sides of the crumbling brick building. He made sure nobody in a vehicle would be bothering him. He had strewn bags of garbage across the narrow pot-holed lane that led back to the rear parking lot. Nothing but a jacked up four wheel drive could negotiate those obstacles and he was sure there weren't too many of them in this nigger land. He had sealed off his lair like any predator worth his salt would have.

He reached into his knapsack and pulled out some beef jerky, a pack of saltine crackers, and a hard boiled pickled egg. Twisting the cap off his thermos, he poured himself a cup of luke warm black coffee. Everything was going better than he had expected. The porky little nigger kid had come home using the exact same path, alone. After this morning, his fat little feet would never leave their tracks on that trail again, laughed Ray Carver to himself. He figured, with this one, the Capital Carver would skyrocket to front page news. If the stupid cops ever knew how close they really were. The first time he had seen it in print he had panicked. It wasn't time yet. Then he had realized the absurdity of the title. It was poetic justice. Carver, the Capital Carver, chuckled Ray Carver. And the dumb bastards didn't even know that it was his name. He had to be charmed. When they found out, it would really frost their shriveled balls.

The nocturnal blanket of night covered the city in a cloak of eternal darkness. Distant stars twinkled dimly in the murky sky. Clouds, black as ebony, gathered on the far horizon, looking like rising plumes from a nuclear explosion. Overhead, the sky was crystal clear. The brisk numbing early morning air was still. The city lay swaddled in a frayed blanket of hushed silence. The streets were quiet. Everywhere, shadows danced under the glowing streetlights. A lucid amber phosphorescence vaguely illuminated the lion's den, Orleans Place.

Ray Carver moved through the shadows, invisible to the un-trained naked eye. Animals always stirred at the dawn's early light. He was no different. He crept through the alley and located the empty storage shed. Sniffing the air, he picked up the fresh scent of cigarette smoke, the odor of men's cologne, the aroma of coffee, and the distinct smell of urine. They had been here, waiting to trap him. No matter. After he bagged this one he'd be moving on to happier hunting grounds.

Once inside the empty shed he shrugged off the knapsack, emptying its contents on to the damp dirt floor. He crawled back outside, dragging the three steel jawed bear traps. Sitting, bent over behind the tangled row of overgrown hedges, he pried open the deadly traps, using his booted foot to force the steel jaws apart. He gently slid the springing mechanism into place and cau-tiously pushed each trap in front of the thick hedge row. Crawl-ing out into the dark alley, he gingerly covered the traps with thin broken branches and dead leaves. He pulled the traps' securing metal chains back through the hedges, towards the shed. Every-thing was almost ready. It wouldn't be long now.

The sun broke over the far horizon. The huge black thunder clouds almost immediately began to cover the dull grey sky, block-ing out the sun's filtering rays. It remained dark, stormy. Nature was brewing up a brutally cold tempest. Ray Carver could feel it in the moist air. By noon, Washington, D.C. would be covered in a foot of wet snow. By noon, he'd be less than two hours away from a shooter and a splash at the Oaktree Tavern.

Ray Carver listened as screen doors began to slam shut. He watched as billowing clouds of hot air poured out of chimneys. The cranking sound of car engines shattered the once silent morning. The shrill whine of sirens faded in the distance. The city was coming to life, while one of its innocent sons was about to be welcomed into the eternal clutches of death.

Ray Carson Carver peered out of the rusted doors of the bent and twisted metal shed. He stared, never moving, as groups of chattering school children took the alley shortcut to the grade school, passing less than twenty feet from his lurking body. He listened silently as they talked about maybe getting a half day off from school if the snow fell like their parents said it might. He remembered the days when he had walked three miles through blizzards to the one room school house, the only heat coming from a pot bellied stove sitting in the middle of the room. He had had a tough life, never getting past the sixth grade. That's when his old man had died, in a cave-in at the Simpson Collieries. Then, his childhood abruptly over, he had started working the non-union strip mines. Before long he was underground, swallowing the gritty dust.

Finally, it was quiet again. He kneeled, spitting a stream of tobacco juice on to the frozen ground. It was time. He crawled back out of the shed and laid the dime store red purse on top of the gnarled vines. He scattered some one dollar bills around the purse, securing them in the tangled branches. To get to the money and the purse the fat fuck would have to step in the leaves and spring one of the traps. Then, Fat Albert would be mincemeat, he figured, backing into the concealing shed. Money, fresh bloody meat, honey, animal urine, it didn't matter. Just matching the right bait to the right game was all that mattered. The rest was child's play.

Ray Carver snapped to attention. The unmistakable sound of a solitary set of footsteps shuffling against gravel echoed across the calm frigid air. The boy was coming, right on schedule. Ray Carver shook with anticipation. He was getting a mild attack of buck fever. He spit nervously, brown tobacco juice running down his chin. The kid was less than twenty feet down the alley. Ray Carver spit again. Now, it was time. One tiny mistake and the moment will have passed, the quarry will have escaped. He pushed on the squeaky shed doors. The high pitched screech attracted the youngster's attention. He looked over in the direction of the shed and saw the purse, surrounded by the scattered money. He stepped toward the purse, never looking at the ground, his eyes fixed on the enticing money.

Ray Carson Carver was nearly wetting his pants with nervous excitement. The anticipation was almost unbearable. He was in the zone, the killing zone. All his senses were on overload. Everything was so crystal clear. He heard the distinct rustling sound of dead leaves. Then the crisp snap of cold wood crackled in the still air. He swore he could hear the rushing metal jaws as they whistled through the air, tearing into the young boy's flesh and snapping his ankle like a piece of fragile peanut brittle.

Reaching outside the shed, Ray Carver grabbed the trap's long chain and pulled with all his might. The terrorized child fell backwards, cracking his ski cap clad head against the frozen ground. Gravel cut into his palms as he tried to break his fall. Tiny stones imbedded themselves into his hands as he backpedaled against the irresistible force that was pulling him through a narrow opening hacked out of the tangled growth less than four hours ago. He couldn't even scream. His head was spinning in torturous pain. His virtually severed ankle was a mangled piece of bloody gristle and bone. His desperate pleas for help died in his gasping throat.

Ray Carson Carver dragged the flailing boy inside the dark shed. The first blustery gusts of swirling wind began to howl. A heavy snow began to fall. He flashed a sinister smile at the groveling boy, circling his wounded prey like a stalking lion. The wide eyed child began to cry for his mother. As he unsheathed the hunting knife, Ray Carson Carver began to sing, "All dem tons. And what'd I git? Cept'n thirty years older. And, up to my ass in debt. The good lord better not call me. Cause I ain't a goin'. I owe my soul to the devil down below."

"Officer. Please help me. He's my only child. He's a good boy. He'd never miss school. He loves school. I just know something bad has happened to him. It's like this feeling has come over me. A feeling that I've lost a part of me. I'm scared. You'all have got to help me," pleaded the hysterical woman, tears welling out of her bloodshot eyes.

Danny Money turned towards the Bud Man. This was a grim task, a dreaded ordeal. The missing boy never showed up for school. The vice principal had tried to call the mother all day. Instead of talking, he was listening, listening to the same I'm sorry that number is no longer in service line from the same smartass sounding voice. Times were tough all over. The boy's mother couldn't pay the telephone bill. Now she sat at home on her day off, needlessly worrying about how she was ever going to scrape enough money together to get him out of this crack house infested ghetto before it swallowed him up and ruined his life forever.

Almost a foot of heavy wet snow covered the ground. The streets were a slushy mess of slippery melting ice. The whole city was staggering under the weight of nature's wrath. Hotels were booked solid. The commuters, unable to flee before the storm hit, crowded every bar and lounge. The ghetto, for the most part, remained the same. Nobody commuted anywhere. Even if they could, where would they go? The snooty, nose up in the air, bitches of the uppity suburban department stores sure weren't eagerly awaiting their shopping pleasure. Not too many of their license plate frames stated I'd rather be shopping at Sak's. So, the everyday life and death struggles of the inner city continued, rain, snow, or shine. Today, it would be a struggle of death.

"Look, ma'am. I understand. I've got three little ones of my own. We're gonna call for another car and start searchin' the area. We'll find your boy," stated the Bud Man, looking at Danny Money, afraid that they really might.

Emancipation Proclamation Jones and Spic N' Span Spiegel pulled in front of 623 Orleans Place, Scout 151 covered with a dirty brown combination of snow and ice. 10-33 Sam, monitoring the police radio from 5D, where he'd been trying unsuccessfully to telephone his cheating wife, decided to respond and set up a command post on the scene. An eight year old boy not at school or home by six o'clock in this weather was definitely a priority.

The Bud Man and Danny Money trudged down the steps, through the blanket of snow, and filled in Jones and Spiegel. There wasn't any other way. They'd have to go house to house, down the whole block, knocking on every door. The word would spread quickly. If he was here, on Orleans Place, somebody would know. Only one person would know where he was if he was dead, thought Danny Money, shivering at the prospect of finding him disemboweled, like the others. He decided to see if Cruiser 311 was on the air. Ronnie might like to get involved in this search.

Plowing through the wet snow, Emancipation Proclamation Jones and Spic N' Span Spiegel crossed the street, their knee high rubber boots sloshing through the melting mush. Even the usually exuberant Jones was somber and determined. He would know the joys and sorrows of raising a child real soon. The anticipated joy at finding the young boy alive and well was overshadowed by the thought of finding him dead or, maybe even worse, not finding him at all, lost forever like the thousands of poor souls that had vanished before him.

The Bud Man and Danny Money started down their side of the street carrying a picture of the young boy with his absent father, who had long since deserted him in the typical tragic ghetto saga of life without father. This was not a stroll down Main Street, U.S.A. The officers knew that behind every curtain and door on Orleans Place lay a surprise, not too many of which were of the pleasant variety.

Rhonda Bell, in Cruiser 311, was making her way to the scene of the search. The drive was agonizingly slow, the traffic snarled in a gigantic pile-up that looked like the first annual D.C. Demolition Derby. Even putting on the red lights and siren would be a waste. She'd be on a code one run that could end no other way than in a slippery slide to the police body shop. Mac would be back any day now. The I.A.D. investigation had exonerated his actions. Ronnie wondered who'd exonerate his mind.

Bow Wow Bowser had ridden her hard. He was going to assign four more detectives to the case. The natives were getting restless. He was getting sick. Ronnie swore she had seen him inhale an entire cigarette in one long sucking breath. The case was going smoothly. Smoothly for the murderer that is. Despite days and nights of knocking on doors they still didn't have a single witness to either murder. The rock and the branch, stuck in the victim's mouths, meant nothing. They were convinced the suspect was a snuff chewing white man. The 30.06 slugs matched. There weren't any fingerprints. So far his pattern of victims couldn't really be established even though his M.O. was the same. Ronnie knew that she had to keep plugging away. She wasn't so sure this one would slip up. Despite the opposite notion, some never did.

Ronnie looked down the long alley in the rear of Orleans Place. The clean fresh snow glistened and sparkled like a pure white sequined blanket. A huge round snowman with a toy gun in his hand was erected on the corner, guarding the alley's entrance. Even in this surreal snow covered environment everything, even the rotund snowman, seemed so sinister, reflected Ronnie, thinking about the Snowman who was trying to ruin her life. He was real. She was afraid that he'd never melt away and disappear like this one eventually would.

At least one car had managed to snow plow its way down the virtually unmarked alley, figured Ronnie, as her eyes followed the set of car tracks that eventually turned into an old dilapidated stone garage not far from where they had found Latisha's hanging body. She decided to park the unmarked cruiser and walk down the dark deserted alleyway. Slinging her purse over her shoulder, she stepped out of the police car into the deep snow, her brown leather riding boots barely keeping her legs dry. Rhonda Bell trudged down the packed snow tire-path, glancing down as a cold swirling gust of wind blew crystals of the powdery granules against her brown wool culotte skirt.

Passing the tree of death, as she now called it, she continued on. Whipping blasts of snow and ice stung her delicate face. Her wool knit scarf trailed out behind her in the relentless ferocious gusts. The portable police radio she carried was strangely silent. Any second now, she feared that it would crackle and fatefully announce that the boy had been found, found dead. Nobody had to tell Rhonda Bell what the boy looked like. She already knew what he'd look like. She didn't need a picture. She carried the image in her mind, an image of grisly sullen death already burned into her head by the previous two gruesome snapshots. A third, she feared, was about to brand itself into her brain.

The wind howled mercilessly. The snow began to harden into jagged crunchy pieces of ice. The temperature began to plummet, and still Rhonda Bell pressed on. She knew something only one other person knew. She knew that the boy was here, in the alley, a hollow empty gutted shell. Ronnie was going to find him and be strong. Inexplicably, she could sense it. The Carver had been here. His werewolf like spirit still lingered in the bone chilling cold. She swore she could almost hear his baleful wail echo in the whipping wind. It taunted her, leaving the fine hairs on the back of her neck tingling with a lurid sensation that made her skin crawl.

All this aside, Rhonda Bell knew that she was soon to face the dead boy's mother, helpless to do anything other than to say that she was sorry, sorry for the evil that still lurked in men's minds. It was her burden and she'd do it like only a mother could, with the pain of the ages resting on her shoulders.

Suddenly, a blast of wind pummeled the alley, snapping

branches like brittle toothpicks. Rhonda Bell put her hands in front of her face as garbage can lids, boxes, empty metal beer cans and twigs hurtled past her like a deadly load of canister. She turned her head down and away, looking at the swirling snow beneath her. First, the creaking sound of straining joints and there the clattering sound of crashing metal caused her to look off to her right just as a door flew off the hinges of an old rusted metal shed and then careened wildly into the desolate blackness. Rhonda Bell was inexplicably drawn towards this tottering shed. She reached her gloved hand into her purse, drawing out a mini mag flashlight. Shining its beam across the blindingly white crystallized snow, she kicked a path through the crusty ice.

Despite the frigid wind Ronnie felt a trickle of perspiration drip down between her ripe full breasts. The smooth skin of her back broke out in a cold sweat. Her knees felt weak. Trembling, she pushed aside the snow covered tangle of branches which concealed the creaking shed. She slipped, trying to inch her way up the icy frozen slope. Finally, grabbing the remaining door of the shed, she steadied herself. And then, bending over, she took a deep breath and entered its belly, the belly of the beast, the vault of terror.

The boy lay peacefully on his back, in his impromptu tomb. Ronnie gazed sadly upon his wide open frightened eyes, determined not to flinch. Every observation she could make was vitally important. Here, in this chamber of horrors, she wasn't a woman. She could only be a police officer. Staring at his throat, she grimaced. The skin was split in a gaping ear to ear laceration. The folds of hardened bloody flesh lay open, curling at the ends. Ronnie looked back up at his angelic face and suddenly gasped in terror.

The image of Darnell was staring up at her through those same frozen eyes. Shaking her head, she tried to calm herself. She had work to do. The only way her Darnell would be safe was for her to catch this monster. She had missed it at first glance. But now, looking again, she spotted the dark lump stuffed in the boy's open mouth. She bent over and gingerly touched the black flaky object. Without ever having used the brittle fuel, she distinctly knew that she was fingering a lump of coal. Why, wondered Rhonda Bell? What does it mean, a rock, a branch, and a chunk of coal? What was he trying to tell them? She forced herself to look back down at the lifeless young body.

The boy's stomach was laid open, the gash cut from his pelvis to the top of his sternum. There, next to him, lay what had made him a human being, his insides, the precious irreplaceable organs of life. Rhonda Bell was not prepared for what she saw next. It shocked her to the very core of her soul. Never had she seen anything so vile, so ungodly. There, in front of her very eyes lay the work of a disciple of the devil. Satanism was alive and well. The sprung jaws of the trap still clasped the boy's mangled ankle in a grip of deadly steel. He had been hunted and trapped like an animal, senselessly slaughtered for somebody's idea of sport.

Rhonda Bell seethed with rage. Her people didn't deserve this, nobody's people deserved this. It was at this moment that Rhonda Bell decided, with God's help, that this butcher, this so called Capital Carver, would never make it to court. If she had anything to say about it his judge, jury, and executioner would be a black woman, born and nurtured in the city he was trying to destroy. Rhonda Bell swore that she would catch this insane murderer and even more than that, she swore that when she did, she would kill him.

Danny Money, the Bud Man, Emancipation Proclamation Jones, Spic N' Span Spiegel and 10-33 Sam all hurried down the alley, alerted to the boy's dreadful fate by Ronnie, over the police radio. It would be almost an hour before the Mobile Crime Lab could get to the scene. Being 150's beat, the Bud Man and Money roped off the alley with yellow plastic tape. It would be up to them to file the P.D. 251 criminal report, just like in the case of the other two victims. The patrol car whose beat the crime or incident occurred in was the unit that was responsible for filing the initial report. If the car was out of service the duty fell to the next closest available unit. In this case, Danny Money, would just as soon have been out of service.

It never occurred to anybody, other than Spic N' Span Spiegel, that there might be other traps set in the area. When he made this announcement Emancipation Proclamation Jones did his best impression of M.C. Hammer and danced back down the alley, following the same footprints that had got him there to begin with. Money and the Bud Man joined Ronnie by the shed. Danny saw the glassy line of dried tears that had run down her cheeks. He didn't care what anybody thought anymore. He reached into the pocket of his dark blue uniform nylon jacket and pulled out a handkerchief. Gently, he dabbed Ronnie's tears away and put his other arm around her shoulders to try and steady her trembling body. Despite his revulsion at the sight of the heinous murder, the Bud Man forced a little grin. The white boy was doin' good. Money was growin' up, thought the Bud Man, making a mental note to have the Bud Lady invite them over for dinner. He had long since given up looking at the attractive homicide detective for anything other than what she was, his partner's main squeeze.

"Damn. Look at this will you," hollered the Mobile Crime Lab officer, sweeping off the snow from in front of the hedges. "He's got two more traps laid here. Shit, this fucker's a real lunatic."

The Mobile Crime Lab officer took the broom and dusted the snow from the tangled vines. "Jesus Christ, Ronnie. Scope this out. This is what he must have used to bait the kid. A Goddamned red purse with some dollars scattered around. This is one sick asshole," added the officer, shaking his head in dismay.

"The snow must have kept some of the money from blowin away," stated 10-33 Sam, squinting as the bright beams from the scout car spotlights scoured the scene.

"How long do you think he's been dead?" asked Ronnie, following the Assistant Medical Examiner towards the morgue wagon. "Look here, baby. I'm just a pick up boy. The man don't rely on me for jack shit. But me, I've bagged plenty of 'em in my day. And I'd say that this young brother bought it early this morning. He's stiff as a board," volunteered the assistant, pulling out the collapsible stretcher from in back of the wagon.

Rhonda Bell walked back towards Cruiser 311, kicking chunks of loose snow as she went. She could use a long hot bubble bath. That was the one time that she could think about things, re-orient herself, find answers. Then she could feel like a woman again. For a few brief moments she could leave the harsh realities of the callous violent world that she both lived and worked in. Tonight, maybe she could walk barefoot in the warm sands of Tahiti.

"You OK?" asked Danny Money, trying to catch up with Ronnie.

"Yeah. I'm OK. Why wouldn't I be? It's just a job. We're not supposed to get involved. It just happens to them. Not us. None of our kids are ever murdered. None of our husbands or wives are ever butchered by these wierdos. We just say 'I'm sorry ma'am. But some freaked out asshole just caught your kid in a trap. Like an animal. Then he sliced his throat and hacked out his guts. You're OK, aren't you?" answered Ronnie sarcastically, her hands buried in her coat pockets.

"Hey. It's me. I care. You know I do. Damn. Don't shut me out. I wanna help you. I wanna be part of you," stated Danny Money, catching up to Ronnie.

"I'm sorry, Danny. It's just that when I looked at that poor child I saw Darnell laying there. He's the only thing that kept me going until you came into my life. Now, I worry about you both. And then there's Mac. He's started drinking again. I called his house today and he was drunk. Now, I'm up to worrying about three men. I don't even have time to worry about myself, not with all of you to try and look after," said Ronnie, reaching for the door handle of the parked cruiser.

"Just remember. Us poor pathetic slobs all worry about you, too. Worry is something that people who care about each other just trade back and forth. Right now, I'm just worried that you won't want to see me tonight, after check off," stated Danny, shuffling his feet in the snow and trying to put on his best teddy bear face.

"Alright. You win. You'll have to come over to my apartment, though. I'll pick up Darnell and see you there," giggled Ronnie, glad that Danny had asked to see her. Right now, she needed to feel wanted.

Ray Carson Carver, getting comfortable with his new nickname, the Capital Carver, pulled his four wheel drive pick up into the snow covered parking lot of the Oaktree Tavern. He needed a little touch. It was time to celebrate. Now, he could officially close coon season and get ready for the next opening day. The albinos were next. He could find plenty of them grazing the lush fields of Georgetown. This time, though, he'd move things along a little. He was makin' the rules, anyway.

He'd put a limit on the albinos, a limit of three. That way he could bag his limit the first day out and go after some fresh game, open a new season. He liked the idea of offing a buck, a doe, and a fawn. That just made good sense. Ray Carver decided that this was one homespun fish and game regulation that he was going to follow religiously.

"Pour me a double," shouted Ray Carver at the owner, Hank Edwards, as he pushed open the door to the tavern and stomped his feet to clean off the snow. He walked over to the woodburning stove and rubbed his rough calloused hands together. It was only a little past ten. This afternoon, coming home, he had made good time, despite the bad weather. Now, he could hole up in familiar terrain and get ready for the next hunt. Most predators only hunted when they were hungry. They killed only what they could eat. Ray Carver's appetite was voracious, insatiable.

"It's cold out there. Hey?" asked Hank Edwards, wiping off a double shot glass.

"Colder than a witch's tit. I could really use me a double header. What you been up to today?" questioned Ray Carver, downing the burning whiskey in one long gulp.

"Not much, Ray. Same old shit. Tryin' to git ahead. But, always endin' up suckin' hind tit," answered Hank Edwards, glancing down the bar at retired railroad man Tony Manola.

Getting the hint, Ray Carver said loudly, "Get ol' Tony whatever he wants. It's on me. You know those retired railroaders. They're useless as tits on a bore pig."

"Thanks Ray. What's the occasion?" asked Tony Manola, raising his glass of Black Velvet.

"Did me a little coon huntin' early this morning. Got me a nice big fat young'un, I did," answered Ray Carver, ordering another double. Maybe later tonight he'd get himself a little piece of poontang. Speakin' of young'uns, his daughter should be sashaying her tight little ass home pretty soon. If he could get rid of the old sow, he'd tap that young child. She was just beggin for it. He'd give her a good old fashioned pants down whuppin'. She needed to be taught a lesson. He'd bring her high and mighty ass back down to earth real quick. She'd been sassin' him lately. Anyway, somebody had to bust that cherry. Might as well keep it all in the family, chuckled Ray Carver to himself. Bellying up to the bar, he downed his second double in one swig, some of the amber liquid dribbling down the corners of his sinister mouth.

Hank Edwards, his back to the bar, glanced at Ray Carver's reflection in the mirror tiles behind the shelves of liquor. Startled, he gasped, dropping an empty beer glass to the filthy linoleum floor.

"Jesus H. Christ," mumbled Hank Edwards, his trembling hand reaching for a bottle of Jack Daniels. If he didn't know better he'd swear that the reflection of Ray Carver's face had looked like a lion's head, blood dripping down from the corners of its diabolical lips.

CHAPTER 11

DANNY MONEY was as nervous as he'd ever been. He was shaking like a leaf. How the hell had he let Ronnie talk him into doing this? Looking over at her beaming face, her ruby red lips curled up into the cutest smile he had ever seen, suddenly, he knew how. She had sucked him in with the same dirty tactics that every woman on the face of the earth had been using since the days of Adam and Eve. She had purred like the proverbial kitten, running her hands through his hair, nibbling at his ear, slipping her leg around his, casually brushing her seductive breasts against his chest and all the time whispering those sweet little nothings that always meant a big pain in the ass something. He had let her impish feminine wiles disarm his usually practical self. Damn it, no matter how resolute he tried to be she could always break him down. She had managed to get him to beg her to let him make love to her and then she had still gotten her way.

Well, here he was, riding into Southeast Washington, into his own personal armageddon, a victim of his uncontrollable lust. He had won one little concession. Tonight, as payment for his services, Ronnie had promised to wear her most erotic lingerie and let him handcuff her to his bed. That had put such a lump in his throat that he would have done anything she asked. Jesus, just sitting in his BMW waiting for the light to change, he was getting hard. He knew what outfit she'd wear. She looked awesome in that sleazy French cut red and black lace teddy with the black fishnets and garter belt. Once she put her red spiked heels on she was actually taller than him. As reluctant as Danny Money was to face the looming disaster, he was shaking in anticipation of the frenzied sexual pay off that awaited him.

Sensing Danny's state of arousal, Ronnie casually put her hand on his thigh, pretending not to notice his lustful gaze. Danny pulled away from the light and cast a quick glance in her direction. He had to admit she was a stunner. She looked as feminine and alluring in the black and white checked double breasted herringbone suit she had on now as she did in her lingerie. He reached over to caress her smooth silky knee. Jesus, she had him going again.

"Danny, honey. Don't you think you should keep both hands on the wheel? We wouldn't want officer friendly to end up wrapped around a telephone pole. Now, would we?" purred Ronnie as she gently worked her fingers around Danny's rock hard shaft and teasingly began to lower his zipper. Finally, she slowly pulled the engorged penis out of his pants and wrapped her milk chocolate colored hand around his white throbbing member. Bending over, she kissed its pulsating head and then abruptly tucked it back in his pants. "We'll just save this for later," she chuckled, zipping up Danny's fly. "By the way, baby. I thought we talked about this before. The Fine Young Cannibals just ain't happenin', hon. Get with the program," kidded Ronnie, removing the annoying tape from Danny's cassette player and slipping in one of her own, her very favorite.

Despite her joking and teasing, Rhonda Bell had never been happier with Danny. She was proud of him. He was showing some concern for the community. He was getting involved. Deep down inside she knew that he would have done this whether she had promised him her body or not. It had just become kind of a game. Besides, she was getting wet herself, just thinking about laying there helpless, handcuffed to Danny's bed. It was turning her on as much as it was him. Tonight, she knew that Danny would stroke and lick her to an orgasmic vacation wherever she wanted to go. Unconsciously, she wriggled in the BMW's soft tan leather seat. Good God, she was both horny and soaked.

"Well. We're here," stated Danny, pulling into the crowded parking lot, still a little unsure of himself.

Ronnie pulled down the BMW's visor and checked her lipstick and makeup in the lighted mirror. This was a big day for her. And, if everything just went OK, it could be an even bigger day for Darnell. Stepping out of the convertible, Danny adjusted his black leather Sam Brown belt, its shiny brass buckle sparkling in the late afternoon sun. At Ronnie's insistence Danny had Brasso'd, shoe polished, spit-shined, brushed and pressed every inch of his uniform and equipment. He had even broken down and cleaned his gun. Securing his shiny black billed uniform cap, he started down the sidewalk determined not to let Darnell, or any of his fourth grade class, know how nervous he really was. Speaking to a bunch of kids about the horrors of drug abuse, on Parents and Teachers Day, was enough to make anyone squirm.

Never again, not even for the pleasure of Ronnie's kinky fun and games, was he going to let her talk him into such craziness.

Watching Ronnie sit down beside Darnell, in the audience, and subtly cross her legs, Danny knew that he was dead meat. She could talk him into just about anything she wanted. The twinkle of glee in Darnell's excited eyes sealed his fate. Damn, loving someone could make you do such simple-ass things, thought Danny Money, as he was introduced by the principal and walked to the podium. Looking out over the appreciative all black audience, his eyes rested on Ronnie and Darnell. They were both glowing with pride, proud that he was a police officer serving their city, proud that he was here to try and make a difference, but moreover, proud that he was theirs.

After it was over, Ronnie hugged him and kissed his cheek in front of the whole gathering. Danny Money glanced over her shoulder at the milling crowd. Most were standing and nodding their heads in apparent approval of his obvious personal involvement. Screw it, he figured as he took Ronnie in his arms and kissed her deeply. Then, placing Darnell's tiny hand in his, he thanked the principal and walked his woman and her son out to his shiny BMW. Pride was a two way street, not to be walked alone, thought Danny Money, gazing at a starry eyed Ronnie.

Rhonda Renee Bell had never been happier. Another hurdle had been crossed. One step at a time, she figured, not wanting to ask too much of Danny. Danny started up the car. The tape came to life, its crisp harmonies gently fluttering like a warm summer breeze. Ronnie listened intently as Norman Connors and Eleanor Mills gracefully, but powerfully, sang their beautiful rendition of "You Make Me Feel Brand New." Without a doubt, Rhonda Bell's favorite tape was Norman Connor's "This Is Your Life," and hers wasn't beginning to look half bad, thought Ronnie joyously, as she gazed back at her infatuated lover.

Briefcase Betty Barnes rolled over in bed and looked at her buzzing alarm clock radio. Reaching over to punch the sleep button, she wiggled back under the billowy down comforter, pulling it over her head. Then, true to her nature, she threw back the covers and got out of her cozy bed. Her toasty warm feet recoiled in shock when she planted them on the cold hardwood floor. When it was time to get up you got up, reasoned Briefcase Betty, slipping her suddenly freezing feet into a puffy pair of lop eared bunny rabbit slippers.

She shuffled across the bedroom floor, grabbed her full length pink terrycloth robe and slid it over her flannel pajamas. One day soon, if everything went as planned, she intended to heave the bunny rabbit slippers and flannel PJ's out the window of her second floor apartment. She eagerly anticipated replacing them with an assortment of sexy lingerie and a pair of those, oh so elegantly sensual, frilly feathered high heeled evening slippers.

You didn't need trap door flannels when you had a man in your bed to keep you warm, thought Briefcase Betty, fully intending to allow Spic N' Span Spiegel that previously unawarded privilege soon, very soon. But, for now, he'd still have to settle for the occasional heavy petting sessions which she enthusiastically initiated and reluctantly withdrew from when they reached their inevitable point of no return. Betty Barnes was almost at her own point of no return. She desperately longed to have a man inside her. No matter if she'd like it or not, she had to know what it felt like to be a woman. And, until she had taken a man, she still considered herself less than the proverbial whole.

The throaty guttural roar of the motorcycle echoed off the brown block walls of the Second District police officer's parking lot. Wisps of hot exhaust spewed out of the tailpipes of its alternately revving and idling engine as the driver methodically backed it into the space designated for motorcycles only. Several passing officers heading into the station house commended the lone motorcyclist on his extraordinary fortitude. The temperature, at three p.m. on this bleak afternoon, was hovering around thirty degrees.

Briefcase Betty, stepping out of her white Honda Civic, glanced over at the dismounting officer. This jerk was just too much, she figured, staring in disbelief at Rambo Roddy, whose helmet clad head immediately turned to follow the derriere of a uniform policewoman who had just sauntered past his leering eyes. She couldn't believe that some asshole would ride a motorcycle to work in this weather. But, Rambo Roddy was not just some asshole, reflected Betty Barnes. He was the ultimate asshole.

Strutting like a peacock with its full plume, Rambo Roddy, dressed in a red, white, and black leather riding outfit which perfectly matched his tri-colored motorcycle, headed for the rear door of the Second District. Briefcase Betty couldn't help but think that the Rod looked like a dismounted ninja warrior, ready for battle. She'd love to walk up to his silly looking motorcycle and kick it over. That would really frost his balls, she chuckled, immediately concluding that she'd like to kick them, too, if she ever had the chance.

Rambo Roddy was in a foul mood, his girlfriend of the past three months having thrown him out of her Fairfax, Virginia condo after he had called her thirteen year old daughter a slut. Well, so what, figured Rambo Roddy, slamming shut the rear glass doors of 2D. Thirteen to thirty, it didn't matter. They were all sluts. It was just his miserable luck to get stuck sittin' next to one eight hours a day. She was totally useless. Her, he couldn't even fuck.

"We shouldn't be over here, Roddy. It's way too far out of our beat. If an official sees us, you know he'll write us up," remarked Briefcase Betty as Rambo Roddy double parked Scout 80 and turned on the emergency flashers.

"Fuck them whiteshirts. And fuck you, too. I'm going in here for a few minutes. You just sit there and shut up. Why don't you play with yourself or something? I'd tell you to file your nails. But, you ain't got any of them, either," laughed Rambo Roddy, looking back as he climbed up the stairs to the entrance of the elegant brick building on Massachusetts Avenue, Northwest. One of his buddies had told him that, during happy hour, this was the hottest meat market in D.C. There was no way he was ironin' his own shirts. So, the answer was simple. All he had to do was find another stupid bimbo to do it for him.

This was definitely a target rich environment, figured Rambo Roddy as he forced his way to the bar, making sure to brush up against as many sets of bodacious ta-tas as he could without any of the fine young ladies filing assault charges against him. Finally, wedging his uniformed body between two luscious blondes sitting at the bar, Rambo Roddy decided that it was time to make his move. He opted for the one on his right. She looked just young enough to appreciate a good cock, but old enough to know how to use it. Besides, her tits were bigger, figured Rambo Roddy, deciding that that was always the ultimate criteria anyway. If it wasn't, why were they all trying to make theirs so much larger? It didn't matter how they got that way, just so they did, he decided, turning around to face the buxom blonde. This one looked like she was ready for the big leagues. He'd use his best line on her. It never failed to get him in their horny little snatches.

"Excuse me miss. Let me dust off your seat for you," stated Rambo Roddy, a mischievous smile on his face as he pretended to dust off the area around his mouth.

The young blonde, having recently divorced a lower than

snakeshit two timing D.C. cop, didn't have any desire to meet another one. In fact, she thought, this one reminded her of that cheatin' son of a bitch that she'd just got rid of. Unfortunately for Rambo Roddy she was drinking a steaming hot Irish Coffee topped with melting globs of whipped cream.

Briefcase Betty looked in her outside passenger mirror. Rush hour traffic was beginning to back up behind the illegally double parked police car, creating a tangled mess for the frustrated commuters. She decided that she better move the car around the corner, out of traffic. Waving her hand at the commuters in an apologetic gesture she ran around the back of the idling patrol car and pulled it around the corner, on to 22nd Street, and then turned into a neatly paved alley. Rambo Roddy would find her sooner or later. Later, was her best hope. She glanced in the rearview mirror. Damn, she knew they should've stayed in their own beat. Cruiser 208 was nosing around the corner right behind her. Now, they'd be getting a counseling session and signing a P.D. 750 dereliction report. She'd never had a black mark on her record.

Lieutenant Harold Bloomington was not very happy about sitting in a traffic jam on Massachusetts Avenue because some asshole was double parked. He hadn't written a traffic violation in the last six years. That was the job of the patrol officers, not the officials. But, in this case he just might make an exception. Then, he had to find out that the double parked asshole was one of his own. Jesus Christ, it was Scout 80, ten blocks out of their beat, observed the enraged lieutenant. He thought Barnes should know better. She'd been around long enough. Well, he couldn't let this shit slide. He'd have to write her up. He motioned for her to walk back to his cruiser.

"Officer Barnes. What the hell are you doing way over here? Are you on a radio run?" asked the infuriated lieutenant.

"No excuse, sir. We're not on a radio run. We shouldn't be over here," answered Briefcase Betty, cringing at the thought of receiving her first P.D. 750.

"What do you mean, we? Is Roddy with you today?" questioned Lieutenant Bloomington, not harboring a whole lot of good will towards Briefcase Betty's cocky partner.

"Yes sir. He went inside the bar to get us a cup of coffee," lied Briefcase Betty, trying to protect Rambo Roddy's behind even though she detested him. Some unwritten codes in the police department were thicker than blood. CYPA, covering your partner's ass, was definitely one such unwritten code.

Lieutenant Bloomington replied, "Yeah, right. I'll bet he did. Pretty expensive coffee isn't it? Knowing Roddy, he's probably gettin a freebie, anyway. If it ain't a police gratuity, or doesn't give a police discount, he ain't buyin' it."

Briefcase Betty smiled politely. Then, looking back down the alley towards 22nd Street, she gasped. Rambo Roddy rounded the corner, the crotch of his dark blue uniform pants smeared with a load of white foam that looked like a premature ejaculation from the Jolly Green Giant.

"What happened to you?" asked Briefcase Betty, unable to contain her laughter at the sight of Rambo Roddy's wet cream stained pants.

"I spilled my coffee," lied Rambo Roddy, looking back over his shoulder to make sure the crazy bitch hadn't followed him out of the bar. Her girlfriend, the other blonde, had added her Pina Colada to his now soaked drawers. Goddammit, he was seething. If it wasn't for Lieutenant Bloomington he'd go back in there and bust her jaw. He'd hurt that worthless cunt. If he couldn't get her, he'd find somebody he could fix up real good, real soon.

"We were lucky to get out of that without a 750," remarked Briefcase Betty as Rambo Roddy sat back down in Scout 80, having just finished putting on a clean pair of uniform pants in the Second District men's locker room.

"Lucky, my ass. That chickenshit bastard, Bloomington, knows better than to screw with me. If he did, he knows I'd fix his wagon, good," angrily answered Rambo Roddy, squealing Scout 80's radial tires as he sped out of the 2D parking lot.

Briefcase Betty figured different. She figured Lieutenant Bloomington, after talking to the irate blonde in the bar, had decided that Rambo Roddy had been punished more effectively than any dereliction notice that he could have ever issued. The whole bar full of people had quietly chuckled at the retreating officer's cream covered pants. Nothing could ever top that, thought Briefcase Betty, wishing she could have been there to see the whole thing. Briefcase Betty Barnes was wrong, very wrong. Very soon, something was going to top Rambo Roddy's recent demise, something that would haunt the cruel officer until the day he died. The beauty of it was that Briefcase Betty would indeed be there to witness the whole sordid affair. Rambo Roddy's day of reckoning was close at hand.

It was dark, awfully dark, when Briefcase Betty answered the radio. For the first time in weeks she was 10-4ing something other than the usual routine assortment of complaints, larceny runs, stolen auto reports, and the occasional disorderly call. Unlike the Fifth District war zone, nothing very exciting ever happened in their little Second District world of the realized American dream. Except for traffic stops, she hadn't even turned Scout 80's red lights and siren on in over two weeks. Now, she was recording the address of a sound of gunshots call on Reservoir Road.

Up here, in the land of milk and honey, this was a code one radio run, red lights and siren all the way. Briefcase Betty realized in the areas where Danny and his nice partner, the one they called the Bud Man worked, these kinds of radio assignments weren't even a priority. Gun shots in the ghetto were a fact of life, a fact not lost on her worried mind as she thought of the endless dangers that her baby, Stanley Spiegel, and his crazy partner, Emancipation Proclamation Jones, confronted everyday.

Anyway, here she was, blasting down Wisconsin Avenue with the freezing wind whipping through the scout car's open windows. The shrill siren yelped its desperate cry, warning cars to pull over, out of the path of the speeding police car. The reflections of the mirrored visibar lights flashed relentlessly off the quaint row houses, painting them momentarily in brilliant red, then passing by in flickering review.

Briefcase Betty Barnes was inwardly excited. But, true to her unflappable character, she remained outwardly calm. Rambo Roddy, behind the wheel, bitching and cussing at every motorist that slowed his break-neck speed as he responded to the emergency call, was unable to contain himself, virtually drooling at the possibility of cappin' a rod- totin' desperado. He skidded Scout 80 west, on to Reservoir Road, and grabbed the inside handle of the patrol car's searchlight with his left hand. Briefcase Betty reached down and flipped off the red lights and siren, carefully surveying the surrounding darkness. Rambo Roddy slammed on the brakes, Scout 80 sliding sideways across the quiet residential street.

"There's the son of a bitch. Right there. I'll nail his black ass, now. Jesus. Can you believe the nerve of this trash? Hangin' out up here. He should've stayed in northeast. Over where that wimpy dork faced nerd of yours works. His kind belong there. His nigger ass is gonna be sorry it ever show'd up here," coldly stated Rambo

Roddy, shining the spotlight on the cowering man and pulling out his nine millimeter.

Not so sure that this poor old man was guilty of doing anything other than walking down a public sidewalk pushing a grocery cart filled with all his worldly possessions, Briefcase Betty sternly remarked, "Roddy. Don't you screw with that old man. All he's probably trying to do is get out of the city before somebody slits his throat. I'll bet he's headed over to the canal. I've seen other homeless people over in the canal area."

"Shut up, bitch. The only way this nasty shit stained mother fucker is gonna get in the canal is when he's floatin' face down in it," angrily replied Rambo Roddy slapping his nightstick in the palm of his hand as he walked briskly towards the slowly retreating man.

"Where you think you're goin, Tyrone? Your black ass lost? Maybe you need some directions, boy. I'm gonna take you to school. Get your hands over your head. And spread em, brother. Now!" ordered Rambo Roddy, pushing the shaking black man against a nearby tree.

"Man. What you be messin with me for? I ain't done nothin'. I be mindin' my own business. Please, officer. Just leave me alone. I don't want no trouble. Look here. I respects the law," nervously stated the spread-eagled black man, turning his head over his shoulder and appealing in vain to the pushy officer.

"We got us a call that there was some shootin' goin down up here. You're beginnin' to look like our only suspect. I don't suppose you got any I.D. on you. Now do you? Your shit's a little flaky, bro. It's in the wind. So to speak," remarked Rambo Roddy, patting down the innocent old man.

Briefcase Betty Barnes walked over to join Rambo Roddy, slipping the portable police radio into her rear pants pocket.

"Look here, miss. I ain't done nothin'. Can't you all just leaves me be? I just wanna go on down to the canal and bed down. Then, in the mornin', I be movin' on. Outta your area," pleaded the worried old man.

"He doesn't have a gun. Does he, Dave? Why don't we just let him go about his business? He's not botherin' anybody," remarked Briefcase Betty, watching as Rambo Roddy sauntered over to the man's heavily loaded shopping cart.

"We don't know if he's got a gun, babe. We ain't searched this worthless pile of shit. I'd say we got us enough probable cause to do us a good thorough search," evilly laughed Rambo

Roddy, raising his black paratrooper boot and slamming it into the homeless man's shopping cart.

Briefcase Betty winced. The teetering cart careened over and crashed into the ground, its contents now strewn across the suddenly littered landscape. Glancing at the horrified man, Briefcase Betty could see the humiliation and pain in his soft brown eyes.

"Whatcha do that for, man? Them's my things. They be all I gots in this world," asked the confused old man, stepping towards Rambo Roddy.

Rambo Roddy grinned smugly. Then, without hesitation, he raised his nightstick and mercilessly cracked it against the side of the pleading man's face. Briefcase Betty watched in horror as the reeling old man staggered backwards, clutching at his bleeding head. Rambo Roddy could almost smell the blood. His eyes glazed over in a look of frenzied savagery. Wielding his nightstick like a bad impression of a bat swinging baseball player, he clubbed the tottering man repeatedly. Unable to fend off the painful blows, the old man collapsed to his knees. Incensed to even greater heights of violence at the sight of the old man's groveling, Rambo Roddy kicked the frail skinny man in the chest and knocked his upper torso sharply back. In excruciating pain, the old man collapsed to the sidewalk.

Briefcase Betty couldn't stand it any longer. She charged Rambo Roddy, bracing herself for the imminent collision. She hurled her small thin body against Rambo Roddy's stout frame, catching the brutal officer totally off guard. Slamming into him with a vicious body block, she tumbled to the cold hard ground. Stunned, Rambo Roddy tried to regain his balance, see-sawing back and forth as he flailed his arms in the crisp night air. Finally, he tripped on the edge of the sidewalk, his body thudding against a thick tree.

"That's enough. You son of a bitch," yelled Briefcase Betty, getting up on one knee, the thin blue lines of her pulsating veins bulging out of the smooth pale skin of her exposed neck.

Rambo Roddy, the palm of his left hand bleeding from the skin ripping collision with the rough bark of the huge tree, looked over at Briefcase Betty's trembling body. The bitch was scared, figured the amused officer, deciding that his career wasn't worth the pleasure of what he'd like to do to her ass licking dog face.

"I'm calling for an official. I've had it with your racist brutality. I'm going to file a report against you," stated Briefcase Betty, her voice cracking with emotion.

"A report for what? Pops, here, ain't gonna say nothin'. Are you pops? Cause if you do, I'll find your stinkin' skid row ass and fix it for good. You get my drift? You old piece of shit?" responded Rambo Roddy, staring at the cowering old homeless wino, a vicious smile plastered across his evil face.

"I don't want no trouble. I be on my way now," answered the unsteady old man, pressing a ripped and torn dirty stained undershirt against his bleeding head.

"Nice shirt. Too bad it had to get all messed up," laughed Rambo Roddy. "That's a nasty fall you took. Better watch those cracks in the sidewalk. Hey, Pops. Maybe you could sue this nigger lovin' city. It just might be their fault that you fell and hit your head. Yeah. That's the ticket. Maybe you could move up here with the white folk. I'm sure they'd just love to have an alley nigger livin' next to 'em," snickered Rambo Roddy, walking back towards Scout 80.

"I'd like to call an ambulance to come and help you. It's for free you know. They'll even take you to the hospital if you want. Please let me call an ambulance for you," pleaded Briefcase Betty, pulling the portable radio out of her rear pants pocket.

"No ambulance. No way. I told you I don't want no trouble. I just fell down and hit my head. I'm just an old drunk. Wants to be left in peace. That there officer. He kill me if it be any other way. I be movin' on soon as I gathers my things," answered the old man emphatically.

Briefcase Betty looked over at the stumbling pathetic old man, knowing in her heart that Rambo Roddy had won. What could she say? The wino would swear that he'd fallen, probably adding that the nice officer had even helped him up. Rambo Roddy would support the old man's story. And she'd look like the most vile piece of crap on the face of the earth, a liberal wave-making female cop who was trying to unjustly snitch on her poor innocent male partner.

Then, there'd be the cracks about her problem. All the other officers and maybe even some of the officials would no doubt conclude that all she needed was a good hard cock. Most, being divorced, would see her as another cold hearted, man hating, conniving bitch, trying to get even with everyman just because one had probably screwed her over. Life, being a woman, was tough. Life, being a woman cop, was sometimes impossible, sighed Briefcase Betty, turning her head over her shoulder as she walked towards the patrol car. Looking back, she watched the old man, down on his hands and knees, trying to salvage whatever he could of the spilled and broken pieces of his tragic dismal life. She sat down in the scout car, her arms crossed in frustration, hoping that she could do likewise with her's.

Ray Carson Carver chuckled to himself. That had been one amusing scene, the white officer trying to cave in the old darkie's head. That female cop, she was a righteous whore. She probably wished that she had a dick, figured Ray Carver, peering through the hedgerow of neatly trimmed evergreens as the patrol car's red taillights disappeared down the dark residential street. He was sorely tempted to finish the job and take out the old wino, just for kicks. In fact, what the hell, figured Ray Carver. He might as well. Rules were made to be broken and besides, they were his rules anyway. The old wino would be a good tune-up for tonight's real game.

It had taken the cops less than seven minutes to get here once he had fired the .357 magnum into the air. He had hoped that these puky la de da faggots that lived up here would call the police. They hadn't disappointed him. Now, he had a rough idea of how long he had if he had to use his revolver to wax their uppity white asses. He'd prefer not to. He had his own first choice of weapon laying on the floor of his parked truck. The old bum had been a lucky break. Ray Carver felt charmed. Too bad the sorry old bastard hadn't decided to go to the hospital like that female cop had suggested. No matter, because now he'd be going to the morgue, courtesy of the Capital Carver, grimly laughed Ray Carson Carver as he reached for the handle of his stainless steel hunting knife.

"Let's check it out. It'll only take a minute," stated Ronnie, turning Cruiser 311 into the pitch black alley, the audible burglar alarm ringing in the crystal clear frosty night. Mac didn't care what they checked out. All he wanted was another hit off the plastic flask full of scotch that he kept in the inside pocket of his blue sportcoat.

In his mind, he was still sitting in front of the three wisemen. The whiteshirted Police Trial Board officials' who virtually held his already ruined life in their hands' were reading. Mac was crying.

"We find the shooting and consequent death of Tactical officer Jeremy Walters by Detective Michael McCarthy justifiable. This board further finds that Detective Michael McCarthy acted within the guidelines of proper police procedure when confronted by an unknown assailant armed with a handgun pointed in his direction. Michael McCarthy, feeling his life and possibly the life of his partner Rhonda R. Bell, were in immediate danger, discharged his service revolver. This action is in no violation of any General Order of the Metropolitan Police Department, District of Columbia, and in turn, Detective McCarthy is totally exonerated."

"Bullshit," muttered Mac under his breath as his mind replayed the gut wrenching scene which had taken place at the solemn tribunal.

"Mac. There's a ladder back here. See it? Maybe they're still inside. You better call for some backup," excitedly stated Ronnie, already stepping out of the unmarked cruiser.

Ronnie stood at the bottom of the tall aluminum ladder which rested against the back wall of the Florida Avenue Liquor store, not far from her old beat, in the days when she had been assigned to Scout 150 with Danny. Even despite the recent murders she had found herself inexplicably drawn back to this area almost as if it unconsciously called out to her for help. Some old timers said that a beat got in your blood, casting a spell over your mind and weaving its mysterious magic on your soul. Ronnie had heard the gristled veterans tell their tales. The obsessive lore of the beat had partially bewitched her, leaving its fiery brand of sorcery on the very fiber of her being. It, like life itself, you could never truly escape.

Glaring back over her shoulder, she started up the rickety ladder. Mac was still sitting in the car. Ronnie knew he was drunk. No amount of breath mints could ever conceal the distinctive aroma of scotch. All she could do was to try to support him through this trying ordeal. He needed her. She knew he'd be there for her if the tables were turned. She'd try to protect him as best she could. Protecting him from the officials, like Bow Wow Bowser, was easy. Protecting him from himself wasn't.

Mac took a long swallow from the flask filled with Dewars. He reached for the radio and reported, "Cruiser 311. We're in the alley rear of the two hundred block of Florida Avenue, northwest. We have a liquor alarm at the burglar store."

"Cruiser 311. You mean you have a burglar alarm at the liquor store?" questioned the amused dispatcher.

"That's what I said. Isn't it? Now, how about some backup," radioed Mac, slurring his repeated attempts at sounding coherent. He just hoped he didn't sound drunk.

"Cruiser 311. Be advised Scout 145 and Scout 146 from the Fifth District are responding," reported the dispatcher, wondering how in the hell the Homicide Squad was going to catch the now famous Capital Carver when they couldn't even handle a friggin' burglar alarm.

Rhonda Bell was on the roof of the liquor store, looking down through a jagged hole where the attic fan used to be. Gazing across the Milky Way of flickering lights making up the city's urban landscape, she could barely envision the dim outlines of Orleans Place. She turned towards the heart of her dying city. Nothing seemed as fresh and as clean as it once had. The monuments, the memorials, the government buildings, everything appeared to have lost its luster. A gritty yellow haze hung over the tarnished city, a haze many were calling Satan's breath, the fog of death, the protective shroud of the Capital Carver.

Ronnie shivered. She reached up and pulled the collar of her black pants suit jacket tightly around her neck. Glancing off into the distance, towards the fantasy land of Georgetown's own little exclusive corner of her otherwise violent world, she shuddered. A black seamy soot hovered over the usually pristine enclave, swallowing up the yellow haze, its thick dark particles totally obscuring the precious land below. Suddenly, in her mind, the fog parted. She was looking down a dimly lit tree-lined street. Almost as if a panning movie camera was zooming in for a close up, her focus was being directed to a lone white house. Now, she could see it clearly. The house, a colonial mansion, had dark green shutters. The long front porch sported smooth white columns, reaching all the way to the wood shingled shake roof. There were trees and bushes everywhere. The long gated driveway circled in front of the gracious southern style home. "Oh God. No," gasped Ronnie. He was there.

"Mac. We've got to get out of here. We've got to get to Georgetown. He's there. I know it. He's going to kill someone up there tonight," hysterically yelled Ronnie, looking over the edge of the building's roof, down towards Mac, as he futilely tried to fumble his way up the rickety ladder.

"What the hell are you talking about? You mean the Carver? What makes you think he's in G-town? So far he ain't been anywhere but Northeast," answered Mac, hastily retreating back down the flimsy ladder, saved by the Carver's grim bell.

Ronnie swung her leg over the edge of the liquor store roof and began to feverishly descend the rungs of the swaying ladder as Mac tried to steady its to and fro rocking motion.

"I just know. That's all, Mac. I can feel it. He's there. Please. Let's hurry," shouted Ronnie over her shoulder as she skipped the last few steps and dropped to the pavement. No matter if he was drunk or not, Mac knew better than to question Ronnie's judgment. He had seen the same insightful gifts in his own wife. Some women seemed to have a vision far beyond the scope of men's understanding, figured Mac, thinking the old adage about a woman's intuition was alive and well.

"You uniform guys can handle this. There's a ladder in the back. Don't know if they're in there or not. Hole in the roof, though. We've got to get going," shouted Mac out the window of Cruiser 311 as the patrol cars pulled on to the scene. Ronnie turned on to Florida Avenue and Mac asked, "Well, kiddo. Where we goin? Georgetown is a pretty big place."

"I don't know, Mac. I'm just going to drive over there. Maybe we'll get lucky. Please don't say I'm some kind of crazy broad. I'm not. He's there. Trust me," answered Ronnie, looking both ways and then running the traffic light at Rhode Island and Florida Avenue.

Ray Carson Carver knew all he wanted to know. Wiping off the bloody blade of his hunting knife on the homeless dead wino's tattered corduroy jacket, he decided it was about time to commence the real hostilities on Reservoir Road. He dragged the gutless old man into the thick bushes, leaving his disemboweled carcass lying, face up, in a rumpled heap. Jesus, the old bastard had stunk when he opened him up. He had smelled like a toilet bowl full of rancid day after wine puke, chuckled Ray Carver to himself as he stared down at the moist steamy pile of innards strung out across the brown grass. He rested the old man's disheveled cart against a nearby tree and headed for his truck, parked behind a vacant house down the block. The little woman of the house should be pulling up in her high and mighty black Mercedes real soon, figured Ray Carver. It looked to him like she had just run down to the market.

He had watched the house for almost two days, sleeping and eating in the back of his truck. It had turned out to be almost too good to be true. The only little problem being that it looked like the rich bitch and her faggot looking dapper Dan old man had two kids, a boy and a girl. Well, he'd decide which one of them to take out when the time came. First things first. He'd wax mommy dearest and then on to mister maggot who was still in the house with the young'uns. Once the dumb blonde had gone out, jamming the sliding gate had been a piece of cake. Everything was set. He should be able to bring down his quarry with one clean shot.

Diana DeBerg didn't know what else could possibly go wrong today. All she had asked her husband, Daniel, do was to stop and pick up some Hagen Daaz on his way home from the office. The children had wanted some ice cream before bed. Was it too much to ask of a man, just to remember to pick up a half gallon of ice cream on his way home? It must be, reasoned Diana DeBerg, because, damn him, he forgot. She hadn't even had time to put on her makeup. Tilting the rear-view mirror to get a look at her face, she hoped that nobody she knew had seen her in the grocery store. She was simply a mess.

If he'd keep his mind off that little miss priss secretary of his and pay attention to her and the children maybe he wouldn't wander around all day with his head up his ass, figured Diana DeBerg, picturing the cutesy little bitch sitting on his desk, her tight skirt halfway up her always wriggling ass. "Damn that conniving slut," cursed the frustrated wife under her breath. If she ever caught the two of them together she'd scratch the whore's eyes out and cut off her husband's balls.

Diana DeBerg turned into the gated driveway entrance to their white two-story colonial home, the bottoms of its tall white pillars basking in a soft shadowy glow reflected from the surrounding amber landscape lights. She reached for the electronic gate opener clipped to the visor of her black 560 SEC Mercedes. The gate began to slowly creak open and then ground to a complete stop. "Goddamn it," shouted the frustrated woman to nobody in particular. Ever since she had spilled the coffee all over Mrs. Randall's lap, during the Country Club's breakfast social, her day had gone to shit. Now, this. She couldn't even get back in her own house.

Opening the door and sliding out of the tan leather interior of the idling car she walked up to the jammed gate, the flat heels of her Cole Hahn loafers clicking distinctly on the paved brick driveway. She was enraged. If she got one speck of grease on her new winter white wool pants she'd have Daniel's ass, the lazy bastard. She pushed against the unmoving black wrought iron gate. It was stuck. It wasn't going anywhere and neither was she. Well, she'd have to use the gate phone and call into the house. Diana DeBerg turned around, her tall graceful blonde silhouette outlined perfectly under the muted glare of the dim driveway lights.

Ray Carver had the perfect shot. Without hesitation he drew back the string of the compound bow, the two index fingers of his right hand tightly curled around the taut line. Unknowingly, she was directly facing his concealed form. The time was right. He released the string, its snapping twang sending the hunting arrow whistling through the still night air.

Diana DeBerg felt a piercing burn penetrate her stinging chest. Stupefied, she looked down at the shaft and feathers of the protruding arrow, the razor like head having sliced its way right through her spurting aorta. She desperately clutched at the foreign object. Grabbing the feathers of the fiberglass shaft, she tried to pull the blood stained arrow back out of her collapsing body. The arrowhead's keen steel edges ripped and then shredded her mortally wounded heart and lungs. She dropped to her knees, smacking heavily against the uneven driveway. Gasping, she doubled over, her forehead cracking against the cold hard bricks. Diana DeBerg thought fleetingly about her husband's sashaying hussy secretary tucking her children into bed, in her house, and then she died.

Ray Carson Carver pulled the dead woman's body to the very spot where, concealed in these same bushes, he had unleashed the hurtling arrow which had ended her privileged life. He walked over to the still idling Mercedes and turned off the lights and ignition. Calmly, he crept back to the woman's warm supple body, glancing down the driveway towards the green shuttered white house. Deciding to have a little look-see, he slit open her gold cashmere sweater, revealing her flattened pink rosebud tipped breasts. Then, grinning, he unzipped her pants and sliced open the soft pliable flesh of her smooth white stomach. One final detail and this gutted pig was absolute history, mused Ray Carver, slipping the tiny red Christmas tree bulb into the dead woman's open mouth.

"Baby. You've got me so hot. I'm as hard as a rock. I think I hear her downstairs. She must be back already. I've got to get going. Yeah, I want you too, baby. I'll see you in the morning. Oh, God. On the desk. You want me to give it to you right on the desk. Jesus, baby. You've got it. See you tomorrow," quietly whispered Daniel DeBerg into the mouth piece of the upstairs bedroom telephone. Damn, that secretary of his was the horniest little broad he had ever known. She just couldn't get enough. Shit, that bitchy wife of his must be downstairs slamming every cabinet door that she could find. Well, he might as well go down and face the music, figured Daniel DeBerg, stepping into the upstairs hallway trying to adjust his throbbing penis so she wouldn't be able to see its stiff telltale outline.

"What the hell's your problem?" hollered Daniel DeBerg, stepping on the top step of the white berber carpeted spiral staircase. He wished he could move that frigid wife of his out and move his horny secretary in. If he knew that he could get away with it he'd have somebody waste his old lady. She was becoming a real drag. Divorce was out of the question. He could never afford it. That cold hearted princess of his would take him for everything she could get her grubby little hands on.

"Jesus," gasped Daniel DeBerg, gazing down the stairway at the hillbilly looking redneck staring up at him from the base of the steps. What the hell did he have in his hands, wondered the shocked home owner. "What the hell are you doing in my house? Get out of my house before I call the police," shouted Daniel DeBerg, watching in horror, unable to move, as the sinister looking man pulled back the bow string and smiled, his yellowed rotten teeth covered with a gritty brown stain. "God. Don't kill me. I don't want to die," begged Daniel DeBerg, backing up the stairway.

Ray Carson Carver turned his head and spit a long stream of tobacco juice on to the white berber carpet, chuckling at the cowering figure above him. His gloved hand released the snapping line. The arrow whirled through the air, its razor like head severing Daniel DeBerg's adam's apple as it ripped through his gurgling throat. Daniel DeBerg died almost instantaneously, his last fleeting thought a mental picture of his secretary on his mahogany desk, her muscular legs spread wide open.

Ray Carver hacked open Daniel DeBerg, inserted a dried tulip into his mouth, and started down the hallway. He still hadn't figured out if he'd take out the youngbuck or the split tail. Whatever his fancy struck him or whatever door he opened first, figured Ray Carver, grabbing the bedroom door knob and slowly pushing open the creaking door.

CHAPTER 12

"DAMN IT, Mac. I know he's up here somewhere. How the hell are we ever going to find a white house with pillars and green shutters?" desperately stated Rhonda Bell, turning Cruiser 311 north on to Wisconsin Avenue.

"I know where there's a white house with pillars. But, it ain't got green shutters," casually remarked Mac, feeling in better spirits since he'd had a chance to take a little nip in back of the liquor store on Florida Avenue.

"Where's that?" asked Ronnie excitedly.

"1600 Pennsylvania Avenue," laughed Mac, suddenly sorry he'd turned Ronnie's crazy hunch into a sick joke. "I'm sorry," he apologized immediately.

"It's OK. That was really kinda funny," answered Ronnie, putting her hand on Mac's bulky shoulder.

Briefcase Betty Barnes didn't care what Rambo Roddy had to say. She was going back to check on that poor old wino. With any luck she could find him an empty bed and a hot meal at the Detoxification Center, if it wasn't already standing room only. The colder it got the more crowded Detox got. It beat sleeping on the grates, figured Briefcase Betty, asking Rambo Roddy to drive back up to Reservoir Road. Despite his constant bitchin' Rambo Roddy agreed. He figured it wouldn't hurt to reinforce his message in case the old stinkin' bastard had second thoughts about reneging on his alleged 'fall down and go boom' story. Besides, maybe he'd trash the old man's U-haul shopping cart again. That would really frost the old geezer's black balls, concluded Rambo Roddy, throwing Scout 80 into an abrupt tire squealing u-turn in the middle of M Street's perpetually congested traffic.

"There's his cart. Over there," exclaimed Briefcase Betty, pointing to the overburdened cart resting against the trunk of a thick tree.

"I don't see the old bastard anywhere. Jig's probably off in the bushes rapin' some old rich bitch white broad. That's every

Sambo's dream. To screw a white woman. Most likely a blonde," sarcastically remarked Rambo Roddy, shining the scout car spotlight along the thick hedgerows which bordered the dimly lit stately mansions that lined the upper class street.

Briefcase Betty was suddenly worried. It wasn't like one of these homeless people to leave their precious cart full of worldly possessions unattended. Most would religiously guard them with their very lives. Something was wrong, awfully wrong, figured Briefcase Betty, opening the passenger side door of Scout 80. She began to feel ill, almost as if the very grip of death was upon her soul, slowly devouring her trembling flesh. Walking over to the abandoned cart, she flicked on her flashlight and pointed its circular arcing light against the cold brownish looking ground. Briefcase Betty stepped on to the frost covered burnt grass, her shoe squishing what felt like a bursting water filled balloon. She slipped on the slimy substance, tumbling to the hard ground, her hand imbedding itself into a moist pile of sticky goo.

Slowly, Briefcase Betty raised her gelatin covered hand and stared at its stringy coating. The rancid smell of death hammered her flaring nostrils. Suddenly, in a blinding flash of horror, Briefcase Betty realized the shocking reality of her ghastly discovery. She desperately flailed her arms and legs, trying to escape the gruesome mess that she was mired in. Screaming, she gagged on a lump of rising bile.

"Jesus Christ. What the fuck? That's a pile of guts you're layin' in. Damn. Look at that. It's somebody's whole belly spilled out like a gutted deer," stuttered Rambo Roddy, backing away from the horrible sight. "It's the Goddamned Carver! He must have smoked the old wino. Shit. Maybe he's still around," shouted the retreating officer, looking down at his ghostly pale white partner as she tried to force her weak trembling knees to lift her to her feet.

"Damn it, Roddy! Give me a hand. Help me get out of this mess. Will you?" pleaded Briefcase Betty, flopping around like a fish out of water.

"No way, baby. Not me. I ain't gettin' that shit all over me. I'm callin' for backup. It's your problem. You get your own ass outta that slop," muttered Rambo Roddy, dashing for the idling scout car.

Briefcase Betty began to cry. What the hell was she doing out here, in the streets? Nobody should ever have to go through this. Now, she'd have to live with this the rest of her life. Whatever happened to those little girl dreams of playing house with her doll-babies, she reflected, trying to stop her damn shaking. She had to get hold of herself. She was better than this. "The best man for this, or any other job, is a woman," resolutely mumbled Briefcase Betty, pushing herself to her feet. Screw Roddy, anyway. The low life pig. She'd show them that she belonged out here, in the street. First things first. She'd have to find the body. It had to be here somewhere.

"We'll respond to assist Scout 80. We're a few blocks away," radioed Mike McCarthy. "Well, Ronnie. I don't know what it was that made you think he was up here. But, I'm sorry to say that your hunch was right. Scout 80's got a dead one just down the street. On Reservoir Road. And he ain't got any stomach left."

"Mac. Over there. There's the house. Just like I told you. There it is. A white house with pillars. And green shutters," excitedly shouted Ronnie, pointing towards the dark unlit house as they sped past.

"Jesus, Ronnie. I didn't know you were psychic. You're startin' to scare the shit right outta my tired old ass. Damn it. How did you know that the dead guy would be a few blocks down from this place? It's weird. Really weird. Wouldn't you say?" inquired Mac, shaking his head in disbelief.

"No, Mac. It isn't right. The dead people aren't a few blocks down from the house. They're in it. We're going back and check it out before we meet Scout 80. It'll only take a couple of minutes. You don't mind. Do you?" asked Ronnie, already slamming on Cruiser 311's brakes and banking the sliding car into a tight u-turn.

"No. I don't mind. Whatever you say. Who am I to argue with the powers that be. Go for it, baby. I'm just along for the ride," answered Mac, hoping he wasn't on the rollercoaster to hell. He had already been there and back, a couple of times.

"Look. Something's definitely wrong. Nobody leaves their 560 SEC Mercedes sitting at the gate to their driveway. The gate's only part open," commented Ronnie, pulling Cruiser 311 behind the abandoned black car.

"This is givin' me the creeps. It's all a little spooky," remarked Mac, reaching for the half empty flask. He didn't care who the hell saw him take a slug of the comforting liquor. He was about ready to piss himself. His hands were trembling. This was way out of his league.

Ronnie calmly walked over to the shimmering jet black car, her soft brown eyes darting toward the flattened line of grass leading over to the mass of tangled bushes. She followed the distinctive trail, already knowing what she was about to find.

"Damn it, Ronnie. How the hell did you know? This is one sick son of a bitch. Jesus. A bow and an arrow. What is this miserable prick? William Tell from hell? We've got to get in the house and notify her family," sadly remarked Mac, looking down at the woman's disemboweled body and hoping that Ronnie would do most of the talking. He wasn't very good at this sort of thing.

"It's no use, Mac. There isn't going to be anybody to tell. Don't you get it? He ambushed her. He's a hunter. A human hunter. He's already killed a black man, a black woman, and a black child. I'm certain of one thing. Before tonight's over we're going to find at least two more bodies. A white man and a white child. And I'm sure of something else, too. They're in the house. What I'm not sure about is who's lying dead, down the street, where Scout 80 is," sadly commented Ronnie, slipping through the small opening in the jammed gate.

Mac, emptying the flask in one long satisfying gulp, scurried after Ronnie, barely able to squeeze his rotund body through the opening in the gate. What a dick life, thought Mac, staring at the lush foliage surrounding the ritzy estate. The only thing better than being one of the privileged nouveau rich was to be one of the lucky snot nosed bastards that was born into it. Those were the arrogant son of a bitches that wielded the real power, he reflected, wondering which category these wealthy ill fated folks fell into.

"Look, Mac. Over there," shouted Ronnie, catching a glimpse of a piece of shimmering broken glass lying in the cedar beds surrounding the quiet house.

Mac, standing at the front door slamming the antique brass knocker against its similarly fashioned plate, finally gave up and walked around the side of the house to join Ronnie.

"Maybe nobody's home. Or, if they are, they sure as hell ain't answerin' the door. My hand's about ready to fall off," stated Mac, staring at the broken window and suddenly knowing that he was about to see in person what Ronnie had already seen in her head. The one thing that he was positive of was that it wasn't going to be a very pretty sight.

Ronnie crawled through the broken window, stepping foot

first into the game room of the massive mansion. Looking carefully around, she wondered if this had been a happy home. It looked so cold, dark mahogany bookshelves lining the forest green wallpapered walls, polished brown planking covering the sparkling floor, everything so perfect, so sterile. If she ever had a home like this, it would be soft, warm, cozy and inviting, thought Ronnie, the heels of her flats echoing in the vast chamber as she walked towards the double wooden doors on the other side of the room.

"Yes, massa. Can I helps you," she joked, opening the front door for Mac and hoping a little humor would break the tension that threatened to strangle her in its nervous grip.

"You be a good nigga and go fetch your master," playfully answered Mac, flicking on the foyer lights. Looking straight ahead, up the white carpeted stairs, he suddenly realized that massa had stood under his last apple. William Tell from hell had aimed a bit too low, skewering his unfortunate target's adam's apple instead.

Ronnie wheeled around and gasped. She stared up the circular stairway at the crumpled body, a dark blackish stain seeping into the white berber carpet.

"Jesus," muttered Mac, his eyes fixed on the dead man's entrails, strung down the length of the curved wooden banister like hanging strands of limp spaghetti.

Carefully stepping around the limp body, Ronnie made her way to the top of the ghastly littered stairs, human organs strewn all around the disemboweled corpse. She hurried down the hall towards the bedrooms, reaching underneath her coat to tightly clench the dangling gold cross hanging around her graceful neck. Praying silently for help, she threw open the door of the first bedroom, her trembling right hand grasping the grips of her two inch .38 special service revolver. Sweeping the room with the revolver in her outstretched arms, she quickly realized that, this time, her prayers would go unanswered. There, stretched across the pink satin bedspread, the eviscerated body of a young child lay serenely, wallowing in its own inner juices.

"Damn him," screamed Ronnie, helplessly gazing at the gruesome scene, the pitiful child's shocked blue eyes staring at the white plaster ceiling, an arrow rammed clear through the sides of her small fragile blonde head.

Mac, huffing and puffing, his pistol at the ready, burst into the foul smelling room, the rancid stench of rotting innards stopping him dead in his tracks.

"The no good bastard. I'll cut out his heart and boil it for dinner," hollered Mac, slamming his first into the wall.

"Jesus. The kid's old lady had a Christmas tree bulb rammed in her mouth. The old man a Goddamned tulip shoved in his. What's that in the girl's mouth? A plant? Or, what?" questioned Mac, trying to calm his frustration and rage.

Ronnie gently opened the little girl's jaw and replied, "No, Mac. It's a sapling. A baby tree."

"There's brown tobacco stains all over the rug. Must be the more he likes it, the more he spits," stated Mac, desperately wishing that he could figure out what the hell was going on.

Walking down the hall towards the other bedrooms, Ronnie wasn't so sure of what was going on either. Right now, the dead wino down the street was throwing her off. It didn't fit.

Easing open the next bedroom door, she sighed in relief. There, bound and gagged, lay a little boy, duct tape wrapped around his head, covering his eyes and mouth, his hands and feet wrapped in coils of baling twine. The pieces of the puzzle were still intact, figured Ronnie, rushing to the bed and dropping to her knees to free the whimpering child. She couldn't believe it, not really. But, if she wasn't mistaken, a hunter always had a limit on certain game. And the Capital Carver was no exception, even if he was the one setting it. Now, at least they knew the limit and the game, thought Ronnie, cradling the crying boy tightly against her bosom and tenderly rocking his trembling body back and forth.

"Too bad the little fella didn't see anything. What a break that would have been. At least we know the murderin' bastard's a drunk. I figure that's what the kid was tellin' us when he said that the bad man had smelled like daddy did when mommy was always mad at him," stated Mac, shuddering as he suddenly thought about the daddy that he had so recently gunned down.

"Poor boy. Who'll take care of him? Money or not, his life isn't going to be too hot. Living with these memories. Speakin' of smellin' like daddy," remarked Ronnie, casting a disparaging glance at Mac and pulling Cruiser 311 in behind Scout 80, still standing by at the scene of the dead wino. They had left the marked units, the morgue wagon, and the Mobile Crime Lab back at the house on Reservoir Road, glad to escape its gruesome visions, visions which were quickly becoming a haunting reality.

"Look, Mac. No clue. Nothing in his mouth. I still think I'm right. The Carver's set on killing a man, a woman, and a child of each race. Just like a buck, a doe, and a fawn. I'm sure he's some kind of frustrated deerslayer," excitedly stated Ronnie, carefully surveying the split open body of the murdered wino.

"He oughtta have an apple in his mouth. The stinkin' nigger pig," mumbled Rambo Roddy, looking at the black bitch detective, his eyes burning with fiery hate.

"What did you say, officer? I really didn't hear you," asked Ronnie, wondering why the white officer kept staring at her, almost as if he'd just as soon see her lying there, her stomach turned inside out like the poor old homeless wino's. Unfortunately, too many times, she'd seen that revolting look of disgust burning in the eyes of the white man, a look not only aimed at her, but at the entire black race. This would be a hard world to change, thought Ronnie. Saddened, she glanced back down at the hollow lifeless body of the dead drifter.

"Jesus. What the hell was that?" yelled the Bud Man, nervously ducking behind a parked K-9 cruiser in the rear of the Fifth District, the incredible noise rumbling the hollow pit of his stomach.

"Shit. I don't know. Sounds like a Goddamned sonic boom," answered Danny Money, looking in the direction of the echoing explosions and wondering if somebody had pipe-bombed the precinct. He only hoped that, if they had, his paycheck had survived.

"Goddamn, man! Will you look at that shit. Just look at that simple-ass motha fucka. Will ya'? I see it. But, I don't believe it," exclaimed the Bud Man, watching in astonishment as Emancipation Proclamation Jones, his black Corvette convertible covered in American flag stickers, pulled into the precinct, the pounding monster jam speakers of his newly installed two hundred watt car stereo thunderously shaking the very ground on which they stood.

Danny Money and the Bud Man continued to stand in the 5D parking lot, both their mouths hanging open in disbelief as Emancipation Proclamation Jones passed in review, the end of his car that goes boom proudly displaying a huge bumper sticker proclaiming "America. Love It or Leave It."

"I am the mother of all fuckers," shouted Emancipation Proclamation Jones, slamming the door of his parked car and shoving his way past the gathering crowd of officers that had already begun to congregate around his vehicle, fascinated by its patriotic display. "It's hot. It's black. And it's beautiful. Like me, baby.

And, it wears the colors just as proudly," he proclaimed, patting the hood of his black Corvette.

"Nice rags, E.P.," chuckled the Bud Man, staring in amusement at Emancipation Proclamation Jones' red, white and blue stars and stripes covered leather jacket and matching leather pants. Unable to contain himself any longer, Danny Money stated, "Why don't you spin around, E.P.? You look like a friggin barber pole."

"Sheet, man. Speakin' of barber poles. I got me more trim than I know what to do with. My pole always be rotatin' up and down. Man. I got me so many bitches I need one of them artificial dick transplants. Then, just like them Reebok commercials, I could pump up and air out," jived Emancipation Proclamation Jones, slapping hands with the Bud Man who was wondering where he could get one of those "America. Love It or Leave It" bumper stickers. He had to admit, he kind of liked that patriotic shit. It gave him a hard on just thinking about salutin' the good ol' Stars and Stripes. He'd have to ask E.P. at roll call. Glancing at his watch, he noticed it was only ten minutes away.

"He's gettin' worse," whispered Danny Money, leaning over next to the Bud Man.

"Yeah. He's still got the pussy palsy pretty bad. He's turnin' into a pussy paraplegic," chuckled the Bud Man, looking across the roll call room and watching 10-33 Sam shudder and twitch his way across the floor, finally tripping over his own feet in a particularly violent spasm.

"Who do you think's nailin' his old lady? You don't really think it's E.P.. Do you?" questioned Danny Money, turning his head to look at Jones and Spic N' Span Spiegel, sitting together in the back of the roll call room.

"No way, man. I heard she likes the whiteshirts. Some guy downtown in the Central Cell Block was tellin' me she's been around. Says the word is, her hole's so big that you better strap a two by four on your ass before you climb aboard. Just so's you don't fall in," remarked the Bud Man, figuring that one of those dickless glamour boy downtown detectives was probably porkin' her poontang. Well, no matter, 10-33 Sam wouldn't miss a slice of bread out of her loaf. No sense worrying Sammy baby, thought the Bud Man. You can't miss what you can't measure.

Pulling up in front of 1723 Gales Street, in Scout 151, Emancipation Proclamation Jones smiled. Just as he thought his luck was beginning to go south. This had to be a sign from God, an omen of good fortune, he figured, staring at the beat up looking Volkswagen Van, faded and weathered bumper stickers proclaiming "No Blood For Oil" and "United States Out of Kuwait" all over its rusty battered exterior.

"And I thought the war ended a few years ago," said Spic N' Span Spiegel, glancing at the bumper stickers and hoping that E.P. could control himself.

"Sheet. I'm stoked, man," exclaimed Jones. "It ain't gonna be over till I personally get a chance to kick some gas right outta one of dem camel jockeys ass."

"What's the address of this here Investigate the Trouble call, brother Spiegel?" asked Emancipation Proclamation Jones, praying that he was at the right house. Because, if he wasn't, he was awfully Goddamned tempted to knock on the door anyway. Anybody that would leave that insulting unpatriotic piece of shit parked in front of their house needed to be slapped upside his traitorous head, figured E.P., fully intending to do the necessary slapping.

"This is it, E.P. . .1723 Gales," answered Spic N' Span Spiegel, looking over at his partner, more than a little concerned about the sadistic looking grin flashing across E.P.'s glowing face.

"Mohammed what!" shouted Emancipation Proclamation Jones, leaping across the urine and vomit stained floor of the rancid smelling row house.

"Yeah. That be his name. Mohammed. Mohammed Abdul Hassan. He be upstairs. In my bedroom. Him and his drunk ass self. He done beat me like I'm one of his Arab whores. I lets him sleep here. He don't pay no rent. He don't do nothin' but sleep here. The garlic breath stinkin' mother fucker. He hit me. Look here. Look at this bruise," hollered the drunken black woman, who'd opened the door, pointing at her puffy swollen cheek.

"Look, ma'am. If we lock him up you've got to press charges or he walks. What did he hit you with? He's your boyfriend, isn't he?" asked Spic N' Span Spiegel, hoping to avoid the impending confrontation that had E.P. virtually licking his lips.

"He went upside my head with that there ball bat. And, he ain't shit to me. No way. His tired ass is history. The Arab faggot can't even get his dick hard. I'm going back to a black man. They know what to do with a hot pussy. And me. I got me one of them," stated the foul smelling black woman, grinning at Emancipation Proclamation Jones, her housecoat falling open to reveal a pair of huge sagging tits.

"Look here, mama. You want this man out of your crib, right? This is your crib, ain't it? If it is, we'll put his ass out on the street. In fact, if you'd like, I'll personally lock his stinkin' butt up for assault," stated Emancipation Proclamation Jones, his white teeth shining in the dimly lit smoke filled house, his foot already resting on the upstairs step.

"It be my house and he ain't welcome no more. I'll press them charges. Yes sir, officer. I sure will. Go ahead on and lock his ass up," defiantly shouted the teetering woman, reaching out to steady herself against the yellowed cracked and peeling plaster wall.

Spic N' Span Spiegel knew the only thing that this disgusting wino was going to press was her Arab boyfriend's shirts when he moved back in tomorrow and beat the shit out of her even worse. Emancipation Proclamation Jones was well aware of this likelihood, but, at this very moment, he didn't give a shit. It was time for a little D.C. Storm, Scout 151 style.

"That your piece of shit Volkswagen Van down there, parked in front of this place?" asked Emancipation Proclamation Jones, prodding the drunken sleeping Arab with the butt of his nightstick.

"Jesus, E.P. This place stinks. Damn, it smells like he shit himself," remarked Spic N' Span Spiegel, pulling back the soiled sheets to reveal a dark brown watery stain.

"You towel headed mother fucker. Get your ass out of bed," shouted Emancipation Proclamation Jones, raising his black combat boot and rolling the snoring drunk's naked body out of bed, sending it crashing to the threadbare carpeted floor.

"What da fuck! What's goin on? Don't you lay your hands on me, you nigger. Who do you think you are?" screamed the rousing drunk, staggering to his feet.

"You don't know shit. Ain't you ever heard of Operation Desert Storm, you rag-headed asshole? It's ancient history. But, this here's Operation D.C. Storm. And me, I'm the thunder. And my partner here, he's the lightning. And we're about ready to explode on your Ahab the Arab ass. You're locked up," delightedly answered Emancipation Proclamation Jones, reaching for his handcuffs.

"You ain't lockin' me up. Don't you lay your hands on me, you black bastard," shouted the enraged drunk, lurching towards Emancipation Proclamation Jones, his hands drawn up into closed fists.

"You throw a couple of them weak-ass Scuds at me and I'll nail you with this here Patriot," answered Emancipation Proclamation Jones, slapping his nightstick against the palm of his left hand and praying that the drunk Arab would do something, anything, to justify the use of a little necessary force to effect his arrest.

Finally, seeing the chickenshit towel head was blowing smoke, E.P. decided to stoke the fire and asked, "You just pull your ugly head out of your camel's ass, or do you always smell like shit?"

Spic N' Span Spiegel stood behind the naked staggering Arab, sure that his over zealous partner had finally succeeded in instigating the confrontation that he so desperately wanted. Spic N' Span Spiegel was right. The Arab lunged at E.P., his grimy hands and arms encircling the reeling officer as they both crashed against the door frame of the stifling hot overheated bedroom. Spic N' Span Spiegel, beads of sweat trickling into his eyes, their salty sting temporarily blinding him, leap-frogged across the dishevelled bed and tackled the back of the collapsing Arab.

Slipping off the hairy man's oily sweat soaked body like a contestant at a greased pig contest, Spic N' Span Spiegel slammed into the floor, his chin cracking against the rancid smelling carpet.

"Jesus. This mother fucker stinks," shouted Emancipation Proclamation Jones, trying to hammer the back of the struggling man's head with the butt of his nightstick. He was missing badly, almost taking out his own pearly white teeth in the process.

"I got him, E.P. I got him," hollered Spic N' Span Spiegel, wrapping his arms around the man's ankles and holding on for dear life.

Emancipation Proclamation Jones managed to wriggle free from the grasp of the flailing man. Reaching down to his Sam Brown belt he pulled out his pistol grip handled mace canister and aimed it directly into the unshaven face of the defiant Arab.

"Here's a little chemical warfare for your Hussein lovin' ass, compliments of D.C. Storm," he yelled, pulling the trigger of the mace canister and gleefully watching as its long arc of mist-like spray splattered against the fighting Arab's thick browed forehead.

Desperately throwing his arms in front of his burning face, the inundated man began howling like a wounded banshee. He fell to his knees, his hands frantically clawing at his stinging tear-filled eyes. Spic N' Span Spiegel, the mace-filled air stinging his watery blinking eyes, pulled out his handcuffs and, forcing the yelping Arab's hands behind his back, locked them on the struggling man's wrists.

"He sounds like a fuckin' wounded water buffalo," laughed Emancipation Proclamation Jones, listening to the man's constant bellowing, not quite sure whether or not Arabs had water buffalo. Finally, concluding that the desert dickheads didn't have any water, so therefore they couldn't possibly have any water buffalo, he began dragging the flailing man down the stairs, making sure that he humped the man's head against every step.

"That'll teach you to mess with me, you limp dicked faggot. You be goin' to jail now, mother fucker," shouted the black woman, standing at the bottom of the stairs and watching her boyfriend's head bounce off each step.

"You nigger whore. You junkie nigger bitch. I'll fix your ass," screamed the enraged man, slamming his foot upward, into her stomach, barely missing Emancipation Proclamation Jones' jaw.

"You done seen that, officer. He kicked me. The nasty smellin' bastard assaulted me, right in front of your eyes," hollered the black woman, staggering as she clutched at her belly.

"That's it. I'm gonna nuke this mother fucker," yelled Emancipation Proclamation Jones, dragging the kicking man towards the kitchen, all the while praying that he could find a microwave oven and somehow figure out how he could turn it on with the Arab's head stuck inside it.

"C'mon, E.P. Give it a rest. Damn, the guy's had enough. Let's just transport him to 5D and do the paperwork. I'll fill out all the reports and you can put 151 back in service," pleaded Spic N' Span Spiegel, convinced his partner had finally blown a gasket.

E.P., confronted with a deal he couldn't refuse, pulled the dazed Arab to his feet and, holding on to the handcuff chain behind the man's back, escorted him out to Scout 151. Spic N' Span Spiegel followed, shaking his head in disbelief as he passed the Arab's rat trap looking Volkswagen Van.

"E.P.'s wild ass self must have started some shit over on Gales," commented the Bud Man, listening to the radio as Spic N' Span Spiegel asked the dispatcher for report numbers and a time check to 5D, one arrest ADW baseball bat.

"Shit. That simple son of a bitch probably managed to find himself a Goddamned Iraqi, wanderin' through the ghetto, tryin' to locate a black camel," laughed Danny Money, not yet realizing how close to the truth he really was as he pulled Scout 150 on to Florida Avenue to see if they could write a few early evening rush hour violators.

"Hey, man. You know about that boy the LAPD beat up on?" asked the Bud Man, pulling his ticket book out of the glove box as Danny Money stopped 150 behind an illegally parked car.

"You mean Rodney, "I can't get no respect," King," answered Danny Money, throwing the gearshift into park.

"Yeah. They locked him up again," stated the Bud Man, stepping out of the scout car to finish writing his ticket.

"What for?" asked Danny Money, looking quizzically at the Bud Man, who, unable to restrain himself any longer chuckled, "They charged him with impersonating a pinata."

"Jesus, man. That's cold," remarked Danny Money, laughing as the Bud Man walked over and slipped the ticket under the illegally parked car's windshield wiper blade.

Danny Money pulled Scout 150 back into the congested rush hour traffic and headed down Florida Avenue, towards Orleans Place. Rambo Roddy, off duty, was already there, long ago considering this vile street the center of the porch monkey universe. Riding around northeast Washington in his black 454 Chevy SS, the pickup from hell, Rambo Roddy was engaged in his favorite off duty sport, writing parking tickets and throwing away the vehicle owner's copy. It was a great little game, a game he had invented, a game that he only played with a deck full of spades, the human kind.

Sooner or later, these unpaid tickets would turn into warrants and another dumb shuckin' and jivin' nigger would be checking into the Central Cell Block, courtesy of officer friendly, chuckled Rambo Roddy, tossing another wadded up owner's copy on to the passenger side floor of his pick up truck. Tomorrow, at the Second District check off window, he'd slip these court copies in with his other tickets and voila, one more phony unpaid ticket would be on its merry little course towards incarcerating another innocent Tyrone-ass jig-a-boo, silently laughed Rambo Roddy.

"Man, look at that pick up, would you. I don't know no brothers that be drivin' that red neck piece of shit," remarked the Bud Man, pointing down the dimly lit street, towards the shiny jet black truck slowly cruising Orleans Place.

"Christ, maybe it's the Carver. They say he's probably a snuff chewin' white boy from the sticks," commented Danny Money, stepping on Scout 150's gas pedal to close in on the suspicious looking truck. Pulling directly behind the slowly moving vehicle, Danny Money shined the scout car spotlight trough the rear window, the Bud Man flicking on the red overhead visibar lights.

Both officers watched intently, the truck's brakelights casting a crimson glow off the hood of their patrol car as the truck pulled over to the broken glass and bottle strewn curb, Scout 150's flashing redlights reflecting off its shimmering surface.

"Be cool, man. It could be him," cautioned the Bud Man, stepping out of the idling patrol car and carefully watching as Danny Money cautiously approached the driver's side of the stopped vehicle, his right hand on the handle of his Glock semi-automatic, his left hand holding up a large black plastic encased flashlight. Taking no chances, the Bud Man unholstered his weapon and slowly sauntered towards the passenger side of the rumbling truck.

"Driver's license and registration, please," ordered Danny Money, shining the flashlight into the dark cabin of the parked truck. Seeing that the driver, true to the Bud Man's instant analysis, looked like a redneck hillbilly shit kicker, he stated, "Step out of the truck, sir. Keep your hands out in the open where we can see them."

"You and that simple ass negro partner of yours oughtta be detectives. What, do you think you've single handedly caught the Carver? I ain't done nothin'. I just like it over here, amongst all these mother fuckers. Makes me feel like I'm in the zoo, surrounded by apes," sarcastically stated Rambo Roddy, grinning as he slowly climbed out of the shiny black truck.

"Shit, what's all this trash? Looks like ticket carbons," remarked the Bud Man, the beam of his flashlight sweeping across the littered passenger side floorboard of the idling truck.

"What can I say? I just love my work. See, I even take it home with me," answered Rambo Roddy. "There ain't no law against a police officer doing his duty, now, is there?"

"You a cop?" questioned Danny Money, glancing over at the Bud Man and hoping that he didn't take this asshole's head off.

"2D," answered Rambo Roddy, slowly reaching into his back pocket and pulling out his badge and ID folder.

"Your shit stinks real bad," shouted the Bud Man, suddenly

figuring out Rambo Roddy's sick little game.

Finally catching on, Danny stated, "I'm going to call for an official. Maybe you can explain what the hell you're doin', writin' tickets, off duty, in our district. There ain't nothin' kosher about that. Man, you're a real jack-off, cop or not."

"Get his name and badge number and let him go. I ain't ever gonna forget his pukey face. The good ol' boys from 2D ain't gonna mess with one of their own. They'll all think its kinda funny. We're all nothin' but niggers, whether we're in blue or not. Ain't that right, asshole?" coldly stated the Bud Man, clamping his powerful hand around Rambo Roddy's throat, the bulging veins of his huge neck standing out against his black skin. Rambo Roddy gagged as the Bud Man lifted him off the ground, pinning him against his Chevy pickup.

"Ain't that right, asshole?" repeated the Bud Man, choking Rambo Roddy in a vise like grip of seething rage, as he continued to hold him aloft by his neck and chin.

Rambo Roddy, his face turning a brilliant crimson, muttered, "Yeah, that's right. You niggers are just like Indians, the only good ones are dead ones."

"See, Danny. That's how a whole lot of you'all still think. Go to school, brother, learn. Because that's the kind of mentality that you and Ronnie face. The good ol' boys are alive and well and you ain't gonna be on any of their party lists because you love a nigger bitch," shouted the Bud Man as he slammed Rambo Roddy against the truck and, releasing his grip, allowed the gasping officer to wither to the ground.

"Just so you don't forget us poor ghetto-warriors, here's a little detailing job, compliments of 5D," coldly stated the Bud Man, removing his call box key and scraping it down the entire length of Rambo Roddy's pick up from hell.

Wincing at the shrill high pitched scraping noise of metal against metal, Danny Money figured he just took an A in that class. He had to admit, the Bud Man sure knew how to make his point. Tomorrow, maybe he'd bring teacher a nice juicy apple, silently chuckled Danny Money to himself. Both officers watched intently as a terrified Rambo Roddy squealed rubber in his haste to leave the wrath of the incensed Bud Man who was waving goodbye with his middle finger raised in the cold night air.

"Hey, Tiny. Get off your big fat ass and pour us another pitcher of Bud, here. We've got us a powerful thirst," roared the Bud Man, walking back to the booth where Money, E.P., Spiegel and himself were all engaged in a friendly game of draw poker.

Tiny, trying to figure out how he could've fucked up so badly, was debating how to explain to the Bud Man that he had run out of Bud. Then, it hit him like a ton of bricks. He had a full keg of Michelob on tap and it was a form of Bud, wasn't it? The Bud Man couldn't possibly tell the difference between Mich and Bud, now, could he? Walking over to the back booth, beer sloshing out of the overfilled pitcher, Tiny filled the officer's glasses, sure that he was off the hook.

"E.P., I hear you nailed some camel jockey, tonight. The boys told me you and Spiegel smoked his no blood for oil ass," stated the Bud Man, eager to hear the much exaggerated story that was already circulating in the station house.

"Man, we stomped some serious butt. I used a little chemical warfare on the stinkin' son of a bitch. Then I kicked that sand nigger's ass all the way down the stairs," bragged Emancipation Proclamation Jones, adding for good measure, "If it wouldn't have been for Spiegel calmin' my black ass down, I'd have nuked the bastard."

"Shit," shouted the Bud Man, turning his head and spitting out a mouthful of foamy brew. "Goddamned your big ass, Tiny. What da fuck is wrong with you, trying to pass off this la de da pinky finger in the air unicorn urine as Bud. Michelob is for Jewish princesses, dykes, and faggots. Bring us some Bud. I don't drink no 'The Night Belongs to Fairies,' man," yelled the Bud Man, slamming his half full mug down on the wooden table top.

"Damn, relax. I'm all out of Bud. And besides, Michelob is my favorite beer," angrily replied Tiny, staring vehemently at the bitching Bud Man who, seeing Tiny's highly agitated state, decided that discretion was, in this case, the better part of valor and quickly relented, stating, "Well, Mich it is, then. Drink up boys. The beer's on me. It's after midnight and we're gonna let it all hang out. Ain't that right, brother Tiny?"

Tiny, unable to contain himself at the Bud Man's eloquent reversal of position, burst into laughter, hoping that the Bud Man was as masterful at extricating his black ass from street squabbles as he was at barroom arguments. "My old lady's turnin' into a LAB, man. The only thing gettin' bigger than her belly is her ass," stated Emancipation Proclamation Jones, reaching down to the table to pick up the three cards that Danny Money had just tossed his way and hoping to improve on his pair of aces.

"What the fuck is a LAB?" questioned the Bud Man, wonderin' where in the hell E.P. picked up half these terms.

"A LAB. Damn, man. You don't know jack shit. LAB. Lot a butt, man. Lot a butt. You know, them sisters that be lookin' like a cottage cheese factory," answered Emancipation Proclamation Jones, carefully shielding the cards he had just picked up from the table.

"Don't be starin' over my shoulder, Tiny. It makes me nervous," suggested Emancipation Proclamation Jones, looking at his certain winning hand.

Glancing down at E.P.'s hand, Tiny couldn't help himself. He slowly placed his forefinger behind E.P.'s head. Then, snapping his thumb in an imitation of a gun's falling hammer, he shouted, "Bang," as he cracked off a fake round in the back of E.P.'s skull.

Startled, Emancipation Proclamation Jones leaped out of his seat, his heart just about rolling off the tip of his tongue. The jittery officer yelled, "What the fuck are you doin', Tiny? Jesus, you just about scared me to death!"

"You're the one don't know shit, E.P. Ain't you ever heard of Wild Bill Hickok?" chuckled Tiny, his huge frame doubled over in laughter.

"What you talkin' about, you giant crazy ass Baby Huey lookin' nigger?" questioned E.P., looking at the other officers who were grinning at the sight of his huge bulging eyes.

"Old Wild Bill was shot in the back of the head, in Deadwood City, South Dakota. Holdin' the same cards as you, he was. Aces and eights, the Dead Man's hand," replied Tiny, suddenly stunned at the look of terror which had crept across E.P.'s shocked looking face.

Emancipation Proclamation Jones instantly turned as pale as any black man Danny Money had ever seen, the unmistakable pall of death hanging over his entire body like a shroud of foreboding gloom.

"Hey, E.P. It's only a joke. Chill out, man. Let's play some cards," remarked Danny Money, hoping to break the tension of the moment.

Tiny, hurrying back from the shelves of liquor behind the bar, slammed a bottle of Hennessey Cognac down on the table, stating, "It's on the house, boys, drink up. I'll be right back with the glasses."

"Free liquor tastes even better than free food," joked the Bud Man, trying to calm down E.P.

"That's a great idea. Let's toast to E.P.'s baby. It'll be here before you know it," stated Spic N' Span Spiegel, shocked to see his usually energetic partner look so somber.

"Let's just pray the little brewski don't look like E.P.'s ugly ass self," joked the Bud Man, pouring E.P. half a glass of the smooth fiery liquor.

Trying to get a hold of himself, Emancipation Proclamation Jones raised the glass, his hands still trembling. Somehow, deep down inside, he had the eerie feeling that he'd never live to see the birth of his child. He felt like his days were numbered, the clock of death just about to strike the final hour of the final day of his life on this earth. Above all else, E.P. knew that he was doomed, a walking deadman on the winding road to the graveyard of eternity. Unfortunately, for Emancipation Proclamation Jones, the fickle winds of life were about to be sucked out from underneath his soaring wings, whisked away by a melting Snowman from Orleans Place.

CHAPTER 13

FROSTY THE SNOWMAN was in a dust storm, the powdered sugar kind, neat rows of coke lined across Ophelia Johnson's glass topped coffee table like dunes in a white sand desert. Slowly, he furrowed each line with the glistening edge of a razor blade, sadistically smiling as he stared down at the precious white powder. Ophelia, her mind already fried from an afternoon of crack and booze, staggered across her white shag carpeted living room. Falling to her knees, next to the Snowman, her short blue jean skirt hiked well above her smooth chocolate brown thighs, she moistened her long nailed finger tip and dipped it into a row of the fine powdery substance.

She raised the bottom of her off the shoulder midriff blouse, seductively rubbing the coke around her long stiffening nipples. "Lick it off for me, baby. It makes me so hot," begged Ophelia, her sultry voice thick with passion.

The Snowman, leaning over, began to encircle her budding nipples with his searching tongue, eagerly lapping up the white powder. Fondling her hard firm tits, he couldn't help but chuckle. Ophelia, out on bail, would never get her day in court. He'd pronounce sentence on her real soon, maybe even tonight.

"God, I'm horny," moaned Ophelia, dabbing her finger back into another row of coke and then erotically running it over the wet folds of her inflamed pussy.

"You'll eat it for me, won't you baby? Please, make me cum. I need it so bad," pleaded Ophelia, laying on her back, her legs spread wide apart.

The Snowman figured he owed her that much. One last trip to the orgasm zone before he offed her useless slut ass, wasn't too much to ask, now was it, silently laughed the Snowman, flicking his tongue into her moist steamy pussy. "Oh, God! I'm there! Shit, I'm cumming," screamed Ophelia, locking her shapely legs around the Snowman's head, her long manicured fingers entwined in his kinky black hair as she held his face tightly against her juicy vagina.

Leaning over the coffee table, Fred Frost snorted a long line of coke up his nostril, immediately repeating the act on the next line, and then the next. Ophelia, spooning the dust up her nose like a steam shovel digging loose dirt, reached between her legs and rubbed her coke-covered hand all over her sloppy pussy.

"God, it's on fire, baby. Put it out for me, please. Give it to me," begged Ophelia, crawling on to her peach colored leather couch and slipping her leg over its cold smooth surface. The Snowman couldn't help but laugh, his head spinning out of control. It wasn't long ago that she'd begged him not to blow her old man's brains out on this very couch. Instead, pleading with him to waste the bastard where his blood wouldn't stain her new furniture. Now, he was fucking her regularly within feet of where he'd capped the pathetic asshole. Jesus, the cold hearted bitch had even screwed him that night, moaning in ecstasy as she rode him to orgasm, her old man laying less than ten feet away, his brains splattered all over the candle lit room.

"Do me," moaned Ophelia, her sensuous body humping into the air, her orange tipped nails pinching her erect nipples in a frenzy of lust.

"Yeah, baby. I'll do you. I'll do you up real good," coldly stated the Snowman, reaching underneath the couch for the handle of his newly acquired .44 magnum, its six inch stainless steel barrel a more than adequate substitute for his wildly throbbing cock.

"No, not that again. I want you inside me. I wanna feel you explode in me. That thing hurts. Please, baby. You can do me with that, but then I wanna feel you shoot," begged Ophelia, sorry she'd ever asked the Snowman to use the revolver on her in the first place. At the time it had seemed so erotic, working the barrel of the gun in and out of her soaking pussy while he watched, all the time stroking his pulsating manhood. Now, he was using the thing on her like a fucking dildo, hardly ever slipping inside himself. She needed hot cock, not cold steel.

Chuckling, the Snowman slid the barrel of the massive pistol deep inside Ophelia's dripping pussy. Withdrawing the wet, glistening barrel, he paused, then shoved it home again. Ophelia groaned in pleasure, her brown eyes rolling back in her head. "Yeah, that's right, bitch. You'll feel a nice big explosion when I shoot, whispered the Snowman, sliding his finger on to the trigger of the pistoning weapon.

"Faster, baby, faster! I think I can get it! I think I can get off," shouted Ophelia, looking down between her legs, still constantly humping the huge pistol, her mind oblivious to anything other than the burning desire in her aching pussy.

"Get it. That's right, baby, get it," encouraged the Snowman, cocking the hammer of the fluid covered revolver. It was almost time to shoot a nice big load into Ophelia's horny little snatch. "Oh, shit! Fuck it, baby! I'm there! I'm cumming," screamed Ophelia Johnson, arching her back, the weight of her whole sweating body suspended on the frame of the slick juice covered weapon.

"Yeah, that's it, baby. Now, I'm gonna shoot, bitch," laughed the Snowman, squeezing the trigger of the loaded pistol.

Ophelia Johnson stared in wide eyed terror, her insides suddenly churning into a mangled mush. The horrendous explosion, muffled by the clamping lips of her vagina, flopped her into the air like a palsied rag doll. Snapped like a brittle toothpick, her spine disintegrated, pieces of bone and gristle splattering against the cushions of the leather couch. A grotesque gaping hole, blown from the inside out, was all that remained of her lower back, chunks of internal organs oozing out of its bloody edges. Totally limp, her body slowly slid off the hideous looking couch, her head crashing face down, burying itself in the unused rows of coke.

Frosty the Snowman, delighted at his most recent handiwork, wiped the gruesome residue off the blood covered pistol. Callously pushing Ophelia's head out of the piles of white powder, he bent over and snorted the remaining lines of coke, eager to get on with things.

"Damn, E.P.. Please can't you at least turn that thing down a notch?" begged Spic N' Span Spiegel, sliding down as low as he could, his head barely visible behind the steering wheel of Scout 151.

"Shit, man. This brother be rappin' his black ass off," shouted Emancipation Proclamation Jones over the thumping rhythm of his gigantic boom box which sat in the back seat of their patrol car, rattling the windows and door handles with its heavy pounding bass.

"I can't even hear the radio, E.P. What if we miss a run? 10-33 Sam will write us up for sure. He's just lookin' for a reason to nail us. Please, E.P. We ain't even supposed to have a radio in the car," pleaded Spic N' Span Spiegel, cruising 151 down H Street and silently praying that the air would stay quiet. Other than a few routine traffic complaints the radio chatter was at a minimum.

"Just one more tune, man. This next one will blow you away. It's radical, dude," hollered Emancipation Proclamation Jones, reaching into the back seat of 151 to crank up the volume even louder.

Spic N' Span Spiegel, his teeth rattling from the vibrating booms, figured the only thing that was going to get blown away was his eardrums. The sonic explosions had half the people on H Street dancing on the sidewalks as Scout 151 drove past, the locals moonwalking all over their little piece of planet earth. Just as Spic N' Span Spiegel thought that he had seen and heard it all, Emancipation Proclamation Jones stepped over the edge, securing himself legendary status in the ranks of D.C. police lore.

Leaning out the open passenger side window of Scout 151, his skinny body about to tumble out of the slowly cruising car, Emancipation Proclamation Jones, in a moment of divine inspiration, decided to lead the H Street choir in a rousing rendition of his favorite jam. "Fuck tha Police. Fuck tha Police," he shouted out the window of the patrol car. The crowd, caught up in the frenzy of the moment, joined in. Enthusiastically conducted by Emancipation Proclamation Jones, the whole block began chanting in unison, "Fuck tha Police. Fuck tha Police." Accompanied by the thunderous background music, they were more than glad to express their true heartfelt sentiments.

Spic N' Span Spiegel, deciding that E.P. had finally crossed the barrier into the land of the loony tunes, so to speak, punched the pedal to the metal, sending 151 careening down H Street. Screeching on to Bladensburg Road, he finally began to slow the speeding police car, hoping that nobody besides an amused group of locals had witnessed E.P.'s latest act of insanity. At least his partner was back to normal, figured Spic N' Span Spiegel, still shivering when he thought of the terrified look he had seen in E.P.'s eyes last night, at the card table in Tiny's.

The terrified look in Darnell Bell's eyes was both genuine and immediate, his whole body shaking in terror. Looking over at his grandmother, blood spilling out of her quivering lips, the frightened child could only tremble. Finally, he screamed, "Don't you hurt my grandma! My mommy will get you for this. She'll lock you up. She's a police officer, the best."

"Your mommy's a bitch, a black bitch. She ain't nothing but whitey's whore, the worthless slut," laughed the Snowman, brutally slamming Ronnie's mother into the living room wall. He ought to cap this meddling bitch, thought the Snowman, looking down at the semi-conscious woman and wondering how she liked baby-sitting her precious little grandson now, while her honky lovin' daughter was off playing cops and robbers.

"I'm gonna let you live. Just so's you can spend the rest of your life crying with that righteous ass bitch daughter of yours. Thinkin' about what it was like havin' a grandson. Because, when I'm done with him he's gonna be one dead sissy. I'm gonna shoot his nuts off and watch him die," laughed the Snowman, kicking Ronnie's mother in the ribs.

"God, good lord. He's your own son, your own flesh and blood," gasped Ronnie's mother, trying to get back up on her feet and desperately struggling to get to Darnell.

"He ain't no son of mine. My son be standin' on the corner, movin' some stuff, makin' a score, takin' care of business for his old man," shouted the Snowman, punching the staggering woman in the side of her head.

"This here ain't nothin but a wimpy faggot, a mamma's boy," he added, grabbing Darnell's shaking arm and mercilessly cracking the cold steel of the .44 magnum revolver across the back of the reeling woman's skull.

"C'mon punk. I'm takin' you to the real world. The world where the Snowman is the main man. The world where who controls the snow is who controls the show and who controls the dough. I'm takin' you home, home to Orleans Place," sadistically chuckled the coked up Snowman, stepping over the fallen woman's unmoving body and dragging a screaming Darnell out the front door, down to his parked car, about to begin a deadly journey into the morbid land of eternal darkness, the street of black magic, Orleans Place.

"I can't believe I let that asshole go. Man, I should've wrote him at least two tickets, running the light and speeding. Jesus, the old bastard just about killed us and I let him talk me out of writin' him up. Said his wife was just taken to D.C. General. Sure, right. I'm gettin' soft. I must be turnin' into a pussy," grumbled Danny Money, throwing his ticket book down on the seat and watching as the elderly man started up the rusty old Buick Regal, a huge cloud of oily smoke exploding out of its dangling tailpipe.

"Just remember. You are what you eat," chuckled the Bud Man, pulling Scout 150 out into the heavy New York Avenue traffic and quickly glancing over at Money to see if his bewildered partner had caught on to his masterful joke.

"You must be wolfin' down buckets of those maggot gaggin' chitlins then. Because you'd have to have a whole lotta guts to come off with that weak ass shit," answered Danny Money, smugly smiling at the Bud Man and figuring that he had evened the score one more time. Despite the levity of the moment, he was unable to shake off the peculiar feeling that something heavy was about to go down. The airwaves were ominously quiet, almost as if the animals had fled their forest haven before the wrath of a raging inferno. The deserted woods of concrete and steel were an ominous harbinger of impending doom.

The Bud Man could sense it, too. The silence of the radio was eerie. Looking up into the twinkling star-lit night, he had to admit that the blood red tint of the full moon was downright weird, almost scary. Both officers felt on edge, the glowing sky appearing to be a forewarning of a boiling eruption from deep within the city's simmering core, an eruption that could only spew forth more death and destruction, an eruption that was about to explode on Orleans Place and dissolve the Snowman in its wake of molten lava and hot fiery lead.

The last place in the world that Emancipation Proclamation Jones wanted to go, at this very instant, was Orleans Place. Having given in to Spic N' Span Spiegel's insistence that they find a nice quiet place, with no music of any kind, E.P. had suggested that they cruise on over to Gallaudet College. His logic was impeccable. Since the school was for the deaf and dumb, it had to be quiet. Currently the center of attention for three fine foxes from the famous college, Emancipation Proclamation Jones was giving a few lessons in his own version of sign language, the pointing and giggling kind. He was just about to score a room and telephone number from a perky little redbone from the rural Virginia countryside, Spic N' Span Spiegel shaking his head in total amazement at E.P.'s lewd, but successful, communication techniques. Unfortunately, for E.P., the bubbling pot of Orleans Place was just about to boil over and painfully scald his happy go lucky, ill-fated life.

"Hey, E.P. We've got a man with a gun on Orleans Place. Let's roll," shouted Spic N' Span Spiegel, recording the information on the radio run sheet and impatiently waiting for his partner to sign off the hot looking campus queen who was eagerly bobbing her head up and down in an imitation of God only knows what, thought the amazed officer, pretty sure he knew exactly what E.P. had in mind.

"Get down on it. Get down on it," sang Emancipation Proclamation Jones, jumping into Scout 151's passenger seat, a huge grin plastered across his smirking face.

"We've got the run with 150," added Spic N' Span Spiegel, slapping the gearshift into drive and squealing 151's tires as he sped out of the Gallaudet campus, turning right, on to Florida Avenue.

"Too bad the ladies can't hear our exit. I'd turn the siren on, just for a little effect, but what's the use? They couldn't hear that either," remarked Emancipation Proclamation Jones, adding, "It's 150's area so the Bud Man and Money will get stuck with the report."

"Geez, did you hear that? Now we've got shots fired, Code One," excitedly shouted Spic N' Span Spiegel, acknowledging the dispatcher's message and reaching down to flick on the red lights and siren.

"Pump up the jam, man. Pump up the jam. Let's rock and roll, baby. Cause that's where the party's at," chorused Emancipation Proclamation Jones, dancing in his seat, his whole body bouncing up and down to the rhythmic beat of the song going through his head.

"What's the address?" he asked, holding on for dear life as Spic N' Span Spiegel wildly pumped the scout car's brakes and slid 151 to a complete stop in the middle of the dark street.

"There it is, right there," excitedly yelled Spic N' Span Spiegel, pointing to the graffiti covered row house to their immediate right, half of its broken windows boarded shut, the other half covered with stained yellowing sheets.

"Nice crib, man," joked Emancipation Proclamation Jones, pulling out his nine millimeter as he led the way up the cracked and broken cement sidewalk, rusted beer cans and broken liquor bottles strewn all over the barren dirt yard.

Looking at the ominous address, Spic N' Span Spiegel couldn't help but feel a twinge of foreboding. All his senses, his years of experience, told him that this was not just another wild goose chase, another bullshit family squabble where they'd end up playing the role of shrinks. This goose wasn't about to lay the golden egg.

"Be careful, E.P. This place is giving me the creeps. Check out the address. I've got the feeling that we're about to walk into the Bates Motel," whispered Spic N' Span Spiegel, staring at the numbers 666 attached to the weathered brownstone row house.

"What you talking about, man? What the hell is the Bates Motel, anyway? Shit, 666 ain't nothin but 999 turned upside down. There ain't nothin happenin' here, nothin' 'cept another junkie beatin' up his old lady. Let's get this over with so's we can boogie on over to Gullaudet. That sweet child be wantin' some of brother E.P.'s chocolate Tootsie Pop," joked Emancipation Proclamation Jones, cracking his nightstick against the ripped and torn screen door and making sure to stand off to one side, just in case the police welcome wagon was not so welcome.

Spic N' Span Spiegel, still feeling fidgety, glanced down the length of the narrow porch, his darting eyes detecting a gentle rustling movement behind one of the dingy sheet covered windows at the end of the deserted looking building. Withdrawing his weapon, he stepped out away from the crumbling brick door frame, trying to get a better look down the length of the littered porch, its surface piled high with plastic bags of reeking garbage and greasy trash filled cardboard boxes. There it was again, the distinct outline of a shadowy silhouette lurking behind the rippling sheet, noticed Spic N' Span Spiegel, cautiously crouching behind a pile of rancid smelling garbage.

"There's somebody behind this window, over here. Be cool, E.P. I'm getting some bad vibes," warned Spic N' Span Spiegel, leveling his weapon at the covered opening.

"Shit, man. Let's clear this run and go 10-8. There ain't nobody home. Color me gone. I'm outta this place," stated Emancipation Proclamation Jones, holstering his gun and turning to walk back down the front porch steps.

"No, E.P., no," screamed Spic N' Span Spiegel, watching in horror as suddenly, the window curtain was ripped aside, revealing a man, his right arm pointing a huge stainless steel handgun at his partner's exposed back, his left, cradling a flailing young child.

Unable to fire at the armed man for fear of hitting the innocent child, Spic N' Span Spiegel hesitated for a split second, frozen in indecision, his partner's life passing before his very eyes. The deafening eruption cracked in the night, sparks flying out of the exploding barrel, the acrid aroma of gunpowder wafting across the foul smelling air. Staring helplessly, Spic N' Span Spiegel watched as the hurtling bullet ripped into his partner's back, its horrendous force staggering the wounded officer.

Clutching desperately at the gaping exit hole in the right side of his chest, Emancipation Proclamation Jones crumpled to the ground, his limp body violently tumbling down the front porch steps. Less than seven feet from the open window, Spic N' Span Spiegel turned back around to confront the attacker, his shocked stare deeply piercing the terrified eyes of the frightened young boy, crying in the man's arms. Standing perfectly erect, Spic N' Span Spiegel began slowly backing down the length of the littered porch, his nine millimeter leveled on the sinister form, his finger still unable to pull the trigger and jeopardize the life of the shaking child.

Laughing at the slowly retreating cop, Frosty the Snowman drew a bead right between the white honky's unblinking eyes. He'd waste this pig, fry his brains in a boiling pot of molten lead. He chuckled as he squeezed the trigger of the .44 magnum, visions of Ophelia's gruesome mangled body dancing in his reeling head. Spic N' Span Spiegel closed his eyes and made his peace with God, praying that his death wouldn't shame Briefcase Betty or the memory of his father. The explosion, like a rolling thunder clap, reverberated through the night air, its booming echo rumbling on the nocturnal wind. The bullet passed by his left ear, screaming through the air, its high pitched whine whistling a merciful tune.

Spic N' Span Spiegel opened his eyes, watching in disbelief as the young boy who had obviously saved his life continued to relentlessly shake the gun hand of the man who held the poor child in his fateful grasp. Seeing his chance, Spic N' Span Spiegel bolted for the far end of the porch. Leaping over the railing, he crashed into the ground below. For the moment, protected by the cement abutment, he was safe. His partner was a sitting duck. Pausing to catch his breath, Spic N' Span Spiegel knew he had no other choice. Suddenly, time stood still, hurtling him across the mystical field of dreams. The ghost of his father stood beside him lighting the way, the way to salvation, the way to glory. To get there, Spic N' Span Spiegel instinctively knew that he had to walk upon the hallowed ground, the few yards of reality that separates obscurity from immortality. The price was high. The reward was immeasurable.

Danny Money and the Bud Man, screaming on to the scene in Scout 150, their flashing red lights casting an eerie reflection of shadowy crimson, looked on in horror, knowing instantly that they had just entered the magical twilight zone of Orleans Place, in all its gruesome splendor.

"Jesus Christ, E.P.'s been shot. Call for an ambulance. Damn,

I can't believe this shit. Spiegel's trapped. He can't get to E.P.," shouted the Bud Man, rushing towards the house and taking cover behind an abandoned car, its stolen tires and rims long ago replaced by cinderblocks.

Danny Money radioed for an ambulance. Then, withdrawing his weapon, he ran over to join the Bud Man, both officers crouching behind the rusted car frame.

"We'll cover you! Make a run for it, Spiegel," yelled Danny Money, grimacing as he suddenly realized whose house he was sitting in front of. "This could be some bad shit. That's the Snowman's place," he said, looking over at his partner, afraid that things were even worse than they had first appeared.

"Don't shoot at the house. He's holding a young boy hostage," shouted Spic N' Span Spiegel, preparing himself to do what had to be done.

Danny Money shuddered, the reality of the situation chilling him to the bone. He instantly knew who the boy was. God, he prayed that Ronnie hadn't gotten word. This would tear her apart.

"Stay where you are, you guys. He's my partner. Please, let me get to him. There's no use in you guys trying. He's too far away. I'll do it. I know I can save him," desperately pleaded Spic N' Span Spiegel, cautiously moving out from behind the protection of the shielding porch, determined, once and for all, to prove that he belonged to this brotherhood of true American heroes, a brotherhood of blue that had already welcomed too many of its brethren to an early grave.

"Good God, almighty. Look at Spiegel. Damn, he's goin' for E.P. Jesus, the kid's got guts," excitedly observed the Bud Man, watching in fascination as Spic N' Span Spiegel stood up, holstered his weapon, and calmly walked over to his partner's ominously still body.

His feet sliding in the puddles of oozing blood covering the dark stained sidewalk, Spic N' Span Spiegel looked down at the silent form of his wounded partner. Then, without hesitation, he bent over and grabbed Emancipation Proclamation Jones' arms, gently pulling the dying officer upright. Emancipation Proclamation Jones moaned, his eyes rolling back, their deathly paling stare unable to focus.

"You're not gonna die. Please, listen to me, E.P. You're not gonna die. You're gonna live to see your baby. Before you're through you'll probably have a whole tribe of little E.P.'s runnin' all over the place. Heck, you'll probably have enough kids to form your own family rap group. You could call yourselves the Declarations of Independence or Emancipation Proclamation and the Constitutions," consoled Spic N' Span Spiegel, desperately trying to force a breath of life into his dying partner. Gently sliding Emancipation Proclamation Jones' limp bloody body over his shoulder and staggering under the weight of the unmoving officer, he turned and began to slowly walk towards the protection of the parked cars on Orleans Place. He glanced back over his shoulder, defiantly locking his vision into the raging eyes of the Snowman who was still struggling with Darnell, unable to draw a bead on their helplessly exposed forms.

A trashman picking up a load of stinkin' police garbage, conjured up the reeling mind of the Snowman as he watched the honky pig pick up the nicely ventilated body of the black Uncle Tom cop. Now, all he'd have to do was smoke this little nigger brat and he could dust off oinker number two, reasoned the drug laced murderer, brutally slamming the cold stainless steel barrel of the .44 magnum revolver into the side of Darnell's painfully exploding head. Dropping the slumping boy's body to the hard floor, the Snowman raised his weapon and aligned its sights between Spic N' Span Spiegel's shoulder blades. With a little luck he could drill both pigs with one round, figured the Snowman, squeezing the trigger of the murderous weapon, its powerful recoil kicking his arm high into the foul smelling air of the dark room.

Spic N' Span Spiegel, his whole body twitching at the deafening roar of the cracking explosion, shuddered as he braced himself for the bullet's deadly impact, fearing that it would plow into E.P.'s exposed form first, probably finishing off his suffering partner. Instead, the sidewalk under his staggering feet disintegrated, flying chips of cement stinging his ankles as the bullet passed harmlessly between his legs and imbedded itself into the rusted body of a nearby abandoned auto. Undaunted, Spic N' Span Spiegel continued on, finally reaching the relative safety of the street, the Bud Man and Danny Money rushing out from behind the protection of the row of parked cars to help him negotiate the last few yards.

"Jesus, you looked like Audie Murphy, out there," gasped Danny Money, helping Spic N' Span Spiegel gently lower E.P. to the cold oily pavement.

The Bud Man, racing back from the trunk of Scout 150, covered Emancipation Proclamation Jones' limp body with a blanket. He was trying in vain to prevent the inescapable onslaught of shock which had already begun to devour E.P.'s helplessly ravaged body.

"That was the bravest thing I've ever seen," solemnly stated the Bud Man, looking directly at Spic N' Span Spiegel, totally unprepared for what was to follow.

Gasping for air, his body totally exhausted, his uniform drenched in sweat, streaks of blood covering his dark blue nylon jacket, Spic N' Span Spiegel calmly stated, "I'm going back in to get the kid. He saved my life."

"I'll go with you. You know that's Ronnie's son in there, right? I've got to go. Call it whatever you want. But, if I'm ever gonna have any kind of life with her, Darnell's gotta be part of that life. He's part of her and I guess that makes him part of me," added Danny Money, knowing in his heart that this moment was frozen in eternity. Only time would tell whether it would ever thaw, returning warmth where right now existed the chilling reality of life.

"Let's boogie," stated Spic N' Span Spiegel, looking down at his wounded partner. The Bud Man, removing his own shirt, pressed it against the gurgling hole in E.P.'s chest, a warm sticky fluid quickly spreading across its light blue wadded form. Instinctively knowing that he would be the one to stay with E.P., he quietly stated, "Good luck. By the way, Danny, what you call it is love."

Danny Money, seeing the sincere look in his partner's eyes, said simply, "That's one four letter word that none of us say as much as we should." Listening to the shrill wail of countless approaching sirens, he could only hope that that love would give him the strength to confront his own imminent death, a possibility which lay upon the horizon, clouded by the mystical fog of Orleans Place, street of the living dead.

Bolting across the dim shadowy street, Spic N' Span Spiegel raced for the protection of the cement porch, Danny Money wildly running right behind. Both officers, their lungs burning, gasped for air as they flattened themselves against the protective abutment. Pausing to catch their breath, they cautiously peered over the top of the littered porch, relieved to see that the far window appeared to be open, but surprisingly vacant. Suddenly, from within the house, a muffled explosion cracked ominously, its reverberating boom echoing out into the crisp night air. The weapon barked again, and again.

Spic N' Span Spiegel looked at Danny Money, both officers

shuddering in fear as they mentally pictured the enfolding drama of violent death being carried out inside the house, one cold blooded act at a time. Danny Money rushed up the porch steps and prayed that he could get to Darnell before his role in the haunting tragedy was canceled permanently. He raced across the littered porch, pieces of wet soggy garbage squishing underneath his pounding boots as he hurled himself through the open window, his Glock nine millimeter at the ready. Tumbling into the musty smelling living room right behind him, Spic N' Span Spiegel leaped to his feet, immediately deciding to race up the stairs.

His heart thumping wildly, a cold sweat beading on his forehead, Danny Money burst into the kitchen, the rancid stench of rotting garbage jumping up into his nose like an acrid dose of smelling salts. Finding nothing, he turned and sprinted back towards the stairway, bounding up the threadbare carpet steps in long desperate leaps. Danny Money followed Spic N' Span Spiegel down the dusty upstairs hallway, noticing everything he touched seemed to be covered with a fine coating of grease. Roaches scurried across the grimy floor, disappearing into dirt-encrusted cracks and crevices.

Spic N' Span Spiegel slowly turned the slimy door knob, wiping his hand on the seat of his pants as he entered the room. A single naked lightbulb hung from the cracked and peeling plaster ceiling, its dim glow casting an eerie yellow pall over the sickening scene. Three bodies lay propped against the dirty bedroom wall, their hands tied behind their backs, a bullet hole neatly drilled between their glassy open eyes. Murdered in cold blood, execution style, the back of their heads were splattered all over the grimy wall like some kind of grotesque art work. The corpses looked so serene that, for a brief second, Spic N' Span Spiegel dropped his guard. Staring at the gruesome spectacle in morbid fascination, he jumped, startled, as Danny Money burst into the room.

"Jesus, that's Frosty's old lady and her kids. Damn, that bastard butchered his own family. We've got to find him before he caps Darnell. Where is that son of a bitch," shouted Danny Money in frustration and rage as he glanced around the room, sure that the Snowman had already waxed little Darnell.

"I'm right here, you fuckin honky pig," yelled the Snowman from behind the startled officer, pushing open the closet door and jamming his monstrous handgun into the back of Danny Money's head.

"Now drop the heat, asshole, or I waste my man, here. I'd love to make his slut a grievin' black bitch," ordered the Snowman, his flaming eyes burning right into Spic N' Span Spiegel's reeling head.

Cocking the hammer of the .44 magnum, he stated coldly, "I was hopin' it would be you, you and pretty boy, here. You don't know me, but I know who you are. You're the dead cop's kid. He used to walk the beat down here, always trying to slip his pathetic white meat into the local bitches. He loved that black pussy so much, sometimes he'd turn his head the other way just so's he could get his dick wet. The whores be laughin' at him, boy, laughin' at his pitiful white ass. One day he wouldn't turn his head, even for my mama, and she was the best. Had his head twisted inside out, she did. He was gonna lock her up, take her to jail cause she was sellin' skag. The mother fucker beat her up, man. Beat the livin' shit right outta her. Then, he raped her. So, while he was doin' my mama one last time, I took the gun outta his holster and I did him, right in the back of his head. The pigs, they covered the shit up. Made him a real hero. My mama spent the rest of her life in jail, takin' the rap for me, her little baby boy. Your old man was my first. Now, you and slick are gonna join him if you don't drop your gun."

Spic N' Span Spiegel was looking directly into the eyes of hell, their bottomless pits scalding his soul. His whole body was trembling. A cold sweat broke out on his back, drenching his uniform shirt. He was confused, deeply shaken by the Snowman's revelations. Totally defeated, he was about to drop his gun, almost relieved to die. He was a loser. Nothing could ever change that. Even his father had been a lie, figured the despondent officer as he began to falter, knowing that to drop his gun meant to die. The Snowman's eyes sparkled. He knew he was just about to roast a couple of pigs. The poor stupid cop was even dumber than his old man, thought the Snowman, convinced that the chickenshit son of a bitch was about to give in.

Suddenly, Spic N' Span Spiegel felt charged with crackling electricity, his whole body tingling with energy. No, damn it, he wasn't a loser. Hadn't he just faced death and hopefully saved his partner's life? Didn't Betty tell him that heroes come in all different shapes and sizes, that he had to stand tall and proud on his own two feet and not carry his father's heavy burden on his back? Well, nobody but he himself knew that he was most likely the best marksman in the whole damn department. While everybody else was out drinking and dancing he was at the range, almost every night, shooting countless rounds at flashing pictures of bad guys and black silhouettes ringed with bull's eyes. Now, it was his time to shine. Spic N' Span Spiegel was in the zone, about to cast his shadow across the legendary sands of time.

"Screw you, you piece of shit," shouted Spic N' Span Spiegel, dropping down to one knee and clutching the familiar oversize grips of his Glock nine millimeter with both hands. Drawing a bead on the Snowman's right kneecap, he squeezed the trigger, the gun's muzzle flash exploding in smoke and flames. The hollow point bullet hit dead center, splintering the Snowman's kneecap in a sickening crunch.

Danny Money, seeing a glimmer of hope, hit the deck, desperately rolling across the floor like an out of control log tumbling downhill, his eyes locked on the steady kneeling form of Spic N' Span Spiegel. Grimacing in pain, Frosty leveled the massive revolver at Spic N' Span Spiegel and screamed, "You're dead meat, just like your old man, punk." He jerked the trigger, the deafening roar rattling the room's window panes, gunpowder and sparks flying through the dense air.

Spic N' Span Spiegel never even flinched, the errant bullet thudding into the chest of the Snowman's already dead common law wife. Before him stood another silhouette target, concentric circles ringing its familiar form. Unconsciously, Spic N' Span Spiegel took a deep breath, exhaled, gently squeezed the trigger and exploded a round into Frosty's heart, staggering the drug crazed murderer.

"Bull's-eye," whispered Spic N' Span Spiegel under his breath as he cracked another bullet into the x-ring, it's soft lead plowing into the Snowman's chest, less than one inch from the first round. The Snowman, wildly clutching at his punctured heart, crumbled heavily to the floor, his collapsing body twitching in uncontrollable spasms. Realizing that Spic N' Span Spiegel had just saved his life, Danny Money got to his feet and rushing towards the Snowman, he kicked the stainless steel revolver across the floor.

Spic N' Span Spiegel, looking like a dwarfed uniformed version of Dirty Harry, calmly stood up and holstered his still smoking weapon as he quietly mumbled, "Go ahead, punk. Make my day."

Walking over to the open closet, Spic N' Span Spiegel found just what he expected. There, huddled in the corner behind the piles of dirty laundry, sat Darnell, trembling in terror, his knees drawn up to his chest, tears streaking down his golden brown cheeks. Bending over, he drew the terrified boy into his open arms, a smile suddenly appearing on his once troubled face. Almost as if the weight of the world had been lifted from his shoulders, Spic N' Span Spiegel carried Darnell into the room and, handing the crying child over to Danny, said simply, "Thanks, kid. You saved my life."

Darnell hugged Danny desperately. Then, looking back over his shoulder, he answered, "You're a nice man, sir. Next to my mommy, you're the bravest police officer I ever saw."

"You're damn right, he is," enthusiastically commented Danny Money. "Ronnie and I will never be able to repay you for what you've done. You've given us back a priceless treasure. But, you're the rich man."

Walking out the front door of 666 Orleans Place, police cars lining the entire street, Danny Money took a deep breath and paused to savor this fleeting moment of life. He watched intently as the ambulance with Emancipation Proclamation Jones on board, still desperately clinging to life, sped off in the distance, headed for D.C. General Hospital, its wailing siren a solitary bugle in the night. Danny Money could only hope that it wasn't playing the mournful melody of taps.

"Goddamn. If you ain't a bonafide hero, I ain't never seen one. You is the cream of the crop. Yes, you sure nuff is," bellowed Tiny across the bar, pushing a heaping plate of smoldering greasy chili cheese fries in front of Spic N' Span Spiegel and winking as he made sure that the heroic officer knew that they were on the house. Danny Money looked down at the gooey oozing mess of bubbling cholesterol. Then, deciding that whatever was good enough for Spiegel was good enough for him, he ordered a plate for everybody.

Ronnie, having just come from the hospital and greatly relieved to have found out that both her mother and Darnell were going to be OK, couldn't do enough for the besieged hero. Offering to cook him the best damn meal he had ever had, cornbread, collared greens, fried chicken, black eyed peas, mashed potatoes and gravy, sweet potato pie, the works, she insisted that he and Betty also allow her the privilege of sending them to Ocean City, Maryland for a romantic weekend get-a-way.

Mike McCarthy sat at a table alone, away from the jovial

group, and poured himself another glass of scotch, glad that the Snowman was dead. He felt grim, somber, never before having celebrated the death of a human being. Amazed at his callous attitude, he shook his head, ashamed of himself. No matter how bad a man was, he had a soul that would be judged by the Good Lord, God Almighty, thought Mac, shuddering as a vision of Ophelia's mutilated torso danced across his mind. As soon as they tied up a few loose ends they could close that case too, he figured, no doubt in his mind that Frosty had wasted both her and her old man.

He watched, somewhat amused, as Briefcase Betty pulled Spic N' Span Spiegel out on the dance floor, swallowing his whole body in a steamy humping grind.

"Go for it, Spiegel," shouted Danny Money, walking over to the juke box to coin some killer jams, figuring Spiegel would be ground chuck once Briefcase Betty had some tunes to grind to.

Mike McCarthy listened to the clink of the coins, thinking of the good old days when he and his wife had played the jukebox, dancing cheek to cheek to the comforting sounds of Perry Como, Andy Williams, Lawrence Welk, and countless others. Suddenly, his blood ran cold, a numbing chill shooting up his spine. He knew this song, but he'd never heard this part. Mac shivered, the frightening words indelibly etching themselves into his mind as the rock country twang of Bon Jovi's Blaze of Glory boomed out of the jukebox.

Instantly, a hunched figure appeared in his mind, bending over a fresh kill, a human kill, blood dripping from between its rotting yellow teeth. Without hesitation, it slid a knife into the belly of the dead carcass. Smiling as it licked its dry weathered lips, it repeated over and over again, "But, Jon. You're wrong. I'm a god. Why don't you pull the trigger and prove it?"

Amazingly, Mac found himself staring at the stubbly bearded hillbilly face of the Capital Carver, laughing as he gutted another victim, tobacco juice drooling down his sinister chin.

"Where are you, you evil bastard, you wicked devil?" shouted Mac, suddenly realizing how stupid he must look, a silly drunken old man loosing his grip, yelling at ghosts, chasing mind shadows that disappeared in the dark.

Rhonda Bell knew who Mac was talking to. The others, they just wouldn't understand, thought Ronnie, walking over to comfort Mac. The nightmares were beginning to devour her too, constantly haunting her with their bewitching reality. It was the clues that were driving her crazy. The answer was there. If they didn't solve the riddle pretty soon the bells would toll again. But, this time they'd either echo the booming gong of Asia or the jingling chimes of Mexico.

Interrupted by the ringing of the phone, her thoughts immediately turned to the welfare of Emancipation Proclamation Jones, virtually fighting for his life at D.C. General, the doctors long ago telling all the officers to go home. There was nothing any of them could do. So, instead, they had congregated at Tiny's awaiting word on the mortally wounded officer. Picking up the telephone, Tiny called for Spic N' Span Spiegel, realizing that he was the one to bear the news, good or bad. Spiegel raced to the phone, wiping a dripping gob of chili cheese fries off his greasy chin with the sleeve of his uniform shirt. A hushed silence settled over the smoky room, the officers crowding around the telephone, awaiting the fateful news.

Finally, after what seemed like an eternity, Spic N' Span Spiegel hung up the phone, jubilantly shouting, "E.P.'s gonna make it. The doctors say he's gonna be OK."

"That tough little nigger is probably already chasin' them cute nurses around the bed," hollered Tiny, proud of his hip new image as, for good measure, he added, "Stop, constipate and listen. E.P.'s back with a brand new edition. Word to your mother."

"Jesus. Tiny. You're just totally rad, man. Simply an awesome gnarly dude," snickered the Bud Man as he turned towards Spic N' Span Spiegel and, in his harshest voice, yelled, "Spiegel, get your butt over here, now!"

Spiegel, shocked at the monstrous Bud Man's callous sounding voice and afraid that he'd done something terribly wrong, ran over to the bellowing officer. Staring at the much smaller officer, the Bud Man turned around in his stool, slammed a long neck bottle of Budweiser on the counter and said it all when he proudly proclaimed, "Hey, kid. This Bud's for you!"

CHAPTER 14

"PLEASE, WE WANT the top down," pleaded Ronnie, running her long manicured fingernails teasingly up the inside leg of Danny Money's Levi's. Glancing in the back of Danny's BMW convertible to make sure that Darnell couldn't see her roving hand, she gently squeezed her boyfriend's balls, driving her point home with more impact than a steaming locomotive.

"OK, like always, you win. Jesus, its gettin' hot in here, anyway," joked Danny Money, both his temperature and his manhood steadily rising in unison with Ronnie's incessant attack. Pulling the gleaming white BMW off the highway into a roadside rest stop he stepped out of the car, stretching his tall lean frame as he watched Ronnie walk Darnell over to the bathrooms, her stacked body attracting the passing head-over-the-shoulder glances of several nearby travelers. Danny quickly put the convertible top down and walked over to a nearby vacant picnic table, pausing to absorb the surrounding majestic scenery. Everywhere he looked, rolling mountains covered with forests of barren dark trees stretched into the horizon, their rounded peaks and valleys dotted with cleared patches of farmland. The distinctive outline of split rail and stone fences bordered their furrowed fields, the whole panorama looking like a huge wavy chessboard.

"God, it's beautiful, isn't it?" sighed Ronnie, sitting down next to Danny, her slender fingers entwining themselves into Danny's as she gently grasped his warm hand.

"Yeah, it sure is. You kind of forget how different things are outside of the city. They're so unspoiled, almost as if time has passed them by," answered Danny, leaning over and kissing Ronnie's glowing cheek. "Over there, off in the distance, straight north, that's Pennsylvania. We'll be there in less than an hour. Then, in another two, you'll be sayin' hello to my family. You're not nervous, are you?"

"No, I'm not nervous," lied Ronnie, squirming in her seat, wondering just how many butterflies it took to make your stomach turn totally upside down. Glancing over her shoulder, she watched Darnell run across the asphalt parking lot, his brand new, 'had to have 'em, mom,' black Air Jordan high tops, kicking up a trail of loose gravel as he sprinted towards the wooden picnic table.

"This is cool, man, totally awesome. Mom, this is bitchin'," shouted Darnell, racing around the table, then charging into the surrounding woods.

"Don't use that word, Darnell. I've told you about that before," hollered Ronnie half-heartedly, unable to bring herself to discipline her son so soon after his terrifying ordeal with his deceased father, the Snowman.

"Don't have a cow, mom. Everybody says it," yelled Darnell, putting a little 'shake and bake' on a nearby tree and then slam-dunking an imaginary basketball over a low hanging branch. Ronnie shook her head, frustrated, but amused, at her son's attempt at being rad. She knew one thing for sure, though. Without a doubt, the Simpsons and MTV were out and Soul Train was back in. Darnell was beginning to sound like some new wave dude from California.

"As they say in the Taco Bell commercials, it's time to run for the border," joked Danny, getting up from the bench and glancing at the sunny, clear blue morning sky. Running over towards Darnell, he pretended to steal the imaginary basketball and do a reverse two handed monster jam over the impromptu basket, making sure to grab on to and hang from the shaking branch for maximum effect.

"The only difference between you two, is that you're taller. Men just never grow up, now, do they?" chuckled Ronnie, calling a foul on Darnell for reaching in on Danny when he tried to steal the pretend ball.

"Well, when do I get to go to the line?" asked Danny Money, arguing with the self appointed referee.

"You'll get a chance at your free throws later, if you know what I mean," laughed Ronnie, winking, as she patted Danny's butt and signaled for a time out. She was elated. There were so many unpleasant things behind her, out of the way. Now, it seemed like there was nothing but happiness in store for her and Darnell. Getting into the idling BMW and slamming the car door, she felt a warm languid flush engulf her body. She looked over at its source, the smiling face of her lover, Danny Money, and decided that she wouldn't have it any other way. Some people went an entire lifetime, searching in vain for what she had found. Love, indeed, was a many splendoured thing, thought Ronnie, reaching over and playfully messing with Danny's wavy windblown hair.

"There it is," shouted Danny over the noise of the wind whipping through the open speeding car. Exuberantly, Ronnie looked up at the sign which read, Welcome to Pennsylvania.

"Damn this place, anyway. If it ain't rainin', it's snowin'. If it ain't soggy, it's foggy," cursed Danny Money looking up ahead, a thick swirling mist totally obscuring the four lane highway. Glancing up at the golden ball of the shimmering sun, Ronnie watched in awe as a towering grey black thundercloud insinuated itself directly across the beaming orb, choking off the warming rays in a dismal blanket of gloom. Dark shadows crept across the passing landscape, their bleak reflections casting an ominous pall on the murky forests lining the winding roadway. Looming off in the distance, down-rutted lanes slashed through the thick woods, massive steel electric towers with huge power lines drooping down from their outstretched metal arms looked like lone sentinels slowly being gobbled up by the encroaching fog.

Ronnie shivered, pulling her black leather motorcycle jacket tightly around her thin graceful neck. She looked in the back seat, making sure that Darnell was buckled in, the collar of his Washington Redskins coat blowing wildly in the whistling wind. Uncrossing her tight blue jean clad legs, she leaned over towards Danny. Gently resting her hand on his thigh, she snuggled her upper body against his and tried to fight off the damp bone-chilling cold which was cutting through her like a knife carving up a plump juicy turkey. Why did she think of that comparison, thought Ronnie, gasping. Suddenly, a vision of a hunched figure lurking over his paralyzed victim and licking his grinning lips as he slid a knife into the body of his suffering prey, shot through her mind.

"This stuff is real thick. Worst I've seen in years," stated Danny, flicking on the foglights as the drizzling mist swallowed up the slowing car.

"Hurry, Danny. Get out of this fog. I feel like he's out there, stalking me like some kind of animal," pleaded Ronnie, desperately clutching at the sleeve of Danny's leather flight-jacket, the car plunging headlong into the blinding fog bank.

"Take it easy, honey. We'll be out of this in a deuce. The top of the hill is just up around this next bend," comforted Danny, putting his right arm around Ronnie's shoulder and pulling her shivering body closer to his.

"There, I told you. We're back in the clear. Look, even the sun's out again. What more could you ask for? Breezewood's only a few miles further. We'll stop there and get some lunch,

OK? Maybe, that'll make you feel better. You want me to put the top back up?" questioned Danny, looking over at Ronnie and knowing that, in her mind, the hunt for the Capital Carver would go on relentlessly until he was captured or killed. Somehow, he had the uneasy feeling that, like marriage, this forced relationship between the Carver and Ronnie was going to last only until death did it part.

"No," stated Ronnie simply.

"No, what?" replied Danny, looking at the speedometer as a Pennsylvania State Trooper sped past, about to nail the tractor trailer that had just thundered down the long winding hill at over eighty-five miles an hour.

"No, I don't want you to put the top back up. I like it down and so does Darnell. Isn't that right, honey?" said Ronnie, glancing back at her son, his eyes beaming with joy as he took in the rural countryside, never before having been out of the metropolitan D.C. area.

"Cows, mommy. Look at all those cows," excitedly shouted Darnell, pointing at the grazing herd of black and white Holsteins lazily meandering across a huge grassy field.

That, figured Ronnie, was answer enough.

"Well, we're finally here. Sure, you're not nervous? How about you sport, you nervous?" asked Danny, looking at Ronnie, then turning around to smile at Darnell.

"No, I told you before. I'm not nervous. Why should I be? I'm used to meeting white folks whose son is my boyfriend. I do it all the time," snapped Ronnie, fumbling with her make-up mirror in one last hectic attempt to make herself look as presentable as possible.

"Your mommy looks pretty good to me. You think she'll pass inspection?" joked Danny, chuckling as he watched Ronnie nervously drop her tube of lipstick for the second straight time, having succeeded in painting everything except her quivering lips.

"I don't think anything's so funny. This isn't a joke to me. I want to look good for your family. They're probably expecting Whitney Houston to walk in the door and I'm not about to give them anything less if I can help it," shot back Ronnie, pulling down the visor make-up mirror to give her tingling flushed face one final look. Then, seeing the smeared lines of lipstick, she started to cry, a steady wet trickle running down her trembling cheeks.

"Hey, take it easy. Go ahead, take a minute and fix yourself up. My family's going to care about what your inside looks like, not your outside. Up here, in the sticks, we check a woman's teeth before we marry 'em and you've got a great set of pearly whites," chuckled Danny, walking around the car to open Ronnie's door.

"There, that's better. Now, I'm ready," stated Ronnie, dabbing her eyes with a Kleenex and stepping out of the BMW, a congenial smile replacing the somber pouting expression on her rich full lips.

Danny opened the trunk, removed the two suitcases, and started up the sidewalk towards the front porch of the two story red-brick house, Ronnie and Darnell following closely.

"It's good to see you, son. Its been way too long. Your mother's always wonderin' why you never come home, anymore. Me, I'd started to wonder myself. But, now I see why. I sure 'nuff do. Your friend is really pretty," stated Danny's father, a smile plastered across his ruddy face as he hugged his only son. Offering his outstretched hand to a relieved Ronnie, he remarked, "Only one thing wrong here, though."

A lump rising in her dry throat, Ronnie prepared herself for the inevitable disaster. She really hadn't expected it, sure that Danny's parents would accept her for what she was.

"The little fella, here. He's gotta lose that Redskins jacket. This here's Steeler country. Maybe later, we'll take him down to the sporting goods store and buy him a Steelers coat and ball cap," laughed Danny's father, rapping his massive arm around Darnell's shoulder and escorting the young boy into the kitchen for a slice of home made apple pie and a glass of ice cold farm fresh milk.

Ronnie sighed, the tension immediately melting out of her tightly coiled body. Looking up the stairs, she watched as Danny's mother bounded down the steps, the attractive congenial looking woman swallowing up her son in a joyous bearhug.

"You look great. A little on the thin side, though," remarked Nancy Money, stepping back to get a good look at her tall handsome boy.

"It's not for lack of good cookin', mom. Ronnie is a great cook. She's a wonderful lady," stated Danny, putting his arm around Ronnie's waist and pulling her body up against his.

"She sure is beautiful. You must be some kind of woman to make Danny as happy as you have. Every time he calls home, all he talks about is you and your little boy. Come on into the kitchen. I've got some fresh baked chocolate chip cookies sitting on the counter just waitin' to make somebody fat and happy," stated Nancy Money, pushing open the swinging cafe style doors and leading the way into the huge country kitchen.

"Darnell, don't eat the last piece of pie. Somebody else might want some," scolded Ronnie, watching as Danny's father plopped a huge juicy looking piece of apple pie on Darnell's plate and offered to top it off with a scoop of home made strawberry ice cream.

"This boy's got a man's appetite. He's gonna do just fine. We'll turn the game on later. I think the Bulls are playin' the Pistons. Did Danny ever tell you he was the captain of the little Indians high school basketball team. Averaged over twenty points a game, he did. His team won the division championship. They lost to the big city boys from Pittsburgh in the state tournament. Little Indiana, Pennsylvania took McKeesport to two overtimes. Danny had forty points, a school record," bragged John Money, excited to have the opportunity to talk sports to Darnell or anybody else who would listen.

"John, these kids don't want to hear about the old days. Why don't you take Darnell out into the driveway and let him shoot some baskets? Hardly anybody's played ball out there since Danny left home," suggested Nancy Money, noticing that her husband had just adopted a new son.

"Don't beat him too bad, Darnell. He's kinda old and slow," kidded Danny, wolfing down his third cookie.

"Who do you think taught him? In your face," scoffed John Money, escorting an eager Darnell out the back door to shoot some hoops.

Danny Money walked down Philadelphia Street, arm in arm with Ronnie, both lovers leisurely window shopping as they browsed through the shops and stores of Indiana's busy main street. Ronnie, watching in amazement at the passing parade of four-wheel drive vehicles of every conceivable description, could only guess as to how anybody could even get into some of their jacked-up cabs, a fork lift or ladder being their only viable option. Pretending not to notice the disconcerting glances of the passing motorists and sometimes obvious gawking stares of the shocked store owners, she walked on, determined to overcome whatever prejudice she faced by continuing to smile and by being polite.

Almost three hours and she hadn't seen a black person yet, thought Ronnie, wondering if this had ever happened to her before. Then, deciding it hadn't, she looked at Danny and bluntly asked, "Honey, aren't there any blacks here?"

"Sure, there's a few. Some go to Indiana University of Pennsylvania, I.U.P. We need a basketball team, you know," kidded Danny, not so sure if more than a couple of black families even lived in the entire area.

"How come everyone of these trucks has a gunrack? I've never seen so many guns in my life. I'm half afraid somebody's gonna shoot me. I feel like a black albino, the last of the species, about to become extinct," remarked Ronnie, pausing to look at a store window displaying a collection of hand made sweaters, its owner furtively peeking out from behind her ancient looking cash register.

"If the men are looking at you, it's because you've got the nicest ass they've ever seen. If the women are looking at you, it's because they're jealous of you. Secretly, they all lust for my hot high school hero bod," seriously stated Danny Money, a grin beginning to spread itself across his boyishly handsome face.

"How about those free throws, now?" asked Danny, pulling Ronnie into a deserted alleyway and passionately burying his tongue into her moist warm mouth.

"Are you crazy? Get on outta here with your horny self. You wanna get us killed?" replied Ronnie, reluctantly pushing Danny away, her female instincts wanting to oblige her lover, but, her common sense telling her that it sure as hell wasn't the right time or place.

At this very same moment, Ray Carson Carver, sitting in his easy chair less than thirty miles away, decided that it was indeed the right place and almost the right time. Burning up with fever, the aching lust to reach out and touch his daughter's forbidden fruit consuming his loins in a fire of boiling passion, he reached down and began to stroke his rising manhood. Stretched back in his recliner watching television, he glanced over at his daughter's ripe young body which was sprawled across the couch, her skin tight blue jeans hugging every single one of her adolescent curves. Jesus, he hadn't had anything that young in years, reflected Ray Carver, unzipping his fly. God, she was probably a cherry, most likely strung tighter than a drum. He'd stretch that skin out real good, thought the lust-crazed murderer, pushing his throbbing cock back into his oil and grease stained Dickey work pants.

Walking into the kitchen, his whole body raked with burning desire, he poured himself his third glass of whiskey, both his hands steadying the shaking glass as he slowly raised it to his cracked lips and gulped the burning nectar. Silently, he vowed that before another day dawned he'd rip open her frilly lace panties and plow his own deep furrow in her tight little uncultivated field.

First things first, though, thought Ray Carver. That meddlin' bitch wife of his had been asking too many questions about where he'd been going on his little asphalt jungle safaris. He'd have to give her a little lesson in manners. In his castle, he ruled the roost, with an iron hand if necessary, no questions asked. Just to make sure that there wouldn't be any further complications, he'd beat the living shit right out of her big fat sow's ass.

"Thanks, mom. We really appreciate it," shouted Danny Money, backing his BMW out of the cement driveway of his parent's house, the sun's rays bathing both him and Ronnie in a soothing warm glow.

"That was really nice of your mom and dad, watching Darnell so we can take a ride and be alone for awhile. Do you think they like us?" asked Ronnie anxiously.

"Sure they like you. Darnell looks like a half pint version of Mean Joe Greene, doesn't he? Dad's got him wearin' just about every item he could buy him that had the Steeler logo on it. Mom's told you at least a dozen times that you're the nicest lady I've ever brought home and, if it wasn't for my modest streak, I'd tell you that I've brought home some fine lookin' babes in my day," answered Danny, smiling as he turned on to Route 286 and glanced at Ronnie, who abruptly reached over and slapped him in the back of the head.

"Thanks for taking us to Pittsburgh. It was really beautiful. I had always pictured it looking like a giant smoke stack with soot covering everything in sight. But, it really was different. We enjoyed it. It was just a wonderful day," commented Ronnie, reflecting on yesterday's drive into the city of the three rivers and the incredible look of joy on Darnell's face when they had ridden up the famous incline plane, the breathtaking view of the entire city stretched out before them like a shimmering oil painting of steel, glass, and sparkling water.

"Jesus," cussed Danny Money, yanking the steering wheel and sending the BMW swerving off the road in an attempt to miss a gigantic pothole that could have almost swallowed them whole.

"I'd almost forgot how bad these roads are. Damn, the only thing worse is that rot gut Iron City Beer they make here. The Bud Man would puke if he had to drink that shit. I think they use sewer water and age it in a cesspool," sarcastically remarked Danny, grimacing as a thundering tri-axle hauling a load of coal exploded past them, down the hill, the whole earth shaking as the truck clattered by.

"Look. Look over there in that field. Deer, a whole herd of deer," excitedly shouted Ronnie, pounding Danny's shoulder and pointing off in the distance, the herd peacefully grazing in an open field at the edge of a tangled forest of pine trees interlaced with thick gnarly bushes and vines.

"Yeah, out here in God's country, if you ain't hittin' a pothole you're hittin' one of them," commented Danny, again carefully maneuvering the car through a jagged edged conglomeration of water filled potholes that must have looked just like the bombed out road to Basra.

Ronnie shivered. Suddenly, the scenery began to change. The miles of peaceful virgin forest began to disappear, replaced instead by an ugly landscape of scarred and barren earth. Gravelly pits of exposed dirt and rock scoured out of the once pristine hillsides, deformed the natural lay of the land. Huge mountainous piles of smoldering ash fouled the clean smelling fresh air, their sulfurous acrid stench causing her eyes to water.

"What are those God-awful things?" she asked, dabbing her eyes with a Kleenex as they rode leisurely past. The polluted air funneling through the open convertible offered little relief.

"They're called boney piles. They're from the coal mines. The damned stinkin' things burn constantly. It's as if they never die," remarked Danny Money sadly, knowing that they'd be there long after he was gone. A sad legacy to leave Darnell's generation, a legacy of a wounded and slowly dying land, thought Danny, wondering if anybody could ever stop the madness.

The madness was alive and well in the house of Ray Carson Carver, his demented mind finally having convinced itself that his daughter was silently cooing the siren's bewitching song, purposely tempting him to enter her forbidden loins. "Damn that little slut," cursed Ray Carver under his breath, crumpling an empty can of Rolling Rock beer as he envisioned her tauntingly seductive body calling out to him, begging him to release her into the fiery world of the devil's unending lust.

"Ray, could you help me down here? I think the washer's broke," hollered Kate Carver from the basement laundry room.

"Yeah, I'll fix it, and you too," chuckled Ray Carson Carver, throwing the crinkled aluminum beer can against the kitchen wall. Opening the refrigerator he popped another tab, swallowing half the beer in one long gulp. Well, this was it, time to get on with things. "Out with the old and in with the new," snickered the evil murderer, descending the creaking basement steps, about to visit his own personal carnival, the carnival of carnage, one more time.

"Sorry I had to bother you, dear. I'd fix it myself, but I can't lift the darn thing. I'm sure it's nothing. I'm already late for church. So whatever it is, I'll look at it later. I just need you to move the washer out from the wall," stated Kate Carver, hoping Becky was upstairs getting dressed for the Sunday Service, not up there laying around watching those God awful music videos. If her father caught her, there'd be hell to pay.

Flustered at running late for church, Kate Carver never noticed the evil flicker in her husband's hollow lifeless eyes, nor the sinister grin plastered across his gaunt somber face. Bending over the heavily loaded machine, a soapy slime covering the water in the tub, she clamped her fingers on the edge of the open lid and tried to drag the washer out from the wall. Without hesitation, Ray Carver slammed the lid across the knuckles of his startled wife, splintering the fragile bones of her bleeding torn hand.

"Oh, my God. Look what you've done," screamed Kate Carver in agony, shaking her crippled hand to try and relieve the excruciating pain.

"I ain't done nothin' yet, nothin' at all," coldly stated Ray Carver, ramming the half empty beer can into his wife's face, breaking her nose and smashing out her front teeth in a sickening blow that hurtled her reeling body against the concrete block wall. The back of her head brutally cracking against the unforgiving cinderblocks, Kate Carver sank slowly to the cold cement floor.

"Guess you ain't a gonna make it to church now, are you, you holy-roller bitch? Praise the Lord. I see the light," mocked Ray Carver, jumping up into the air and slamming his black steel toed work-boot into his wife's snapping ribs. Mumbling, "A man's work is never done," he kicked her again and again. Finally, her limp body slumped to the floor, its battered torso knocked totally senseless.

Walking calmly up the painted wooden basement steps, Ray Carver licked his lips in anticipation. Now, he would take her. He'd take her to Sunday school and make her pray, pray to God that he didn't kill her after he was finished. He paused in the kitchen to grab another beer and then started for the stairway to the second floor bedrooms. When he'd finished quenching his powerful thirst for her tight young flesh then he'd need something to wash the taste out of his mouth, something to quench his other thirst, figured the cold hearted murderer as he climbed the last steps to fulfilling his own tormenting lust.

Flinging open the bedroom door, he leered across the room at his startled daughter, her voluptuous young body sprawled across the pink and white lace comforter draped over her disheveled bed. She got up to her knees, removing the earphones off her rhythmically swaying head.

"What's wrong, Daddy? Why are you looking at me like that? Where's mother? What have you done to mother?" desperately questioned Becky Carver, slowly backing away from her advancing father.

"Your mother got what was comin' to her big fat ass. Now, little girl, you're a gonna git what you've been beggin' fer. I can see it in your eyes. You want daddy to stick his pecker in you. All them school boys been tryin' to git in yer pants but you, you want a real man, not some fuzzy faced sissy. Now, ain't that right, honey?" stated Ray Carver, unbuckling his belt and unzipping his fly as he started towards his cowering daughter.

"No, daddy, no. Oh, please God, no. Don't hurt me daddy. Go away. Leave me alone. You're just drunk again. I know you really wouldn't hurt me or mama," cried Becky Carver, rocking back and forth in terror, her mind unable to accept the agonizing humiliation about to be wreaked upon her trembling body. Kneeling on her bed, her arms locked around her knees, her whole being numb with fear, Becky Carver started to cry.

"I've never seen so many poor white folks. It's kind of comforting to know that poverty comes in all different flavors. When you've lived in D.C. as long as I have, everything that's poor or underprivileged begins to taste like chocolate," remarked Ronnie, turning around in her seat to catch one last glimpse of the ramshackle shanty which, to her, looked like a school bus with a porch, one long black stove pipe sticking out of the middle of its tire covered roof.

"Hey, there's poor whites and then there's white trash. They're two different entities. It isn't any different in D.C. or anywhere else. Just because you're poor doesn't mean you're a piece of crap. And just because you're black doesn't mean you're a dope dealer, or a hold up man, or a pimp, or a prostitute," added Danny, turning down a narrow bumpy tree lined lane, happy to see that there wasn't another human being in sight. Pulling the car off the desolate roadway, he leaned over towards Ronnie, sliding his hand inside her sweater and up her silky smooth back. Danny raised her chin, covering her moist lips with his in a long lingering kiss. Unsnapping her bra, he reached around and cupped her supple breasts, gently pinching her swiftly hardening nipples.

Ronnie groaned, lost in the intense passion of the moment, the crotch of her french cut panties beginning to moisten with desire. She attacked Danny's mouth, entwining her searching tongue with his. Reaching down to the hard bulge in his bluejeans, she unzipped his fly, desperately trying to grasp his rising manhood.

"God, I couldn't stand it, thinking of you laying in the next room, all alone. Jesus, I was one horny dude. If I wasn't afraid of waking up the whole house I'd of gone for it," panted Danny, slipping his lips over one of Ronnie's budding nipples.

"Gone for what? And just what made you think that I was alone?" joked Ronnie, leaning over to lick Danny's throbbing shaft.

"Next time, damn it, we ain't worryin' about keeping up any goody two shoes image. Jesus, who's gonna take care of my EMHO," sighed Danny, his eyes rolling back in his head as Ronnie slid her lips over his glistening manhood.

"The back seat," moaned Ronnie, pulling her sweater off, over her head, the gentle breeze caressing her wet saliva covered breasts.

"What, what the hell are you talking about?" panted Danny, trying to unzip Ronnie's skin tight blue jeans.

"The back seat. I want it in the back seat. Do you want me to draw you a picture or are you gonna let me screw your brains out in the back seat. Because, if you wait much longer, you're gonna be taking care of this yourself," stated Ronnie, squeezing her fingers around Danny's bulging rod.

Pulling off her pants and rolling into the back seat of the BMW, Ronnie invitingly spread her legs, her glistening vagina leaving no doubt as to her eagerness to welcome Danny's thrusting manhood. She moaned as he entered her, her shapely legs clamping around his waist as she moved in unison with his pistoning shaft. Pounding her unmercifully, Danny rode the winds of passion to a final shuddering climax. Exploding in a boiling orgasm, his entire body breaking out in an instantaneous sweat, he buried himself in her, trying to touch the very depths of his lover's soul.

"That was fantastic. I didn't know you had a thing for back seats. You should've told me sooner. I'd have probably bought a friggin Fleetwood Brougham if I'd known. Lot more room," chuckled Danny, pulling on his pants and watching as Ronnie, deciding to let it all hang out, tossed her bra into her purse.

"I've got a lot of things you don't know about. Some are a lot better than this," wryly stated Ronnie. Winking at Danny, she settled back into her seat and added, "Let's go get a drink. And maybe after you rest up a little, we can find one of those nice little cute red barns with a stack of hay."

"Dry as a bone bitch, Goddamned dead fish, just like your old lady," muttered Ray Carson Carver, wiping the blood off his shriveled limp dick. Looking over at his humiliated daughter, the damp sticky bedspread pulled up to her quivering chin, her eyes red and swollen, he could only shake his head in disgust. Next time, if she wasn't any better, he might have to wax her squirming ass. He felt hollow, empty, unsatisfied. Yeah, that was it. He'd drive on down to the Oak Tree Tavern and wet his whistle. Damn, he'd almost forgot it was Sunday. Good ol' Tootsie Hale would be down there, hanging around, trying to get her snatch stuffed. He could use a good piece of ass for a change.

"I guess young stuff just ain't all that it's cracked up to be," chuckled Ray Carver, flinging the back of his hand through the musty smelling air, its distinctive crack knocking his cowering daughter's face sideways, a trickle of blood flowing out of her lacerated lip.

"One word of this to your mama and you'll be rottin' in an early grave, before you can spread your legs for all them boys wants in your pants. You understand, girl? Cause, if you don't, I'm a gonna take the razor strap to your tight little ass right now and teach you some manners. You obey your papa. You hear me, child?" shouted Ray Carver, leering down at his terrified flinching daughter, his eyes dark bottomless pools of smoldering rage.

"Yes, daddy. I understand. I won't tell mama. You'll never

hurt me like this again, will you daddy?" replied Becky Carver, her voice quivering with fear as she gazed up at the menacing figure of her domineering father, unsure if her life would ever be the same.

"Now that we've got that straight, go clean yourself up and git your ass downstairs to help your mother. I think she had a little accident in the basement," remarked Ray Carver coldly, a sinister smile briefly flashing across his amused face. Abruptly, he turned around and walked down the stairs and out the back door. Slamming the screen behind him, he sauntered towards the comforting confines of his four wheel drive pick up truck. As he started up the dirt and mud covered truck he reached up on the dash and grabbed himself a pinch of Copenhagen. He sure enough hoped ol' Tootsie was in the mood for a little drillin', thought Ray Carver, pulling out his lower lip and inserting the small wad of gritty tobacco. Shit, she was always ready to be put on the rack for a greasy lube job, laughed the demented killer, pulling out of his driveway and heading for the Oak Tree Tavern.

"Good to see you, Ray. What'll it be, the usual shooter and a splash?" greeted Hank Edwards, hoping he would indeed be glad to see the evil looking mean old bastard. At least he shelled out a lot of coin, buying drinks like there was no tomorrow, rationalized Hank Edwards, figuring another paying customer was better than nothing, no matter who, or in this case, what it was.

"Tootsie, git that nice ass of yours over here so's I can buy you a drink, woman," yelled Ray Carver down the length of the bar, the few other customers chuckling as Tootsie slid off her stool and slowly strolled over next to the retired coal miner, purposely brushing her well rounded buttocks up against his outstretched knee.

"Them jeans is tighter than a virgin's pussy," remarked Ray Carver. "Bring ol' Tootsie, here, a double and git her whatever else she wants."

Hank Edwards, hoping Tootsie's old man didn't walk in the door, slid the shot glass in front of the flirtatious woman, his eyes constantly shifting towards the swinging front entry in nervous apprehension. Up here, in the backwoods, adultery was punishable by death.

"What would you know about a virgin, honey? The only ones left round here are the ugly third graders," commented Tootsie Hale, resting her left hand provocatively on Ray Carver's thigh while she gulped the whiskey with her right.

"You'd be surprised at what I know bout cherries," snickered Ray Carver, thinking about his deflowered daughter, a lurid grin plastered across his pale greyish looking face.

"Bring us the bottle, Hank. Me and Tootsie's goin' in the back room. Got us some business to take care of, we do. Ain't that right, Tootsie?" said Ray Carver, running his grimy hand all over Tootsie Hale's generously proportioned ass.

"Anything you say, baby, as long as you keep buying the drinks. It ain't like you and me haven't been there before. Hell, you're given it to me more regular than my old man. That sorry bastard ain't been able to get it up for years," answered Tootsie Hale, grabbing the bottle of Seagrams 7 as she led the way to Hank Edward's back-room. The little cluttered office, its only piece of furniture a ripped and torn recliner, often served as the barroom's version of a no tell motel, the satisfied customers leaving a ten spot on the musty smelling stained seat.

"Goddamned, Tootsie. Your ass is gittin' broader than a barn," chuckled Ray Carver, savagely slapping the palm of his hand against Tootsie's undulating buttocks, the sharp crack drawing an amused murmur from the sparse crowd of onlookers.

"Pull my pants down and spank me. I've been a bad girl," laughed Tootsie Hale, dragging Ray Carver into the dark dingy room, her ponderous frame flopping into the squeaky chair as she eagerly groped for his steadily rising manhood.

"That place is really cute. Let's stop there for a drink. It's just how I pictured a country bar, a lot of wood and stone, almost looks like a log cabin. Takes me back to the pioneer days," mused Ronnie, studying the rustic building as Danny sped past, hardly even slowing.

"You'll be a pioneer, alright, the first black ever to set foot in that red neck joint," joked Danny, negotiating a sharp curve in the meandering country road as he glanced over at Ronnie, her pouting bottom lip mischievously stuck out in a comical display of disappointment.

"Jesus Christ, I give up. We'll stop," relented Danny above the whistling sound of the wind rushing through the open convertible. Ronnie, a wide grin suddenly appearing on her playfully sullen face, seductively licked her finger and marked an imaginary line in the air as she said, "That's one point. One more and we can hit the hay, if you get my drift, big boy."

"Yeah, I know. Sit up pretty and the nice little doggy will get a bone," answered Danny Money, pulling into the dirt and gravel parking lot of the Oak Tree Tavern.

"No, honey. Just like most men, you've got it all backwards. In this game, if the nice little doggy sits up pretty he gets to give the bone," chuckled Ronnie, getting out of the parked car and heading for the front door, her inviting profile sensuously swaying back and forth as she walked across the barroom parking lot.

Pushing open the heavy wooden door, his eyes adjusting to the dim smoky interior of the greasy smelling bar, Danny Money motioned for Ronnie to enter. Ronnie, removing her sunglasses, looked carefully around, somewhat taken back by the hateful intimidating stares of the leering customers. Deliberately, she walked over to the nearest table, making sure to graciously smile at the shocked coal miners, most of their mouths hanging open in total disbelief. Danny walked up to the bar and ordered two screwdrivers, half convinced that they would have to fight their way out of this redneck rendezvous before this version of tea at the Ritz was over.

Tootsie Hale, lustfully groaning, her sweat soaked body feverishly pounding up and down on Ray Carver's glistening pole, accidentally kicked the unlatched door. The creaking door slid partially open. Sitting in the squeaking chair, his face buried between Tootsie Hale's ponderous breasts as he brutally pinched her hardened nipples, Ray Carver felt the queasy pangs of animal fear stab at his throbbing heart. Withdrawing his head from Tootsie's heavy undulating breasts, he glanced over her pistoning shoulder, startled to see the tall voluptuous silhouette of the black woman from the McDonald's in D.C. This time the black bitch was with a different man, noticed the shocked murderer, shoving Tootsie Hale's heaving body on to the coal dust covered floor.

"Goddamned you, Carver. I was just about to cum," gasped Tootsie Hale, desperately reaching out to grasp Ray Carver's slick juicy shaft in a frenzied attempt to slide the greasy pole back into her well oiled slit.

"The nigger bitch is a pig, just like you, you old whore," muttered Ray Carver, looking at the clean cut white man sitting next to the cocky looking spook, and finally putting two and two together. The old fat dude from the Golden Arches must have been a cop, too, figured Ray Carver, everything suddenly coming into crystal clear focus.

Tootsie Hale, in a fog of passion, asked, "What, what did you say? Look, if you've got to go, you'll come back later and get me off, right. I'll finish you, the way you like it best. You know, in my mouth." Looking up into the icy cold stare of Ray Carson Carver, his devious eyes fixed on the two city slickers, Tootsie Hale abruptly decided to shut up. More than once she had looked too deeply into those cruel eyes and had sworn that she was staring into two cesspools of murky death.

Suddenly, Ronnie felt a cold chill race up her tingling spine. She shuddered, feeling like she was sitting in an arena of death, the stalking lion circling her helpless body, drawing ever closer, ready to sink its blood thirsty fangs into her soft yielding flesh. Looking around the tension filled room, her mind recoiled in fear. Dark images of a gruesome meat locker filled with frozen hunks of human carcasses hangin' on gristly blood covered hooks began to appear in her frightening apparition of doom. Terrified, Ronnie clutched Danny's hand, almost yanking his arm out of its socket as she pulled him and his chair across the floor, right up next to her body.

"What's wrong, baby? Are you alright? Let's get out of here. This place is really givin' you the creeps, isn't it? You don't need this redneck aggravation. Let's blow this joint," suggested Danny Money, mistakenly assuming Ronnie's anxious behavior was a result of the hate-filled stares of the local yokels.

"No, no way. I'm not leaving until I'm good and ready. Something's wrong here. I feel like I'm being watched. No, stalked. That's the right word. Stalked by some kind of beast," replied Ronnie, her eyes combing the room, looking for some kind of an answer to a question her mind couldn't seem to grasp.

Hank Edwards looked out the open back door of the bar, gasping as the beast like image of a lurking prowler crept across the shadows, spooking the living daylights right out of his startled body. Squinting, his eyes unable to adjust to the bright sunlight, he looked again. Damn, if it wasn't old Ray Carver sneakin' out the back yard, into the woods. Probably busted his nut and crawled out the office window, thought Hank Edwards, figuring Carver was smart enough to avoid any possibility of being greeted by a load of double aught buck, compliments of Tootsie Hale's cockholed old man.

Ronnie's chill began to wane, its frightening horror slowly giving way to a warm tingling glow from the combination of alcohol and the incessant wanderings of Danny's finger which was slowly tracing a sensuous line up her long graceful neck. Just a simple over reaction to the cold prejudicial stares of a bunch of

UMWA mountain men, sitting around the bar, sizing her up like some high price filly at auction, figured Ronnie, trying to rationalize her frightening apparition.

Determined to milk it out to the very max, both Ronnie and Danny slowly sipped their drinks, torturing the leering rednecks until, finally, they emptied their glasses and deliberately walked out of the tension filled bar. Hopping into Danny's BMW, Ronnie leaned over and licked his ear, both lovers laughing as she whispered in her most sultry voice, "Well, you've got your two points. Now, let's go find us one of those cute little red barns." Glancing back over her shoulder as they pulled out of the parking lot, Rhonda Bell couldn't shake the eerie feeling. Somehow, deep down inside the tightening pit of her stomach, she knew she hadn't seen the last of the Oak Tree Tavern.

CHAPTER 15

"PLEASE, RODDY, don't say anything to that lady. We don't need to spend our time cruising up and down Massachusetts Avenue, harassing women just because they happen to have a nice ass," sarcastically remarked Briefcase Betty, thoroughly disgusted with Rambo Roddy and his continual crude behavior.

"That one up ahead ain't just got a nice ass. She's got the finest ass I've ever seen. What an aerobic butt. She must work out every day to keep that thing as high and tight as it is. Damn, she's a friggin' Amazon goddess," excitedly stated Rambo Roddy, pulling Scout 80 over to the curb lane. Briefcase Betty shrunk as low into her seat as humanly possible, cringing at the thought of how she was going to manage not to look this woman in the face when Roddy laid one of his lewd offensive lines on this statuesque blonde.

"Hey, you. You, baby," shouted Rambo Roddy as he pulled the creeping scout car up next to the sashaying blonde, his roaming eyes starting at her satin gold high heels and slowly inching themselves up her extraordinarily long muscular legs to the hem of her clinging tan miniskirt.

"Me. You want to talk to me, officer?" asked the striking blonde, pausing on the sidewalk, afraid that she'd done something wrong.

"Oh, an English lass, are we? A little crumpets and tea," wise-cracked Rambo Roddy, immediately picking up the unmistakable British accent and then motioning the stunning woman over to the police car.

"Yes, officer. What can I do for you?" questioned the woman nervously, afraid that she was about to get her first jaywalking ticket of the new year.

"What you can do for me, baby, is put a little lipstick on my dipstick," crudely remarked Rambo Roddy, a wide grin spreading across his beaming face.

Shocked, the radiant Englishwoman stared at Rambo Roddy in disbelief, her finely chiseled jaw dropping to the sidewalk. Then, regaining her stately composure, she bent over provocatively. Leaning her head inside the rolled down scout car window she looked directly at Rambo Roddy and calmly replied, "Truly, mate. I'd bloody well rather go down on a Pit Bull with AIDS."

Briefcase Betty, startled at the woman's outrageous reply, cracked a broad ear to ear grin. Suddenly, unable to contain herself any longer, she burst into raucous laughter and slapped her knees with the palm of her hands. For good measure, she yelled, "Tally Ho, baby!"

Infuriated by the insulting remark, Rambo Roddy meekly replied, "Go screw yourself, you uppity limey bitch."

"Your arse, mate," shouted the woman over her shoulder as she saucily flipped her undulating buttocks from side to side and then slowly sauntered into the British Embassy Compound, making sure to turn her head over her shoulder and mockingly smile at the frustrated officer.

"Shit," screamed Rambo Roddy, pounding the steering wheel of Scout 80 with his fists, his face turning the brightest shade of brilliant crimson that Briefcase Betty had ever seen.

Where do you go when you want to find a greasy wetback? You go to the taco stand, thought Ray Carver, slowly cruising his Dodge four by four through the crowded streets of D.C.'s predominantly Hispanic area of Mount Pleasant. The rice and beaners were everywhere, stuffin' their pudgy faces with every form of burrito known to man. Fattenin' themselves up for the slaughter, laughed the Capital Carver to himself as he squinted in the bright afternoon sunshine, his eyes never really recovering from all those years underground, in the mines. But, what if you want to find a whole family of spicolas? Then, you go to a sitdown Mexican restaurant and wait until Jose and Maria come in there with their little crumb snatcher, he reasoned, pulling into the parking lot of a graffiti covered corner market, all its walls painted in a pink, orange, and fluorescent green potpourri of Spanish gang slogans.

"Damn, this Goddamned Spanish gibberish is really gitten' on my nerves. You greaser sons of bitches shouldn't be allowed in this country if you can't speak decent English," cussed Ray Carver under his breath, disgustedly listening to a group of chattering Mexican women as he walked over to the pay telephone next to the cluttered looking run down market. He couldn't believe his good fortune. The thievin' wetback spics hadn't stolen the telephone book yet. He scowled as he flipped through the yellow pages to find the listing for restaurants. America, his America, was dying a slow agonizing death just like he was.

"Yeah, that one sounds good, El Tio Pepes, on M Street, over in Georgetown," he muttered, fatefully resting his chipped and broken dirt encrusted fingernail underneath the address of the fancy sounding eatery. At least this way he could gut out a high falutin' beaner, probably a nice fat juicy one at that, he reasoned, ripping the page out of the telephone book and walking back to his parked pick-up truck.

"Goddamn it! This shit is gettin out of hand! The whole city's about ready to explode. The newspapers got pictures of this Bigfoot looking creature stalkin' the streets, tearing up its human prey with its claws. How about this headline in the Post. When Will The Carver Carve Again? How long before you two nail this bastard?" ranted Bow Wow Bowser, staring menacingly at the two cringing detectives and lighting up his sixth cigarette in the last five minutes.

"Jesus, lieutenant. We've even got the computers tryin' to figure out the connection between the clues he left at each of the scenes. We're on it big time. It won't be long now. We think he just might be an out of towner, a hillbilly that comes into the city to do his huntin'," defended Mike McCarthy, fanning his hand in front of his face in an effort to get one decent breath of fresh air, the whole room looking like one gigantic swirling fog bank of smoke.

"That's wonderful, just wonderful. Thousands of tourists come into this city every day and you're gonna check out everyone of 'em. Maybe we could lay barbed wire and land mines around the city and then funnel all the people through Fourteenth Street or bring 'em in down New York Avenue. In fact, the goddamned business owners are startin' to call the mayor. Business is down. The Chief's on my ass. And you tell me some redneck mountain man just ain't a happy camper no more, so's he disembowels people for fun," yelled Bow Wow Bowser, hacking as he sucked down half a cigarette in one long drag.

"Lieutenant, we'll lock him up soon. I can feel it," cut in Ronnie, trying to take some of the heat off Mac, her eyes burning in the smoke filled room.

"And you, you take a couple of vacation days right in the middle of the worst slaughter in the city's history. What, are you feeling the deep pangs of a broken relationship? Or, have you got PSM? That's every Goddamned woman's excuse nowadays. You all are either on your period or just about to start," raved

Bow Wow Bowser, the veins on his forehead standing out, looking like they were about ready to take off the top half of his head in a crimson explosion.

"That's PMS, lieutenant. And no, I don't have it, my period, or a broken relationship," answered Ronnie, shaking her head in disbelief.

"Jesus, my head's spinning. Damn, I can't breathe. I think I'm havin' a heart attack," excitedly shouted Bow Wow Bowser as he desperately clutched at his heaving chest, his heart pounding wildly, his face suddenly turning a washed out pale ashen hue.

"Call an ambulance. He's having a heart attack," yelled Ronnie out the front door of the detective lieutenant's smoke filled office as she helped Mac lower the gagging official to the ash and butt covered floor.

"The smokestack finally blew," tersely stated Mac, unloosening the lieutenant's tie and unbuttoning his collar.

"A priest. Get me a priest. I'm dying and I want to confess," gasped Bow Wow Bowser, desperately wanting to cleanse the adulterous demons from his sinner's soul before he stood before his maker.

Pulling into the emergency room driveway behind the ambulance, Mac and Ronnie watched in silence as the paramedics wheeled Bow Wow Bowser's unmoving body through the electronic double doors and into the midst of the doctors and nurses descending upon him like frenzied buzzing bees. The two detectives took a seat outside the emergency room, anxiously awaiting word of the lieutenant's fate. Finally, unable to stand it any longer, Mac headed for the hospital cafeteria, concluding that this just might be a five cream and five sugar day, before it was over.

"Isn't that Bow Wow's wife and kids?" asked Ronnie, reaching up to take her cup of hot water and tea bag out of Mac's extended hand.

"Yeah. That's them, alright," answered Mac, settling his bulky frame into the slick plastic chair and raising the scorching cup of coffee to his lips, proud that he had shown restraint, using only four creams and four sugars.

Both detectives watched silently as the two nurses, trying to calm the lieutenant's distraught family, ushered Bow Wow Bowser's hysterical wife into the emergency room. Within minutes, the somber faced family priest walked into the crowded waiting room, clutching at the crucifix dangling around his white collared neck, his leather bound bible tucked tightly under his left arm. Calmly, he pushed open the swinging doors and entered the emergency room, prepared to do his faithful duty and administer the last rites to one of the less devoted parishioners of his flock.

Fearing that the wheezing lieutenant was about to expire, Ronnie and Mac pressed their faces against the oval windows in the emergency room door and silently prayed for Bow Wow Bowser's deliverance.

"What the hell's Bow Wow's old lady doin in there? She ain't supposed to be in there. Not when he's giving confession," observed Mac, incredulously.

"I don't think the priest knows she's in there. She was behind that curtain. Trying to get herself together. He couldn't see her," answered Ronnie.

"And she couldn't see him. Uh, oh. The shit's gonna hit the fan now," said Mac.

"I think it already has," suggested Ronnie, noticing the shocked look on Bow Wow's old lady's face.

"Jesus, watch out," yelled Mac, yanking Ronnie back from the door and staring in amazement as an enraged Mrs. Bowser suddenly wheeled and stormed out of the tension filled emergency room, her body crashing wildly into the swinging double doors.

"I hope the cheatin' bastard dies. Because, if he lives, I'm going to make his life so Goddamned miserable he'll wish he was dead," shouted Mrs. Karen Bowser, rounding up her children and stomping out of the room full of shocked bystanders.

Looking back over her shoulder at the two stunned detectives, she icily stated, "If the scumbag lives, tell him he'll be hearing from my attorney. Confession isn't going to be good for his soul. He should have kept his mouth shut. If I find that slut, 10-33 Sam's wife, she's gonna end up lying next to dickless in there with both her eyes scratched out!"

Initially wondering what was going on, Ronnie suddenly put two and two together. No way. Bow Wow Bowser couldn't have been screwing her old sergeant's wife. No way, she figured, anxious to check with Danny to see if 10-33 Sam was being cockholed on the side.

"He's gonna make it! The skinny old cancer stick is gonna make it," hollered Mac, interrupting Ronnie's train of thought and wondering what the hell he was so happy about. Bow Wow

Bowser was a prick. Who really gave a shit if he croaked, thought Mac, patting Ronnie on the back. Ronnie, remembering the vengeful hate filled look in Mrs. Bowser's eyes, figured the lieutenant had just committed the most grievous mistake of his life. He had lived. Before that woman was done, Bow Wow Bowser was going to die a thousand deaths.

"Hell hath no fury like a woman scorned," mumbled Ronnie under her breath, deciding it was time to get back to work. They had a Carver to catch and they better find him before he sliced up another one of her city's terrified children.

Hope the fat greaser and his family had a nice dinner, because it was going to be their last, figured Ray Carver, a brown line of tobacco juice dribbling down his stubbly bearded chin as he watched the three Hispanics leave El Tio Pepes and walk down M Street, towards their car parked on the dark residential streets behind the fashionable restaurant. They shouldn't have been so cheap, parking on the street to save a couple of bucks, instead of using the valet parking. It was going to cost them a whole lot more. That little mistake was going to cost them their miserable stinking lives, thought Ray Carver, calmly stalking his prey through the first twilight shadows of an unseasonably warm and humid D.C. night.

Reaching underneath his loose fitting red and black checked shirt and down his baggy canvass hunting pants, Ray Carver caressed the worn wooden stock and smooth blue steel barrel of his twelve gauge Ithaca pump shotgun. He felt sorry that he had had to hurt his baby, sawing off the already shortened barrel of the famous Deerslayer model which he had cherished for so many years. Well, sacrifices had to be made to bring the hunt to a successful conclusion, he figured, as he waxed back to the cold wintry days when he had patiently sat in the tree stand, waiting for the shouting row of drivers to spook the whitetail bucks towards him, towards the dreadful fate that awaited the poor unsuspecting animals, towards their own gruesome death.

Now, he had to be more cunning, tracking down his own kills like he had tracked the bloodsign of the wounded deer. I'll finish them off by cutting their gurgling throats, he decided, a gleaming twinkle sparkling in his cold callous eyes. Even this was getting too easy, the thrill beginning to diminish in the lust for more challenge. The challenge of the one final hunt. He sought the final quarry, the ultimate thrill, predator versus predator, cop versus killer, the Carver versus the nigger pig. In this, his last safari, the killing fields would be the familiar landscape of his own turf, the friendly hills of Pennsylvania, and in them the black bitch would die.

Shaking his head as he carefully crept through the bushes and trees across the street from the laughing forms of his unsuspecting victims, Ray Carver forced himself to concentrate on the immediate task at hand, the liquidation of three wetbacks. Intently, he watched as the man opened the door of the Chevrolet Caprice for his wife, then joyfully picked up his daughter and tossed her giggling body into the sticky night air.

"Ain't that sweet," muttered Ray Carver, a sadistic grin crossing his lips as he stepped out from behind the trunk of a huge tree into the dim shadowy glow of a flickering street lamp.

It was the twilight hour, the haunting time of ghouls and demons. Death's magical mystery tour was about to begin again in the pristine streets of Georgetown. The Capital Carver was about to sign another of his works with his grisly trademark. The air hung ominously heavy as Ray Carver stepped down off the curb and began to walk across the dark deserted street, towards the parked car, his mind having already enacted the bloody doomsday massacre of his pitifully weak quarry, over and over again.

Moving quickly, Ray Carver closed in on the unsuspecting family, his nostrils flaring as he lifted his head, snorting into the moist still air. Unconsciously, he glanced up at the semi-circular orb of the half moon, its eerie faint glow filtering through a solitary bank of ominous black clouds. He felt the urge to bay, to howl in pronouncement of his power, the ultimate power of the primeval call of the wild. "The meek shall inherit jack shit," chuckled Ray Carver, stepping up to the driver's side window of the now idling car. Only the strong shall survive in this jungle and he was the king of the beasts.

"What, what do you want, señor?" asked the man, slightly cracking open his upraised window and nervously wrapping his arm around his wife's trembling shoulder.

"I want you, you fat greasy porker," laughed Ray Carver, whipping the sawed off shotgun out of the leg of his pants. Instantly, he flipped the gun around, slamming its wooden butt into the car window. Pieces of shattered glass exploded into the car's interior as he cracked the window a second time, clearing a path for the deadly weapon. Shoving the barrel of the shotgun up against the cringing man's forehead, he squeezed the trigger. The gut wrenching roar dissolved the man's head in a smoke filled vacuum of bloody liquid and splintered bones.

Looking inside the car, at the gruesome mess, Ray Carver grinned and then spat a stream of tobacco juice against the driver's side door. He pumped another round into the chamber, disappointed to see that the deafening explosion of lead pellets had failed to finish off the headless man's old lady and her fat little rug-rat.

Kicking and screaming wildly, the wounded woman looked up at the crazed killer. Suddenly, her whole body went limp. She stared at the murderer in calm silence, morbidly resigning herself to her untimely fate. Protectively laying her blood covered body over her hysterically sobbing baby girl she crossed herself, pleading desperately, "No, dios Mio, ami ninita, no!"

"Yeah, you old whore, you and your little baby, too," coldly stated Ray Carver, his gloved finger slowly pulling the trigger of the shotgun, its flesh and blood covered barrel pressed tightly against the cowering woman's ripped and torn earlobe.

"Oh, my God," gasped Briefcase Betty Barnes, staring in mesmerized horror at the blood splattered windows of the shiny white Caprice. Pushing her way through the gathering crowd of curiosity seekers, none of whom had any inclination whatsoever of approaching the grisly mass of flesh and bones which, without question, lay inside the still idling vehicle, Briefcase Betty walked over to the car and reluctantly looked inside.

"Holy, shit," muttered the shocked officer, immediately turning her head aside and desperately gasping for a breath of fresh air.

"It looks like the son of a bitch had a gut wrestling contest with the headless horseman," remarked Rambo Roddy, looking over Briefcase Betty's shoulder into the wet steamy mess of innards and body organs strewn all over the tan velour seats. "Man, he must be one wet stinkin' dude," he added, guessing that the Carver must have really liked wading into this greasy grimy mess of spic spare parts.

"We better wait for Cruiser 311. They're on their way. Dispatcher says ETA of three minutes," commented Briefcase Betty, anxious to turn over this slaughter to Homicide Squad.

"That must be those assholes, now. Jerk and the Fatman," sarcastically laughed Rambo Roddy, hearing the distant wail of a shrill yelping siren and deciding that he ought to send Hollywood a script for his satirical version of the once popular weekly show.

Rhonda Bell took a deep breath and stuck her head inside the shattered window, the foul rank air still cloudy with wispy trails of gunpowder and smoke. The hair on the back of her neck tingled with static electricity. She knew he couldn't be more than a few miles away. She was close, but something deep down inside her told her that she had even been closer to the butchering bastard, sometime, somewhere.

"The clues. Check their mouths for clues. He must have left something," suggested Mac, putting his arm around Ronnie's waist to steady his trembling partner. The brown streak of tobacco juice, running down the driver's side door had already sadly answered one of his questions.

"Mac, two of them don't have any mouths. They don't even have any heads," blurted out Ronnie, gagging as a sour lump of mucus caught in her gasping throat.

"They're here somewhere. I know it. I know he'll leave a trail. They always do," stated Mac, positive that the Carver was after something more than simply murdering people like a modern day avenger of Noah's lost arc.

Turning her head towards the blood splattered front windshield, Ronnie glimpsed the precious trail. They were still in the hunt. There, sitting in a neat row on the red streaked dash, lay three more tracks, the tracks to a fearful destination that loomed ominously closer with each victim's last gasp. The judgment day was almost at hand, thought Ronnie apprehensively, wondering how a key, a shotglass, and a cherry fit into this sickening bizarre jigsaw puzzle of death.

"He must have really worked fast. They can't be dead for more than twenty minutes or so. The bodies, or what's left of them, are still warm," observed Mac, frantically trying to maintain his professional demeanor in the face of the horror of an urban guerrilla battle the likes of which he had never seen.

Ronnie staggered back from the blood stained car, her wobbly knees almost giving out completely. Finally, the horrendous slaughter had begun to sink in, taking its heavy toll on her sensitive mind and body. She looked emotionally over at Mac, a solitary tear trickling down her smooth brown cheek. Sadly, she stated, "Damn him, Mac. All I can think about is doing the same thing to that bastard that he's done to them. I'm sorry, but I want to watch him die at my own hands, not watch him laugh at us in court."

Mac hugged Ronnie tightly against the side of his body, his pudgy arm wrapped around her shoulder. Comforting his besieged partner in this, her time of need, made him feel useful for a change. Somebody needed him. Maybe, just maybe, he didn't really need the bottle anymore, thought Mac, walking Ronnie back to Cruiser 311. Warfare was truly a terrible thing. No winners or losers. Only a never ending parade of maimed and mutilated victims, he mournfully concluded as he opened the passenger side cruiser door and helped Ronnie into her seat.

"Don't be sorry. It's no sin to want to kill a man like this. Anyway, he's already dead on the inside," comforted Mac, reaching into the jacket-pocket of his wrinkled navy blue sportcoat to get out his notebook. All he kept seeing, over and over again, was the little girl's blood stained pink lace dress and shiny black patent leather shoes. Later tonight, when they went to her house, he'd get his first look at her undoubtedly angelic face. That's what he dreaded the most, piecing together bubbly smiling pictures of the victims to mutilated headless bodies. Nothing in God's world could ever prepare you for that grim task, reflected Mac, shivering as he slowly walked back to the scene of the slaughter, almost afraid to find out what precious happy memories this brutally snuffed out family would be sharing with him and Ronnie, tonight, through their inevitable collection of photo albums and VCR tapes. God, he hoped the tapes wouldn't have sound.

"Scout 150, respond to 903 6th Street, Northeast, and see the complainant, Jones, regarding an alleged assault, 2153 hours," stated the dispatcher.

"150 is 10-4," answered Danny Money adding, after he unkeyed the mike, "Shit, not again. Damn that wild woman. She slices up more of the brothers than every other broad that lives in our whole Goddamned beat."

"Chanelle's just like the perfume. She's sexy and she's sweet. But, man, can she be deadly," joked the Bud Man, turning on to 6th Street as Danny recorded the fourteenth radio run of this busy four to twelve shift.

"Can you believe this nigger? He brings two whores, two no account bitches, into my crib and decides he's a Goddamned Playboy photographer," shouted Chanelle Jones, pointing to a cowering young black man, huddled in the corner of the living room, his left arm dripping blood on to the soiled beige carpet.

Walking through the open screen door, behind Danny Money, the Bud Man glanced over at the slightly wounded young man, then looked back at the violent, incensed woman, still holding her trademark straight razor in her right hand.

"Alright, Chanelle. Put the razor down and we'll rap. No sense anybody gettin' hurt worse than they already are," politely ordered the Bud Man, anxious to get to the juicy details of this latest sexual escapade.

"You got it, brother Bud," answered Chanelle, folding up the pearl handled straight razor and laying it down on the dust covered coffee table.

"He ain't got nothin' more than a little scratch," stated Danny Money. "You want us to call an ambulance?"

"No way, man. I can take care of myself. That bitch be crazy, shit," answered the man, furtively glancing over at Chanelle, afraid that if the officers left anytime soon he'd be going to the morgue.

"Go ahead, Chanelle. You tell us your side of the story," stated the Bud Man, looking around the room for the alleged porno snapshots.

"He be doin' some nasty things with those two whores. They be using all kinds of sick lookin' things on each other, in my house, in my bed. You'all know I pay the rent here, not that faggot-ass queer. I want him outta my house," angrily stated Chanelle, threateningly pointing at the nervous young man as he slowly began to get up on his feet.

"The pictures. You said he took pictures. Where are the pictures? I, er.. I mean we, need to see 'em to confirm your story," anxiously pressed the Bud Man, virtually licking his chops at the chance to get a good look at some amateur porn.

"The nasty-ass things are over there, on top of the TV. I found 'em underneath the mattress when I was changin' the sheets," answered Chanelle, sitting down on the couch, her short tight skirt riding halfway up her shapely thighs.

"Damn, would you look at this! These two foxes are riding on the same rail," excitedly exclaimed the Bud Man, looking at the photograph of two naked women, each imbedded on the opposite end of a two headed dildo.

"Jesus, I didn't know that you brothers had such small dicks. This poor boy's got less than me," joked Danny Money, pointing at the wounded man as he handed the snapshot to the Bud Man.

"Well, brother. If we lock up Chanelle we'll have to confiscate these pictures and show 'em to the judge and jury and they'll all see what a pitiful little pecker you've got," laughed the Bud Man, eagerly flipping through the rest of the photos.

"Sheet, man. Ain't no simple ass jury crackers gonna be lookin at my dick. I don't wanna press no charges against mama. She's my main squeeze," answered the young man, a phony smile plastered across his nervous looking face.

"You ain't squeezin' me, or anything else, in my place. Now go on about your business and get your useless black ass outta here," shouted Chanelle, shaking her fist at the retreating young black man who was slowly inching his way towards the front door.

"Hey, Chanelle. You sweet child. Whenever you retire from slicin' and dicin' look me up. I swear you're about the hottest looking wild thing I ever did see," remarked the Bud Man, winking at Chanelle as they fell in behind the nervous young stud, now in full flight running down the sidewalk.

"Don't let the door hit you in the ass you big bullshitter," chuckled Chanelle, discreetly sliding the straight razor back into her skirt pocket, wholeheartedly convinced that she liked slashing the worthless bastards more than she liked screwing them.

"10-8. No report. Complainant advised," radioed the Bud Man, pleased with his handling of this assignment, having judiciously avoided both a ton of worthless paperwork and a long day in court, all in one smooth stroke.

Echoing his sentiments, Danny Money stated happily, "Well, we got outta that one slick as shit. Let's head on over to Micky D's and get us a double cheese. I think we still qualify for the police discount."

"Absolutely. One hundred percent of nothin' equals nothin'," answered the Bud Man. "Maybe a little later we can slide on over to Tiny's and do us a little exercise."

"What the hell are you talkin about? Tiny ain't got any workout equipment. You plannin' on doin some aerobics with that old toothless bag lady?" questioned Danny Money, looking over inquisitively at the Bud Man as they stopped in the long line of traffic backed up at New York and Florida Avenue.

"Don't have a cow, man. I just thought we might wanna do some curls, some twelve ounce curls," chuckled the Bud Man, licking his lips at the thought of an ice cold glass of Bud, its foamy head slowly trickling down the side of the wet frosty mug.

"Look at that red-neck son of a bitch! He's got some nerve, bustin' that light right in front of us. Let's nail his ass. That country bumpkin needs a little schoolin'," excitedly stated Danny Money, sticking his arm out the passenger side window and waving it up and down to slow the traffic approaching from their rear as the Bud Man flipped on the red lights and floored the gas pedal.

Skidding sharply on to New York Avenue, Scout 150 fell in behind the speeding Dodge pickup, steadily accelerating as it lurched forward in pursuit of the grey four-wheel drive truck.

"Shit, I can't read the tags. But, they're Pennsylvania plates. And I know I saw a UMWA sticker on that piece of shit," remarked Danny Money, squinting in an effort to read the dirt covered numbers and letters.

"What the hell is UMWA?" asked the Bud Man, desperately swerving to avoid nosing up the tailpipe of a braking Mercedes.

"United Mine Workers of America," answered Danny Money, leaning forward to try and get a better look at the rear end of the bumper sticker covered truck as they passed under the Brentwood Road overpass, still gaining ground on the speeding truck.

Changing lanes like a spastic version of Parnelli Jones, the Bud Man darted out from behind a black cloud of sooty exhaust fumes, deposited by an accelerating Metrobus, and punched the pedal to the metal. They were less than fifty yards directly behind the camper top pickup and closing fast. All that stood between them and a date with the haunting winds of death, the grim deadly face of the Capital Carver, was fifty yards of open roadway.

"Let's nail this asshole," shouted Danny Money, flicking the siren on to wail and picking up the mike to the outside speaker.

Suddenly, almost as if by magic, the winds of death shifted, bringing with them the cold bleak reality of life.

"Look out," screamed Danny Money, slamming both his hands against the dash and bracing himself for the imminent collision.

The Bud Man, glancing to his right, watched in horror as a school bus filled with pom-pom waving cheerleaders made a wide right turn on red, ponderously swinging into their lane. Pumping the brakes like a Tasmanian Devil, the Bud Man cut the steering wheel to the left, the rear end of 150 abruptly skidding to the right on the slick oily pavement. Frantically fighting to bring the sliding scout car under control, he locked the brakes, 150 spinning completely around like a giant top moving in slow motion. Helpless, both officers stared out the front windshield, a confusing blur whirling past the careening police car as they suddenly slammed into the curb, blowing the right rear tire.

Viciously bouncing back off the curb, 150 began to slow, finally coming to rest facing the wrong way in the middle of New York Avenue. Both Danny Money and the Bud Man paused to take a deep breath, neither officer able to instantly shake the cobwebs out of their reeling heads. Then, realizing the likelihood of eating the front bumper of an oncoming car, Danny Money, his knees still wobbly, got out of 150 and stopped the creeping flow of curious onlookers, enabling the Bud Man to limp the virtually unscathed car on to a quiet side street.

On his knees, pumping up and down on the grease covered jack handle, the Bud Man bitched, "Goddamned fuckin' tourists. Forget the Golden Arches. After we're done changing this tire I'm headin' for Tiny's. Gonna get me a tall cold one."

"Why ask why?" chuckled Danny Money, plopping down the spare tire from 150's cluttered trunk and somehow wondering if maybe they weren't better off, not having stopped the speeding pickup. Something about that truck reminded him of people and places that he had left a long time ago in a frightening evil hate-filled world frozen in the sands of time, a world where the cruel law of the land was simply survival of the fittest.

CHAPTER 16

"THIS MIGHT BE IT, Mac, the break we've been waiting for. Maybe our luck's changing," enthusiastically remarked Ronnie, glancing over at Mac from behind the steering wheel of Cruiser 311.

"Well, I sure hope so. Because, whatever he's trying to tell us with those clues sure isn't sinkin' into my big fat head," drolly stated Mac, slowly flipping the pages of his notebook as he poured over his detailed synopsis of each murder for the thousandth time. He looked up. "Here we are. Home sweet home. The land of the elusive American dream. The mythical world of milk and honey," joked Mac, looking over at the enormous stone mansion as Ronnie pulled up to the wrought iron gates of the sprawling estate.

"Yeah, sure. You must mean the land of the white American dream. And you sure as hell aren't talking about chocolate milk, because this is whitey's exclusive turf up here in this part of Georgetown. Us colored folk, all we be dreamin' 'bout is welfare checks and Cadillacs," mimicked Ronnie, getting out of the detective cruiser to hit the buzzer of the intercom.

Driving up the circular driveway, Ronnie caught a glimpse of Scout 80, parked behind the six car garage, hidden out of view. No doubt at the snobby homeowner's insistence, figured Ronnie, immediately sorry that sometimes, she too, harbored unwarranted prejudice against her fellow human beings. These people were probably just decent folks who had had a few breaks in life, she reasoned, trying to convince herself that the kinder gentler nation was not a cruel hoax like so many others that had been perpetrated on her abused race.

Before Ronnie could even ring the bell, the heavy dark oak doors creaked open, a uniformed maid appearing in the shadowy inner light. Mac looked over at Ronnie, his eyeballs rolling back in their sockets. The maid's eyes riveted on Ronnie, staring right through the back of the attractive detective's head, almost as if not to even acknowledge her presence. Turning around to glance at the mistress of the house, the maid shook her head in disgust. Then, addressing her remarks at Ronnie, she stated coldly, "Madame Farnsworth asks that you use the service entrance in the back of the house."

Ronnie started to reply. But, before she could utter the choice words that she had in mind for the maid and her asshole boss, Mac gently grabbed her arm, answering, "We'll be glad to use the back door. No problem. We should've realized our faux pas."

"You, sir, can use the front door. I was speaking to the colored woman. Madame Farnsworth asks that she, or any other niggas, use the back door," astonishingly answered the maid in a sickening southern drawl.

Ronnie, deciding that she wasn't using anybody's back door, ever, rushed back up the steps. Forcefully, she plowed aside the stuttering maid and entered the dark old musty smelling house. Mac lumbered up the stairs, right behind his enraged partner, hoping Ronnie wouldn't be using the startled maid to mop up madame's shiny floor. Standing face to face with the shocked socialite, Ronnie smiled sarcastically, glaring at the aristocratic woman, every conceivable part of her body displaying a gaudy menagerie of diamonds and gold.

"Well, I guess there goes my invitation to the gala ball," wisecracked Ronnie, unable to restrain herself despite her resolve to remain professional and calm.

"There's always the bathrooms to clean out, afterwards," haughtily answered the middle-aged socialite, giggling as she turned her head towards the chuckling maid.

"That's it. I've had it with you, you arrogant bitch," shouted Ronnie, grabbing the front of the woman's dress.

"Get your hands off me, you lowlife nigger. I'll sue your black ass," screamed the flailing socialite, desperately trying to imbed the pointed toe of her high heels into Ronnie's shins.

Rambo Roddy, hearing the commotion, rushed out into the foyer, his mind still focused on the tight round ass of the Farnsworth family housekeeper that he had just left behind in the huge country style kitchen.

"Get your hands off that woman. Who the hell do you think you are, laying your dirty black hands all over this fine upstanding white woman, you black bitch?" shouted Rambo Roddy, bolting across the room towards the entangled couple and figuring, for this, Mrs. Farnsworth might even remember him in her will. Grabbing the collar of Ronnie's khaki green suit jacket, Rambo Roddy spun her around and viciously slapped the side of her face with the back of his hand.

Enraged, Mac charged Rambo Roddy without hesitation, literally wanting to tear the arrogant officer's head off. Plowing into

Rambo Roddy with the full weight of his thundering frame, Mac swung his clenched fist upward, cracking it into the underside of the reeling officer's jaw. Staggered by the crunching uppercut, Rambo Roddy stumbled backwards, grabbing at his throbbing chin.

Briefcase Betty, returning from the library of the stately mansion into the middle of this wild melee, immediately rushed towards the struggling women and thrust her busty frame between the two groping combatants. Slowly, out of total confusion, the absurd drama began to wane until it gradually reduced itself to a level of controlled hysteria.

"What the hell's going on here? This is ridiculous," shouted Briefcase Betty, separating Ronnie and Mrs. Farnsworth with a powerful jiggle of her ponderous breasts. Rambo Roddy, rubbing his swollen jaw, leered at Mac, his shifty eyes revealing his desperate desire to put a bullet right between the chubby detective's puffy fat cheeks.

"Just a little misunderstanding. Nothing serious. I'm sure we can work it out," answered Mrs. Farnsworth, deciding that if this incident went public her nomination for a position on Georgetown University's board of trustees would be out the window and so would her chance to get the prestigious school back to its white Aryan roots. Her appointment was essential in shifting the balance of power and nobody knew that any better than she did.

"I called because I thought that I might be of some assistance in finding this Capital Carver maniac. Not that I wish to be involved any further in this dreadful matter," stated Lillian Farnsworth, gloating as she knew she had the black bitch and her fat nigger loving partner by the proverbial balls.

"And how is that?" questioned Mac, flipping open his dilapidated notebook and subtly stepping over beside his heavily panting partner.

"The other night when that horrible man must have butchered that poor unfortunate Mexican family I was driving down that very same street. Not that I'll ever take the Rolls through that part of town again. Anyway, I saw this disgusting looking hillbilly truck racing down the street. Almost sideswiped my car with his rusty looking wreck. The newspapers had reported that the police thought the killer was some kind of mountain-man type and that truck certainly didn't belong to anybody that would live in Georgetown. And I know for a fact that coloreds don't drive those kinds of cars. They prefer Cadillacs," sarcastically stated

Lillian Farnsworth, a smirking grin plastered across her aristo-cratic face.

"Can you describe the truck?" anxiously pressed Mac, to-tally forgetting about the recent racial outbreak in his euphoria over this possible dramatic break in the gruesome case.

"I certainly can," answered Lillian Farnsworth. "It was a grey beat up looking thing, covered with dirt and mud. It had those big knobby looking tires and one of those aluminum camper tops. Really, it was barbaric looking. It sat way off the ground, ridiculous."

"Did you see the license plate or anything else?" excitedly questioned Mac, looking at Ronnie, who, despite herself, was reflecting his unbridled enthusiasm in her sparkling brown eyes.

"No. The plates were covered with mud. But, I did notice a couple of bumper stickers on the disgusting looking thing. One was an NRA sticker. That, I know for sure. My husband and I are avid gun enthusiasts and like you, I'm sure, support that type of worthwhile association," stated Lillian Farnsworth, a phony smile crossing her ruby red lips as she smoothed her skirt and sat down on a nearby chair.

"No, I don't support the NRA and really am not into guns," remarked Mac, poking Ronnie in the ribs with his elbow and smiling back at a flustered Lillian Farnsworth. "Now, was there anything else?"

"I sort of remember one other sticker. It had four letters on it. Something like UMVA," commented Mrs. Farnsworth, rising from her seat in an unconcealed gesture at terminating the inter-view.

Mac, escorting Ronnie out the front door, glanced back at Lillian Farnsworth as he walked down the grey marble steps and asked, "Could it have been UMWA?"

"Yes, that was it," answered Lillian Farnsworth, looking admiringly at Rambo Roddy and gratefully stating, "And you, my good man, are welcome in this house anytime."

"What a bitch," screamed Ronnie, pounding her fists against the faded dash board of Cruiser 311 as Mac turned on to Foxhall Road and headed for Homicide Squad, convinced that they were one step closer to terminating the Carver's grip on their terrified city.

"White trash. She ain't nothin but a garbage can full of shitty white trash. Me, personally, I ain't nothin' but a black man in a poor white man's Armani, an inside out Oreo cookie. I be diggin' on the sisters, specially the one's that be fine, like you," joked Mac, evoking a twinkling gleam in Ronnie's cold staring eyes.

"You are one trash talkin' dude. Let me get my boots on, cause the shit's startin' to flow deep, real deep," answered Ronnie. Unable to hold back any longer, she burst into a chorus of unrestrained laughter, the absurd humor of the whole comedy of errors finally hitting home with its own personal brand of pathetic reality.

"Well, we got us a killer to catch. Let's get back to work," stated Ronnie, playfully punching Mac in his flabby shoulder.

"Fer sure, fer sure, a killer that drives a grey pickup," jokingly replied Mac, trying to cover up his fear that there was sure to be more killing before they found the insane murderer who sat behind the wheel of that mysterious truck.

"Would you look at that. It's enough to make me puke, a Goddamned uppity nigger bitch driving a car like that. I couldn't even afford the insurance on that ride," sarcastically muttered Rambo Roddy, watching in disgust as a stunning looking black woman pulled up next to Scout 80 in a brand new shimmering red Ferrari.

"What's your problem? The woman probably worked her ass off to get that car. It's none of your business what she drives," remarked Briefcase Betty, finally deciding that she'd had all she could stand. Tomorrow afternoon she'd see a whiteshirt, maybe Captain Carlson, he was a square shooter, and take a foot beat. Anything was better than serving eight hours imprisoned in a patrol car with an asshole like Rambo Roddy.

"I'm gonna make this Magnum P.I. bitch my business. If she worked her ass off, it was on her back. The only spooks that can afford a car like that are drug dealers, prostitutes, or pimps," coldly stated Rambo Roddy, pulling Scout 80 behind the sleek looking shiny Ferrari, about to make the biggest mistake of his miserable life.

"What are you gonna stop her for? Lookin' good in a good lookin' car? She hasn't done anything wrong. Just let her go on about her business and we can go on about ours," cautioned Briefcase Betty, an aching knot beginning to tighten in her fluttering stomach at the thought of the impending confrontation which Rambo Roddy seemed determined to provoke. He just couldn't let sleeping dogs lie. As if they didn't have enough problems, mutilated bodies strewn all over their beat and yesterday's run in with good ol' Lillian Farnsworth. Now this dickheaded dork wanted to start some more shit, reasoned Briefcase Betty, feeling her blood pressure begin to rise.

"Looks to me like she just failed to properly signal that left turn she just made," smugly stated Rambo Roddy, following the Ferrari as it turned on to Cathedral Avenue.

"Big deal. We could stop every motorist in the city for not using their turn signal. You didn't use yours," observed Briefcase Betty, silently praying that she'd suddenly wake up and find out that her time sitting next to this backwater jerk-off was all simply a bad dream.

"Yeah. But, I'm the man, the sheriff of this here town. I do whatever the hell I want, whenever the hell I want to," answered Rambo Roddy, flipping on the red lights and signaling the Ferrari over to the curb.

Briefcase Betty, her nervous stomach doing an incessant barrel-roll of continuing somersaults, silently watched the reflection of the mirrored red lights flickering across the quiet tree lined lane, the dusky rays of the yellow sun glinting off the sleek racy looking car.

"Well, it's time I dealt with this coon. I'm gonna tighten her ass up, real good. Real damn good," cruelly stated Rambo Roddy, slapping his nightstick against the palm of his hand. As he picked up his ticketbook and opened the scout car door, he fully intended to lay some lumber on the attractive unsuspecting black woman.

"Looks to me like she just might get a little disorderly. Wouldn't it be a shame if I had to lock her black ass up for Disorderly Conduct? Maybe even have to use a little necessary force to make her see the light? Praise da Lord, hallelujah, brother," mimicked Rambo Roddy, snickering as he got out of the patrol car and walked up to the idling Ferrari.

Briefcase Betty felt the dry lump in her throat and desperately tried to swallow. Somehow, she had to stop Rambo Roddy from beating this poor defenseless woman to a bloody pulp. The dreaded confrontation was finally at hand.

Juanita Daniels looked back over her shoulder at the approaching officer, feeling very uneasy as she watched him continually slap his nightstick against the palm of his hand, a sinister smile pasted across his smirking lips. Her husband, I.A.D. commander Deputy Chief Marvin Daniels, had told her at least a thousand times. If you're stopped, just stay in your car and co-operate with the officer. Most likely he'll just give you a verbal warning and a polite slap-on-the-wrist-type lecture. Juanita Daniels took a second look back at the swaggering officer and instantly concluded that, before he was done, she'd be getting a crack on the head, not a slap on the wrist.

"Get out of the car, you jungle bunny," ordered Rambo Roddy, reaching for the door handle.

Shocked, Juanita Daniels replied defiantly, "I'm not getting out of this car and who the hell do you think you are, talking to me like that? What are you, some kind of nazi Neanderthal?"

"Listen, baby. I'll talk to you however I feel like. In case you hadn't noticed I'm one of the white occupational army that you jive-ass niggers is always complainin' about. And I think I'm gonna start a little jungle warfare on your lazy welfare ass," bitterly remarked Rambo Roddy, opening the car door and grabbing Juanita Daniel's wrist.

"Get your hands off me before I carve you up like the turkey you are," responded Juanita Daniels, hoping that she could avoid chopping this arrogant prick into mincemeat pie. Owner of a chain of Okinawan karate schools and holder of a tenth degree black belt, Juanita Daniels, true to her discipline, tried to avoid confrontation and the use of violence at all costs. But, for this asshole, she just might digress a notch or two and lay a good old fashioned hurtin' on his racist macho butt.

Incensed at the woman's defiance, Rambo Roddy jerked on her arm. He yanked her struggling body out of the car and laughed as the well dressed lady tumbled to the pavement.

"That's it, mister macho. You're history. Listen, honey. You better call an ambulance, because your asshole partner here is about to take a little ride, compliments of Sister Sledge, Sister Sledge Hammer, that is," shouted Juanita Daniels cockily, looking over at Briefcase Betty and winking as an unspoken understanding passed between the two women.

Briefcase Betty, sensing that a divine moment of monumental significance was close at hand reached into the scout car and opened her ever present briefcase. Strangely excited, she removed her Panasonic Camcorder from its leather carrying case. Something told her that she was about to film the rise and fall of Rambo Roddy's Third Reich, all on one little VCR tape. Ecstatic, she pressed the button and began rolling. Juanita Daniels pressed her own button and began chopping.

"Eeeeyah," shouted Juanita Daniels, quickly raising her trousered right leg and abruptly slamming her low heeled pump into Rambo Roddy's kneecap. Without hesitation, she leaped into the air and whipped her left leg into the shocked officer's ribcage, snapping several bones with a sickening crunch. Staggering backwards, Rambo Roddy wildly swung his nightstick and frantically tried to fend off the attacking woman.

Showing no mercy, Juanita Daniels pressed her attack, catching Rambo Roddy with a sharp blow to the side of his reeling head. Following up, she leveraged a vicious downthrust, crumpling the bridge of his nose with a savage closed fist punch. Rambo Roddy's nightstick fell to the ground, clattering as it rolled down the street. Clutching at his face, Rambo Roddy dropped to his knees, cowering as he awaited the next staggering blow.

Juanita Daniels, finding it hard to pity the trembling beaten officer, decided that this class was not quite out. She opened her hand and slapped the bent over officer across the face, repeating the action across his other cheek. Rambo Roddy, his head throbbing with intense pain, his cheeks stinging from the continual slaps, pleaded, "Please, no more. I've had enough. Don't hit me again. I'm beggin' you, please don't hurt me anymore."

"Make sure you get it all, honey. I know you won't wanna miss this. It'll make your day," hollered Juanita Daniels at Briefcase Betty as she reached down to Rambo Roddy's Sam Brown belt and removed his handcuffs. Clamping one of the cuffs tightly on to Rambo Roddy's wrist, she dragged the stunned officer over to Scout 80 and snapped the other handcuff over the steering wheel.

"Now, I suppose you'll have to lock me up. Don't worry. I'll take my medicine. It was worth it. I can imagine how horrible it must of been to have to sit next to that disgusting slob," calmly stated Juanita Daniels, holding out her hands in submission.

"No way. Aren't you Deputy Chief Daniel's wife? I know I've seen you before," inquired Briefcase Betty, finally releasing the record button on her continuously running VCR.

"Yes, I'm Juanita Daniels. I'm sure my husband isn't going to be too pleased when this hits the newspapers. The Post will have a field day with this one. Hell, he's been talkin' about retiring, anyway. Maybe this will get him off his butt and out the door," answered Juanita Daniels, wondering why she wasn't already wearing the same bracelets as her vanquished foe.

"I don't think there's been any problem here. As far as I'm

concerned, my partner was chasing a suspicious juvenile and ran into a tree. I'm sure he'll see it my way when I show him a copy of this tape and threaten to send it to all the news networks. He'll never be able to face up to the fact that a woman, especially a black woman, kicked his ass. I got it all, even him beggin' for mercy. Rambo Roddy will resign before he lets anyone know about this. And that's just what I plan to suggest," happily stated Briefcase Betty, finally seeing a ray of hope in her once bleak situation.

"It's OK with me. Mum's the word. I'll never tell a soul, including my husband, if that's the way you want it. You're doing me one big favor," remarked Juanita Daniels, ecstatic at her good fortune.

"No, it's you who's done me a big favor," countered Briefcase Betty, even more elated at her good fortune.

"Fuck both you bitches," bitterly muttered a humiliated Rambo Roddy, already hoping that Lillian Farnsworth might be able to give him a good reference. He had a feeling that, pretty soon, like it or not, he'd be looking for a new job.

Looking down at the mutilated body of Li Wong, the Capital Carver's eleventh victim in less than six months, Rhonda Bell could only shake her head and silently reaffirm her personal vow to kill the animal that had committed this unspeakable act. His pattern had become almost predictable. The only question, what race was next. His was a deadly game of multi-ethnic selectivity, figured Ronnie, fearfully wondering if his decision to go back to using the rifle meant that he was about to start the whole cycle of killing again.

"He must have followed the guy from the Chinese restaurant down the street. Just like he did when he took out the Mexican family," stated Mac, grimly surveying the gruesome scene, the eviscerated body of the Oriental male laying spread-eagled across the blood streaked hood of his Mercedes Benz sedan.

"Damn. He's got this poor dead soul trussed up like a trophy kill. Back in the woods, that's how they prove they're macho. The mighty white hunter drives around his little hick town with his kill, the poor gutless buck, sprawled across the hood of his car. Here I am, see me, the king of the jungle. What a challenge, huh, to bring down a poor defenseless deer from two hundred yards with your good ol' high-powered rifle and scope," bitterly commented Mac, the frustration and strain of their fruitless hunt showing in his quivering voice.

"Hey. Chill out, baby. It's OK. We're gettin' close. I can feel it. Pretty soon, it'll be him, layin' across the hood of our car," soberly stated Ronnie, the deadly conviction of her statement sending a cold shiver up Mac's spine.

"Why the hell would he park in this deserted alley? It's darker than hell in here. Doesn't he know there's a maniac on the loose? Jesus. Every newspaper and every news channel in the whole damn metropolitan area was predicting that he was goin huntin' for an Asian male next. And this idiot falls right into the trap," shouted Mac, kicking the tire of the ghastly looking Mercedes, his puffy face turning a brilliant shade of crimson.

"It will never happen to you. That's the way it's always been and that's the way it'll always be," answered Ronnie, desperately raking her brain to figure out why in God's name the killer would have hacked off both the victim's hands at the wrist and then placed them next to his head, on the hood of the car, interlocking their fingers like some bizarre handshake of death. The clues were becoming as gruesome as the murders themselves, dejectedly thought Ronnie, turning around to walk back to Cruiser 311, the shrill whine of the approaching mobile crime lab van echoing in the distance.

"It ain't safe in the city and it ain't safe in the country. This sure as hell is a sad commentary on our miserable lives. Us, the superior beings. Shit," sarcastically remarked Mac, following Ronnie back to the cruiser and wondering if it wasn't time for him to retire. He'd had just about a belly-full of humanity. Maybe dogs were indeed man's best friend. At least they wouldn't kill you, figured Mac, a wry smile crossing his face as he thought of his two precious children, the kids, Hoss and L'il Joe. They'd both be waiting at the back door, sitting up pretty, eager to see daddy. If only they all still had a mommy to come home to, lamented Mac, despondently thinking about his deceased wife. Maybe, just maybe, it was time for him to retire from life and join her, sadly figured the brooding detective, his eyes starting to water with tears of sorrow.

"What's wrong, Mac? Are you alright?" questioned Ronnie, glancing over at her dejected looking partner and immediately sensing the unmistakable aura of sadness surrounding Mac's slumping form.

"I'm OK. Just thinking about the good old days. But, I guess, the only thing good about them is that they're gone," answered Mac, a forced smile slowly appearing across his slack lips.

"Hey. Aren't you the one who always told me to keep my chin up, cause it's always darkest before the dawn?" kidded Ronnie, trying to cheer up her despondent partner.

"Yeah. I guess I was. Life's a bitch and then you're dead," quipped Mac, plopping down behind the wheel of Cruiser 311, his bulky frame leaning heavily over the steering wheel, his eyes blankly staring out over the ghastly murder scene.

Ronnie patted Mac on the shoulder and walked around to the passenger side of the parked car. In her heart, she wondered if he was really joking. She was more than a little concerned about his present state of mind. At least he'd slowed down on the booze. Tonight, she'd say a prayer for both her and Mac. God willing, they'd nail the Carver before he wounded their city again, thought Ronnie, hoping that this would be the cure for both of their debilitating illnesses, the illnesses caused by a society bordering on the brink of total madness. Sadly, God was not willing, not just yet.

CHAPTER 17

"WHAT'S WRONG HONEY? Jesus, you sounded hysterical on the phone," shouted Danny Money as he flung open the door and burst into Ronnie's apartment, his nine millimeter clasped in his trembling hand.

"I saw him. I saw the Carver. He's just butchered a young Oriental girl. Oh, God. It was awful. I watched the whole thing. He was laughing at me, taunting me," cried Ronnie, throwing her outstretched arms around her frightened lover.

"Darnell, is he OK?" asked Danny, looking over Ronnie's shoulder, towards the back bedroom.

"He's fine. He's still sleeping," answered Ronnie, hugging Danny tightly against her cold trembling body.

"You better get something on. Where's your robe? I'll get it for you. You're freezing," stated Danny, finally realizing that, except for the Redskins football jersey draped over her lean frame, Ronnie was totally naked.

"I don't need a robe, just you. You'll make the dreams go away," answered Ronnie, inserting her fingers through Danny's and leading him towards her bedroom.

Slipping off the Redskins jersey, her golden brown skin glowing in the diffused wash of luminous moonbeams flickering through the window blinds, Ronnie slid underneath the puffy silken bedspread and seductively motioned for Danny to get undressed and join her. Not needing a second invitation, Danny stepped out of his blue jeans, dropped his brown leather flight jacket on the carpeted floor, and climbed into bed next to Ronnie, his whole body tingling at the silken touch of her smooth skin.

"So, it was all a dream, a nightmare?" said Danny, deeply breathing in Ronnie's intoxicating scent.

Snuggling up against the comfort of his warm naked body she replied, "It wasn't a dream. It might have been in my mind, but it was real. Dreams are things that disappear when you wake up. They're just little pieces of your imagination, pasted together in a sort of weird jigsaw puzzle that you can never really solve. This was different. All I can tell you is that when I wake up in the morning this dream is going to become a living nightmare of reality. Somewhere out there, lies the mutilated body of a poor young oriental girl, and . . ."

"And what?" pressed Danny, almost afraid to ask after seeing the sullen look in Ronnie's misty tear filled eyes.

"And her little unborn baby," replied Ronnie, choking as she fought back the torrent of emotion welling up from inside her trembling body.

"You mean you think he murdered a pregnant woman?" he asked, instinctively tightening his arm around Ronnie's slender waist, a lump suddenly appearing in his dry raspy throat.

"I don't think. I know," unerringly answered Ronnie without hesitation, her whole body quivering in fear, goosebumps breaking out on her forearms.

"Jesus," he muttered, stroking the subtle curve of Ronnie's lower back, hoping to calm her shaking body.

"I'm so tired. All I want to do is go to sleep. Please, promise me when I wake up I can roll over and kiss you. Please stay with me. I need you," she whispered, turning over and backing in against Danny's warm hard body, her mind slowly drifting off into the throes of a disturbed restless sleep.

"I'll be there for you. I'll always be there for you. I love you," murmured Danny Money, gently kissing the back of Ronnie's slender neck, his arm draped over her already sleeping body.

"Well, good morning. You look as beautiful as ever," remarked Danny Money, looking up from the breakfast table, Darnell at his side wolfing down an overflowing bowl of Lucky Charms mixed with Cocoa Crispies.

"Don't you smooth talk me, you BS'er. I know how I look," good naturedly countered Ronnie, wrapping her robe around her waist, now wishing she'd at least put on some make up.

"That's how she always looks in the morning. Not too hot, huh?" nonchalantly stated Darnell, chomping away on a spoonful of the grotesque mixture, milk dribbling down his steadily moving chin.

"And you, young man. What is that you're eating? I don't buy any of that junk food cereal, now do I?" scolded Ronnie, casting an accusing glance at Danny, who was pretending to be reading the *Washington Post*.

"Don't have a cow, mom. Danny went out this morning and got it for us. He's already had two bowls," tattled Darnell, pointing his spoon at the cowering off-duty officer.

Slinking down in his seat, Danny remarked, "I couldn't decide on which one, so I got them both. It isn't too bad. They taste pretty good mixed together."

"You two are beyond help. Both of you are bad boys, aren't you? joked Ronnie, feeling a glowing warmth that perhaps they were very close to becoming a real family.

"Maybe you can punish me later. You know, the handcuffs again. Hurt me baby," kidded Danny, winking at Ronnie as she walked over to put the tea kettle on the burner.

"I know what he's talking about. He wants you to do him," innocently stated Darnell, proud of his newly acquired worldliness.

"Don't you talk like that. Where did you ever learn something like that? I can't believe it," uttered Ronnie. Despite herself, she almost busted a gut at Darnell's offhand remark.

"Get with the program, mom. BBD, Do Me Baby," sang Darnell, mimicking the once popular song.

"Well, you just tell your partner in crime, there, that I know my music pretty well and he isn't going to be doin' any foolin' around with me this morning, cause he Can't Touch This," laughed Ronnie, pulling the robe tightly around her body as she sashayed through the kitchen, teasingly flitting her firm rounded buttocks.

"By the way, speaking of music, me and the Bud Man were talking to Spiegel the other day. He says E.P. is doing great, but he's changed his tune. Seems he's takin' a liking to John Denver and been singin' Take Me Home Country Road," commented Danny Money, smiling as an absurd picture of E.P. plowing a cornfield, hitched behind a team of horses, popped into his mind.

"What are you talking about?" asked Ronnie, looking quizzically at Danny.

"I'm talkin' about love and marriage go together like a horse and carriage. E.P.'s gonna tie the knot, put on the old ball and chain. I guess he's going to marry his girlfriend and take her back to his home, the wild and wonderful state," humorously replied Danny Money, wondering if it wasn't about time he did the same with Ronnie.

"What's the wild and wonderful state?" inquired Ronnie, pouring herself a cup of hot tea.

"West Virginia. Mountain men. You know. Take me home down dem good ol' country roads," sang Danny Money, walking over to Ronnie and adding, "God, you look so sexy, standing there over the sink. Let's go for it."

"What about Darnell?" teasingly asked Ronnie as she seductively rubbed the crack of her buttocks against Danny's growing member.

"Don't kids ever go out to play, these days?" said Danny, glancing over his shoulder to make sure Darnell wasn't looking and then gently cupping both of Ronnie's firm breasts in the palms of his hands.

"Maybe for a little while," replied Ronnie, knowing that on Saturdays all the local kids were down at the park, at least one parent always standing by as part of the Neighborhood Watch Program.

"Hey, Darnell. Why don't you go on down and shoot some hoops? I'll be down there to join you in a little while. Me and your mother need to talk about some things, adult things," suggested Danny, sure that Darnell would get the hint.

"Don't make it too quick. I don't want the dudes thinkin' you can't hang in there with mom," answered Darnell, beating a hasty retreat out the front door before he got his butt chewed out for being a smart ass.

"Man, it's scary. These kids know more at eight or ten than we did at twenty," remarked Danny, shaking his head in disbelief.

"What you mean we, white man? Speak for yourself. I knew plenty by the time I was a teenager. How'd you like me to play teacher for awhile?" giggled Ronnie, massaging Danny's hardened shaft.

I'd just love to be teacher's pet. Keep that up and I'll drag you back up to the Keystone State and make you live with all those rednecks, you nasty girl, you," replied Danny, slipping the robe off Ronnie's shoulders.

Suddenly Ronnie froze, the words slamming into her head with the force of a shattering explosion.

The what?" she excitedly shouted, her whole body about to explode in nervous anticipation.

"You know, the Keystone State. You've got a friend in Pennsylvania," replied Danny Money, startled at Ronnie's abrupt change in mood.

Her heart slamming against her chest, rivulets of perspiration streaming down from the underside of her sweating breasts, Ronnie gasped for air and desperately struggled to maintain her outward composure. Slowly, she backed away from Danny, her head spinning in confusion, trying to sort things out. Not a rock, but a stone. A key and a stone. Keystone, thought Ronnie, staggering as she dashed into the living room and grabbed her briefcase. The severed hands, locked together in a ghastly handshake, that had to be the You've Got a Friend, concluded the excited detective, opening up her briefcase and grabbing the sheet of clues.

"Danny, sit down, baby. I think I've got the scent. I'm on to him," hysterically shouted Ronnie, motioning for Danny to join her at the kitchen table.

"Whoever you're on, sure as hell isn't me," sarcastically stated Danny, wondering what in the world was going on. A minute ago he was just about to get laid. Now, it looked like he was going to get screwed. No sex involved.

"The Carver, the Capital Carver. You've just hit the nail on the head. All along, he's been trying to lead us to his lair. If we can figure out the rest of the clues, we'll know exactly where he lives. He's from Pennsylvania. No doubt about it," excitedly stated Ronnie, quickly running her finger down the worn tattered list.

"Tell me more about Pennsylvania. The clues have to be some sort of symbols for local slang or customs. Maybe even places," she pressed, looking desperately at Danny and praying that he could provide some more pieces to the mysterious puzzle.

"Well, I'd say he had to be a coal miner. He left the lump of coal and it's the kind they mine in Western Pennsylvania. I sure as hell saw plenty of that stuff in my younger years," he replied, staring at the typed list of clues and penciled in notes.

"What about the Christmas ornament, the tree bulb? What could that mean?" she asked, eager to zero in on the callous murderer.

"I hate to say it, but my home town, Indiana, Pennsylvania, in fact the whole of Indiana County, prides itself on being the Christmas tree capital of the world, if that's any help," answered Danny, somehow, deep down inside, afraid that it indeed had been of help.

As calmly as possible, Rhonda Bell walked over to the bookcase, pulling out two volumes of her son's encyclopedia set. Opening the first one, she leafed through the P's and stopped to read the information on Pennsylvania. The second volume, the I volume, held more promise. She flipped the pages until she came to the section on the state of Indiana and began to skim through the paragraphs. There it was. The state flower of Indiana was the Tulip Tree. Crossing tulip off the list she now knew that, most likely, her killer either lived in Danny's hometown or, at the very least, in the vast expanse of rural Indiana County.

"Danny, he's from up in your area somewhere. I can feel it. I know we're on the right track. I'm certain of it," resolutely stated Ronnie, almost jumping out of her seat at the startling ring of the telephone. Picking up the receiver, her stomach churning, Ronnie already knew what she was about to hear. In her mind she had seen it all. She only needed to know where the young girl's body was and what clue had been left at the scene.

"OK, Mac. I'll meet you down there. We've got a break. I'll tell you about it when I see you. Give me an hour," stated Ronnie, hanging up the telephone and looking sadly at Danny.

"They found the Oriental girl over by the canal," she despondently remarked, a solitary tear trickling down her dark brown cheek.

"What about her baby?" asked Danny, anxiously staring into Ronnie's wounded eyes.

"It was right next to her. The bastard cut it up into little pieces," sobbed Ronnie, rushing into Danny's outstretched arms, her whole body raked with trembling spasms of anguish and grief.

"God, Mac. It only gets worse," sadly stated Ronnie, turning her head away from the gruesome scene.

"Yeah. I know what you mean. I've never seen anything like it. If he counts this as a two for one bluelight special, what race will he go after next, the Arabs, the Jews, maybe the American Indians? This is pathetic," somberly responded Mac, surveying the grisly massacre.

"Did she have any I.D. on her?" questioned Ronnie, dreading the moment when they would have to draw back the sheet and watch the agonized pain grip the poor girl's husband, his whole life passing before his very eyes.

"She sure did. Her purse is laying over there, next to what's left of her baby. I managed to reach inside and get her wallet. Once the Mobile Crime Lab finishes dusting the scene we'll take a ride and notify her husband. The Morgue Wagon will be here any minute. They were runnin' a little late. Had to pick up two dead junkies from some crack house over in Southeast," soberly answered Mac, trying to figure out how in God's name you could tell a man that his wife and baby had just been gutted out, both butchered like a side of hanging beef.

"I'll tell him. I can answer a lot of questions that you can't. Mac, I know you'll think I'm crazy, but I saw this whole thing in a dream, everything, right down to the smallest detail," stated Ronnie, hoping that Mac didn't think she had lost her marbles.

"Look. I don't think you're crazy. I just think you're special. After you called that bow and arrow nightmare at the Georgetown version of Elm Street I'll never doubt your intuition or instincts again. Baby, if you've got it, flaunt it," remarked Mac, trying to add a little levity to this whole morbid stinking mess.

Watching as the crew of the morgue wagon, assisted by two uniform patrol officers, shoveled the remains into a plastic body bag, Mac looked over at Ronnie and, shaking his head, asked, "Now, what were you talking about on the telephone? You think you've got a lead, a suspect, what?"

"Not a suspect, but his lair, his haunt, the place that the bastard hangs. I think I know where he lives," excitedly answered Ronnie. "I'll tell you all about it in the car, on the way over to the victim's house. We're almost on to him, Mac. I can feel it. In a couple of days he's mine."

"You mean ours, don't you?" questioned Mac, afraid that Ronnie did indeed mean what she had said, just exactly the way that she had stated it.

"That's interesting. It makes sense," responded Mac as Ronnie finished spinning her intriguing theory, most of the clues falling into place with astonishing simplicity. Summing up the incredible trail of bizarre clues, he added, "Well, that leaves us with a branch, a sapling, a shot glass, a cherry, and tonight's friendly reminder, two empty bottles of Rolling Rock beer, minus any incriminating fingerprints."

"That should convince you that I'm not crazy. It says right here on the bottle that it's brewed in Latrobe, Pennsylvania," stated Ronnie, certain that she had made her point.

"Alright. You've convinced me. Our murderer is from Pennsylvania, Indiana, Pennsylvania, either the town or the county. Now, where do we go from here? How do we find him? The other clues have to hold the answer," reasoned Mac, glancing over at Ronnie as she turned Cruiser 311 on to 22nd Street.

"That, I haven't figured out yet. I guess we better contact the local Indiana police and the Pennsylvania State Police. Maybe they can shed some light on the situation. It's a start," replied Ronnie, deciding that she ought to pick Danny's brain a little more. He might just hold the key to the kingdom of the Capital Carver's own personal hell.

"Good idea," responded Mac, stepping out of the car in front of the victim's apartment and looking back at Ronnie. He knew one thing for sure. He had better crack this case before she did or her whole world would come tumbling down in an avalanche of violence. In his mind, Mac had no doubt that Ronnie fully intended to kill the Carver, whether he was armed or not. She would be his judge, jury, and executioner. Or, worse yet, the Carver would be hers, reasoned Mac, ringing the doorbell, his stomach tied up in knots. God, he prayed, please don't let the man be home. He was having enough trouble holding back his own tears. Slowly, the door cracked open and Mac began to cry.

CHAPTER 18

IT HADN'T BEEN all that hard, thought Mac, rolling down the window of his refurbished 1966 Mustang as he sped northwest on Interstate 70 towards the hometown of the Capital Carver, the damp swirling wind slapping his face with sobering reality. All he had had to do was get out his maps and pour over the endless number of boroughs and burgs which dotted the western Pennsylvania countryside and there it had been, staring him right in the face. It had almost been too easy.

In another three hours he'd be in the dinky little borough. Then, all he had to do was find the murderin' red neck's truck and the deadly game was over. Or, had it just begun in earnest, feared Mac, looking up at the dark ominous sky, half the orb of the luminous moon swallowed up in a towering black thunder cloud. Windblown specks of water began to appear on the streaked windshield. "Damn," cursed Mac, turning on the windshield wipers. That's all he needed. It was beginning to rain.

"Spiegel put in his transfer papers to go to 2D. They told him he could go anywhere he wanted, any assignment. Can you imagine? First, a medal from the President himself, and now this. He's takin' that asshole Rambo Roddy's place in Scout 80, next to Briefcase Betty. That's a match made in heaven if I ever saw one," commented Danny Money, glancing over at Ronnie who was blankly staring out the car window, her mind millions of miles away, desperately trying to put the final pieces of the Carver's puzzle in place before the heinous murderer struck again.

"Yes, I can imagine. We used to sit next to each other, didn't we? Don't you ever miss those days? There were times when I couldn't wait to get to work, just so I could see you. Now, I'm not so sure I ever want to sit through another roll call. Nothing's as clear as it used to be. Things seem to be out of our control. All we do is mop up everybody's mess. We don't prevent problems. We don't even solve problems. It seems like all we do is try and cover them up, so everybody thinks that it's just one big happy world we all live in. I'm getting tired of the whole damn thing," dejectedly responded Ronnie, her mind and body drained, her muscles aching from lack of a good night's sleep.

"Hey, cheer up. Life goes on. Hell, this war's been goin' on for thousands of years and the police haven't won yet. What makes you think that it's all on your shoulders? As long as there are people like you, that care, someday it will all be different. Maybe we'll win, maybe we won't, shit happens, you know, but we've got to hang in there. You're not doin' it for us. You're doin' it for them," soberly stated Danny, pointing out the window of his BMW at a group of kids playing basketball in a neighborhood park.

"Yeah, I guess you're right. Why don't you drive by Tiny's. I could use a drink. Maybe it'll help me sleep tonight," suggested Ronnie, looking at her watch. In less than twelve hours she'd be back on the job. It really didn't matter, thought the exhausted detective. Whether you punched a time-clock or not, this was one job that worked you twenty four hours a day.

Mac wound his way through the twisting country roads of rural western Pennsylvania. A light mist continued to seep out of the low hanging grey clouds which hovered above him like a wispy shroud of damp bone chilling doom. This whole place is depressing, thought the venerable old detective, his weary bones beginning to ache in the cold moist air. Just a few more miles and he'd be there, staring into the very eyes of death, grimaced Mac, totally willing, if need be, to trade in his own tired old useless ass life for that of his beautiful loving partner. Ronnie had so much to give to life. She still dared to dream of a better world, not only for blacks, but for her people, the entire human race, decided the tired detective, glancing over at the passing road sign.

Johnstown, Pennsylvania, reflected Mac. The home of the famous incline plane. The home of the hot fiery forges of the slowly dying steel mills. The home of one of the nation's highest unemployment rates. The home of the sadly fading American dream, despondently thought Mac, pumping the brakes as he cannonballed down a steep hill and decided to rejuvenate himself with a bolt of good old Jolt java. Pulling the car into a deserted neon lit Burger King, he decided that he'd have the mother of all cups, a six creamer with seven sugars.

His whole world was turning into a churning mish-mash of bright exploding lights and bottomless black holes. "Was it over?", hoped the exhausted detective, his bulky frame slumping over the Mustang's steering wheel. Suddenly, the blaring horn of a rumbling coal truck startled him. Opening his heavy sleep-filled eyes' he looked out the car's smeared windshield at a blinding white glare approaching him head on. "Jesus," he muttered. Yanking the wheel hard right, he swerved back over the double yellow line and barely missed a head-on collision with the thundering coal truck.

Shaking the cobwebs out of his dulled brain, Mac pulled over to the side of the road, the car skidding in the loose gravel as he locked the brakes and slid to a complete stop. Damn, he couldn't help anybody if he ended up as a mangled hood-ornament on some local yokel's tri-axle, cursed the weary detective under his breath, disgusted with himself for being such a foolish old man. He turned around to look in the back seat and smiled. Two sets of sparkling brown eyes looked eagerly up at him from their warm cozy blanket, both the kids curled up in blissful contentment. He knew he should have left them at home, but he just couldn't bear the thought of never seeing them again.

"How's daddy's big girl and his little fella?" he asked, handing both Hoss and L'il Joe a milk bone as he pulled back on to the dark deserted highway, the do-not-enter, one-way, road to hell.

Restlessly tossing from side to side, her tense body alive with high strung anxiety, Ronnie threw back the covers, got out of bed, and started to pace back and forth in the small bedroom.

"Hey, it's four in the morning. Come on back to bed. You need the sleep," whispered Danny, propping his lean naked body up on one elbow as he stared at Ronnie's nervous pacing form.

"I've got to admit, you don't look like a lineman and you're certainly not a wide receiver so you must be a tight end," he joked, commenting on the Redskins football jersey which hung almost to Ronnie's knees.

"Something's wrong. I can feel it. It's just eating at me, tearing up my insides. The game has changed. We're not the home team anymore. No more homefield advantage. It's time for a road trip. Now, we're the visitors," remarked Ronnie, her mind reeling as she tried to put a finger on the queer tingling sensation racing up and down her spine.

"Come on, honey. Lie down for a little bit. We'll talk about it before we head for roll call. We've got a couple more hours of sack time," pleaded Danny, motioning for Ronnie to crawl back into bed. Not wanting to say anything more, for fear of dragging

Danny deeper into this whole sordid mess, Ronnie slipped into bed and, running her fingers through Danny's wavy hair, nestled her head against his smooth muscular chest. Listening to the rhythmic beat of Danny's slowly pumping heart, Ronnie closed her eyes and pretended to go to sleep. Soon, she'd answer a different roll call, the roll call of death, the ominous roll call of the Capital Carver, feared the frightened detective, her mind suddenly conjuring up disturbing images of the insides of a bone chilling meat locker, bloody human carcasses hanging from its cold steel hooks, the scent of blood wafting through the thick frigid air.

"Have a good day, baby. Take care of yourself. I'll call you later," lied Rhonda Bell, hugging Danny as she kissed him deeply, passionately. Then, stepping back, she looked longingly into his soft warm eyes and prayed that it wouldn't be the last time that she ever held the man she so desperately loved.

"Don't start anything you're not going to be able to finish," he humorously stated, somewhat taken back by Ronnie's intense passion.

"It wouldn't take me long to finish you off if I wanted to, believe me," coyly replied Ronnie. "By the way. Last night I was just thinking about that bar, up in Pennsylvania. You know, the one with all those nice friendly open minded guys who would just as soon have sent me back to Africa, probably in a pine box."

"You mean the Oak Tree Tavern," answered Danny, chuckling at Ronnie's remarks as he slid into the seat of his BMW and turned over the ignition.

"Yes, that's it. The Oak Tree Tavern," she nervously replied, fully realizing the prophetic significance of her instant replay of the terrifying meat locker vision. Mentally crossing the shotglass, the empty beer bottles, and the branch of oak off the shrinking list of clues, Ronnie waved good-bye to Danny and began to emotionally prepare herself. As soon as she dropped off Darnell at her mother's, she'd be heading for the Oak Tree Tavern and a rendezvous with her murderous quarry, the heinous butcher who had enchained her city in the throes of terror. Now, she could truly set her people free.

Mac pulled off the narrow road, into the dirt parking lot of an ancient looking red brick school house, its dark weathered walls lined with hairline cracks, mortar crumbling from between the endless sagging rows of chipped and broken bricks. Stretching as he stepped out of the idling car, he took a deep breath, the crisp scent of pine needles invigorating his drained body.

Looking up at the ominous grey sky, wisps of swirling mist eerily drifting through the endless panorama of rounded mountains, their slopes covered with thick shadowy forests, Mac looked over at the road sign. Well, here he was. The sign said it all. Welcome to the Borough of Cherry Tree, Population 253. "Welcome my ass," muttered Mac, an icy shiver coursing through his entire body as he kicked a small rock across the empty parking lot. Figuring out these two clues had turned out to be relatively simple. He had scoured the entire Pennsylvania map, concentrating on Indiana County, and there it had been, staring up at him, the innocent sounding town striking terror into his very heart.

Before the sun set, this little hick town, the cherry and the sapling, the tree, would make its mark in the bloody annals of criminal history, never again remaining the innocent little-play world untouched by time, feared Mac, as he instinctively reached under his rumpled navy blue sportcoat for the comforting feel of his two inch Smith and Wesson revolver. The other three clues, the shot glass, the beer bottle, and the branch still didn't make any sense. But, no matter, he'd find the Capital creep. This backward burg wasn't big enough for the both of them.

Leaving the car parked at the archaic looking school house, Mac leashed up Hoss and L'il Joe and began to walk. It was only a matter of time. The murderin' bastard's truck would be here somewhere, figured Mac, grinning as L'il Joe lifted his leg and peed all over the metal leg of the welcome sign. "Piss on it, piss on it real good," encouraged Mac, carefully surveying the peaceful quiet town, the slowly rising sun unable to break through the low hanging blanket of thick grey clouds. A light drizzle began to trickle out of the stormy looking sky. Undaunted, Mac slipped on his beige rain coat and continued on. The damp air crackled with static electricity, an ominous clap of thunder echoing up the socked in valley. There would be two storms today, figured Mac, a sheet of rain and a hail of lead.

"I haven't seen anybody do that in years," stated Mac, watching a tidy looking woman, bent over on her knees, pulling dandelions out of her front lawn.

"We just love them, boiled, then covered with vinegar," answered Kate Carver, wiping the light misty rain off her wrinkled brow as she stood up and straightened her knee length frock.

She smiled, a warm friendly glow covering her handsome weathered face.

"Not a very pleasant morning for a walk, is it? Are you visiting? Oh, excuse me. I don't want to seem like some neb nosing old biddy," she remarked.

"It's OK. You're not being nosy, only friendly. And you certainly aren't an old biddy," politely stated Mac, taking an immediate liking to this attractive down-to-earth woman.

"Yes, I am visiting. Well, actually I'm just sort of passing through and my dogs needed a little watering break. This seemed like a nice friendly town," answered Mac, trying to avoid an outright lie.

"The little darlings are so cute. What are their names? I don't think I've ever seen that kind of dog before," commented Kate Carver, instantly deciding that this was a very nice man, indeed.

"They're Lhasa Apsos. And the fat one, her name's Hoss. The little fella, that's liftin' his leg on your nice flowers, is L'il Joe. My wife, God bless her, and I, used to love Bonanza and I have to apologize for L'il Joe. I'm sorry," sheepishly replied Mac, tugging at L'il Joe's leash.

Giggling, Kate Carver said, "You don't have to apologize. I'm sorry about your wife. I'm sure she was a beautiful God-fearing woman. I bet you miss her, don't you?"

"I sure do. I miss her so bad. It's been a while now, but, the hurt, the sorrow, they never really go away," sadly answered Mac, strangely finding himself hoping that, maybe too, this fine woman was without a loving partner.

Suddenly, Mac cringed as he caught a fleeting glimpse of the yellowish bruises circling Kate Carver's graceful neck, the indelible marks of abuse obvious to the veteran officer. Shocked, he looked deeply into her soft brown eyes, almost able to feel this humiliating pain and suffering oozing out of her brutalized body.

"How about a cup of coffee? I'll bet you like your coffee, don't you? I've got a fresh pot in the house. Why don't you sit yourself down on the porch, outta the rain, and I'll get you a cup," pleasantly offered Kate Carver, instinctively pulling up the collar of her neatly pressed dress.

"Yes, I'd like that. I'd like that a whole lot. By the way, my name's Mike McCarthy, but my friends, they call me Mac," stated the venerable old detective as he plopped his rotund frame down on to the cushioned porch swing and tied Hoss and L'il Joe to the wrought iron banister, both dogs immediately assuming a spread-eagled position on the soft damp grass.

Kate Carver pushed open the screen door and, turning her head back around, asked, "And what should I call you, Mr. McCarthy?"

"You can call me, Mac," answered the smiling detective without the slightest hesitation.

"Glad to meet you, Mac. You can call me Kate, and the impolite young lady here, this is my daughter Becky," stated Kate Carver, watching in amazement as Becky, totally ignoring Mac, bounded down the steps and instantly endeared herself to the two canines by offering each of them a leftover piece of breakfast sausage.

"Excuse me, Kate. Would it be alright if I used your bathroom before I saddle up and head out? There's not too many public restrooms in these parts and I'd like to finish my walk before I leave town," asked Mac, the moderate three cream three sugar coffee having already run through him.

"Go ahead. You're welcome to use it. It's down the hall to the right," answered Kate Carver, nervously glancing at the kitchen clock and praying that her husband didn't get back from the feedstore before this pleasant man left her house. He'd beat her ass for sure if he knew another man had been in his house.

Ray Carson Carver slammed on the brakes. Throwing the pickup truck into reverse, he skidded across the narrow highway. The huge oversized tires squealed as he backed the four wheel drive up the middle of the road and slid into the schoolyard parking lot, loose gravel spraying against the red-brick walls of the weathered old school. "Son of a bitch," muttered the surprised murderer, staring down at the out of place Maryland tags. They were here. It had to be them, the black bitch and her fat partner. He had expected an unmarked police cruiser with D.C. tags, but no matter. He'd have to move fast. No telling how close they really were. Burning rubber, the screeching tires smoking on the wet oily asphalt which was shrouded in willowing wisps of rising steam, Ray Carson Carver sped towards his house just as Mike McCarthy closed the bathroom door.

"Who the hell's mutts are these?" shouted Ray Carver, leaping out of his still idling truck and brutally slapping his daughter, the vicious force of the savage blow knocking her to the wet slippery ground.

"The nice man. He's inside the house using the bathroom. Please don't hurt him or mommy. He doesn't mean anybody no harm," stammered Becky Carver, a thin trickle of blood oozing out of the corner of her mouth as she watched the enraged dogs desperately trying to sink their teeth into her father's leg.

"What's going on out here?" hollered Kate Carver, opening the screen door just in time to absorb a staggering punch that dropped her to her wobbly knees.

"I'll deal with you later, you worthless slut," coldly stated Ray Carver, insanely driving his steel toed work boot into his wife's painfully cracked ribs.

Rushing down the hall, Ray Carver quietly slipped into the den. He opened the glass doors of the gun cabinet, hurriedly sliding the .44 magnum Ruger Blackhawk revolver out of its western style leather holster. This would be easier than he had figured. The helpless prey was simply no match for the steel-nerved predator. He had sucked the fat pig right into his lair. Now, he'd open him up and give him a good enema, Carver style. He'd clean the shit right out of porky pig and then he'd trap the bitch, just like he had planned it. Her, he was gonna sample, try some of that nice juicy black meat before he left her guts strung out like crepe paper at the senior prom.

"Kate, you never mentioned your last name or whether you were even married," hollered Mac down the hallway, the noise of the flushing toilet drowning out the terribly beaten woman's agonizing moans of warning. "I'm sorry I took so long, but I didn't think you'd mind if I washed up a bit, kinda shake off the road grime," added Mac, wondering what had got the kids all riled up. They were yipping away like a couple of crazy-ass banshees.

"It ain't a gonna matter what her name is, buddy boy, cause your name is mud," chuckled Ray Carver stepping out into the hallway, the .44 magnum leveled at Mac's startled form. Standing face to face with the grinning madman, Mike McCarthy instantly knew that he was history, about to become the Capital Carver's next victim.

"You. You're the dude from the McDonald's. Long way to drive for a Big Mac attack. Why? It doesn't fit. You've already killed three whites. I thought you sickos always followed a pattern," disdainfully remarked Mac, figuring what the hell. He was about to be butchered, anyway, disemboweled like all the others.

"Well now, ain't you ever heard of the three little piggies?

Well, I'm the big bad wolf and I'm a gonna huff and puff and blow three of you away," roared the Capital Carver, cocking the hammer of the deadly handgun, his hollow lifeless eyes unable to conceal the cold hearted bloodthirsty killer that lurked within his soul. Slowly, the life was being sapped out of his emaciated body, the Black Lung having almost totally eaten away his entire respiratory system.

"Jesus, no! Where does it end?" shouted Mac, crossing himself.

"For you, porky, it ends here," stated the Carver in deadly earnest, spitting a long arc of tobacco juice across the six foot space that separated the two adversaries.

"I'm a goin' down in a bloody blaze of glory. Just like you said, Jonny. Just like you said. I'm gonna make myself famous, now draw!" shouted Ray Carver, his sinister eyes dancing with glee.

Mac, realizing it was now or never, desperately reached for his revolver, the .38 special tucked away in the shoulder holster dangling underneath his left arm.

Skillfully raising the murderous handgun, Ray Carver smiled and then squeezed the trigger. The thunderous explosion, spewing forth an acrid plume of smoke and fire, erupted with deadly finality. The speeding bullet plowed into Mac's flinching chest, his gun flying out of his hand before he even had a chance to draw a bead on the snickering killer. Stuffing the revolver down the front of his Dickey work pants, Ray Carver reached around to the side of his belt and slid the shiny blade of the hunting knife out of its dirty worn sheath. He'd better git ol' fatso's car keys before he messed the poor boy up, laughed the confident killer, already setting the bait for his next trap. The bitch was close. He could feel it.

"Run, Becky, run! Your father's gone mad. Go get help. Get away from here. He's gonna kill us all," screamed Kate Carver, momentarily regaining her senses, her whole body throbbing with excruciating pain. Distracted by his wife's desperate cry, Ray Carver rushed to the front door and watched in frustration as his fleeing daughter raced across the front yard, Hoss and L'il Joe playfully nipping at her heels.

"Damn you, you old whore. You're gonna mess everything up, you good for nothin' bitch. I'll fix your ass," raged Ray Carver, a huge glob of bloody phlegm choking off his raspy breath as he began to hack. Raked with burning spasms, his insides began to explode with crippling ferocity. Kate Carver, seeing her chance, crawled down the porch steps and staggered to her feet. In excruciating pain, she clutched at her side as she limped across the yard towards the nearest neighbor's house.

He had to get moving. One down, two to go, decided Ray Carver, regretting that he hadn't had the time to finish the ritual gutting of the dead porker. "You just have to take your losses and get on with life," he wheezed, tobacco juice and blood steadily dribbling down his greasy bearded chin.

"Hey, Hank. That nigger bitch been in here again?" shouted Ray Carver, a sadistic grin covering his oily dirt streaked face as he walked into the Oak Tree Tavern.

"No. The spook ain't been around. She sure had a nice ass though, didn't she? You think that white boy was porkin' her? Bet she's one hot split tail. I heard tell them there colored babes is like Jew bitches. They're both hotter than a smokin' pistol," answered Hank Edwards, wondering if he'd ever have a crack at some black snatch. "The usual?" asked the daydreaming bartender, licking his lips at the very thought of getting a taste of forbidden fruit.

"No, not the usual. You just git your big ass out from behind the bar. I'm gonna take over and tend bar for a little while. That, or I'll shove this smokin' pistol right down your pants and blow your pecker clear to hell," coldly stated Ray Carver, grinning as he spit on to the stained wooden floor.

"Git on over there and watch the door. Soon as the nigger gets outta the car you skeedaddle out the back door. I'll take care of everything else," ordered the crazed murderer, methodically pouring himself two fingers of Old Grand Dad.

Hank Edwards was shaking in fear, his bowels about to lose themselves all over his three day old unwashed Fruit of the Looms. He was glad he hadn't put on clean drawers. Before it was over, he had a feeling that he'd be throwin' this pair in the trash.

"You make sure you tell anybody else that comes to the door that you've had to close for a couple of hours. I don't want no customers except the darkie. She'll be my treat, on the house," laughed the Carver, his eyes turning as blank and lifeless as a solitary lump of pitch black coal.

"There it is," sighed Rhonda Bell, rounding a sharp bend in the road, the Oak Tree Tavern less than a hundred yards away. She felt ashamed. The thought of lying to Danny about going to work and then calling in sick went against everything she stood for. She had even betrayed Mac. She should have told him how she had finally put together the clues and figured out that the Carver was either in, or near, the Oak Tree Tavern. Instead, she had decided to spare him the final confrontation. The poor man had already endured so much pain for so little gain. At least she walked into her own little valley of death sharing life's greatest joy, the joy of having a man love you as much as you loved him. No matter what happened, she could, if need be, go to her grave smiling, knowing that for even a brief second in time she had felt the winds of love beneath her wings.

Maybe that was all just a bunch of crap, relented the beleaguered detective, braking as she approached the parking lot of the dark ominous tavern. Maybe, deep down inside, she really was selfish, wanting nothing short of watching the sick murdering bastard crawl at her feet, in his own blood, and then die a slow agonizing death like those that he had butchered with his own hand. No maybe about it, thought Ronnie. Despite herself, despite her reverence for life, she had made the decision long ago. Today, she would be God. Today, she would send the devil back to his own fiery hell.

"Oh, no! No, not this," audibly gasped Rhonda Bell, pulling into the muddy pot hole filled parking lot of the Oak Tree Tavern. There, parked beside the corner of the run down wood and stone bar, sat Mac's car, a rack of deer antlers resting on its shiny white hood. How could he have got here before her? He couldn't have possibly known about the clues, about the Oak Tree Tavern, figured Ronnie, stepping out of her car, a shocked expression evident on her stunned face.

Side-stepping a muddy puddle, she cautiously walked up to the parked car, her black riding-boots squishing in the oozing mud and gravel of the rain-soaked lot. "Damn, the hood's still warm," gasped Ronnie, resting her palm on the wet metal, its entire surface covered with bead like drops of shimmering crystal-clear rain water. Shivering as a moist gust of cold damp air swirled across the virtually abandoned parking lot, she pulled the collar of her waist length black leather motorcycle jacket up around her neck. Now, she was really scared. It was up to her to stop this madman. Obviously, Mac had already tried and failed, the antlers a sick symbol of the Carver's victory.

It could mean nothing else, she figured, reaching into the waistband of her skin-tight blue jeans and pulling out the black Smith and Wesson nine millimeter semi-automatic pistol which she had decided to bring along in place of her two inch .38 special police issue revolver. Thrusting her hand into her jacket pocket she retrieved one of the two clips and abruptly slammed it up into the handle of the nine millimeter. She yanked the slide of the pistol back as she chambered the first of its fourteen rounds. Grimly, she strode towards the tavern's front door, her whole mind and body solely committed to end the Capital Carver's cold reign of terror in a fusillade of hot scalding lead.

"She's coming! The black bitch is comin'! God, she looks like a sweet thing. How about I git a taste of her, Ray? Ain't never had me no dark meat. Can't say as I ever had nothing looks as good as her," excitedly hollered Hank Edwards, watching as the beautiful curvaceous black woman slowly crossed the muddy parking lot.

Mesmerized as the striking woman neared the front door, he stated, "She's got a gun! Damn, Ray! She's got a fuckin' hogleg! Jesus, what's going on here?"

Suddenly more concerned about dying than about skinnin' any babe, black or otherwise, Hank Edwards started slowly backing away from the front door. His head began to spin. Turning, he gasped in shock. There, at the end of the bar, stood Ray Carver, looking like a B-Movie version of the Good, the Bad, and the Ugly all rolled up into one.

"Jesus Christ, Ray! What's the cowboy get-up for? What's goin' on here? You're plumb crazy! I'm gettin' outta here," screamed Hank Edwards, wildly rushing for the back door, his whole body covered with the stale odor of sweat.

"Not alive, you ain't. Now, slap leather," shouted Ray Carver, quickly drawing the .44 magnum out of the holster tied down around his leg.

"Oh, God. I don't want to die," begged Hank Edwards, racing for the kitchen behind the bar.

Drawing a bead on Hank Edward's exposed back, Ray Carver calmly stated, "Everybody's gotta go sometime." Then, he slowly cocked the hammer and squeezed the trigger, sending Hank Edward's twitching form tumbling head first into the yellowed porcelain sink, its cracked bowl slowly filling with the dead bartender's gushing blood.

Flinching at the echoing explosion, Ronnie hurled herself against the rough wooden planks of the bar's exterior wall, slivers of wood cutting into her smooth palms. She tried to still her wildly beating heart by taking long deep breaths. God, she was so alone. No police radio, no back-up, no partner, nobody to call the local police, nothing; nothing except those footprints in the sand. "This time, please God, let there be just one set of footprints in the sand. Carry me through this, please," prayed Rhonda Bell, stepping away from the wall and momentarily hesitating in front of the heavy wooden door.

"Go for it," shouted Ronnie under her breath as she slammed her shoulder into the creaking door and burst inside the dim gloomy bar, the hazy air still thick with the acrid smell of spent gunpowder. Dropping down on one knee behind a chalky blue dust covered pool table, she leveled her gun across the spooky looking room, the faint glow of flickering red candlelights casting an eerie pall over the entire tavern's dusky looking interior.

Her eyes still not adjusted to the dim hazy light of the windowless bar, Ronnie grimaced as she heard the distinct metallic click of coins dropping into a jukebox. Squinting, she watched as a shadowy figure walked slowly across the dirty wooden floor. What was that strange noise, wondered Ronnie, listening intently. Damn, the lunatic was dressed up like Billy the Kid observed the frightened detective, a fine sheen of nervous perspiration coating her forehead. That was it, spurs, the jingle jangle of spurs, concluded Ronnie, the bizarre scene gripping her in the clutch of mind numbing terror.

The jukebox suddenly began to play, Ray Carver having hit E-3 five consecutive times. Jon Bon Jovi began to sing. Ray Carver began to laugh. Rhonda Bell began to cry.

"You ain't a gonna shoot me in the back, now is ya?" chuckled Ray Carver, leaning over the bar and pouring himself a double header. Downing the burning whiskey in one long gulp, he turned towards Ronnie's cowering form and stated, "You've come after the lion in his own den. Now, that wasn't very smart was it? Your dead-ass partner, he made the same mistake as you and he paid for it with his life. This here's the jungle, baby. Survival of the fittest. Only the strong shall survive. Kill or be killed. Me, I kill. You, you be the prey."

Ronnie swallowed and tried to steady her trembling hands. She wiped the tears out of her eyes, images of her hardened ghetto past dancing through her reeling head. With Blaze of Glory blaring out of the crackly sounding tinny jukebox she stood straight up and stared across the room at the callous killer, her whole body boiling with rage.

"So, you're him. The big bad Capital Carver. The country bumpkin from the Golden Arches. And to think I almost felt sorry for you that night. You, the son of a bitch who cuts up little children with his bad ass self. Well, you ain't jack shit to me. McDonald's or not. You don't deserve a break today. You ain't gonna spill my guts you stinkin' bastard. I'm gonna string you up by your redneck balls," defiantly shouted Ronnie, both her sweaty palms tightly clasped around the handle of the nine millimeter.

"Yeah, that's me, you nigger whore. Ray Carson Carver, the God of hell-fire," answered the crazed murderer, his hand slipping down towards the butt of the .44 magnum.

"Who do you think you are? You're not a god," yelled Rhonda Bell, wondering what had ever made her utter such a strange phrase. And, what about his name? How could it be?

"Why don't you pull the trigger and we'll both find out," coldly challenged Ray Carver as he slickly drew the massive handgun out of the well oiled holster before Ronnie could even draw a bead on his crouched form.

The acidic burning pain of hot lead ripping through soft flesh blinded Ronnie in a searing bolt of excruciating agony, her head instantly exploding in a brilliant burst of white light. She desperately grabbed at her wounded thigh, shreds of her ripped and torn blue jeans imbedding themselves in the gaping wound. Rapidly blinking her eyes, she drew herself back from the perilous brink of total collapse, determined, if need be, to die like she had lived, with pride and dignity. She squeezed the trigger of the nine millimeter. Three empty shell casings clattered on to the cold hard floor, the bullets harmlessly plowing into the back wall.

Another deafening explosion tore up the felt cover of the pool table, chunks of slate and jagged pieces of the careening balls flying past her undaunted form. Catching a glimpse of movement off to her right she cracked off three more rounds, the unmistakable dull thud of a bullet impacting human flesh like music to her ears. There he was, over by the jukebox, a dark stain spreading across his chest. Eight more times she pulled the trigger. The sound of exploding glass and the baleful howl of a stricken terror filled animal pierced the smoke laden air as three rounds ripped into Ray Carver's writhing body, the other five killing the jukebox and Jon Bon Jovi's blaring "Blaze of Glory."

Rhonda Bell hit the ejector button that sent the empty clip rattling across the shell covered floor and rammed another clip home. Keeping the nine millimeter in front of her as she limped towards the slithering torso of the Capital Carver, his bleeding body leaving a bloody wake as he slid across the moist streaked floor, Rhonda Bell cautiously closed-in on the writhing murderer.

"You got me good, you black bitch, but, not good enough. I ain't gonna die," hacked Ray Carver looking up at Ronnie's towering form, an evil mocking grin plastered across his sinister face.

"Twice in the belly, a couple in my legs, and one in my chest. Pretty good shootin'. I'd have toasted your black ass 'cept'n for this here damn black lung. I had me a bead right between yer eyes I did. Gonna bust your head wide open, splatter what few brains you porch monkeys got. Damn cough did me in," rasped Ray Carver, slipping his hand underneath his body, pretending to be holding his wounds.

"You ain't got the stomach to finish it," he taunted, waiting for the chance to pull out his belly gun and waste the stupid nigger.

"You're right. I don't have the stomach for it. It's what makes us different. We're not different because of our skin color. We're different because of what's inside of us. I'm beautiful because I care, not because I'm black. You're ugly because you're a murderer and I'm not ever gonna be that," stated Ronnie, bending over to pick up the Carver's blood-covered revolver.

"I figured the same. You nigger broads think you're holier than thou. Always trying to be better than the white massah. Well, you ain't nothin' but a slave, baby. A slave to your own stupid dreams. I'm gonna lick my wounds and I'm gonna kill some more of you darkies before I die," coldly stated Ray Carver, reaching for the .32 caliber revolver stuffed down the front of his pants. Bent over, picking up the .44 magnum, Ronnie realized that she had just committed the biggest mistake of her life. He had her dead to rights, the small handgun pointed right between her unblinking eyes.

"Wrong!" shouted Kate Carver, stepping out from behind the bar, a .38 special held out in front of her advancing form.

"Yes sir, mother. I'm sure glad to see you. This here blackie is trying to kill me," lied Ray Carver, deciding that if he played his cards right he could kill two birds with one stone.

"Well, she isn't doin' a very good job of it, now is she? 'Cause you're still chirpin' away. This is for Becky. I know what you did to her. A woman's work is never done," calmly stated Kate Carver, exploding six rounds into her husband's jitter-bugging body, and then dropping the empty revolver on to the blood splattered floor.

"I suppose you're a police officer," stated Kate Carver, wrapping a tablecloth around Ronnie's profusely bleeding leg.

"Yes, Washington, D.C., Homicide Squad," answered Ronnie, wincing as Kate Carver twisted the impromptu tourniquet and tried to stem the flow of blood.

"Was your partner a big man with wavy grey hair, goes by the name of Mac? A real pleasant gentleman?" asked Kate Carver, already knowing the answer.

"Yes. Have you seen him? Is he alright?" pressed Ronnie.

"No, I'm afraid my husband killed him, right in our own house. God, Mac was such a nice man. Sort of like the one you always dreamed you had," despondently answered Kate Carver, wishing things in her life could have been different, wishing that a Mac would have come into her life.

"Oh, God," cried Ronnie, tears streaming down her golden brown cheeks.

"I'm sorry, officer. I'm sure you two were very good friends. Probably very close. Law enforcement is such a terrible job. It must be awful. You know we're pretty far out in the sticks. The ambulance and the police won't be here for another twenty minutes. Why don't you tell me about it. How many did he kill?" inquired Kate Carver, almost afraid to hear the gruesome tale of murder that was sure to follow.

"Counting Mac, I guess he killed fourteen. Fifteen, if you include an unborn child," grimly answered Ronnie, preparing herself to relive the somber story for the first of many times to come.

"Don't count me out, yet. I think I'm still alive," stated Mac, grinning as he propped himself up against the front door of the Oak Tree Tavern, Becky attempting to steady his wavering body.

"Mac, you're alive," excitedly shouted Ronnie, forgetting about her wounded leg as she tried to get up. Then, unable to support herself, she collapsed back down on to the gritty floor.

"As alive as I'll ever be. Thanks to my wife, God bless her soul. It's the last thing she ever bought me before she died. Promised her I'd wear it, too. But, I never did. Not until night before last when I had this strange feeling that she was begging me to put it on," stated Mac, pulling back his torn shirt, the bullet proof vest barely covering his rotund belly.

Bounding over to Ronnie who was helplessly lying on her back, Hoss and L'il Joe immediately began licking her face. In their own way, they too were soothing her tired wounded body with the gift of an unbridled enthusiasm for life. Mac walked unsteadily over to the bullet riddled corpse of the Capital Carver, politely asking Becky to stay outside. Seeing his own gun lying in the grisly mess of thick blood, he asked, "Are any of my slugs in him?"

"Yes, I killed him with your gun. I found it laying in the hallway. I figured my husband had dragged you off somewhere," answered Kate Carver, her voice quivering as the tears welled up in her reddening eyes.

"You did no such thing. How could you? I shot him with my own gun. Isn't that right, Ronnie? Kate wasn't even here, was she? She was in town trying to find her daughter, now wasn't she?" emphatically stated Mac, winking at Ronnie who was already nodding her head in agreement.

"God bless you for saving her from this. I think it only right that I tell you. He raped her, you know. He raped my baby girl," cried Kate Carver, wrapping her arms around Mac's bulky frame.

"You've come a long way, baby. Go check on your daughter. Take Hoss and L'il Joe with you. She really takes a shine to the kids and they sure do like her," suggested Mac, reaching down to pick up his empty service revolver, the tangled web beginning to neatly unravel itself in his detective oriented mind.

Carrying Rhonda Bell out to the awaiting ambulance, the two paramedics motioned for Mac to join them, the massive bruise on his chest most likely signifying some minor internal damage. Both detectives waited patiently as the Indiana County Coroner walked past the bagged body of Ray Carson Carver, about to take the same final journey that he had sent so many others on.

"Excuse me, Mrs. Carver. Would you and your daughter like to ride with us?" awkwardly asked the coroner, not knowing how to handle such a delicate situation.

Looking back at Mac, then glancing down at her daughter, the two women sharing their inner most thoughts without uttering a single word, Kate Carver answered, "No. I don't think so. If Mr. McCarthy wouldn't mind, I think we'd both like to ride to the hospital with him and his partner."

"I wouldn't mind a bit ma'am. And that's Mac, to my friends.

So it's Mac to you," cheerfully stated the beaming detective as he glanced over at Ronnie and winked. Then, whistling, he opened his arms as Hoss and L'il Joe leaped into the ambulance, both dogs ignoring him and, instead, jumping all over their new found friend, Becky Carver. "Man's best friend my ass," humorously muttered Mac, smiling at Kate Carver as the ambulance pulled out of the bumpy parking lot and turned onto the main road to Indiana.

"You crawled out of what?" laughed Ronnie, grimacing as a bolt of pain shot through her cleansed and sutured wound, the bullet having passed right through her flesh, barely missing her thigh bone.

"I crawled out through the bathroom window," sang Mac, breaking up as he tried to explain how he had managed to squeeze a forty six inch waist out of a forty two inch wide window in the bathroom of the Carver's house before the killer returned and sliced him open.

"Don't you know a good man always builds a shed over his tool," joked Mac, looking over at Ronnie.

"You're not going to try and tell me that the bigger the shed, the bigger the tool, are you?" giggled Ronnie, the cobwebs gradually clearing from her groggy sedated mind.

"Mom," shouted Darnell, bursting into the hospital room, his outstretched arms encircling Ronnie's graceful neck.

"Jesus, are you alright? Why didn't you tell me what was going on? I could have helped. You almost got yourself killed," pouted Danny Money, uncertain as to how he should feel.

"Thanks for bringing Darnell with you. It was really kind of you," stated Ronnie, wanting to apologize for lying to Danny, but not knowing what to say.

"What the hell are you talking about? It was kind of me? I thought we were supposed to be a family. What else would I do?" sharply remarked Danny, knowing he was about to be an asshole and start an argument.

Looking over at the nurse that had just entered the overflowing room at the Indiana Hospital, Mac suggested, "Well, folks. If Nurse Ratchet will wheel me out of here we can cruise on down to my room and call out for pizza."

"That's Cratchet," curtly replied the stoic nurse. "And there certainly will not be any pizza while I'm on duty."

"Looks like we'll have to slip out of this overgrown M.A.S.H. unit and find us a nice greasy spoon then," replied Mac, motioning for Kate, Becky, and Darnell to join him. He figured the two young lovebirds needed a little time to themselves. Once they quit flapping their wings and their jaws, they'd do just fine, figured the wily old detective, casting a quick glance at Kate's undulating buttocks as Nurse Cratchet wheeled him down the hall.

Ronnie looked up at Danny, afraid to say anything. Danny stared down at Ronnie, too hurt to speak.

"Well," stammered both lovers at the same time.

"You go first," stated Danny.

"No, you go ahead," answered Ronnie.

"All right. All the way up here, in the car, worrying about whether you were dead or alive, everything about us was spinning through my head. You know, all the problems we'll face. Having kids of our own, everything. So I made a decision. I've got to tell you like it is," he emotionally stated.

"I'm a big girl. I can take it. Go ahead," answered Ronnie, her heart sinking into oblivion. Her whole world about to come crashing down around her.

"I've decided that I am absolutely head over heels in love with you and I want you to be my wife. Will you marry me so we can have a handsome baby boy," asked Danny, bending over and kissing Ronnie's forehead.

Startled, Ronnie looked up at Danny and then replied, "No way!"

"What? You don't want to marry me? Damn, I thought that was what this was all about, commitment, dedication, sacrifice. How the hell could you do this to me?" he asked, a crushed look plastered all over his handsome face.

"Honey, I didn't say I wouldn't marry you. It's just, that lately, I've been dreaming a lot about frilly pink and white lace dresses and pigtails and shiny patent leather shoes. Why don't we get married and have a beautiful baby girl?" answered Rhonda Bell, reaching up and pulling Danny's pouting lips down to hers, a long sigh passing between both lovers as they lost themselves in the throes of ecstasy, about to enter into an even more binding oath than the one they had sworn to uphold so many years ago in a city that seemed so very far away.

Great S.P.I Books
Fact And Fiction

SPi.
BOOKS

☐ **The Super Swindlers: The Incredible Record of America's Greatest Financial Scams** *by Jonathan Kwitney.* They say that crime doesn't pay, but it has paid quite handsomely, thank you, for some of America's greatest swindlers and con-men. Acclaimed investigative journalist Jonathan Kwitney (The *Wall Street Journal, The Kwitney Report*—PBS TV) tracks down these notorious paper pirates who have taken individuals, corporations and governments to the cleaners. In The Super Swindlers we find out how these con-men have been operating and how so many of them have avoided prosecution. (ISBN 1-56171-248-5) $5.99 U.S.

☐ **First Hand Knowledge: How I Participated In The CIA-Mafia Murder of President Kennedy** *by Robert D. Morrow.* We still have far more questions than facts about that dark November day in Dallas. But now out of the shadows, comes the only inner-circle operative not to have been mysteriously assassinated. The author's information was the basis of the House Select committee on Assassinations 1976 investigation. Morrow finally feels the danger to himself and his family passed and he is ready to talk. (ISBN 1-56171-274-4) $5.99 U.S.

☐ **Love Before The Storm: A True Romance Saga in the Shadow Of The Third Reich** *by Roslyn Tanzman.* They were two young Jewish medical students, in love, and studying medicine in Europe's greatest medical schools. The future looked rosy, until the German economy tottered and the right-wing forces marched into power. In this moving, true retelling of her parents' actual love story, Roslyn Tanzman recreates their love at first sight, their class-war between the family and the shadow cast upon the lovers by Hitler's Germany and impending World War.
(ISBN 1-56171-240-X) $5.50 U.S.

Hot Hollywood Titles
from S.P.I. Books

☐ **Sweethearts**   The inspiring, heartwarming and surprising stories of the girls America tuned in to watch every week in the 60's. These glamorous and sexy stars made the 1960's a "time to remember" and long for, featuring Goldie Hawn and Judy Carne, Sally Field, Barbara Eden and more.
(ISBN 156171-206-X) $5.50 U.S.

☐ **Hollywood Raw** *by Joseph Bauer.* Wouldn't you like to know how **Christina Applegate** and **David Faustino** (Kelly and Bud Bundy on *Married With Children*) live in real life? *Hollywood Raw* also includes informative sections on **Kirstie Alley**, **Rosanna Arquette** and **Arsenio**. Author Joseph Bauer was there on the sets as the studio teacher to the young stars. He saw first hand all the never-reported details of their shocking private lives.
(ISBN 1-56171-246-9) $5.50 U.S.

☐ **Who Said That? Outrageous Celebrity Quotes** *by Ronald L. Smith.* Here is the largest collection of memorable quotes from America's top pop icons, stars of the big screen, the small screen, the music scene and more. Readers are challenged to identify the sources of unforgettable quotes.
(ISBN 1-56171-228-0) $4.99 U.S.

☐ **Hollywood's Greatest Mysteries** *by John Austin.* Hollywood columnist and author John Austin takes the reader well beyond the prepared and doctored statements of studio publicists to expose omissions and contradictions in police and coroner's reports. After examining these mysterious cases, you will agree that we have not been told the truth about Elvis Presley, Marilyn Monroe, Jean Harlow and others.
(ISBN 1-56171-258-2) $5.99 U.S.

To order in North America, please sent this coupon to:
S.P.I. Books •136 W 22nd St. • New York, NY 10011
Tel: 212/633-2022 • Fax: 212/633-2123

Please send European orders with £ payment to:
Bookpoint Ltd. • 39 Milton Park • Abingdon Oxon OX14 4TD • England
Tel: (0235) 8335001 • Fax: (0235) 861038

Please send____ books. I have enclosed check or money order for $/£ ____
(please add $1.95 U.S./£ for first book for postage/handling & 50¢/50p. for each additional book). Make dollar checks drawn on U.S. branches payable to **S.P.I. Books**; Sterling checks to **Bookpoint Ltd.** Allow 2 to 3 weeks for delivery.
☐MC ☐ Visa # _____ Exp. date _____
Name _____
Address _____